ISLANDS OF TIME

ISLANDS OF TIME

BY JACK DANN

CEMETERY DANCE PUBLICATIONS

Baltimore

2023

Islands of Time

Trade Paperback Edition

ISBN:
978-1-58767-923-0

Cemetery Dance Publications
132B Industry Lane, Unit #7
Forest Hill, MD 21050
www.cemeterydance.com

The stories and short novel contained in *Islands of Time* are works of fiction. The characterizations and incidents presented are totally the products of the author's imagination. Accordingly, these stories should be read solely as works of fiction.

ACKNOWLEDGMENTS

"Introduction" by Pamela Sargent, copyright © 2023 by Pamela Sargent.
"Mr. Death Goes to the Beach" by Jack Dann, copyright © 2019 by Bantam Doubleday Dell Magazines. First published in *Isaac Asimov's Science Fiction Magazine*, March/April 2019. Reprinted by permission of the author.

"The Mirror In the Mirror" by Jack Dann, copyright © 2021 by Jack Dann. First published in *Relics, Wrecks & Ruins*, edited by Aiki Flinthart. Reprinted by permission of the author.

"In re The Strange Fate of Samuel Langhorne Clemens" by Jack Dann, copyright © 2019 by Jack Dann. First published in *War of the Worlds Battleground Australia*, edited by Steve Proposch, Christopher Sequeira, and Bryce Stevens. Reprinted by permission of the author.

"Mohammed's Angel" by Jack Dann, copyright © 1986 by O L Society Ltd. First published in *Overland*, Spring 2009. Reprinted by permission of the author.

"The Island of Time" by Jack Dann, copyright © 2013 by Jack Dann.

FOR ABSENT FRIENDS…

Wanda June Alexander, Susan Casper, Gardner Dozois, Dennis Etchison, Tom Dupree, Harlan and Susan Ellison, Michael Engelberg, Keith Ferrell, Wendy Foldes, Jay Haldeman, Paul Haines, David Hartwell, Mark Levy, Joe Lindsley, Anne McCaffrey, Peter Nicholls, Skip and Jean Radecker, Mike Resnick, Bob Sheckley, Lucius Shepard, Len Wein, Gene Wolfe, and Roger Zelazny.

The author would like to thank the following people for their help and support:

Veny Armanno, D. Avraham, Paul Brandon, Richard Chizmar, Pete and Nicky Crowther, Rjurik Davidson, Bob Eggleton, Kate Eltham, Andrew Enstice, Aiki Flinthart, Mary Greene, Gerry Huntman, Rob Hoge, Jay Lake, Deborah Layne, Pat LoBrutto, Kevin Lucia, Barry N. Malzberg, Steve Paulsen, Steve Proposch, Jean Rabe, Rob Reginald, Mike Resnick, Pamela Sargent, Christopher Sequeira, Deborah Sheldon, Allan Dyen-Shapiro, Tony Smith, Cat Sparks, Bryce Stevens, Jonathan Strahan, Dirk Strasser, Sheila Williams, George Zebrowski, and, as always, my partner Janeen Webb.

CONTENTS

INTRODUCTION BY PAMELA SARGENT:

JACK DANN and I met in a college astronomy class, which seems appropriate for two students who went on to write science fiction. "Who *is* that guy?" George Zebrowski, another aspiring writer (who has been my life partner for a few decades now), whispered to me after Jack, more nattily dressed than most of our classmates, waved his fingers at us from his seat a couple of rows down in the lecture hall. I replied that he was just a friendly guy, which was my first impression, somebody who seemed curious and open to any interesting people or experiences that came his way, maybe even a happy-go-lucky-hail-fellow-well-met type of person.

True to a degree, but also misleading. Jack Dann is someone who takes whatever he does very seriously, even if he only seems to be having fun. A better way of putting this is that he's having fun while at the same time devoting some serious effort to whatever he's doing. I first noticed this when he and George and I were starting out as writers. Jack and George would often get together to do what amounted to jamming together on their typewriters, trading off drafts as they produced sentences that might become either the beginnings of collaborative efforts, stories that one or the other would take over and finish, or else pieces that would finally be abandoned. To me, this process often looked as though they were just fooling around, but it was actually two hopeful and determined young writers experimenting while honing their craft. A number of these stories by Jack and George sold and were reprinted, and Jack went on to collaborate with several other writers of note on later stories. Four recent collaborative pieces of his are included here, and this kind of collaboration is trickier and more difficult than it may seem, as it requires the writers to create a third writer temporarily, an entity who is both of them and yet neither.

As for the art of writing fiction, Jack took that seriously enough back then to take college courses in comparative literature, and, decades later, to earn a Ph.D. in creative writing at Australia's University of Queensland after emigrating there from his lifelong home in upstate New York state; his doctoral dissertation on alternate history was the basis for his recent nonfiction book *The Fiction Writer's Guide to Alternate History: A Handbook on Craft, Art, and History* (Bloomsbury, 2023). Jack is somebody who is open to experience, eager to explore whatever might be open to him, a quality I've always envied.

Jack moves through his stories the way he has traveled through life. To read a story by him is to enter a place where a lot is going on and all the reader's senses are engaged, to experience in depth what he has imagined and depicted, to start out thinking you're reading one kind of story only to find out that the story has reached beyond itself and become something else. There might be a trace (or more than a trace) of darkness or horror in the humor, or an unexpected glimpse of beauty or hope in a grim landscape. The stories here can be classified as horror, but there's also much more to them that this particular label doesn't capture.

Among the fictions in this collection are "Spirit Dog" and "Under the Shadow of Jonah," two stories connected to a couple of Dann's novels that also stand alone as stories. In "Spirit Dog," a piece from the novel *The Silent* (1998), he draws on the history of the American Civil War to imaginatively depict its horrors; any writer dealing with this well documented and still controversial period of U.S. history faces a formidable challenge, which Dann meets and overcomes. "Under the Shadow of Jonah" is clearly inspired by his acclaimed novel set in Renaissance Italy, *The Memory Cathedral* (1995), a book so rich in well-researched detail that it can serve as a guide to Florence, as it did for me when I visited that city and sometimes felt I was viewing it through Dann's eyes. A third story, "The Last Maskil," is part of his most recent novel, *Shadows in the Stone* (2019), also set in Renaissance Florence; influenced by Gnostic theology, this novel might be classified as an alternate history of human religions and theology and indeed the universe.

Homage to one of science fiction's masters, H. G. Wells, and his novel *The War of the Worlds*, is here in the form of "In Re: The Strange Fate of Samuel Langhorne Clemens," a delightful and even amusing, if also frightening, story depicting the Martian invasion of Australia and featuring Mark Twain as one of the main characters. Other stories inspired by fine sf writers are "Waiting for Medusa," which calls a notorious story of Harlan Ellison's to mind, and "The Island of Time," *hommage* to the late and great Gene Wolfe. "The Carbon Dreamer," a story written at the beginning of Dann's writing career, reveals an already formidable talent, while "The Hanging" is set in upstate New York, the background and setting for much of Dann's writing. "Mr. Death Goes to the Beach" is a haunting tale that contrasts a child's view of the world with the suddenness and finality of death, and "A Perfect Summer for Baseball, Tentacles, Mutants, and Love," written with the redoubtable Barry N. Malzberg, reveals Dann's gift for humor.

And there are more stories here, along with afterwords to each story, remembrances of how they were written and what inspired them.

All of these stories show off Dann's ability to draw the reader completely into his settings and into the minds of his central characters; even when we're not sure of where we're going, we're compelled to go along for the ride. This technique, which gets readers so far into the perceptions of a story's central character that they can feel surrounded and even closed in by the wealth of detail at the beginning, until the story opens up, also serves to underline the theme many of Dann's otherwise diverse works have in common, namely the struggle of an evolving consciousness to confront, understand, and apprehend its surroundings and the universe while thoroughly enjoying the quest along the way.

PREFACE: ROWS OF BOOKS

I REMEMBER ANNE McCaffrey's* tiny office on the ground floor of her grand old Victorian house in Sea Cliff, New York. I was standing in the doorway, taking in the books on the narrowly spaced shelves that covered the walls. Annie was sitting behind her desk and staring hard at a row of books beside her.

It was 1969.

I was twenty-four years old; Annie was forty-three.

"These books are mine, Tawny Lion," she said and then paused. "It's as if every year is on this bookshelf. One day you'll be counting the years of your life by the number of books you've written. And that's what you end up with, a row of books, the years of your life."

"A row of books, the years of your life."

So now it's 2023, and I'm sitting in my own office in the country… in country Australia, which is, I suppose, as far from Sea Cliff (and my home town in upstate New York) as one can get. Although Annie has been gone for a while, her books and words stay with me; and now I,

* Anne McCaffrey (1926-2011) wrote the still-popular *Dragonriders of Pern* series. She was the first woman to win the Hugo and Nebula Awards, and her novel *The White Dragon* was one of the first SF novels ever to appear on the New York Times Bestseller list.

too, have those shelves of books, which are, indeed, also constructions of dreams and nightmares and memories.

When I was choosing the stories for this collection…as I pulled down volume after volume, looking wistfully at the covers of the magazines and anthologies in which they appeared, rereading the words I had written in different places and different times, I could *see* the years. I could see once again those strangers called 'me' who wrote those stories. I could remember the thought-processes, the dreams, the catalyzing ideas that birthed those improbable stories; and so I became, for a while, a time traveler. And once again, I swam in those warm, often dangerous seas of memory. I was once again privy to the how's and why's of my creative life, that sea in which—to continue to stretch the metaphor unmercifully—I'm still submerged. Although I'm 'talking' directly to you now, oh perspicacious reader, I am still engulfed, still living multiple lives, still dreaming worlds and words onto paper and screen. It's been a privilege; and it's a privilege not only to share the stories contained in this volume, but to share my recollections of how these fictions came to be.

Needless to say, these recollections—these afterwords that follow the stories—are optional add-ons: if I've done my job and dreamed the stories correctly, they will stand on their own metaphoric feet and give the bird to that constructed identity often referred to as the author.

So…welcome, dreamers…

24 February 2023
Windhover Farm
Victoria, Australia

MR. DEATH GOES TO THE BEACH

RAPHAEL LEWIS Goldsworthy couldn't stop coughing. The familiar tickle was deep down in his throat—tickle tickle cough cough—and his back hurt with every barking convulsion.

"Where's your inhaler?" his mother asked, casually patting the orange striped beach blanket as if the device had somehow migrated into the sand below. Without acknowledging her, Raphael pulled a Ventolin inhaler out of the pocket of his swimming trunks and inhaled a puff of the acrid chemical mist.

"Take another puff," his mother said.

He pressed down on the inhaler again, held his breath, exhaled, and squinted at the ocean. The waves weren't very high, but the ocean seemed to extend right up to the sky. Raphael felt his lungs open up into chilly rooms inside him. He breathed deeply in and out—shutting his mother in, shutting his mother out—and wondered whether the ocean was actually blue...or green.

The sky was certainly blue, except, of course, for the clouds that seemed to sail across it like fluffy boats; but the water, well, that was something else again. It looked dark blue one minute, then green, and then it looked like part of the sky. That didn't make sense to Raphael and he shook his head, something he did when he was perplexed. He could ask his mother, of course, but she wouldn't know the answer and would just tell him to take another puff on his inhaler (which he didn't need to do) or put on more sunscreen. And then, her motherly obligation completed, she'd forget about him entirely.

"Raphael...take another puff on your puffer!"

Raphael continued to stare at the ocean, and then to distance himself from his mother, he turned his head just a bit to the right and stared with all his might at the orange and purple granite boulders that looked like huge, rounded huts sticking up from the sand. He saw a boy who looked to be around ten—Raphael's age, although Raphael was *almost* eleven—standing in a cleft between two rocks. It didn't look like there was much space: the kid must have squeezed himself hard between those boulders...and a few feet away Raphael saw a rather clownish looking man standing on top of one of the rocks, a blood-red rock. The man was dressed in a white suit. His shirt was open at the collar, and he wore a wide-brim Akubra hat at a jaunty angle. But his pale, rosy-cheeked face was...odd: too narrow, somehow, as if someone had pulled his hair so hard that it had stretched his head. Raphael shook his own head again, swallowed the tickle that would cause a cough, and wondered: how the hell did that guy climb up that rock? He would have needed a ladder or something.

"Raphael, will you stop daydreaming and put this sunblock on," his mother said, holding out a greasy tube of ointment.

"See the guy standing on that rock?" Raphael asked. "How'd he get up there?"

"I'm sure I don't know. He probably found a way to climb up from the other side. Now take this damn cream and put it on your nose and your ears. They're already starting to get burned. You want to look like a clown?"

He turned to his mother and looked at her as if for the first time. She was deeply tanned, and her jet-black hair was pulled away from her face and held in place with a Cartier comb his father had given her. Her eyes looked very, very blue set in that tan, and Raphael could see why all his friends at the academy always turned up when she visited on weekends. She had once been a famous model and still looked like a movie star, and she always wore low cut dresses to show off her breasts. Right now she was wearing a white bikini, white as the pristine sand all around them. Raphael knew what pristine meant. His mother certainly wasn't that. When she left his father to "take a permanent vacation in Australia," all sorts of people called her names on social media; and Raphael had to bash Sammy Walton right in the nose for calling her a slut.

He squeezed a handful of sand until he could feel it crunch.

His hand felt hot, and he imagined that the grains of sand were so sharp that they were cutting holes in his palm; and if he bled to death, then he and his mother could go back home, and he could see his father again. Well, he'd probably be a ghost or something, but at least he'd be back with his father in America.

His father was a U.S. senator and a Republican.

"Why do they call this place Squeaky Beach?" he asked his mother.

"How the hell should I know?" she said. "You need more cream on your nose. You've got skin like your father's, pale as a sheet."

"I can't help that."

"That's why you need sunblock."

"*I* know why they call it Squeaky Beach," Raphael said.

"Then why ask me?"

"I just wanted to know if you knew."

His mother removed her comb, and her thick, luxuriant hair fell across her shoulders. She slipped the comb halfway into her bikini top, and the diamonds sparkled like wet sand in the sun. Raphael noticed that a man with gray hair and black swimming trunks had just walked past them again. He was quite a walker, that guy.

"I would suppose it's called Squeaky Beach because the sand squeaks," his mother said.

"And do you know *why* it squeaks?"

"Stop the Platonic dialogue bullshit. You sound like your father. It's very annoying. He can get away with it. You can't."

"He's a senator, and you're not."

She looked away from Raphael and smiled at the gray-haired man who was already on his way back toward them again.

"Well," Raphael said, "the sand squeaks because it's made out of quartz and all the grains are rounded, you know, like worn-down, and they're...pristine. The sand by our house in Fort Lauderdale doesn't squeak because it's polluted, and so the grains can't rub against each other as well and..."

His mother wasn't listening.

Raphael shook his head: he couldn't even get her to pay enough attention to piss her off. She said hello to the gray-haired man, who made some awkward small talk with her and nodded to Raphael almost every time he ended a sentence. His name was Ronald; and he owned a company in Thailand that built yachts, and it didn't take him long to ask her if she would like to take a swim; and he made a little bow, as if he were asking her for a dance; and she smiled the smile that made her dimples squinch.

Raphael considered it all disgusting.

After the requisite amount of coaxing, she stood up and said, "That would be very nice. It's a very hot sun today, isn't it?" and before Ronald could extend the obligatory invitation to her son, she said, "Would you be a dear, Raphael, and guard our belongings? We're just going to take a very quick swim to cool off, and when we come back, you can take a dip. And later we can drive to Moo's Restaurant for a steak dinner. How's that?"

Raphael grunted and looked sullen. What was there to guard, anyway? A cheap paperback book about the President, a clutch-bag of lotions and other stuff, and, okay, there was her wallet. It made sense to guard her wallet from wallet thieves in this dangerous place full of health food nuts and ecotourists. He watched his mother and Ronald step carefully through the squeaky sand to the breakers, and then he looked back toward the red-streaked boulders that cut into the sea and rose into the sky. He was keeping an eye on the man who had mysteriously climbed to the top of the rounded rock. And he noticed that the boy who had squeezed between the rocks had disappeared. But he was there just a minute ago...and the clownish man was no longer standing on top of the rounded granite mound: now he was standing right there in the cleft where the boy had been. How the hell could he fit in there?

Raphael went to investigate. He could keep an eye on the blanket, and there wasn't anybody sitting in that area, anyway.

He purposely crunched the sand with his heel every time he took a step: there was something delicious and satisfying about its scrunch under his feet. He walked to the cleft where the boy and then the man had just been standing, but neither one of them was there anymore. It was as if they had *both* simply...disappeared.

"Hello."

Startled, Raphael turned around, and there was the man. His hat cast a shadow over his face, so that even though Raphael was looking right at him—and they weren't even two feet apart—he couldn't quite make out his features. It was as if he could discern the man's features better from a distance than up close. He might as well have been looking at a grainy close-up photograph of the man's face.

"Hello," Raphael said, reflexively backing away. Although his mother had carried on about not speaking to strangers, he didn't feel nervous. In fact, he felt quite relaxed, contented, sort of. This was man-to-man stuff. One man saying hello to another man, and the other man saying hello back. Like that. Raphael glanced toward his mother's empty beach blanket and said, "I've got to keep an eye on my mother's blanket. Her wallet and stuff is on it."

The man nodded and said, "Yes, you never know, although it's pretty safe around here, not like in Fort Lauderdale."

"How'd you know I'm from Fort Lauderdale?"

The man smiled, a thin smile that didn't show any teeth. "Well, if you were Sherlock Holmes, and if you were cognizant of every detail, how would *you* discover the truth?"

"Well..." and Raphael smiled and nodded. "Okay, yeah, okay, it's my swimming trunks, right?" There was an emblem on the pocket: Ft Lauderdale, FL.

The man smiled.

But Raphael's teeshirt covered his trunks...it was too large for him and only good for the beach. Of course, the wind probably caught it and revealed the emblem.

"I suppose you also know my name," Raphael asked. "Do you know my name...?"

"Well, Sherlock Holmes would have very good hearing, and would have heard your mother talking to you." He smiled thinly again.

"No, that's a trick," Raphael said playfully. "Come on, Mr...Holmes, tell me my name."

"Nope, I can't make it out, Raphael?"

Raphael giggled. "That's pretty good. Now tell me *your* name."

"Don't you want to guess?"

"Give me a clue."

"Okay," said the man, tilting his head back...but that didn't help: Raphael still couldn't make out his features. "Do you remember the boy who was standing in the rock cleft behind me and watching you?"

"I don't know if he was watching me," Raphael said. "If he was watching anybody, it was probably my mother. Everybody watches her." He thought he could see the man smile again.

"Well, do you know what happened to him?"

"What's that got to do with your name?" Raphael asked. "Is he your son or something?"

The man shook his head and laughed softly, a deep yet soft laugh. "No, Raphael, he's certainly not my son."

Raphael looked around, but couldn't see the boy.

"He's drowning," the man said, matter-of-factly as he pointed toward a dark spot in the ocean far beyond the rocks. "I'll pick him up later."

Raphael felt the tickle of a cough, which exploded. He took a puff of Ventolin—the sand carried by gusts of wind must be irritating his lungs—and said, "I can't see anything. And…and if he's drowning, we should find a lifeguard or something."

The man smiled. "I'm afraid it's too late for that, but don't worry, everything is in hand. I've slowed things down over there so that we can chat for a bit longer."

Raphael shook his head and started to say, "You're really—"

"Now that I've given you all the clues you need, I think you should be able to discover my name."

"I think I'd just better get back to my mother's blanket. It was very nice meeting you, Mr."

"Yes? But Mr. who…or Mr. what?"

Raphael wasn't having any more of this. This was…weird, and although he hated to admit it, his mother was probably right about talking to strangers. But weird as it was, Raphael *liked* talking to this guy. It was…well, it was sort of like the feeling you get when your feet are scrunching in the squeaky sand. But Raphael started walking away, anyway.

"Come on, Raphael, take a guess," the man said; and even though the man was behind Raphael, it was as if his voice was right in front of him.

Raphael stopped and felt a tingle of excitement, the thrill of prior knowledge; and he remembered something in the Bible about an apple. He turned around and said, "Okay, so maybe you think you're some sort of a ghost. Like an angel."

"Yes…?"

"Like death or something, but you'd have to be nuts and I don't believe in—"

"That's very good, Raphael. I can tell you're a smart boy, a veritable sleuth."

Raphael didn't know what a sleuth was, but he glowed with the compliment. That was more than he ever got from his mother.

"Okay," the man said, taking Raphael's hand and leading him towards the shoreline. Raphael didn't resist because it felt like holding hands and walking with this man was the most natural thing in the world to do. But Raphael couldn't help but notice that the man's hand was cool; it felt just like when you first stepped into the ocean on a beautiful, warm day. As he took a deep breath of the warm, fragrant air, the tickle in his throat disappeared; and his back didn't hurt as it usually did when he had been coughing.

"You're pretty close to figuring out my name," the man continued. So, since we're friends now, why don't you just call me Mr. Death. I'd tell you my given name, but I think you're a respectful boy, and 'Mr.' is a reflection of respect, don't you agree?"

"Yes, I suppose," Raphael said, suddenly wondering what it would feel like to drown.

ISLANDS OF TIME

MR. DEATH ALWAYS enjoyed the beach. It was one of the few little recreations he allowed himself, for his schedule was always full. His life's work, if one could put it in such whimsical terms, was the death of human bipeds; and today was like every other day, except the numbers always differed slightly. So far, he had taken 126 thousand and change... well, actually 126,365; and his day wasn't over yet. That doesn't mean, of course, that he was consciously or even 'physically' present at every death. Suffice it to say that it was all a matter of iteration.

And that Mr. Death was nothing more than an algorithm.

But he was certainly present right here and now...presently enjoying the sea-scented air, the long afternoon warmth of the sun, the fullness of breath in his disincarnate lungs, the salty perfumes of sweat, the small acrid invasions of perfume and suntan lotion, and the bracing presence of this transplanted boy from Fort Lauderdale.

Mr. Death led Raphael right past his mother and gray-haired Ronald who were both sitting on the beach blanket. Raphael's mother didn't even call out to him as he passed...and she was looking straight at Raphael, who stopped right in front of her and was about to say something when Mr. Death gave him a gentle tug. "Come along, Raphael, your mother can't see you right now. And neither can her boyfriend."

"He's not her boyfriend," Raphael said. "She's only known him for five minutes."

"Actually, it's more like a half-hour, but he'll be her boyfriend eventually."

"And what about my father?"

Mr. Death shrugged and said, "Oh, I suppose I should pay him a visit."

"You mean kill him?"

Mr. Death stopped, as did Raphael, who was still holding his hand. Mr. Death gazed contentedly out to sea and closed his eyes for a few seconds, enjoying the life-giving warmth of the sun. He thought about

Raphael and glanced into his prospective future: the bronchiectasis would soon reveal itself as a symptom of an aggressive form of cystic fibrosis...unless, of course, he did the unthinkable and intervened.

"I don't kill anyone, Raphael. I just, well, take them...just as you would take a peanut out of a jar."

"My father isn't a peanut."

"You're all peanuts," Mr. Death said, tugging at Raphael hand to continue their stroll along the beach. "Well, actually, numbers."

Raphael dragged behind a bit, shaking his head as if he were trying to figure things out, then asked, "Why couldn't my mother see me? Am *I* dead?"

Mr. Death laughed and picked up a little segmented sand worm out of the sand, which he then flicked into the water. "Why, do you feel dead?"

"I don't know what that would feel like."

"Neither does anybody, I suppose," Mr. Death said as he continued to walk.

"If I'm not dead or anything, then why didn't my mother see me back there?" Raphael felt something warm churning inside him, inside his chest. "Is *she* dead?"

"No, nobody's dead," Mr. Death said sharply. "Your mother didn't see you because no one can see you right now. You're not in time. When you're with me, you're free."

"I don't *feel* free," Raphael said, but he knew that was a lie as soon as he said it. He felt...like he was jumping on a trampoline and was in mid-air defying gravity for a heart-stopping instant. Except this wasn't for a second: it just went on and on: holding Mr. Death's hand and feeling the sun all over him as if he wasn't wearing shorts and a shirt. And his lungs felt as light as...light!

They walked and walked, the ocean forever on their right; trees and stone headlands shifting shape ahead of them, as if everything was almost transparent and apt to change its shape at any time; and then Mr. Death suddenly surprised himself by saying, "We'd best get you back to your mother now."

Was this an act of mercy? he asked himself, feeling the boy's soft hand in his; and then he laughed at himself, as only an algorithm could.

Well, a single act of mercy out of 126,365 iterations seemed fair enough.

As they walked back along Squeaky Beach, Raphael asked, "You said nobody's dead. But that's a lie, right? You told me that the kid who was looking at me—or at my mother—was drowning. What are you going to do? Undrown him?"

"No, I'm going to take care of him right now," Mr. Death said softly, smiling to himself; and as they approached the spot where Raphael's mother was sitting, he squeezed Raphael's hand and disappeared.

"AND WHERE THE hell have you been?" Raphael's mother said, her face tight with anger. "You were supposed to guard our stuff, not go…well, where the hell *did* you go?"

"Just around," Raphael said, suddenly feeling alone and somehow bereft. He shook his head and sat down on the far corner of the blanket. Everything, even the air, seemed heavy, claustrophobic once again.

"So what happened to your boyfriend?" he asked his mother.

She laughed. "You mean Douglas?"

"I thought he said his name was Ronald."

His mother shook her head, and her hair moved across her shoulders like a shiny black wave. "Whatever. He was just some guy looking for the main chance. And he's certainly not my boyfriend. I'm married to your father, remember?"

"Can we go back home and see him?"

"Maybe," she said, looking suddenly and uncharacteristically pensive. "Maybe we can...sometime. We'll see. But right now let's get packed up. Are you hungry?"

Raphael helped his mother fold the blanket and put everything into a carry bag: he was actually a little hungry.

And as they made their way along a path through coastal scrub toward the car park, Raphael heard a woman scream "*My baby, oh, my God, no,*" or something like that. Although distant, the shrill voice sounded just like his mother's.

"What's going on?" his mother asked, stopping. "Maybe we should go back and see."

"No, it's okay," Raphael said, remembering something, remembering feeling free, as if he could walk invisibly right through the ocean and the sky or the red granite boulders. "Someone probably just drowned or something." He took a deep breath, inhaled the salt-washed air as if with new lungs. "But there's really nothing we can do to help. Really."

His mother looked at him for a second, looked at him as if she could really see him and then nodded. And as they continued on to the car park—and as the sun burned down on them without mercy—Raphael wondered when they would be able to go back to the beach again.

AFTERWORD TO "MR. DEATH GOES TO THE BEACH"

MR. DEATH GOES to the Beach" appeared in a special Gardner Dozois memorial edition of *Asimov's Science Fiction*, a magazine that Gardner edited for twenty years. Gardner was one of my closest and dearest friends. Family. In a Q & A that I did for Asimov's at the time, I was asked "What is the story behind this piece?" And I wrote:

"This is one of those short stories that just sort of slipped out of my unconscious. That rarely happens, and I'm sure it has something to do with the death of my dear friend Gardner Dozois. I remember waking up from a night of bad dreams, one of those exhausting, seemingly sleepless nights; and as I propped myself up in the bed, I imagined the idea of death as the personification of a harried bureaucrat. And this combined with the ocean and the beach, which I associate with comfort, freedom, and…fear: the idea of drowning, of the pull of deep water, that sort of thing.

"Over the next few days, I kept thinking about death, my image of 'him'; and as I did so, the so-called texture of the image took on the coloration of a deadly story I admire by J. D. Salinger: 'A Perfect Day For Bananafish'. It's a mood-piece of a story with an ending that shocked the hell out of me. I knew 'Mr. Death Goes to the Beach' wasn't going to have that kind of a shock ending, but I wanted to contrast the quiet joys of peace and relaxation with the undeniable finality of sudden death. I wanted to create a story that would be warm and familiar…so warm and familiar that it would chill like an ice-cube dropped into the collar of an unsuspecting bather. Whether I accomplished any of this will have to be determined by my readers.

MR. DEATH GOES TO THE BEACH

"So I think—and this is just a bit of pop-psychological self-analysis—that 'Mr. Death Goes to the Beach' was this writer's natural way of working out grief and guilt and all those subterranean emotions that accompany the death of a loved one."

THE MIRROR IN THE MIRROR

SO, LIKE most things, it began and ended in the bathroom. Specifically, a bathroom in Lighthouse Point, Florida and a bathroom in the dilapidated Lucerne Hotel on West 79th Street in New York City. (It might also be noted that there is a third bathroom involved in this story, located in the swanky Pierre Hotel on New York's Upper East Side. However, I will leave it to the reader to determine whether this one is an integral part of the story's resolution or merely an epilogical literary device.)

And I should tell you that all these bathrooms were the very same bathroom. Sort of, but not really. To explain, allow me to introduce you to Norman and Laura Gumbeiner, who on Wednesday, November 10th, 2020, at 9:30 in the morning, were standing beside each other in their ensuite bathroom located in their stucco, pink, single-story, two-bedroom house overlooking the Intercoastal Waterway.

"Can't you see I'm in the bathroom?" Norman asked, as he swished his chrome safety razor in the faux-antique marble sink's frothy hot water. He was a spry eighty-five-year-old hypochondriac, who often deflected his wife's sarcastic remarks about his attention to body, mind, and receded hairline by repeating the canticle that "What you call hypochondria is what has kept me alive all these years." Or he would ask, "Do you think colonoscopies where precancerous growths are discovered every time should not be performed?" Or, if he was in a really expansive mood, he would soliloquize about his encounters with Fuch's dystrophy, urinary infections, arthritis, irritable bowel syndrome, amongst a host of other undeniable empirical 'proofs'—all that to crush, to utterly crush his white-haired (with a touch of hairdresser's blue), seventy-nine-year-old assailant.

Laura looked intently at her husband's reflection in the bronze framed mirror, which was a family heirloom (her family) and would be out of place in any bathroom, except perhaps one in Windsor Castle. She was already dressed, showered, and perfumed. A handsome, if rather overweight woman, Laura Gumbeiner smelled like happy memories of Coney Island.

"You're mowing the lawn today," she said sweetly, talking directly to the reflection, as if by doing so, she wouldn't have to interact with the familiar stranger beside her.

"You're not my boss. And I'll mow the goddamn lawn—"

"Today," Laura, said, recasting what he was about to say.

In response, Norman nicked his chin with the razor, then jutted his jaw forward so that his life mate could apply the styptic pencil she already had in hand.

"Okay, I'll do it this afternoon."

"Not in that heat you won't. You'll do it this morning." She smiled wryly. "And after that, who knows? If you're not exhausted, maybe a little hanky-panky."

He smiled back at his wife in the mirror. "But if I take one of those get-up-and-do-your-duty pills and have a heart attack, it'll be on *your* head."

"I'll take that chance," she said. Then she made an odd gurgling sound and suddenly stepped backwards, as if she had just seen a ghost, which, in a sense, she had.

"Whasamatter?" Norman asked, turning towards his wife. He still had patches of shaving soap under his sideburns.

"*Look!*"

"At what?"

"At yourself. There." She pointed at the mirror, then stepped forward, looking intently into it. "At *us*."

Norman complied, looked at their reflections in the mirror, and repressed a fart. "Yes, I see you, and I see me. Now what the hell's the matter with you?"

"Look at us. We're...young."

"Okay, if you say so, we're young. We're as young as we feel." He scowled at himself, just now remembering the film *As Young as You Feel* with Monty Woolley and Marilyn Monroe. He grimaced. He had a gray age mark on his left cheek, folds in his neck—what the hell did they call them? chicken somethings—and what he thought of as old-men's earlobes. And when he looked at his wife in the mirror, he could see that she, too, had spots and the selfsame chicken skin under her chin. But he considered her pretty, nevertheless.

"No, Norman. *Look!*" She looked at him directly for an instant, saw the old man that he was, shook her head in disappointment, and then turned back to the mirror. "My mother," she said, talking to the mirror, "may-she-rest-in-peace, was right. She once told me that this was her second-chance mirror."

"What the hell does that mean?" Norman asked, pulling a monogrammed washcloth from the heated towel rail and wiping the soap off his face.

"I never knew what it meant until now," she whispered, mesmerized, for the reflection in the mirror was that of a sleek, ash-blond young woman: her face slightly asymmetrical, full lips, large boat-blue eyes, a somehow quizzical face that most people—men especially—found charming. She smiled at herself and then extended her hand toward the mirror…into the mirror.

It was blood warm, viscous and slippery as mercury; and as she felt its palpable adamantine suction, she grasped Norman's arm. Although he resisted, reflexively, she pulled him right through the mirror. Pulled him over to the other side. Pulled him right back to their old apartment situated in 1965. November 10th.

The day before, a distant Canadian power station had failed at 5:27 p.m., plunging New York City into star-ceilinged darkness until 3:30 a.m.

3:30 a.m. today.

It was now 9:35 a.m., New York time.

I WON'T BURDEN you with the astonishment that the Gumbeiners felt at that isometric moment of transition. Whatever it was, you've just imagined it according to your own cultural frame of reference. And after their initial gob smacking, disorienting shock subsided…after they made what might be referred to as mad, passionate love before they could even reach the bed…and after they, finally, showered and changed into their 'old' tight-fitting sweater and jeans vestments; Laura found a jar of instant Sanka decaffeinated coffee and boiled some water.

They sat quietly at the kitchen table in their respectively bewildered states of continued shock and sipped the acrid brew out of chipped mugs. Norman sniffed the flat black liquid and wished for a strawberry latte from the cappuccino machine that was sitting on a counter in what had once been their kitchen on the other side of the mirror. He looked at the young woman who had been his wife for almost sixty years and felt yet another non-chemically induced stiffness. And so they watched the traffic on West 79th Street and Broadway. And they listened to the horns blaring, listened to the background roar of the city until Laura broke their trance of silence.

"I've told you what Mother said the last time I saw her in the nursing home."

"That was a terrible nursing home," Norman said, remembering how the hallway doors clicked shut and locked.

"Pay attention, Norman! You're not eighty-five anymore. You're—"

"Thirty." Yes, that was right, he thought. He was here…and he was there. It was like seeing double images. You're thirty and you're in law school. And you hate it. You want to be a writer, but your father's will specified law school, all expenses paid, or no bequest. (I might add that Norman became—or had been, depending on your perspective point—a war correspondent and the editor-in-chief of a second-tier local news magazine. He never managed to finish law school. But all that was now in the future, and Norman's problem was that he had already lived it… unless, of course, it could be changed.)

(Supplemental: Although Laura had no grand aspirations to be a writer, she would attend literary gatherings with her husband and begin what she called "noodling" after meeting an editor at a writers' conference. Thereafter she would make a very comfortable six-figure income writing a series of best-selling novels in her spare time under the pseudonym Candy Cartman. All of this, of course, being dependent upon the above-mentioned reader's perspective point and the mutability of time and alternity.)

"Norman!"

"Yes, I'm listening! And I remember: your mother told you to remove the mirror from the room as soon as she died and that you only live twice."

Laura looked at him coolly, her eyes now blue green, her face perfect and unblemished.

No wonder old people want to be young, Norman thought, then said, "But as I've told you a thousand times, she was not in her right mind. She thought that *she* was James Bond. It wasn't her fault, it—"

"It was true," Laura said, musing, "and Mother was right. We lived once, and this—right here, right now—is twice. And, incidentally, Mr. Armchair Psychoanalyzer, she never thought she was James Bond!"

"It's crazy, that's what it is. You and I are hallucinating. Maybe we just died, and these are my last thoughts like in that *Twilight Zone* episode where the guy is being hanged, and the rope breaks or something; and he runs around happy as Larry until the last scene when his neck is broken because it was all a dream. Like that."

"So we both just died in the bathroom. Both of us. At the same time."

"No," Norman said, "*I* just died. You...you'll live to a hundred and twenty. Or, more likely, I'm asleep and right now this minute I'm having a dream, or a nightmare about your mother."

"*My* mother?"

"Yes, your mother and her mirror. So, I'll tell you what...I'm going to go back into the bathroom, and maybe if I can push myself back through her *fakakta* mirror, I'll wake up."

Laura sipped her coffee, looked at him coolly again, and shrugged. "Knock yourself out. But why on earth would you want to go back to being..."

"To being what?"

"Old and smelling like an old towel."

"Okay, that's it!"

Norman rose, told Laura he really was going back 'home' (for a decent cup of coffee), admitted that the dream part of getting laid was terrific, and then shambled into the bathroom: his unconscious hadn't quite caught up to his new situation, and he still thought his right knee was arthritic.

He stared at himself in the mirror. Pretty good looking: prematurely graying hair, manly scars from a terrible case of pimples in adolescence, cleft chin, well-defined pecs instead of saggy man boobs. He pressed his hand against the mirror. It was cool, actually cold. He pressed harder and told himself to wake the hell up. The mirror frame creaked from the pressure of his hand on the mercury-coated glass it surrounded. But he couldn't push back into his old, or, rather, his other bathroom in Lighthouse Point.

And he didn't wake up into his Floridian future.

He grimaced at himself, then raised his arms into a bodybuilder's pose—he was scarecrow skinny, but muscular—and said, "Maybe this isn't such a bad dream. Maybe…"

But he knew…oh, he knew.

He remembered the lines of a poem by Juvenal that he had inserted into a one-act play that never saw the proverbial light of day:

Like warmed-up cabbage served at each repast,
The repetition kills the wretch at last.

THUS THE MINUTES, hours, days, and years passed; and repetition it was, repetitions of repetitions, (accompanied, of course, by the ever-pivotal soupçon of *non*-repetition): shower, morning coffee, Norman rushing to catch the D train to St. John's Law School in Brooklyn, hot bagels and late-night study sessions with his five-member study group; and Laura kissing Norman goodbye before leaving for the advertising agency that just bordered on the Bronx, an advertising agency that she one day owned and relocated to the West Village (after she had signed Maria Chorale Cosmetics and Raimond International Resorts); and she worked late and met Norman at the Stage Deli to share a bowl of matzah ball soup and an enormous hot pastrami sandwich; and Sundays walking around the 79th Street Boat Basin, and movies, and cooking in the grease-stained kitchen; and Norman graduated law school with honors and (of course) passed the New York Bar exam and joined the law firm Hensley, Lowry, Graham & Gallagher, and started climbing the ladder to partnership, and then moving to Sea Gate in Brooklyn, and as every hour and every day of another life slipped from memory, they were replaced by the real moments of the ever-moving, punishing, dog-eat-dog present; and then moving back to Manhattan, this time to the Upper East Side, to a seven-figure-price-point, four-bedroom 'residence' in the Pierre on Fifth Avenue; and Laura opened satellite agencies in Boston, Palm Beach, and West LA, and…

…and as evidenced above and repeated again (for repetition is one of the leitmotifs of this story) they forgot. Forgot their old life, forgot all the joys and pains of what we might call their first life, as their trajectories toward another futurity worked themselves out.

And, yes, as you might have guessed by following the trail of metaphorical breadcrumbs I've left, they separated.

In 1985.

Well, it wasn't really much of an adjustment, as they were rarely in the same place at the same time. In February of 1999, however, Norman was having lunch (yes, with Laura, for they were never formally separated or divorced, just "detached") at Barbetta's on West 46th Street when he inhaled a bite of aged Wagyu filet steak. The waiter, an elegant-looking young man from Ecuador, performed a perfect Heimlich maneuver, which worked, but for the fact that Norman suffered a massive heart attack just as the half-chewed piece of steak shot out like a projectile, smashing one of the electric candles in the overhead crystal chandelier.

Laura, heartbroken, gave a moving valediction at his exquisitely tasteful funeral, supervised his burial in the Mount Hebron Cemetery in

Flushing (the very same cemetery in which Emanuel Weiss, an ex-member of Murder Incorporated, and Selig Grossinger, founder of Grossinger's Resort, resided), and commissioned a monument commensurate with his status.

As Laura's mother had always said, "Well, dead is dead."

MOTHER'S APHORISM, HOWEVER, wasn't strictly true.

Norman was certainly dead, and Laura grieved for his loss; grieved as we all do for all the "could have beens," and then, as most of us do, she slid back into life, slid back into the moment-by-moment, numbing comfort of repetition and regularity until, yes, you guessed it: Wednesday, November 10th, 2020, at 9:30 in the morning.

Laura had elected to skip her Wednesday Morning Club: she just wasn't in the mood for mahjong, chamomile tea, and the usual array of finger sandwiches, scones, marmalade, lemon curd, herbed butter, and pickled salmon. And she wasn't in the mood to spend the usual time painting her face and coordinating an appropriate wardrobe assemblage. So she slept in, then took a wake-up Adderall and made her autogenic way to the bathroom for a pee.

Her bathroom in the Pierre was large and ornate enough to give her mother's mirror an appropriate rather than garish pride of place. She leaned her pelvis against the lip of the sink and looked at her reflection. Then, as she had done once before, a lifetime before, she made an odd gurgling sound and suddenly stepped backwards, as if she had just seen a ghost—or, rather, two ghosts—for reflected in the ornately framed mirror was herself...and Norman. Both old. Together.

Norman's face was partially lathered with shaving soap. He winked at her, or perhaps he just blinked. She could see a powdery white spot of aluminum sulfate on his chin where, theoretically, moments ago she had applied a styptic pencil.

"Norman?" she asked.

"Okay, I'll do it this afternoon," Norman said, looking blankly into the mirror. He was referring to Laura's previous request to mow the lawn—that being the Laura on the Lighthouse Point side of the mirror.

And Laura, second-chance Laura, if you like, extended her hand toward the mirror. She expected the surface to be blood warm and viscous, expected it to be as slippery as mercury...expected to feel the mirror's palpable adamantine suction. She pressed against the glass, which felt cool, actually cold. Resistant as time itself.

She pressed harder, pushed against the mirror, which was nothing more than a large, impermeable object affixed firmly to the bathroom wall; she pushed against it with both hands until her arms ached from the pressure and her palms felt hot, as if pulsing in time to some unknown rhythm. Finally, she gave up, stepped back, and stared intently, desperately into the mirror.

But there was nothing there, nothing to see and regret, just an empty reflection of the other side of the room...

AFTERWORD TO "THE MIRROR IN THE MIRROR"

IN 2019 AUTHOR and editor Aiki Flinthart was diagnosed with terminal cancer. Her generous response—and her last project—was to edit an anthology of original stories called *Relics, Wrecks, & Ruins: Futures and Pasts, Fearless and Frightening*: a percentage of the royalties would help fund a writer-in-residence mentorship program for five years. When she asked me to contribute, I told her that I had a title, but no story to go with it; and then, for reasons known only to my unconscious, a story idea flashed in my mind after I did a podcast gig about Avram Davidson. As I told Aiki, "Avram's ghost kicked off the story."

When I showed an intermediate draft of the story to Barry Malzberg, my dear friend and occasional story collaborator, he wrote that the protagonists "twist in and out of that mirror like senile acrobats or crippled ballroom dancers. *This* is the meaning, the purpose and the end of life. They are Schrodinger's Children."

I had intended "The Mirror in the Mirror" to be a sort of cosmopolitan Fred Astaire/F. Scott Fitzgerald romp; but my characters had other intentions, as did, I suppose, the story itself. The last section came as a surprise to me, and showed me how the surface can reflect some dark depths. Or, I suppose, how my unconscious knows more than I do. I don't think I will ever figure out those dark, unconscious, oceanic processes that enable us to create stories out of...aether.

IN RE THE STRANGE FATE OF SAMUEL LANGHORNE CLEMENS

"Way! Way! The Martians are coming!"
—H. G. Wells (The War of the Worlds)

I FIRST SAW the redoubtable author, speaker, and raconteur Samuel Langhorne Clemens, otherwise known by his more recognizable nom de plume Mark Twain, when he spoke to a 'packed house', as they say, at the Melbourne Athenaeum Library Theatre on Collins Street in Melbourne city.

The invitation to hear and meet this man was proffered by his devoted wife (and my longtime catechumen and friend) Olivia Langdon, who had suffered from Pott's Disease as a child. I had been charged by my diocese and her influential parents to administer to her secular and religious educational needs when she could no longer attend classes at Thurston's Female Seminary in Elmira, New York; and we formed a life-long bond, which we have maintained through a lively correspondence over the years.

As I was not able to comply with Olivia's request to perform her marriage to Mister Clemens—that back in 1870—because I was administering to the aborigines of this great colony of Victoria, and as she had once again fallen ill and could not accompany him on this antipodean speaking tour to heal their finances, she was most insistent that her husband should finally make the acquaintance of 'the rector who had brought her ever closer to science and the Lord'.

I must confess to the reader that I have had but little to do with Olivia's literary, intellectual, and (it pains me to say) reformist accomplishments; and as I shall prove later in this recountal, I no longer even deserve to wear the clerical collar. Be that as it may, I fulfilled this particular obligation to Olivia by making the trip by rail from my parish in the gold mining town of Foster to Melbourne, where Mr. Clemens had kindly reserved a suite for me at the Grand Hotel, which was but a short walk from the Athenaeum. And although I was greeted with the usual civilities by the hotel staff, I must admit I was surprised that Mr. Clemens hadn't left me his card or a note to accompany the theatre ticket that the concierge handed me upon arrival.

"No, sir, I can assure you that the ticket was all we received," and that was that.

Well, Mr. Clemens must have had more on his mind than paying his respects to his wife's correspondent and former curate: I could not in good conscience have expected any more courtesy than the ticket and sumptuous hotel suite, the latter being certainly more expensive than anything I could afford on my own. As the lecture wasn't to begin until 9:00 pm, I entertained the idea of exploring the Royal Botanical Gardens, but thought better of it in case Mr. Clemens might yet try to call upon me at the hotel. Olivia had told me that he was prone to eleventh hour appearances. And as no such appearance eventuated, I dressed and enjoyed a stroll down Collins Street. I arrived at the theatre in plenty of time and, again, inquired as to the whereabouts of Mr. Clemens, but was told that he never sees patrons before he performs. With that I gave my ticket to a uniformed porter who guided me upstairs to my seat in the exclusive section of the balcony dress circle.

The star performer was late, and only when every seat was filled and the audience began shifting in their seats and talking in louder and louder voices did Mr. Mark Twain step out from behind a curtain decorated with the stars and stripes of the United States. The audience seemed to be struck dumb, for I could not hear a sound except for the breathing of the woman beside me and the general rustling of clothes as people shifted positions, suddenly coming to attention en masse.

Mr. Clemens was dressed immaculately in evening clothes and his patent leather shoes flashed in the glare of the lime lights, but his clothes belied his affect, which at first blush seemed unsure and seemingly provincial. His uncut gray hair looked like it was hastily combed, if it all, and he looked frail, far older than his years, and somehow unkempt. And yet...and yet, as I have just noted, he was perfectly dressed. Perhaps the combination of frizzy hair, thick mustaches, and bulbous nose gave me that impression...and the way he initially moved, as if he was surprised to have stepped onto a stage. He took a few awkward, tentative steps across the platform, blinked at the lights, and then suddenly pivoted toward the audience, as if he now recognized every soul seated before him and was absolutely sure of himself and his elevated place in the world. The audience roared in appreciation, and I found myself clapping along with everyone else.

"Now I know that all you good people are here to be entertained," he said, walking purposely back and forth across the stage like a ship's captain pacing his quarterdeck. "And I would guess that you're all probably waiting for me to tell a story or two, as it seems that I've been known to do that from time to time." He waited for the laughter and shouting to subside, and then continued: "Now I do not claim that I can *tell* a story as it ought to be told. I only claim to know *how* a story ought to be told.

There are several kinds of stories, but there is only one difficult kind, and that's the humorous story, which is the one I'll talk to you about. And the humorous story is American…of course!"

After the applause died down, he called for a chair which was brought out to him by a stagehand. Then he sat down, lit a cigar, and began talking to us as if we were at an intimate gathering. "The art of telling a humorous story—understand, I mean by word of mouth, not print—was (as I said) created in America, and has remained at home. But I consider it my paramount moral duty to bring it here to you."

Perhaps it was the temperament of the crowd, the anticipation of hearing the great man speak, the great man who had travelled so far to be here, but all those around me were ready to laugh at every intonation, at every calculated pause; and to my surprise, I found myself absorbed in the hilarity, if hilarity it was, for as I listened I could not help but understand that he was in actuality giving us an American version of an Aristotelian lecture on the nature of humor. I knew we were being mocked, but I could not ascertain exactly how he was doing it, nor could I prove what I've just alleged. I remember him saying, "Let me set down an instance of the comic method, using an anecdote which has been popular all over the world for, oh, maybe twelve or fifteen hundred years. The teller tells it in this way…"

And I was amazed, as transfixed as were my neighbors, as he took on the aspect and intonation of an elderly farmer from the Midwest of his country telling his story of a wounded solder. I won't bore you with my fragmented recollection of the story: suffice it to say the tale received a standing ovation. What I wish to relate happened after the telling, after he explained (in what I considered a condescending manner) the art of stringing incongruities and absurdities together in a wandering and seemingly purposeless way.

As I mentioned earlier, I was comfortably seated in the exclusive dress circle: my seat was in the very center of the center section, first row. Mr. Clemens crossed to a position directly before me and looking up at me—I'm certain he knew who I was as I was wearing my clerical collar—he said, "When I was in Sydney I had a large dream, and in the course of talk I told it to a missionary from India who was on his way to visit some relatives in New Zealand." He smiled, nodded (at me?), and continued: "I dreamed that the visible universe is the physical person of God; that the vast worlds that we see twinkling millions of miles apart in the fields of space are the blood corpuscles in His veins; and that we and the other creatures are the microbes that charge with multitudinous life the corpuscles."

I felt more than a little uncomfortable at this profane turn of his lecture, and I might add that his penetrating upward gaze actually felt hot on my face, as if he were directing poisonous igneous rays toward me from his squinted eyes. Did I detect the ghost of a smile? I could not be sure.

"Now this missionary, whom we'll call Mr. X., considered the dream awhile, then said: 'It is not surpassable for magnitude, since its metes and bounds are the metes and bounds of the universe itself; and it seems to me that it almost accounts for a thing which is otherwise nearly unaccountable—the origin of the sacred legends of the Hindus. Perhaps they dream them, and then honestly believe them to be divine revelations of fact. It looks like that, for the legends are built on so vast a scale that it does not seem reasonable that plodding priests such as myself could happen upon such colossal fancies when awake.'

"And then," continued Mr. Clemens, "when I asked my pious missionary about his personal belief, he told me that—and I quote—'There are many nations in the world, and each group of nations has its own gods, and will pay no worship to the gods of the others. Each group believes its own gods to be strongest, and it will not exchange them except for gods that shall be proven to be their superiors in power. Man is but a weak creature, and needs the help of gods: he cannot do without it. So, too, do we as Christians know when a man is working by God's power and not by his own. We know, for instance, that there was a supernatural property in the hair of Samson, for when it was shorn, he was as other men...'"

With that, the speaker shrugged and raised his hands in supplication, obviously enjoying the stunning effect upon his audience, which had suddenly become as silent as the proverbial mouse. However, I took his words and manner and intense, focused stare as a personal insult, as I'm sure it was meant to be. I know not why he had chosen to disparage me, although I must admit even now that he did it with such subtlety that no one else could have or would have guessed the insult or his motives. Nor could I understand his motives. Had I not been anything but friend and counselor to his helpmate over the years? Surely it could not be jealousy on the husband's part. Surely not. I did find out the truth, but not on that particularly devastating night, for even as Mr. Clemens looked up at me with such ferocious intensity, the world was about to come to an end, and resurrection would seem infinitely distant to those such as myself, who might be compared with the transient creatures that swarm in a drop of water.

For it was at that very moment that Melbourne exploded, or to be specific, I felt a change in temperature, as if I and the entire company around me had been transported into a boiling hell; and I heard a strange roaring, a machine-like stuttering such as I had never heard before. Then the theatre shook as if the hand of God had slapped it: surely, this must be an earthquake. But that would not explain the sudden, intense blast of heat.

A portion of the ceiling collapsed right before me, falling on the hapless assembly below, and I was literally thrown out of my seat as the balcony began shaking and cracking. Panicked neighbors to my left rushed toward the immediate safety of the exit door wing, while a heavyset woman seated to my right elbowed me back into my seat in her scramble to get to the doorway. As I struggled for breath, others pushed roughly past me and disappeared through the double-door exit. I got up to follow and felt a terrible stabbing pain in my foot, which had been stepped upon, and as I fell back onto the cushions of my chair, I experienced the prolongation of what could have only been seconds into a long moment: the stage and seats below were veiled in swirling plaster dust, and I looked for Mr. Clemens—this occurring in an instant, mind you—but could not see him. Patrons behind me and below were shouting and clamoring to escape, and the heat...the heat was suffocating.

Someone shouted "Fire!"

I heard crashing, saw the far wall to my right bulge, then crack open like an egg to reveal tongues of flame—this vision of the fires of Hell was my recurrent nightmare, and now it was fact!—and I pushed myself down into the aisle, foolishly and irrationally hoping for the protection of the seats, which were, of course, constructed of flammable fiber. I did indeed feel a fiery breath streaming above me. I closed my eyes tight and held my breath, as an overpoweringly acrid smell burned my nose and throat. But I certainly couldn't remain curled up in the aisle like a child; I had to face whatever the Lord had prepared for me.

Rising, I found myself staring right through a rupture in the ceiling and the wall behind the proscenium arch. I can only describe what I saw as some sort of enormous armored spider, which must have been taller than a house. Although plaster dust impeded my view, I could see that the metal machine or creature had extended a long, flexible, glittering tentacle no thicker than a walking stick. It whipped across the stage and captured a pitiable figure trying to escape: I could only pray that it wasn't Mr. Clemens.

But I had no time for further contemplation because I reflexively ducked as the shining silver spider directed a beam of intense heat and a contained stream of foul-smelling black smoke into the theater. And then, wreathed in its *own* miasma of unearthly green smoke and still hoisting the poor soul caught in its grasp, it moved away into the distance, prancing on long, thin metallic legs as if it were wearing seven-league boots.

So the demonic phantasm had seemingly finished with us.

But, alas, it had left us a terrible offertory...

The stream of roiling black smoke the creature had ejaculated now covered the first floor. It was oily and shiny and heavier than the densest fog, and it poured smoothly over the floor, seats, stage, and what was left of the audience scrambling for the exits. What happened next is akin to a dream, a nightmare where cause might (or might not) follow effect, but perception is skewed in such a way that words might become objects and ears might see. It was in such a state that I watched the doomed people below me fall screaming into the poisonous black ocean of smoke, none to rise thereafter; but I couldn't *hear* their screams: I just *knew* the unfortunates were calling, pleading, shouting, for my psyche was so overwhelmed that my ears were stoppered and my eyes recorded their pleas for help as exudations of the poisonous sea that overwhelmed them. The black smoke moved like a living thing, or like carbolic gas pouring from a volcano until all the surfaces below me were covered; and even then it flowed rather than diffused as any earthly gas would be wont to do.

It pains me to relate that I could but gaze helplessly at the extinction below me. As I mumbled the first line of Psalm 46, I noticed that the gas was forming into layers: the bottommost streams were diminishing, turning a sickly ochre color, and settling. Perhaps the deadly stuff was dispersing! I experienced a small surge of hope and an obscenely selfish relief as I surveyed the dead and gauged my chances of getting out of this theater alive. Then the balcony began to tremble as if it was a live thing; and I feared that in moments or perhaps seconds, it would indeed collapse...or the rest of the ceiling would collapse. I was, to coin a phrase, *incidit in scyllam cupiens vitare charybdim*: caught between Scylla and Charybdis: if I remained where I was, I would certainly fall to my death; and if I could manage my way downstairs, I would die of lung poisoning. But the gaseous, eddying lake *was* diminishing. I could see that where the gas had completely changed color, it became transformed into floury dust.

Slowly, cautiously, I made for the exit. There was no one left at this level: those who had made their way downstairs were certainly already dead, although I comforted myself with the thought that they might have escaped the building before the metallic spider had released its heavy poison. I waited beside the exit, my back against the wall, as if a solid object could somehow protect me; and when I heard another portion of the ceiling collapse, I quickly made my way down the stairs. It was a miracle—if, indeed, such a word should even be spoken in such circumstances—that the stairway itself hadn't collapsed. Holding my soiled handkerchief over my nose and mouth, I then ran through swirling black dust, almost tripping over the corpse of the heavyset woman who had earlier elbowed me back into my seat, and escaped the theater directly through its front door. Escaped into a blast furnace, for Melbourne was on fire. Buildings had exploded (and were exploding!). What had been Collins Street and Little Collins Street and Bourke Street were now rubble, and an unearthly green glow emanating from the heavens above illuminated this hellish transmogrified city.

People were running in every direction.

A patrol of soldiers shouting "Out of our way, out of our way" pushed past me, and I barely escaped being run over by a hansom cab. I sought momentary shelter against a building wall so that I might get my bearings and found myself staring, transfixed, at the huge armored spiders, or tripods, if you will, that were moving steadily and purposely in the distance. I could but glimpse them through the smoke, fire, and glowing haze. I would learn soon enough that they were not automata, but buttressed war vehicles: the steely integuments that contained the octopoidal Martian invaders. Their movements gave the impression of synchronization and choreography, but I admit to describing them in this manner because I have never served in the military. I'm sure a more astute observer would describe their movements more precisely in terms of maneuver and strategic advantage.

And as the tripods moved, they swept streets and lanes with their heat rays. Buildings exploded as if bombs had been placed inside them. Omnibus cable trams burned and melted, their tracks transformed into molten rivulets. Yet, perhaps, just perhaps, all was not lost, for I also heard the booming of artillery and saw one of the tripods come under fire. A projectile smashed into its silvery plating, and the tripod lost its footing whilst firing its heat ray from one of its metallic arms. As the monster toppled, the green-flashing heat ray voluted: not only did it set fire to the surrounding buildings, but it also struck one of its comrades. Both tripods collapsed to the jubilant shouts of everyone, including myself. This was a short-lived joy, however, for it was as if the creatures' minds were telepathically connected (which indeed they were) because other tripods immediately blasted our troops and converged upon their fallen comrades. Perhaps it was an afterthought, but then they turned their heat rays on everything around them. As children might whirl weighted skip ropes around their heads, so did the tripods deliberately and purposively begin to spray a large circumference with death. And I could see that the Martians' green-flashing heat-ray funnels were turning in my direction.

As did everyone else around me!

Chaos ensued. Horse guards appeared seemingly from out of nowhere and rode through the pedestrians as scythes through wheat. Motor cars and horse drawn vehicles rushed this way and that. Some were boarded, their drivers and passengers thrown into the street. Carriages were overturned. The screaming, frightened crowd had turned into a maddened mob. The hoi polloi as well as the more affluent pushed and punched each other in a mad rush to escape the oily flames; and I must admit that I was no different than any of the other panicked pedestrians. I ran, ran madly, pulling and pushing past others as the world turned red around me. I felt the searing heat, felt my face burn and itch, and the coins in my pocket became so hot that I screamed in pain. I tore the pockets open, all the while running with no sense of direction or purpose other than that given to all threatened, fleeing animals. But I was lucky: I had escaped the direct ray. I was only blistered: my frizzled beard came away like confetti when I touched my stinging cheek.

A cyclist careened past, knocking me down; and an instant later I found the cycle overturned. The rider's clothes were on fire, and the poor man stood up as if he could run away from the flames devouring him. Without considering right or wrong (although, may God forgive me, it was too late for him), I grabbed the bicycle, set it aright, and rode off as fast as my legs could push the pedals. And then I, too, was knocked off my perch, so to speak, by a drunkard, who swung an empty bottle at my head, then kicked at me. I got up as quickly as I could, lest I be trampled by those rushing past. The bicycle had, of course, disappeared.

I heard a woman's scream; and, finally, I regained not only my balance, but what I like to think of as my moral compass. I hurried around a corner and saw two men trying to drag two ladies out of their little pony-chaise while a third man dressed in what was no more than rags held the frightened pony's head. I could see that it was an older, stout woman who was screaming while her courageous, young companion was fighting a black-bearded tough off with her whip. A scruffy-looking red-haired man came around from the other side and tried to pull her out of the chaise.

I shouted "Desist!" and ran toward them. Although I am now in my late middle years, I was an expert boxer in my youth; and when the wretch closest to me rushed toward me with brass knuckles, I gave him a roundhouse kick and a punch to the jaw. I then approached the one holding the pony. He let go of the chaise, and the young woman smacked the carriage horse with her whip.

As the carriage receded down the lane, I was struck from behind. I saw a brief yet brilliant flash of yellow light as I fell. Although I was dizzy and concussed, I remained conscious. And then I heard gunfire, or rather a shot being fired nearby. I looked up to glimpse my assailants running away helter-skelter.

Well…?" asked a gentleman looking down at me as he leaned out of a charred, square phaeton buggy. He had been dressed in evening attire, which was now scorched and grey with ash; his black hair and mustaches were singed and frizzled, and his forehead and clean-shaven cheeks were burned and blistered. He was slender yet powerfully built and held a double-barrel howdah pistol, which was little more than a sawed-off rifle. "The world is on fire, Vicar. Do you wish to burn or bolt. The choice is yours."

As he spoke, he snapped his whip impatiently; and I gladly climbed into his carriage.

HE TOLD ME his name: Herbert Wells.

"And what's yours, Vicar?"

"Langdon McDowell, at your service, sir." I said, striking out at a thug wearing a torn Salvation Army jacket who appeared seemingly out of nowhere and tried to pull me out of the carriage: no doubt, intending to insert himself in my place. Every street, lane, and avenue was teeming with frightened, coughing people, many limping and bandaged, as most (including Mr. Wells and myself) were burned and blistered by the Martians' fire. But I suspected that terror-stricken mass of humanity had its own intent and direction. Like iron filings attracted to a loadstone, pedestrians as well as the more fortunate in wagons, drays, cabs, carriages, and motor cars were heading south: away from the immediate conflagration and toward the monolithic Flinders Street Station: Melbourne's rail terminus.

We, however, moved east across the crowd. After seeing the destruction to the tram tracks, Mr. Wells and I both agreed that our best prospect would be to find relatively near shelter and wait (and hope) for the Martians to move on…or for our armed forces to strengthen, regroup, and destroy them.

Thus did we travel through this unearthly cityscape as particles of dry red dust—the exudation of the Martians—roiled in the air, covering everything. We proceeded slowly and carefully, mindful of our stout-hearted horse, past Parliament House and into the Treasury Gardens. The red-hued atmosphere began to gave way to true darkness, to the comforting susurration of insects and the leaf-crunching movements of ringtail possums. A cloud of flying foxes flew overhead. Mr. Wells and I did not utter a word in the woods; it was as if—for these few moments—we had escaped not only the Martians, but time itself. There were people running about (mostly soldiers), but their movements were hushed; and by the time we reached the broad avenue of Powlett Street in East Melbourne, the only indication that the Last Days were upon us was the boiling red sky behind us. The streets and laneways were empty; the terrace-style homes devoid of light. Had everyone left? Were the residents hiding? Could they be…asleep, unaware of the horror surrounding them?

We heard reassuring, rumbling noises and then artillery wagons materialized out of the dust. The wagons were flanked by Victorian

Mounted Rifles, Rangers, artillerymen, and sappers in wide-brimmed slouch hats and small round caps. The soldiers' red, blue, or khaki jackets and dark trousers looked crisp and well-kept: they had not yet been stained with blood and the evil-hued dust produced by the alien invaders. Columns of fresh faced volunteer and professional troops, all marching smartly toward us, marching down Victoria Street, Albert Street, Grey Street. A young fuzz-faced soldier shouted to us from a carriage truck hauling a huge Maxim gun, "Halloo, we're the beast-tamers!"

And another: "To the front…to smash the beasts!"

Laughter. "Away with you, boyos"—this also directed to us—"or you'll get eaten!"

Mr. Wells waved back, then shook his head and said, "They're green as twigs. They think they're going to a picnic. But there won't be enough ground to bury them all in."

I nodded, admittedly feeling an appreciative security as I watched the troops massing and marching past and listened to the ringing clop-clop of the cavalry horses: thickset stocky bays known as Walers, and the rumbling of numberless carriage trucks, wagons, and hospital carriages. Mr. Wells fell silent, for he suddenly had his hands full trying to quiet his carriage horse.

"Hey, you two," shouted a sergeant in a practiced, stentorian voice, as he cut away from his men and rode over to us. His green and gray uniform was anything but well kept, and he looked grizzled, dirty, and exhausted; he wore a flapped ammunition bandolier and carried a lever-activated service rifle over his shoulder. "Unless you've got state or military business here, off with you both! This area has been cordoned off, and you're not safe here."

"We're safer than where we were," Mr. Wells said softly, glancing back at the western sky, which seemed to be on fire.

The sergeant stared fixedly at my companion, then nodded. "I got caught up in Kew: we lost the 1st Militia Battalion there and most of the 4th in less than an hour. I just hope we can smash them's tripods before they can turn their heat rays at us again." He shook his head, as if he had acquired an exaggerated facial tic; and although he continued talking to us, he seemed to be directing himself to some faraway presence. "Yes, I know they's nothing but slimy octopus things once you get them out of their machines. They got no natural defenses. I killed one with my boot, yes I did: stepped right on its slimy head—they're mostly just big heads, anyway—and it squelched like a big huntsman spider." He turned away and mumbled, "Just like a big huntsman spider." The sergeant had a welt that extended across his ruddy, sunburned face; and because his eyebrows had been singed away, he appeared goggle-eyed: as if he was in a state of constant surprise. He regained himself and told us that all the residents had been forced to lock up and leave their houses. "Any that are still here…well, it's on them if they get burned out or eaten by them monsters."

"Eaten?" I asked.

"That's what I said. Well, maybe get dranked rather than eaten. They're bloodsuckers. I seen it, I did." Then his expression changed; he nodded blankly and mumbled, "I seen them, I did. They burned out Kew, just like they're going to burn us down." He now stood motionless as a store mannequin.

Mr. Wells thanked the sergeant and gently tapped the carriage horse on its rear with his whip and told it to 'Step'. Once we were away, he said, "Seems the old soldier has a bit of war nerves, poor sod."

I could but nod, and we rode: we rode past the troops moving west, and the forage capped artillerymen who were deploying medium field guns and old smooth bore brass howitzers were too preoccupied to notice us. Unlike the fresh-faced boys marching to the front, these men were as bedraggled and hollow-eyed as the sergeant who had stopped and cautioned us. Nevertheless they looked to be setting up their machines quickly and efficiently.

"How could we have been going about our business in Melbourne City when entire shires and townships were being destroyed by these… creatures?" I asked.

Although that was, of course, a rhetorical question. Mr. Wells responded thoughtfully: "If what we've experienced is anything to go on, I would suspect theirs is a strategy of containment." He made a guttural, laughing noise. "Destruction is certainly containment. 'And where ignorance is bliss, 'tis folly to be wise.'" When I didn't react as he no doubt expected, he said, "I should have thought you'd know Thomas Gray for his 'Elegy Written in a Country Churchyard'. He was quite a good poet."

Under different circumstances I would have attempted some sort of persiflage; but as I was not in a proper state, I simply stared toward the ominously empty streets ahead. After we turned down Clarendon Street, I commented that the residents could not have all left the area. They must be ensconced in their homes, in their cellars perhaps. They must be too afraid to turn on a light or—

"Whoa," Mr. Wells said as we approached the imposing grand entry of a very dark two story bluestone dwelling. "Would you be so kind as to inspect this house, Vicar? If it is occupied, surely one of its neighbors will provide us safe haven." Meantime, I will tend to the horse and hide the buggy from view."

"Shouldn't we stay together?" I asked.

"I will find you."

ISLANDS OF TIME

I KNOCKED ON the arched front door; and when no one answered, I found a rock with which to smash its stained-glass window and gained entry. Cognizant that my criminal activity would not pass unnoticed in Heaven, I guiltily felt my way through every floor, through every room of this sumptuous alcazar. I called out softly with each few steps I took, just in case the owners were hiding in one of the cavernous chambers, but I was certainly and surely alone...until Mr. Wells found me when I returned to a drawing room that overlooked the north portico.

"I've investigated two of the other terrace houses on the street," Mr. Wells said. "I sense something very wrong here, as if—"

"Yes...?"

"As if we're being watched. Can you feel it?"

"Do you mean here, in this particular room?" I asked. I could easily make out his features, red-tinged in the crepuscular light streaming through a high window.

"Yes," he said impatiently. "On this street, in this room, everywhere around us." I looked around the shadowy salon with its velvet sofas and formally placed ottomans, its grand piano and pool table which awkwardly faced each other; but I could not sense anything other than a sudden pounding in my head.

"Well, except for a sudden mi—"

My suggestion that I might be experiencing the onset of a migraine headache was cut short by the muffled booming of artillery and the rattle of Maxims, and then the very floor heaved under us as the room seemed to explode into brilliant white light. And then deafening explosions as Martian heat-rays struck our artillery projectiles, melted our armaments, destroyed buildings nearby, and transformed cobblestones into the lethality of canister shot.

"Downstairs, quickly," Mr. Wells said, and we didn't stop until we reached the basement story. A small barred window near the ceiling allowed the sickly green light to suffuse the room, a portion of which was devoted to the storage of root vegetables, hanged meat, wine, and other foodstuffs.

"Well, at least we won't starve," I whispered, as if the Martians were standing just outside the barred window.

"If we can survive long enough to experience satiation," Mr. Wells said, seating himself across two crates.

"Well—"

He told me to be quiet, and, of course, I acceded to his wish. We listened to the faint screams of men hurt or dying, to the occasional clatter of horse and wagon, to the distant roar of a fire: most likely the Treasury and Fitzroy Gardens we had passed through earlier. And the percussion of cannon, the dull distant noise of battle and death, and my own heart-stabbing fear and panic stretched all emotion into a sort of regularity, a metronomic steady beat of resignation. It was in that state that I broke bread with Mr. Wells, for we had found enough victuals in the larder cupboard to provide us with a rather sumptuous cold dinner of cured ham, smoked bacon, some limp lettuce, stilton, nesselrode pie, and a half-bottle of very good Madeira.

We ate sparingly, however, as we knew not how long we might have to take advantage of the bounty of our unknown hosts' home. And even though I was no better than a thief in another man's house, *Corinthians 9:27* flashed into my mind: "Discipline the body and keep it under control, lest after preaching to others I myself should be disqualified." Ah, the Lord is certainly capable of great irony...and that ironical thought was followed by a blinding glare of green light and then a punishing blast, a concussion that knocked me unconscious.

I woke up to see Mr. Wells' green-shadowed face near my own.

"Well, after a cursory examination, I don't believe any of your bones are broken," he whispered as he knelt over me. His breath smelled fetid "Now try to remain quiet, for there is smashed crockery everywhere. And if you move, you'll make a noise, and—"

I nodded, for I could see beyond the collapsed wall which had once supported the barred window: five or six crablike excavating machines with jointed legs, levers, and metallic arms that could reach, clutch, and dig were working in smooth coordination to turn the pit caused by the explosion into some sort of hippodrome or coliseum. Everything, including our prostrate selves, was bathed in the auroral greenish light of the open air, for the house had collapsed backward. The floor above was completely destroyed: all that remained was the scullery which we inhabited. We were in effect buried in the earth and ruins, buried on every side except that facing the excavation, of which we were now a part of.

And we could clearly see, up close, as it were, the actual Martians denudated of their metallic integuments. The brain-addled sergeant who had stopped our carriage on Powlett Street was right when he said that the Martians were mostly just big heads. Their huge heads or bodies—it was difficult to discern one from another—were about four feet in diameter. Their faces had no nostrils, just great, owlish eyes above beaks that seemed to be composed of hardened flesh. And below their beaks were bunches of long reticulated tentacles arranged around small adipose lips the color of raw liver. These sinewy appendages functioned as hands and feet do for us, but our greater gravity made it difficult for these creatures to use them propulsively. The Martians were gathered together in groups around open, makeshift pens, each containing equal numbers of inert and probably drugged human captives; every once in a while one of the Martians would make a whistling noise; but for the most part they seemed to be communicating without words...communing telepathically, one head to another.

I thought at the time that perhaps my migraine symptoms and Mr. Wells' earlier perception of 'wrongness', of being watched might be side-effects of the Martians' telepathic 'noise'. But such an errant thought—and, indeed, my need to describe it here—are symptomatic of my reaction to the horror I witnessed from the vantage of the basement larder. To this day I try to escape, to bury and suppress that terrible vision...that vision of Martians reaching into the pens with their proboscide tentacles and feeding on the human beings they had captured; and even as we watched this abomination in fascinated disgust, the Martians' crab-like automatons had begun to herd hundreds of men, women, and, God protect them, children into a newly finished and closed section of the pit. Presumably, the entire pit and many more like it would become holding stations for the cattle they had come to Earth to feed upon.

And Merciful Heavens feed they did.

They didn't need to chew flesh; there was no cracking of bones, no mastication; no, these foul, globular creatures simply inserted a dart-tipped proboscis into their living captives and imbibed their blood directly. They literally drank them dry! And their human fodder did not—or could not!—twist or shudder or utter a word.

Unlike we more composite humans, the Martians had no need for glands, digestive organs, and hormonal regulation: no need for what an astute author of my acquaintance had described as the organic fluctuations of mood and emotion. These creatures had left tooth and claw and emotion behind, along with their need for digestion. No ructions of love or fear or hatred for them. They were in simplicity and complexity giant brains, fleshy intelligences that could create ideas and machines to fulfill any and all of their ghoulish, dispassionate dreams...and they dreamed of us...as food.

Which they would cultivate and farm and slaughter.

ISLANDS OF TIME

I AWAKENED TO a wickedly roseate dawn tinged with the greenish aurora of the previous night. For a moment I could not determine where I was; and then memory overcame my mind's resistance. I felt ill as I gazed outward into the pit, which was now compartmentalized into holding pens, feeding and forcing yards, waiting bays, circulating catwalks, and gates. Beyond the processing facility a spherical unit arrayed with heat ray funnels burned blood-drained bodies into ash.

The smell of burning flesh was overwhelming.

Mr. Wells was kneeling beside me; how long he had been there watching the machines, I could not tell.

"They've gone," he whispered. "They've all gone."

True enough: there was not a Martian to be seen. Only their machines, which crab-walked around and through the facility as they executed their assigned tasks. We could no longer see any of the human captives, for the pens were empty and discarded and the pit was now a completed walled facility.

"The Martians must only feed at night," Mr. Wells continued. "That is only a guess, of course, as we have only been here for—"

"We must leave before they return," I said, feeling a sudden, inexplicable surge of impatience. "Right now."

"No," Mr. Wells said, looking calm and focused, as if he were simply contemplating whether to move a bishop or a knight on a chessboard. "I believe we should wait a bit longer. Get the lay of the land, so to speak. Watch and see if their machines are capable of surveillance, and if so how we might best circumvent them." Then Mr. Wells bent low so as not to expose himself to outside eyes—either machine or alien—and crawled away from me. I noticed that while I had slept, he had cleared a rough path free of any shards of glass, shattered crockery, plaster, and splintered wood: a path past where the larder cupboard had stood to the stairway which might give us entry to the uppermost tier of the excavation and possible escape. But I did not have a chance to whisper, "No, I don't think we should wait." I didn't have a chance to tell him that I, too, had felt as if we were being watched...and that I felt the pitiless stare of something cold and calculating and very near right this very minute.

And thus we, or rather he lost any chance of escape...

UNFORTUNATELY, MR. WELLS was wrong: the Martians could and did feed day or night, for, as I was to learn later, they had no need for sleep as we know it; and as I watched Mr. Wells carefully crawl past the area where the wan morning light streamed into what was left of the larder, I saw a grayish tentacle slithering silently down the stairs as fast as water sluicing into a well. Reflexively—and without even considering the possibility that I might endanger myself—I shouted to warn Mr. Wells of his immediate danger.

No, that is a lie! Even now my mind still seeks to bury my misdeeds, even at the very moment my pen touches paper, even as I try to expiate myself by composing this true and scrupulous narrative. No, I did *not* warn Mr. Wells of immediate danger!

I watched, transfixed and in abject terror, as the snaking tentacle paused in the stairwell for an instant before lashing itself around Mr. Wells and evulsing him upward and out of my line of sight. And then my turn came, for two or three more tentacles slithered down the stairs, waving back and forth, searching, crawling, investigating, as if their extremities had eyes. I backed away, but there was nowhere to go except into the excavation itself. But anything would be better than being seized by those grasping feelers.

It was then that I heard a strange, alien shrieking, a hellish sound that I can only describe as something like a combination of chittering cicadas and baying hounds. And at that instant the tentacles furiously began slapping against the ceiling, walls, and floor in what I could only imagine as some sort of convulsive death throe before being pulled—or so it seemed—back up the stairwell to where they had originated.

Then silence, except for my bellows-loud breathing. Silence and the greenish light of sunrise. But I could not hold back my guilt, disgust, and panic. I had to get away from this place, and as we had not seen anything but the Martians' automata in the pit, I thought to take my chances and find a gate or outlet through which I might escape. But as I stood up, a voice sounded in my head, as if I was hearing the internal vocalizations of my conscience.

"Move away from the opening! Immediately!"

Even as I did so, I thought I could recognize that voice and its particular accent. "Who…or what are you?" I asked.

"Come up the stairs where you will be safe, and I'll explain."

"Safe? My companion just—"

"Mr. Wells might well survive to tell the tale, even though I fear he will suffer a bit of amnesia for a time."

"How do you know who he is and what he is about? How—?"

"Lower your voice. Just think what you wish to say, and I'll hear you. You might have already given your position away. You must choose: remain here and die, or trust what you are hearing and climb the goddamn stairs!" Then I heard the voice again and somehow I knew it was an afterthought: *"What you believe to be machines working in the excavation are not automata at all. They are Martian slaves and can perceive any change in their surroundings as well as any armored Martian. And I am not strong enough to protect you from the lot of them."*

I knew that voice! It was…Mr. Clemens.

But how could *that* be possible?

"Move!"

IN RE THE STRANGE FATE OF SAMUEL LANGHORNE CLEMENS

After I heard the clank and creak of metal in the excavation beyond, I obeyed: I crawled to the stairway where Mr. Wells had been seized and climbed the stairs.

"*Keep going.*"

"Can you see me?"

"*In more ways than you could ever imagine.*"

I climbed the stairs, then climbed over what seemed like a mountain of earth, bricks, plaster, and smashed and broken household objects. I tripped over the protruding leg of a buried settee and fell, sliding backwards down through the rubble. I might well have broken my back on the cement stairs below me, but my fall was arrested by tentacles that encircled me and drew me upwards to the relative safety of what was now high ground (and what had previously been street level). Shivering with fear and disgust, I nevertheless registered that the tentacles pressed and squeezed around me as if they were fingers kneading bread. And then, released by the tentacles that had saved me, I found myself as close as I ever want to be to a dead Martian: its two-story armor carapace was burn-blackened where it had been sheared almost in half, and its three metallic legs were bent, splayed, and broken. Although still partly connected to its lower carapace, gravity had brought down the torso; and the hood that had contained the Martian rested on the ground, which was saturated with a striated greenish-black ichor. The Martian—presumably the one that had attacked Mr. Wells—stared upward with dulled owl eyes, as if staring at the kindred creature that had so recently felled it: the monster that kneeled before me on its tripod legs.

The monster that bowed until it was low enough to the ground to open its hood and reveal its dual nature, for the victorious Martian looked as pallid and dull-eyed as the creature it had destroyed; but tethered to this Martian was the limp, corpselike body of a man: Mr. Samuel Langhorne Clemens.

"Mr. Clemens," I cried.

"*Direct yourself to me, parson…to the tentacled creature that has not yet breathed its last breath.*"

"But—"

"*Desist your verbalization. For your safety and*"—I swear I could hear his sardonic laughter—"*for mine.*" Those thoughts hurt, as if every word, so to speak, compounded the migraine throbbing in my brain.

I nodded and said, or rather thought, "*How have you become this… this thing?*"

"*The 'I' which once inhabited the rusk of my body*—my *body, which is barely alive and will not live for much longer—was poached, shall we say, by the Martian within whom I presently inhere. This Martian is, or rather was, special: a telepathist who could enter alien minds. Most Martians can only commune amongst themselves, but this one ranked high in their scientific estate. He and others like him would rule our minds and restrict our thoughts.*"

"*And yet…?*"

"*Ah, yes,*" said this composite Martian and Mr. Clemens, "*but these creatures have a tragic flaw: hubris. How could they even consider their cattle as their equals? But I am—or was—a very bullish sort of kine; and while the Martian drained my blood, drained just enough to pleasure himself and weaken me, while he probed and investigated my psyche, my thoughts and memories and knowledge, I insinuated myself into* his *psyche. I hid inside his great brain and twisted his thoughts into my own. Who is the slave and who is the master now? I ask myself. But such a question has no relevance, for both of us will soon cease to exist. My remains, which are strapped to this Martian body, are nothing more than a faded memory. And the Martian who talks to you now as myself is dying.*"

(This sibylline conversation, which I have tried to render as just that: a conversation, was, in fact, more of an 'immanence', an almost instantaneous sequence of revelations, which I don't believe lasted for more than an instant. I must beg the reader to forgive both this narrative intrusion and my inability to describe this singular experience.)

"*And* we," continued Mr. Clemens, "*must ask you a favor in return for saving your life, Vicar.*" I could sense a smile, which I visualized as a flower blooming and then dying, turning from resplendent red to black and rot. "*And we, or rather I, have a confession to make.*"

"*Yes...?*"

"*Do you remember when our eyes met during my talk at the Athenaeum Theatre? Of course you do!*"

"*Could you read my mind even then?*" I asked.

"*No, but I can now...and your memories: those I can read...*" Although Mr. Clemens gazed at me, or perhaps through me, the Martian through which he communicated looked intently at me with its great owl eyes. "*And I must acknowledge my jealousy of you, acknowledge that I have* always *been jealous of you. It was because of my misplaced jealousy and anger that I could not bear to rendezvous with you at your hotel, could not shake your hand nor welcome you to Melbourne. I can now but beg your forgiveness.*"

"*But why on earth would you be jealous of...me? You who—*"

"*Because for all the years of our marriage, Olivia talked of you, talked incessantly about your faith and friendship and...*"

"*Yes?*"

"*Friendship and love.*"

"*Platonic love,*" I insisted. "*Platonic love.*"

The creature that had tethered Mr. Clemens to itself did not have the facial musculature to express emotion, but those eyes drilled into my own; and I saw that he knew...he *knew* that I had been in love with Olivia, that every letter I wrote her was an expression of that extramundane love. And perhaps, just perhaps, she might have felt something more than a modicum of affection for me.

Again I insisted, "*But it* was *Platonic!*"

"*Yes, I can see that.*" The Martian's eyes seemed to change color. "*But as a last request, I must ask you to share your love with her.*"

"*What?*"

"*Olivia is dying, Vicar.*"

"*Dying?*"

"*Her old enemy—Pott's Disease—has worsened considerably,*" Mr. Clemens continued, "*and she is now permanently bedridden. I will not be able to look after her. But you can...and must. Ironic, isn't it, that a Martian has given you your heart's desire.*"

I won't burden the reader with the humiliating complexity of my emotions at that moment, if, indeed, this recountal—which tries to translate what occurred instantaneously into a sequential conversation—can even be considered accurate. I can say that before we—or I—returned to what we know as sequential time, I knew that I would do as he asked: I promised never to tell Olivia the truth of what had happened to her husband.

It was then that the Martian, that grotesque life form that now contained Mr. Clemens' will and spirit, closed its metallic hood, rose to its full height, and released—or rather discarded—the now dead body of Samuel Langhorne Clemens. As he did so, armored Martian slaves clambered over the lip of the pit compound, and Mr. Clemens raised his metallic arms and melted the Martians with his heat rays as if they were glass. However, more slaves appeared, like insects swarming, as did their Martian masters: tripodal in their armored integuments.

And the world seemed suddenly to be boiling and melting in the flames.

To this day I have no idea how I survived that doomed and abbreviated battle of the one against the many. All I remember is Mr. Clemens, his incorporeal presence calm as a summer's day, whispering or perhaps shouting, I know not: "*Run, Vicar...find my Olivia, comfort her, and tell her that I—*"

IN RE THE STRANGE FATE OF SAMUEL LANGHORNE CLEMENS

ALAS, I COULD not try to complete Mr. Clemens' last sentence in Olivia's sweet presence, for she passed into the arms of the Lord while I was in transit to America; and after putting her affairs in order, I returned to Elmira, New York, where I once again became a tutor at Thurston's Female Seminary and preached on Sundays to a small congregation in one or another of the parishioner's homes.

And the Martians…?

Should they return, we who survived can envision their fate: by the blast of God shall they perish, and by the breath of his nostrils shall they be consumed.

Amen!

POSTLUDE:

It was with great pleasure and trepidation that I read Mr. Wells' excellent account of the Martian invasion of Australia, and I am most grateful that he referred to me as a physician named Doctor Moreau rather than Langdon McDowell the cowardly vicar. And although our paths have never crossed again, I can but wish him crowning success and long life.

Rev. Langdon McDowell
Woodlawn House
Elmira, New York
3 October 1901

AFTERWORD TO "IN RE THE STRANGE FATE OF SAMUEL LANGHORNE CLEMENS"

I'VE BEEN LIVING in Australia for almost thirty years, yet it took about ten years before I began to feel comfortable/secure/established/stable enough to write about my new land. Although I'm a dual citizen, although I talk, gesture, and act as if I've just left New York, I'm nevertheless a stranger, albeit a comfortable one, in my country of origin. Australia is also a strange and exotic place for me, even after all these years; but I think I've osmosed enough of the culture and feel enough kinship with the axiomatic "Australian mindset" that my unconscious finally and firmly began to settle into this 'second phase' of my lived experience. I found myself writing stories set in and about Australia, stories such as "Mr. Death Goes to the Beach", "Trainspotting in Winesburg", "Mohammed's Angel", and…"In re the Strange Fate of Samuel Langhorne Clemens."

In fact, quite a few of the stories in this volume feature Australian settings.

In 2018 Steve Proposch, Christopher Sequeira, and Bryce Stevens asked me to write an alternate history story in which H. G. Wells' aliens invade Australia; this for their anthology *The War of the Worlds: Battleground Australia*. Although my initial response to their email was to say, "No, sorry, but keep me in mind for your next project," my fractious unconscious had another agenda entirely.

In the following days—or, rather, nights—I began to dream of Melbourne, Martians, the Victorian goldfields, Mark Twain, and (well, of course) Mr. Wells himself. These conflations soon began to cohere into a plot; and I developed an insistent urge to reread Wells' *War of the Worlds*, investigate the life of Mark Twain and his visit to Australia, and research the gold rush country town where I live (and the city of Melbourne, where I also live).

When I wrote back to Steve, Chris, and Bryce to accept their kind invitation, I was in the throes of a reading binge. I had just finished *The Warden*. That might explain why I told them that I'd be channeling Anthony Trollope to write this tale.

If my unconscious and Mr. Trollope (and H. G. Wells and Mark Twain) hadn't been in cahoots, this story might never have been written!

MOHAMMED'S ANGEL

THE AUSTRALIANS LOVE VEGEMITE, BUT WE LOVE DEATH.
—PLACARD WAVED AFTER BALI SETTLEMENT
MASSACRE BY MOHAMMED GHANDOUR, JR.
4 JULY 2019

LAURA MCKENZIE Langer, tall, blond, and handsome in her teal-blue *Suzi Marchette* housedress, leaned against the cast iron railing of her balcony and looked out at Wilson's Promontory. Laura had loved the Prom since she was a child. She used to imagine its landmass was a stone-grey dragon rising from the sea. It still looked like the mythical creature, especially now, when it was on fire. Smoke billowed up from the eastern tip of the national park like dragon's breath.

It was another stinking hot morning. The air was bitter and autumn-dry.

Laura went back into her air-conditioned study, ordered her live-in housemaid—whom she had nicknamed 'Helpless'—to bring her another cup of tea and a Turkish cigarette, and then tried calling her mother again. Large fashion photos in white mats and black lacquered frames covered the walls. All photos of her. Laura was *Suzi Marchette, the Suzi Marchette,* even if her mother had created and established the couturier brand.

"Hello, Mother," she said, directing Helpless to put her tea and cigarettes on the cloisonné table beside a chair with carved spiral arms where she had been sketching. The maid was a tall, fair-complected, almost pretty girl from Wales who had presented herself to Laura's husband Jason as a legal entrant. But it was easy to see that her entry papers were forged. Laura suggested to Jason that he hire her as a provisional indentured at half-wages.

"Mother…?"

"Yes, dear, I can hear you very well." The voice seemed to come from nowhere and float in the cool, breezy air.

"I've been *trying* to reach you all morning," Laura said, agitated.

"Well that's very kind of you, dear. I appreciate your concern."

Laura motioned to her maid. "I need an ash-tray. And matches."

"That's why you called me?" her mother asked.

"No, Mother," Laura said, resigned and frustrated. "I was talking to Helpless. Turn on the visual. Please… I can't stand talking to a disembodied voice."

"You called *me*, remember? And I'm not ready to be presentable."

The maid brought the matches and a cut-crystal ashtray. Laura waved her away. "Yes, and I'm your daughter, remember? I don't care how you look. I was terribly worried about you."

"Thank you, darling."

Have you seen the news?"

"Again with the news. Always with the news. I told you never to marry a politician, remember? I told you to marry Murray Taschen, who had his own money and would have given you a happy life."

"Murray Taschen is *dead*, Mother," Laura said.

"May he rest in peace, you would have been a wealthy widow; and you wouldn't have to work yourself to the bone and prostitute your talent so the Schmuck can afford to stay in office."

"Don't call him that."

"*You* do."

"Mother, goddammit, turn on the visual right now. I can't talk to you like this."

"If you want to see me, come back to Melbourne and buy me lunch at Vito's. I'm dying to walk down Collins Street again. I haven't done that since the riots."

"You know I can't do that."

"And why not?"

"Well, first of all, I've got Hanna home today. The school called another day of prayer because of the shortfalls, and it's the nanny's day off."

"You're too lax with your help," her mother said.

"She's always off on Wednesdays, Mother; and as you well know, my travel-pass is good only for Thursdays and Saturdays."

"The Schmuck has his diplomatic pass. You're his wife. God, even the Premier's wife has an unrestricted pass."

"I'm not the Premier's wife," Laura said.

"Obviously."

"Mother, I *only* called to see if you were all right...and, obviously, you're all right, so I'll hang—"

"And why shouldn't I be all right?" her mother said placatingly.

"Because your *shahid* neighbor martyred himself in your temple this morning."

"*My* temple?"

"Unless there's another Beth David Synagogue on Grey Street, half a block away from you," Laura said. "Don't tell me you didn't hear the explosion...or feel the vibrations"

Her mother didn't respond.

"You shut down your implants, didn't you," Laura said, sighing.

"It's the only way I can get a good night's sleep," her mother said.

"Well, thank the good Lord you weren't there. I was so worried because you're *always* at the temple on Wednesday mornings."

"I slept in," her mother said very quietly.

"Mother, turn on the damn visuals."

"I haven't been feeling up to par," she said vaguely. Then, "Did anyone survive the martyrdom?"

"No, Mother, the synagogue and the Catholic hospital complex next to it were completely destroyed," Laura said. "Worse than the Opera House. *Now* do you see why I was calling you?"

"My neighbor...you said my neighbor. You don't mean the Ghandour family? You don't mean Mohammed, do you...?"

"Yes, I think his name was something like that."

"He's such a lovely boy. He lives right next door in 11 E. He always brings me presents."

"He brings you presents?"

"Yes...presents."

"What does he bring you...what did he bring you?

"Just presents," her mother answered; and then dead silence.

Laura called to her.

The line was still intact.

"Mother. Mother...? Are you all right?"

"Yes, dear. Don't be so impatient."

"I was just about to call emergency. I think I'd better call a doctor for you anyway."

"I just checked the news," her mother said, ignoring Laura's threat to call the doctor. "Terrible...terrible. Yes, it was Mohammed. He saved me. I told him I was going to stay home today. I'm sure that's why he picked today. Well, he told me that paradise was right in front of his eyes. I should have known something was up when he said it was just beneath his thumb."

"You're talking utter nonsense."

Her mother sighed and said, "Your sister Lorraine was always the smart one in the family, but she wouldn't call me if I was dying."

"Yes, she would, Mother."

"So now you've got the business and most of my money, and you're as dum—" She stopped herself and said, "I haven't got your university education, and *I* understand what Mohammed meant."

"And what was that, mother?" Laura said coldly.

"He meant that a detonator lies beneath his thumb." She paused, then said, "I *must* have some flowers sent to his parents."

"I thought you said you checked the news. His mother and father were both in the temple."

"Whatever for? They're Muslims."

"How would I know?" Laura said. "You know all the answers. Go find Lorraine and ask her."

"Wait," Laura's mother said and checked the news again. "Ah…it was the ecumenical breakfast. It's a big deal. The mayor and the bishop and that blind teli-minister who speaks in tongues—and God only knows who else—will have been there. I'm surprised your husband wasn't in attendance."

"He's in Canberra, Mother."

Laura's mother sighed and said, "Mohammed shouldn't have carried his parents away with him, but he once told me—"

"Told you what, Mother?" Laura insisted.

"That he belongs to God…and that an angel came down from Heaven to tell him that God is going to take revenge on *all* religions, on all the churches, mosques, and synagogues."

"And you never thought it might be an idea to report that to the authorities?" At that moment little Hannah ran into Laura's study. She had her mother's white-blond hair and dimples, and she was wearing pearl pink jodhpurs and a matching pearl-neck cardigan.

"Mommy, who are you talking to?" Daddy?" The little girl looked around and said, "He's not here." Then in a hushed voice: "Are you talking to...Grandpa?"

"Grandpa's in Heaven, honey, remember?"

Hannah nodded sagely. "Uh, huh, I remember, that's why I thought maybe you were talking to him."

"Go put some shoes on. You'll get a sliver in your foot running around like that."

She balanced on one foot and held the other one in her hand. "Were you talking to Grandpa's ghost? I talk to angels in the garden, but you can *see* them."

"No, Hannah, I wasn't talking to Grandpa's ghost. At least he would have made some sense. I was talking to your pigheaded grandmother, who is in the process of going completely mad and has forgotten all her manners."

"Grandma doesn't have a pig head, and she doesn't get mad all the time like you," Hannah said, scowling and dropping back onto two feet.

"That's right, baby," Laura's mother said.

Her image suddenly appeared big as life and in high-definition color and contrast in the center of the room. She wore an appropriate sea blue night-dress, privacy veil, and a satin mourning scarf. "Mommy's being very mean to Grandma," she said to her granddaughter as she petted a brown and white masked beagle puppy that was wriggling around on her lap.

"She's mean to me, too," Hannah said; and then suddenly realizing that there was a *puppy* on her grandmother's lap, she shrieked with joy. "I want to pat the puppy too is that your puppy where'd you get him Mommy I want a puppy too why can't I have one is that one for me, Grandma?"

"This puppy's mine, sweetheart, Hannah's grandmother said. :He was a present. It's up to your Mommy and Daddy whether or not you get a dog. She turned her gaze meaningfully to Laura.

"Go put your shoes on. Mommy's talking to Grandma."

"What's the puppy's name, Grandma?"

"Henry, he's named after your grandfather."

"If I had a dog, I'd name him after you, Grandma," Hannah said.

"Lorelei would be a nice name if you have a female dog, but what if it's a male?"

"It won't be," Hannah said with authority. "And when I get one, I'm going to name it Old Oar after you."

"That's not my name, Lorelei said, smiling. "Now where on earth did you get that name from?"

"From Daddy."

"Ah…"

"Shoes. Now!" Laura shouted, and Hannah skipped out of the room, banging the Hindu temple door back against the wall.

"Old Oar, hey?" Lorelei said.

"Mother…"

"I may be a whore, darling, but I am certainly *not* old. The fact that the Schmuck always talks to my bust proves that *something* about me must be youthful." Indeed, Lorelei looked as young as her daughter who had her mother's features, especially the thin, aquiline nose. Although Laura was attractive, Lorelei was beautiful. Perhaps that explained why the media, especially the paparazzi, still called out for Lorelei at *Marchette* mannequin parades.

"Mother, Jason is just—"

"A schmuck."

"Look, Mother, I've got to go. As long as you're all right, that's all that concerns me."

"Don't you want to know who gave me the dog?" Lorelei asked.

"No."

"And what's this business about Hannah talking to angels in the garden?"

"All children have imaginary friends," Laura said.

"She's not getting enough attention."

"That's all she gets is attention."

"She needs a companion."

"I'm not buying her a dog."

"I miss your father," Lorelei said, as if it was something she just remembered.

"Yes, Mother, I know you do."

Then Lorelei smiled with nostalgia and mumbled to herself, as if she had forgotten she was still on the line with her daughter. "At least Mohammed was interested in the ways of the flesh…if not in the ways of the world."

With that, Lorelei ended the connection; leaving Laura with nothing to do but light another Turkish cigarette, sit back down on her blue mohair velvet settee, call Helpless, and watch Hannah sneaking shoeless back into the garden to talk with the angels.

AFTERWORD TO "MOHAMMED'S ANGEL"

I WROTE "MOHAMMED'S Angel" for a special "Future or Alternative Melbourne" issue of the Australian literary journal *Overland*. My working title for the story was "Angels in the Green," but "Mohammed's Angel" was a better fit for the story.

As I wrote to the editor:

"As with my alternate history James Dean novel *The Rebel*, I've been experimenting with writing SF as mainstream fiction; and 'Mohammed's Angel' is written in the form of a *New Yorker* story. The horror, which permeates the story, is in the background...is the background; and the trope is that the future reader would accept it as mundane.

"The quote at the beginning of the story is derived from a placard waved by an Afghan in Pakistan in 2001: 'The Americans love Pepsi Cola, but we love death.'"

THE ISLAND OF TIME

For Gene Wolfe, who
grew us all from a bean

YOUR NAME is John Carter—Captain John Carter of Foster, Victoria—and you're twelve years old. Actually, you're twelve and three quarters, almost a teenager. It's a June night, and the Australian winter cold has settled deep into your bones, making you shiver as you stand in the sunken garden, just as you shiver when you're in your own bedroom: you're not allowed to keep the space heater on because it uses too much electricity.

Above you, an impossible eternity of distance above you, the gauzy span of the Milky Way is almost as bright as the moon. You've turned your head upside-down to see the face in the moon before, but not tonight. Tonight you are desperate to become the *real* you…the grown-up you. Tonight you must focus; and so you stand under the starry sky, staring as hard as you can at the black expanse of the Southern Ocean until you sight the island landmass known as Barsoom. Although Barsoom can't be seen during the day, you know it's green and lush; the great gold and crystal spires of the city Helium on the river Iss reflect so much light that it's hard to look at them. You know that because you've seen them. Now, as you raise your arms and concentrate, as you silently call to the *real* you to come and help, to transform you, you can see the far away city's lights twinkling and spinning. Your outstretched arms begin to ache as you shiver in the moonlight and await an answer to your call.

But there will be no answer.

Not tonight.

"Stop that, Jonathan!"

The lights of Helium blink out.

You lower your arms and turn around. "Stop what? I'm not doing nothin'."

Your sister Julia is wearing torn jeans and the navy blue sweater that your grandmother, may she rest in peace, knitted for her. Her blond-streaked hair is pulled back tightly into a ponytail, and her ring-pierced lips look swollen and bruised. She's two years older than you and has breasts—you've seen them—but you would never know it by looking at her in that sweater.

"You know what," she says, poking you in the ribs, "you've just got to stop it. I heard Mother talking with the dickhead about taking you to see a shrink. Is that what you want?"

You shrug. "How would I know? I've never seen one, and you know as well as I do that the dickhead wouldn't never allow it, anyway. He'd be afraid that—"

Your sister gets that closed, dangerous look. "Go back to the house before—"

You know you shouldn't argue with her, not after she's been hurt; but you can't help yourself. "Before what?"

She pushes you with both hands. "Before I—" and then she just walks away. You want to go after her, but she's all closed up. Angry and sad and somehow a little dead. So you take one last look out over the sea (but all you can see now are the ruddy lights of the drilling rigs off the coast of Barrie's Beach); and then you climb the stone perron, cross the manicured lawn with all its silly fluted topiaries, and quietly sneak back into the Dickhead's faux Greek Revival mansion. The rooms on the first floor all have high ceilings and chandeliers and marble fireplaces, which always impress guests and, as the Dickhead is so fond of repeating: "It's good for business." But the maroon carpets are threadbare in spots, and you once heard someone say that all of the really good furniture and paintings have been sold long ago. Nevertheless, it's the most impressive house *you've* ever seen.

You take the stairs that lead into the servant's quarters. You skip certain steps because you know which treads creak; you know every inch of this part of the house, which is always "closed off," probably because your mother hates house cleaning and probably because it saves on fuel bills. Although your mother thinks that the Dickhead is rich—which is probably why she married him—he claims that all he's got left is the house and the cars and a small annuity, which will keep them all going until he sells his first novel for seven figures. You don't quite know what seven figures means, but you figure you'll find that out eventually.

When you reach the third floor, you duck under a low archway and carefully open the door so it doesn't squeak; then down the hall to your room, to safety...except that the Dickhead has been watching you all along. Watching you from your own window. Waiting for you in your room.

"What in God's good name are you doing out there at this hour?" he asks in his conversational voice, as if he were saying "Good morning".

He's wearing a heavy white bathrobe with his initials embossed on the pocket; your mother has one just like it. His bristly gray hair is neatly combed and still damp. Your mother tells you that he's very good looking and his cleft chin is a sign of strength and resolve; but he reminds you of a silly, gangly guy you used to watch on television when you were a kid. His name was Mr. Cracker, and he lived in a house that was painted like a barber's pole. However, you suppose that the Dickhead looks nice. He has an old, crinkly, and happy kind of face, which makes you hate him all the more.

"Well, are you going to answer me?"

"Yessir."

"How many times do I have to tell you, call me Dick...or Dad."

You already have a father, and he's not dead, just gone away, so you say, "Okay...Dick."

"Now, tell me what were you doing out in the sunken garden at this ungodly hour?"

"Nothin'. Just looking out, you know."

"Without a jacket? You're shivering even now."

You can't tell him that it won't work if you have too many clothes on. By rights you should be naked when you make what Tars Tarkas calls the *sak* of transformation. (*Sak* means jump in the language of Barsoom's green men; more about all *that* later.) But the *sak* of transformation works sometimes, even when you're just wearing pants and a shirt: no socks or underwear.

"Well...?"

"Yeah," you say, sloping your shoulders, "it was pretty dumb."

"But why on earth would you go outside like that to freeze your butt off in the middle of the night?" He's earnest now, earnest and caring; and you know just what to say. But as you say it, you hope that your mother is awake, so he won't...linger:

"I dunno, sometimes I wake up thinking about my Dad, and I get scared and then I find myself outside and—"

"Well, get undressed and try to get some sleep," he says in what you think of as his forgiving voice. But he's sly. You know that about him.

"You'll have to be up in a few hours for school."

You try not to wince as he gentles your hair and pats your face. He sees you into bed and pats you again. You pretend to fall asleep and don't open your eyes until he leaves; and then you listen to the floorboards creak as he slowly walks through the hallway. You hold your breath as he passes your sister's room because you know she's not in there. You hear the doorknob squeak like a mouse as he opens her bedroom door, then silence—the silence of the stars: one beat, the silence of the moon: two beats, the silence of deep black you're-dead-forever water: three beats—and finally you hear the door close and the creak of footsteps fading down the hallway. You exhale.

"Darling…?" It's your mother calling the Dickhead. "Are the kids all right?"

"Yeah," says the Dickhead, his voice soft but clear in the echoic darkness. "Jonnie couldn't sleep, poor kid. But he's all tucked up now."

"And Julia?"

You wait for it…

"She's fine, honey," he says with a chuckle, and you hear the sticky sound of their bedroom door closing.

Although you can't hear anything now, you *know* what he's saying.

"That little girl of yours is pretty near a grown woman."

"Pretty near," you whisper guiltily. *The Dickhead was pretty near, but he's gone now.*

You squeeze your eyes closed and dream of Tars Tarkas and the *real* you.

TARS TARKAS IS three-hundred and seventeen years old and weighs about four hundred pounds. He stands fifteen feet tall, has a perpendicular slit for a nose, a fanged mouth framed by four enamel-white tusks the length of your arms, and two crimson eyes that bug out of the sides of his head: if he needs to (and he often does because he's a green blooded warrior chieftain), he can see in two directions at once. His scaly skin looks like rough-cut jade; and he's your very best friend...or, rather, he will *become* your very best friend once you grow up into what you're supposed to be.

You first met him on the school bus.

Well, you found his four-armed picture on the cover of a magazine scrunched under the cushion of your seat. The wrinkled, yellow-stained magazine was thick as a book and still smelled of lemon cordial. And there he was, the one and only Tars Tarkas—scimitar, spear, carbine, and sapphire pommeled battleaxe in hand—holding back an army of slavering, reptilian centurions. Beside him, but not dwarfed by the jade skinned Barsoomian, stood a sandy haired, broad-shouldered earthman; and right then and there—without even having to read the magazine—you knew who that earthman was. It was *you*, the grown-up you, the real you; and there you were, standing tall and unafraid, army knife gleaming under the silvery light of the twin moons, protecting a half-naked princess—who looked just like your sister—from a leaping, two-headed Martian tiger.

Your sister told you to leave the dirty, old magazine on the bus, but you stuffed it into your book satchel; and at lunch break you sneaked away to Pearl Park, sat under the gazebo near the stream, ate your peanut butter and jelly sandwich, and read the magazine until you knew it by heart. Then you buried it because now it was *yours*; you wouldn't need paper and pictures to remember who you really were. And no matter what the dickhead might try to do to you, the real you (who stands six-foot-seven and can jump thirty feet in the air on Barsoom) would be able to protect your sister.

It doesn't matter that you are skinny and pimply and only twelve and three-quarters because the real you and your companion Tars

Tarkas have given their solemn word that they will come to help whenever you call. All *you* have to do is follow proper procedure: raise your naked arms at just the right hour, encompass the night sky, and remember the proper sequence of incantations taught to you by Tars Tarkas in the sacred language of his people, the green Thants.

But unless you do it right, unless your thoughts are properly focused and calibrated to the exact telegraphic frequency, you will just stand there like an idiot in your birthday suit; and there will be no *sak* of transformation.

No Barsoom.

No adventures with Tars Tarkis and the grown-up Captain John Carter.

And...no help here on Earth.

YOU'VE BEEN CROSSING out the days on your free pocket calendar from *John's Meat Emporium, Foster 03-5675-0000*; and now it's the Queen's Birthday weekend, which means trouble because the dickhead is home and prowling about. The weather has become unseasonably warm, and tonight—Saturday nights are *always* the worst—you hear the dickhead's footsteps, the squeak and squeal of doorknob and door, and the consequent soft banging noises in your sister's bedroom. Quiet as a snake and angry as a two-headed tiger, you sneak out of your room. The dickhead won't hear the tap-click of your bedroom the door latch, not with all that stentorian breathing, and then you're free and breathing the cool, unstrangulated air of the sunken garden.

But you've no time for air and freedom.

You need to save your sister, so—difficult as it may be to concentrate—you raise your arms to embrace the star-spangled night and pray (in the sacred Thantian language) for the familiar, blindingly bright flash of transformation.

THE ISLAND OF TIME

This time the gods of Mars grant your wish.

But something is terribly wrong...

YOU'RE STANDING IN familiar surrounds on a yellow, mossy plateau overlooking Helium. The huge city is in flames, its crown of gold and crystal spires shattered. Gaily colored, fire-bombing aerostats circle in the smoky sky above; two-masted catamaran warships crowd the River Iss; and armies swarm like ants around Helium's breeched fortifications. Although the wind is high at this elevation—keening and whistling through the stunted blood colored trees and quartz outcrops—you can still hear the distant thunder of bombs exploding, arms clashing, and men screaming in blood-fury.

Your eyes burn and tear in the strong Martian sunlight as you look around your Tars Tarkas' camp. There are no chariots, mastodons, warriors, women, or children to be seen. All the tents are gone, except yours; and the campfires are long dead. You turn your gaze back to the burning city. You are certain that your friends, human and Thant alike, are down there fighting the invading hoards of lizard men and white apes; and you must find them. They rode to battle upon their mastodons and eight legged, white-bellied riding beasts; but yours is nowhere to be found. No matter, because your muscles—which are conveniently adapted to the much stronger gravity of Earth—give you the strength to vault and leap as if you were wearing seven-league boots.

As you've no time to waste, you dress quickly. You collect your saber, knife, and carbine (which shoots radium projectiles); and then you step outside and take a deep breath of the clean Martian air. Now you finally, finally *feel* like your true self.

You're the John Carter who saves his friends.

You're the John Carter who *will* save his sister.

And so you run, bounding over gullies and crevasses that ordinary Martian riders would have to go around, vaulting over hills, trees, and settlements. With every gravity-defying step you take, the clangor of iron and steel and the cries of men and monsters become louder and louder...and the clouds of dust and smoke kicked up by the fighting hoards and carried hither and thither by the wind become incrementally closer. After an hour, your legs begin to ache; you're out of breath; and a wall of dust and smoke looms up and over you. One step, two steps, three; and now you're right in the fray. Lizard men astride two-headed octopeds the size of hippopotamuses attack you, but you have no time to waste: you must find Tars Tarkas.

With lightening-fast sweeps of your saber, you decapitate the heads of the nearest octoped and, in quick succession, shoot three of the reptilian beast-riders with your carbine. Then you take a great leap over the other beast-riders and land just inside the breached fortifications; but you are almost knocked to the ground by a mob of deserters. You're surprised because the warriors are wearing the emblems, brassards, and purple and rose colors of Helium guards. You stop one of the deserters and ask him for the whereabouts of the Thant fighters. He looks at you, shakes his head, laughs, and then disappears into the dust-swirling miasma of fighting men and beasts.

You press forward toward an open area where the clash of weapons is the loudest; and it is there—in the slaughtery that had once been the Queen's private gardens—that you find Thant warriors fighting lizard men and white apes. Although greatly outnumbered, the jade skinned Thants—unlike men—will not retreat.

And neither will you.

"TARS TARKAS," YOU shout as you cleave and hew, as you and the outnumbered Thant warriors begin to turn the advance of these beast-riders and white apes into a rout. "Tars Tarkas".

Your voice is hoarse. Your hands are slippery with blood.

"Tars Tarkas!"

"Ah, welcome, John Carter of Foster. I was afraid we would not look upon each other again."

You feel (rather than hear) his responding call; and you fear the worst, for you know that Tars Tarkas is loathe to reveal his telepathic sigil to anyone.

"But you must make haste, Earth friend, if we are to fight and—with the blessing of the great River Iss—die together in battle."

You leap across the gardens and fight your way past the Queen's treasury and the shattered halls of governance, but you're too late: no Thant (not even Tars Tarkas) standing alone without carbine or cannon could overcome a troop of lizard men astride their two-headed, shark-jawed octopeds. Before you can reach your friend, one of the octopeds bites through his lower right arm and slams him to the ground. But Tars Tarkas slashes at the creature with his other arms. The huge beast rears backward, squealing in pain and dislodging its rider, who was positioning himself to take Tars Tarkas' head as a prize.

You shoot the stinking, flesh-hungry beast.

It dies open jawed, revealing Tars Tarkas' dismembered arm, which seems to be reaching out to you from the rows of bloodied, needle sharp teeth. Its dismounted rider rushes toward you. You barely have time to deflect his poison-tipped spear. But as you decapitate him with a roundhouse swing of your saber, you hear someone sound the call. A dozen Thant warriors materialize out of the smoke and dust; and as they slaughter the lizard men and their beasts, you try to carry your friend to safety.

"No, John Carter," Tars Tarkas says in a thick, raspy voice. He presses one of his remaining large, nail-less hands against his wound to stem the flow of blood. "I must die *here*, standing and fighting. Gird me to fight. Help me, Earth friend, as I would help you."

You tourniquet his wound with your belt and then gently lift him to a standing position. Leaning back against a blood-smeared wall, he grimaces—which is the Thant version of a smile, grips his sapphire pom-meled battleaxe in one hand and his scimitar and spear in the others, and says, "I suppose these will have to do. One of the octo's ate my rifle, any-way." Then he shakes his head twice, a gesture of great sadness and serious import. "You came to help us in our time of need, but, alas, I will not be able to reciprocate. Your sister…you must save her yourself, you must—"

The white apes attack; and as you stand together fighting, you sense the instant that Tars Tarkas dies. You *feel* the whisper of good-bye, and you know that the greatest Thant warrior on Mars was not defeated by his enemies: his two great hearts simply stopped beating. And still, even in death, he stands upright.

But you…you fight on alone until a war-hammer crashes into flesh and bone. *Your* flesh and bone.

And thus you fall back to Earth.

Back into the sunken garden…

Into the long sunlight of a winter afternoon.

YOU OPEN YOUR eyes and then turn your head away from the sun. You have a terrible, pounding headache, and your arms and legs feel stiff and tingly. You look toward the Dickhead's house and wonder what happened.

Every other time you've gone to Mars, even when you've spent days and weeks there, you'd always find yourself back on Earth within a few minutes (Australian Eastern Standard Time). This isn't Saturday night and you *know* you're in trouble. No sense trying to sneak back into the Dickhead's house; you'll just have to think this through.

But you don't even know what day this is. It could be Sunday or next week. You can tell Mom and the Dickhead that you fell asleep and somehow got amnesia like Arnold Schwarzenegger in *Total Recall* or Gregory Peck in *Spellbound*. Or that you were abducted like the kid in *Ransom*… or that you ran away because you want to be an entrepreneur or a writer and don't want to go to school anymore; but then, hallelujah, you saw the light of reason (the Dickhead's reason) and decided to come back home.

Or you can just tell them that you were on Mars—they would believe that!

As you stand up, your mind suddenly reels with memory and grief. Now you feel it. Now you know it. Now you believe it.

Tars Tarkas is dead!

Although you feel small and weak and alone, although you feel every one of your twelve and three-quarter years, you walk big as life through the garden to the house. You open the front door with such force that the brass knocker bangs up and down; and as you stand in the checkerboard tiled hallway, you feel exactly as you did when you heard Tars Tarkas' telepathic whisper of farewell.

You walk into the reception room.

"Hello? Is anybody home?"

You check the living room, library, study, kitchen, mudroom, pantry, and dining room; then you run upstairs, up the curved staircase and through the hallway, past the guestrooms and entertainment center. Click, you open the door to your mother and the Dickhead's bedroom. You smell strong, sweet perfume: *Joy*. The mirror on the wall over your mother's dressing table is all cracked, and a triangular splinter sparkles on the carpet. Perfume bottles and your mother's favorite jade lamp are also all over the carpet. The bed isn't made, and your mother's bras, stockings, underwear, and dresses are strewn across the pink and black sheets. You don't see any of the Dickhead's clothes, though; and suddenly you're scared.

Something is wrong, very wrong…

You step on a yellow-lined notepad—what's *that* doing on the floor?—as you rush back into the hallway, pass under the archway and up three steps into the servants' quarters. You open the door to your sister's room. You know it's silly, but you're afraid that she's dead, that the Dickhead has hurt her again, only this time…this time…

The room is empty, the house is empty, and you imagine—silly as it is to have such thoughts—that the *world* is empty, and you'll be alone forever. You call out your sister's name, just to hear the sound of it.

"Julia."

You listen to the house sounds and call again, "Julia? Sis…?" You want to tell your sister that you *tried* to bring Tars Tarkis back to help her.

If only…if only you could have returned to Earth as your true self this one time: but you *always* return as the small and weak and guilty you; and right now you wish that you could keep getting smaller and smaller and smaller until you just…disappeared.

You go back to the Dickhead's and your mother's room. Something is niggling at you. The yellow notepad. You pick it up and see the indentations like writing without ink on the top sheet. You know the trick of reading secret writing, so you take the pad back to your room, sit down at your built-in desk and ever so lightly rub a soft, Number two pencil over the indentations.

Dear Mother,

I'm sorry I'm really sorry but I have to leave. You <u>KNOW</u> why and if you really don't ~~then you must be blind~~ well then I just don't know.

Dick hurts me and he hurts Jon and I would have taken him with me if he hadn't already run away somewhere. You should get

That's all you can make out, but it's enough, enough to let you know that it's all your fault and that she thinks you ran away and left her with the Dickhead.

You hear the door open downstairs.

You shiver and your hands are shaking; but you go into your closet, reach up, up, stretching, and grab a hammer that you've hidden behind a bunch of stuff on the top shelf. It's just a regular hammer, not a war hammer like the one you carried on Barsoom; but it will have to do. Quiet as a cat, you slip out of your room and down the hall. Your only chance is surprise. You'll have to jump out and crack the Dickhead on the head before he knows what happened. Then you can...well, you'll worry about what to do once he's dead.

But it's not the Dickhead. You can tell by the clattery-clack of your mother's high-heeled shoes on the tiles. You see that she's alone, and you drop the hammer onto the carpet. When she sees you, she shouts, "Oh, God, oh, thank God you're alright," and she drops her keys, patent leather handbag, and groceries, and smothers you with a hug. Then she pulls away from you, but doesn't let go of your arms. Her eyes are glossy with tears, her usually clean and frizzy autumn brown hair is straggly and pulled back with an amberina comb, and her right eye and cheek are swollen and black and blue. "Where *were* you, Jon? I was so sick with worry." She hugs you again, and you can smell a kind of sour-sweet perspiration on her blue cashmere sweater.

"I...I didn't mean to be gone so long," you say. "What day's today?"

She looks at you the way she does when she thinks you're telling a whopper. "It's Wednesday. You've been gone four days. You must be starving."

You are kind of hungry.

"Where's the...where's Dick?

Your mother gets a closed, almost sly look...just like your sister's. "You don't have to worry about— He won't be back. I promise."

"Cross your heart and hope to die?"

"Cross my heart and hope to die." She hugs you again and makes a wailing sound. When she's done, you pick up her groceries and follow her into the kitchen. You notice that there are dirty dishes in the sink: she's never left dirty dishes in the sink before.

"What about Julia?" you ask as you put the plastic grocery bags on the counter. Just saying her name makes you want to cry; but *you* don't cry, even though it's all your fault.

"Oh, she's out. But she'll be back soon." Your mother doesn't look at you when she says that. She takes a stack of frozen dinners out of one of the bags, puts them in the freezer, and then she looks at you. "Now, Jon, you must tell me where you've been. Did your stepfather try to...did anybody try to—" She sobs, and you don't want to worry her, so you tell her that nobody tried anything and you ran away because you didn't want to go to school. But you finally saw the light of reason and came back home.

"But...where did you go? Where did you sleep? What did you eat?"

You make something up that doesn't involve Tars Tarkas—you can't say his name either without feeling like something hard has caught in your throat—and after dinner you promise that you'll never, ever leave her again.

Even though you know that's a lie.

THE RADIUM DIAL on your alarm clock glows 3:07 AM THURSDAY 14 JUN. Without bothering to dress, you get up and quietly go downstairs.

You open the door to the garage; pull your 6061 aluminum frame, 18 speed pearl white mountain bike off the wall rack; and then walk it back into the house and out the servants' side door. It's a chilly moonless morning, and clouds obscure most of the stars. You look out over the Southern Ocean, but can't see Barsoom; and even if you could, there would be no lights spinning and twinkling in Helium. You turn away, walk your bike over the lawn to the laneway, and you're off, peddling hard through the gears, now peddling down O'Grady's Ridge Road, and then Fish Creek Road. Half an hour later, you come to your turn-off. You go around the big sawhorses blocking the dirt road that winds its way to a high perch overlooking the sea. From there you can see *everything*.

It's your secret place...yours and no one else's.

When you reach the embankment, you lean your bike against a gum tree, throw your pajamas down beside it, shiver, and then walk over to the edge. Although you've never been able to jump from here—the *sak* of transformation only seems to work in the Dickhead's sunken garden—you don't care.

You gaze at the night-black water in the distance below, whisper a prayer in the sacred Thantian language, and then, arms outstretched, you lean out into the cool darkness.

You couldn't save your sister.

Perhaps you can save yourself.

AFTERWORD TO
"THE ISLAND OF TIME"

IN MY INTRODUCTION to "The Island of Time", which was first published in J. E. Mooney and Bill Fawcett's anthology *Shadows of the New Sun: Stories in Honor of Gene Wolfe*, I wrote:

"I know two Gene Wolfes. One is an affable, taciturn, witty convention companion, whom I can't resist hugging every time I see him. The other Gene Wolfe scares the living hell out of me. He's the one who writes SF and fantasy with the skill and depth of a Nabokov, Borges, or Joyce, a literary genius ferociously bending and twisting genre tropes into high art.

"A blessing on both your heads, Gene Wolfe!"

When I was asked to submit a story for that volume, I knew immediately what I wanted to write: a homage to Gene's brilliant short story "The Island of Doctor Death and Other Stories." Gene's story was a tour de force, and it was, impossibly, written in the second person. I often tell new writers to start writing in the third person—he said such and such; she said such and such; they said such and such—and to foreswear writing stories in the first person until they have a bit more experience with the craft. Why? Because first person *seems* easy. It's easy to write, "I did this and I did that," and off you go. The problem is that you are stuck with the narrow "I" perspective. And too often the prose reads like the amateur banter that can sometime be found in corporate trade magazines. Third person gives the writer the room to be an omniscient observer, to be a minor god and bequeath to the readers everything they need to know. But second person—*you* did this and *you* did that—is simultaneously direct, narrow as a tunnel, and expansive as the damn universe. It's a voice rarely used in fiction because...because it's nigh impossible. Well, it's impossible for everyone except Gene Wolfe.

I've never been able to get Gene's story out of my head, and here was a chance to try *my* hand at writing in the second person**. I knew that it would be dangerous to try a story such as this, to risk comparison with Gene's classic story; but I didn't—and don't care! We stand on the shoulders of giants; or, rather, I should say that we try to keep our balance as we stand on the shoulders of those giants. Sometimes we get to breathe the air of the empyrean. And, yes, sometimes we fall flat on our respective asses!

It's always been a balancing act. But I think it's worth it!

SADLY, GENE PASSED away in 2019. I miss him.

This story was and is dedicated to Gene, who grew us all from a bean.

* I've written only one other second person POV story. It's called "Summer" and is included in this collection.

GRIEVING THE SPIRIT

For Keith Ferrell

I LISTENED. OF course I listened: that's what I'm paid to do, but it seemed that I was listening to everything, listening to the slight rattle of the window behind me (the weather report had predicted storms for the next few days); listening to the hollow sighing of the ductless air conditioner, and listening to the clock, to the electric ticking of my Mr. Bean clock, a silly plastic doodad that actually keeps good time and functions as an anxiety-reducing talking point for new patients.

But the immaculately dressed and coiffured patient sitting and scratching on the leather barrel chair beside me was definitely not a new patient, and, frankly, I was at an impasse: she really wasn't a good candidate for CBT therapy.

So why did you take her on?

Because I did. Because I did!

Blame it on the pregnant mommy brain.

I glanced at the half-moon clock face that divided a smirking Mr Bean from the numbers above him: three-thirty, or thereabouts. One had to guess if the minute hand was beneath the nine and the three.

"But Doctor Strauss—"

"Melinda, remember?"

"Oh, yes, of course, Melinda," Sondra said, her voice smooth, refined, and somehow condescending. "But I can *feel* one of the demons moving under my skin right now." She pulled up the sleeve of her drape-necked silk dress and extended her arm towards me. "Can you see it?" Her voice instantly changed, lost all its practiced mellifluousness. "There, right there; it feels wet. They always feel wet."

I clasped her hand and felt an instant and somehow nauseating shock. Static electricity, I reasoned. But the baby huddled inside me must have felt it too, for she kicked. Hard. It was as if we were both repelled by the contact. I made a mental note, for that had never happened before, then carefully examined Sondra's arm, which was spotted with minor excoriations from scratching. I released her hand and feeling immediate relief, told her (as I had told her in every other session), "No, Sondra. I don't see anything moving. Can *you* see it?"

"No, *I* can't see them. I just feel them moving around like…"

"Like snakes?" I asked, massaging my hand, as if to restore life back into it.

"Yes," Sondra said, sitting back in the chair, her relief obvious. "Exactly. Like snakes."

I listened to the tinnitus sussurating in my ears, hissing like one of Sondra's imagined snakes and asked, "Have you been practising the strategies we discussed?"

She straightened in her chair and nodded. She looked like she had been stunningly beautiful in youth. I remembered seeing a photograph of Kim Novak after her failed plastic surgery, then pushed the image aside. Age had not been kind to Sondra…and probably wouldn't be to me either, for that matter. My arm itched with a numbing, serpent antipathy for Sondra; and I noticed that the assortment of roses in the flute on the side table needed changing.

"And have you kept your appointment with Professor Kim?"

The dermatopathologist.

Sondra didn't respond, which meant *no.* I had noted in her folder the number of specialists—and therapists—she had seen. An educated guess. I figured her for a functional psychotic with a base somatic disorder of delusional parasitosis who presents with a rational affect.

"Okay," I said. "Do you want me to give Professor Kim a call? He might be able to prescribe something else to stop the itching."

"How many times do I have to tell you…Melinda? It's not itching, it's demons. And I'm not depressed, or schizophrenic, or obsessive compulsive. We've established all that; and I'm not taking any more medications. The last magic bullet Kim prescribed made me shake like I had Parkinson's."

I nodded.

"And it didn't do a damn thing to stop the…'itching'," she said sarcastically. "So…no more Kim."

I nodded again, repressing a sigh, then shifted to more productive concerns. "But didn't you tell me last week that you know the demons aren't real?"

"No, Melinda, I think what I told you is that I *tried* to believe they're not real."

"But didn't you also tell me that you've been successful in just thinking them away?"

"Yes, you taught me how to do that, and it does work…sometimes."

"Can you try to do that now? Can you try to think the demons away?"

She gazed vacantly at a botanical print on the wall, then nodded, closed her eyes, and lowered her head. After a moment she jerked awake and, looking disoriented, said, "No!" She extended her arm again. "They won't leave, and *you* know why."

"I know what you've told me before…but I think it's better if you can describe what you told me."

"They came after I killed my baby."

I felt a false labour contraction, a sudden, painful cramp. I nodded to Sondra, trying, forcing myself to give her my full attention.

"But didn't you tell me that you had a miscarriage? That's not murder, Sondra; it's just a terrible circumstance." I realized I was patting my stomach.

Stop that!

Oh, God, let it happen to other people. Not to me. Not to me…

Selfish, narcissistic bitch!

"The miscarriage certainly wasn't your fault," I continued. "You cannot, must not, blame—"

"Yes…it was my fault, Melinda. And you know why that's true."

"I do…?"

"I told you I had an illicit assignation, and you know what happened after that."

I nodded again, reflexively confirming that I accepted what she said without any suggestion of agreement, but my thoughts drifted. Sam was cooking tonight; it would be either bolognaise or paella. I felt the baby moving…Sam's baby kicking determinedly inside me as if she had been listening to this entire session and was prodding me to get rid of this patient. I felt a sick, fluttery sensation in my stomach as if, impossibly, my baby was radiating fear and hatred.

Pregnant mommy brain.

No, just get rid of the patient!

"But that didn't cause the death of your husband," I said, ignoring my foetus's calcitrating invocations, forcing myself to maintain a professional demeanour. "Your husband never knew about that assignation… or the miscarriage. We covered that in an earlier session, remember? Didn't you tell me that you understood that there could be no rational connection between your one-time tryst and your husband's death?"

"Yes, Melinda, I *know* there's no rational connection. But I also feel demons crawling beneath my skin. The man who fucked me—the man who was not my husband—gave me the dead foetus. Gave me the demons. Well, I suppose we both gave me the demons. I know that's not rational, too. But that doesn't make the demons—the goddamn snakes—any less real. How would *you* connect the dots? By telling me they're not real? By telling me there's no correlation between fucking and demons? Telling me that black is white doesn't really help." She looked directly into my eyes; and for an instant I felt that our roles were reversed. I felt that she was in control. That she was someone—or something else.

Get her the fuck out of the room.

Something sly and serpentine was looking at me through those hazel eyes of hers. Narrow eyes that seemed to shift from brown to green to achromatic black. Something was peering out at me as if from behind a dark window, and I gasped inwardly—no intake of breath, no sign of surprise—for I too had learned to look out from behind my own protective window. Professional discipline. I had learned how to radiate warmth. I had learned how to empathise rather than sympathise: the former disguised distance, the latter was simply unprofessional.

The baby kicked again, warning.

The session is almost over.

Another few minutes, then a pee and a latté.

"However, I did see the demons...once," Sondra said.

What? A fresh confession?

"You did?" I asked, surprised.

"Yes, in the blood and viscera I had expelled into the toilet. I saw them swimming in the porcelain bowl. Did you know that all demons are snakes?"

"Only that you have told me that's what you believe."

Sondra's demeanour suddenly changed, brightened. "Well, I'll admit I extrapolated from my own experience…my own experience of reality." She looked away and chuckled.

I felt another cramp, and another: strong, insistent.

"And what about your baby?" Sondra asked.

"My baby…?"

"Oh, I'm sorry, Melinda. In context, that sounded quite untoward." Then Sondra looked at her diamond-inlaid watch and said, "Oh, my, our time is up." She smiled at me, a generous smile suggesting empathy and affection. "But aren't *you* supposed to be the one to say that?"

I returned her smile, forcing it; and as we stood up, I said, "Yes, I suppose that's true."

I felt another cramp. This time it definitely wasn't the baby. No, I was sure this was something else, something slippery and infectious. Something was moving, snaking, tearing its way into my shivering womb.

Something Sondra had been very determined to leave me.

AFTERWORD TO "GRIEVING THE SPIRIT"

IN 2019 KAARON Warren, Sean Williams, and I were asked to headline an anthology of original Australian stories. The anthology was edited by Deborah Sheldon and *called Spawn: Weird Horror Tales About Pregnancy, Birth, and Babies.* Needless to say, this subject matter is not up my street, to coin a phrase; but I was immediately hit by a story idea: twenty years ago I was going to write a story about a doctor who discovers that he has a demon floating around in his bloodstream. It was, no doubt, a catchy idea; but, like so many ideas writers come up with on a daily basis, it never became front of mind...until I read Deborah's invitation. But how could I fit my old demon idea into a story with a pregnancy theme? Of course! A pregnant doctor seeing patients. And I was going to write a novelette about a general pratictioner seeing patients...until I found myself researching cognitive behavioral therapy and delusional parasitosis. Needless to say, the process didn't go anywhere near the way I had anticipated. So here's the skinny—or, rather, the rest of the skinny—on how "Grieving the Spirit" came to be.

This from a brief interview I did about story inspiration to promote the anthology:

"As I've learned over the long years (to my Brobdingnagian chagrin!), the writer doesn't tell the story; the story tells the writer. Which is exactly what happened with "Grieving the Spirit". I was certain that this would be at the very least a novelette; but the story, or, rather, the characters had very different ideas. They took—or, rather, stole—my premise and most of my dialogue and then decided to narrate their own story. They decided that conciseness and precision were more important than the author's predilection to gild and re-gild the proverbial lily. Oh, they happily used my notes, plot arc, and research; but the story—its cut and thrust and emphasis (and most of the dialogue)—is all theirs.

"About a quarter of the way into the story, their whispers became shouts: they told me where to go in no uncertain terms…and then they told me where to stop.

"So, gentle and empathetic reader, don't blame the author. The characters (in their infinite wisdom) made him do it!"

THE TOWERS OF EDEN (WITH BARRY N. MALZBERG)

7216 ANNO DOMINI: RUSTICATING IN THE DESERT, DRIVING ON THE WINE RED SEA

AND HERE, with extraordinary punctuality: here the millennium comes to die.

Michael Evreux Brevard driving along the hardpan packed channels of his ever-receding desert, driving at what once would have been considered to be a hundred and ninety-two kilometers an hour (top speed), driving what once would have been known as a 1963 Cadillac De Ville Series 6300 Convertible: a plum-colored streamlined megalith, a small-finned shark that inhaled petroleum and exhaled the most sensual and poisonous hydrocarbons and particulate matter. Brevard inhaled, luxuriated in the irradiated wind soughing over the windscreen, tasted the acrid fumes, the desiccated dryness of the ever-mobile desert, which rushed past him as if he, the president, king, owner, and ruler of sky and sand were sitting still in this leather and chrome accoutered living room. Ahead, twisting like sand devils in the dying sun were the desert's fairy chimneys, enormous amorphous extrusions of stone, as mobile—and as stationary—as Brevard in his Cadillac. As the tuff cones and heady spires danced for Brevard's pleasure, so they also changed color and texture: the kaleidoscope desert.

THE TOWERS OF EDEN

"Are we there yet?" asked Zahia Falaise, his ghost-creation who had the guileless face of a child made perversely sensual—an ultimatum of sensuality—by her poise and presence. She sat next to Brevard, her long bare legs squelching on white leather as she crossed and uncrossed them annoyingly. She wore an iridescent blue Bali gown with a sheer black top. Her breasts were too large for such couture, but she was Brevard's creation. Although he was father and lover, she was her own. He could not inhibit, nor channel her behavior.

As a creator he was a merciful, if broken god.

Brevard didn't answer her, and the two startlingly beautiful women in the bolstered back seats laughed, asked the same irritating question, and then continued their intense discussion of the topology of six-dimensional manifolds.

Thus for minutes hours perhaps days of concentrated pleasure, for time itself, for the soft subtle thrill of anticipation did Brevard drive. He drove until their chimed question was answered in the darkness of a moonless night, answered by the constellations of city lights in the great distance, a haloed phosphorescent cloud, which imitated the coruscating stars above. There...there were his towers, his mechanical city, which, should he will it, would move like fog or settle like dust; and as he drove on, the sun rose purple and red, blinding the enormous glass city of sky-tipped towers.

"Are we there yet...?"

No, he said, seeing a sudden flare in the distance, "No we are not, and we had better hope that we never will be."

NAKED LUNCH REDUX

HAVING REACHED THE desert, his penultimate goal, Brevard decided to prepare a picnic for his ghosts. Zahia was to his right: his archangel, his muse perched like a flamingo on an extrusion of silica. To his left, reclining on the soft blanket of ferrite sand were his back-seat angels: Leandra Cassiel and Denise de la Calle. The two sylphs had Brevard's complexion and features. They were his adolescent fantasies of self transformed: his sisters, his lovers, himself. Their long blond hair was braided and piled atop their heads, their skin—his skin—was faultless. Brevard was indeed his own Botticelli. He removed his clothes to allow his body to burn in the sun; and Leandra and Denise, his differentiated selves, repeated his every movement. Only Zahia remained as she was; and as a result, Brevard's desire could not be shared: it was forcibly focused entirely on her; and as the promised platters of food materialized around them, she stared him down.

Leandra and Denise continued to argue topology, Denise insisting that she was unique, that the mathematical paradigm of the many in the one did not—could not—hold true here; and when they all finished eating, when they finished sunning themselves and comparing blisters, they made love.

Later, as Brevard perceived the undetermined flow of time, he stared at the women, unblushing in his own nakedness. He had long ago, eternities ago, moved past lust to a kind of safe, sterile place in which desire and departure commingled: the radiation suntan, burns, and attendant crepuscular sickness had no context in this consciously generated, post-apocalyptic place.

"Wake up, Michael," Zahia said forcefully. "You are not dreaming this. This *is* happening…this is how the ruins of the millennium speak."

Leandra and Denise giggled. They had since agreed that each was indeed singular. Brevard felt the itch of radiation as a warm wash of light. "Ruins of the millennium?" he said. "There *is* no millennium."

Zahia laughed at him. "What an utter fool you are, Michael."

Once, perhaps, her laughter would have disconcerted him, but not now, not in this known landscape, not in this endless desert where moments trudged past like little messengers.

ZAHIA: REDACTED TIME AND UNINTENDED CONSEQUENCE

IN THE LAST hours (that is how he described it to himself) Zahia had been all insistence, all strategy as she argued him toward what she took to be the only possible protocol. "We cannot do this alone," she said. "We must not do this alone. We need help, lest we repeat what was and will be."

Brevard continued to quote Genesis to her—the first gospel of events that followed the Towers of Eden—but she was dismissive. "We need to expand the perimeters of possibility," she insisted. *You* need to expand the perimeters of possibility."

"I already have, darling," Brevard said, laughing ruefully, "which is probably the reason why we are back here once again." Later again, when they were in the car driving west, ever west, he said to her, "Oh, by the way, we are utterly and absolutely alone."

ON THE MATTER OF BEING ABSOLUTELY ALONE

HANDS ON THE clock of his destiny, Kennedy preens before a large crowd of reporters, nosy parkers, and fans on the tarmac at Love Field in Dallas. "Perhaps you will remember me," he says to Bob Walker of WFAA-TV 8, "or perhaps this is how I will be remembered: as the man who accompanied Jacqueline Kennedy to Paris." He flushes with satisfaction, nods to the thin applause. It is going well. Everything is going well. Soon he will be eating a good Texan steak and delivering a speech to the local government, business, religious and civic leaders at the Business and Trade Mart downtown and his triumph will be complete. Someone hands him a hat, one of those enormous, grotesque constructions which the Texans seem to equate with being a really great fucker. Kennedy knows better. Being a really great fucker has more to do with prestige and positioning than a silly hat. He feels a twinge in his back and is suddenly reminded of old perils. "We are joined together in a great task" he says to nobody in particular and everyone in general. The Mayor gestures: he wants Kennedy to don the hat. Screw that, he thinks. "I'll take it home, wear it in Washington," he says. Perhaps he is imagining this, perhaps it has not happened; or, then again, perhaps it has already happened so drastically that he was/is/will be impelled by its ragged consequence. Is he standing on the tarmac or has he just given his Chamber of Commerce breakfast speech at the Hotel Texas? Is he enjoying his steak at the Dallas Business and Trade Mart luncheon, or is he sitting with Jackie and John and Nellie Connally in the Presidential limousine approaching Dealey Plaza? Complex and twisted, all of it.

Whether here, there, or everywhere, someone invisible as clean air whispers into his left ear: "*Destroy time and chaos may be ordered.*"

A TWENTIETH CENTURY LITERARY REFERENCE WITH ATTENDANT FOOTNOTE

"DESTROY TIME AND chaos may be ordered," whispered Norman Mailer's ghost, the aforementioned Sergius O'Shaugnessey, to the hapless Svoboda in an infinitely distant century.** That had seemed like good advice in the penumbra of Nagasaki, only a dozen years earlier; but

* Sergius O'Shaugnessey is the narrator and guiding intelligence behind Mailer's short novel *The Man Who Studied Yoga* (1956), conceived as a prologue to his most (typically) grandiose unfinished project: an eight-part novel on the human condition to be observed by the mythical O'Shaugnessey. And Sam Slovoda is a helpless, hapless, lost, middle-aged man observed by the aforementioned all-seeing externalized O'Shaugnessey.

this was a new gleaming era, an era in which technology had become interchangeable with both death and life. Didn't matter! Brevard knew that Mailer's strange and megalomaniacal ghost had had it right for this century as for every century: "Destroy time and chaos may be ordered" is was and will be inevitable truth. But Brevard had a powerful intention. He could and would destroy chaos by re-enacting a new sequentiality, a glittering new sequentiality for an ever-new eighth millennium. Thus, for example, sacrifice John Fitzgerald Kennedy again and again (and again) until you get it right, until the act through repetition is rendered numb to any past, present, or future emotive significance. Until it is remembered by no one but perhaps a first citizen/president/god/creator/king such as Brevard. Then (now? before? after? ah, sequence, where is thy sting?) kill the king and kill him and kill him until he is no longer the king and in fact no longer dead but merely a character or a scrap of dialogue in the story. But Kennedy *was* the century...*was* the story, the life the death, the character, the scrap of dialogue. Born in one wartime, came near death in another, a projectile then to the boundary of what could have been the third and last war but was instead talked off that peak, screwed the sister deities who spun the threads of fate and destiny with single-minded abandon if with no *real* emotion (like a grounded V-2 rocket he could only be a simulation of flight and flame) and then, as a kind of gift to the hundreds of millions of future observers, left with a flourish. The mission was always to leave with a flourish, then exit left and leave 'em laughing; and if Sergius O'Shaugnessey had uttered the utter truth, the 'golden rule', then the 'mission' was its corollary: destroy the weavers of chaos and (the threads) of time may be ordered.

DIMENSIONS OF MEMORY IN A STANDARD 4/4 TIME SIGNATURE

BREAKFAST IN THAT huge, closed hotel restaurant space, then the empty air itself, everything heated like stones in a fire, and then, and then the great limousine prowling to the edges of consciousness. Most of the time now he had to fuck passively because of his godamned wrecked back, but he comforted himself: this was an age of fundamental passivity, of submission, of diminished resistance to the waves lifting into a tsunami of implacable force. On the ocean, clinging to a raft, he had learned of dimensions of passivity so cruel that inert fucking by comparison was a goddamned pleasure.

THE 1812 TRACKLESS STEAM POWERED SYMPHONY

OF COURSE MAILER'S ghost, the doomed O'Shaugnessy, might have been dead wrong. Nothing could be certain in Heisenberg's world, a world refracted by the sprawl of the Grassy Knoll

So much, more than enough, for Brevard being all knowing...so much for the frailties of omniscience, the vicissitudes of the godhead, the mediated difficulties of the local imperator creator. Perhaps Zahia was right: perhaps he was not creator-in-chief, the isometric dreamer of realities; and perhaps he might be existentially rather than absolutely alone. But alone or multitudinous it was (or would soon be) a crowded solitude containing all manner of ghostly constructions, all or some or perhaps none of his own making; and what a troupe-band-bevy-collection it would be: geologists, paleontologists, physicists, astronomers, et al.; a diverse collection of expertise from the applied, earth, life, and natural sciences; and, too, all manner of philosophers, religious quacks, and humanitarians. All these ghostly constructions willingly contained in the twelve caboose-red first class carriages of a steam train powered by a Salamanca locomotive that is being driven by none other than its inventor Matthew Murray of Holbeck, Nottinghamshire, Great Britain, England, Europe, the great globe itself, the solar system, the galaxy, the universe, the mind of God. Address a letter to him in this way and await its return: ADDRESSEE UNKNOWN.

As yet unseen by Brevard or his angels, Murray is chasing Brevard, the coupled drive wheels of his locomotive and the free wheels of the carriages following in the fused indentation trails of the atomic Cadillac. Matthew Murray of Holbeck has enormous plans of his own. He follows Brevard not as a supplicant approaching his god, but as a spider running along its web after its prey.

However, it might also be noted that Murray is no less grotesque or dangerous than the atomic catalogue driving them all to a disaster so encompassing, so final, that it will render irresistible its fetching answer to this iterated century of flame.

A SHORT PAUSE BEFORE THE RECRUDESCENT CRASH

IT SHOULD BE noted that (if O'Shaugnessy is right and Zahia wrong) all which occurs previously and prospectively has been planned, researched, extrapolated, simulated, and engineered by Brevard. Of course the crux is whether this depiction is a (fictional) reconstructed simulation or an authentic iteration of the great work of time and possibility. Either way Brevard is trapped. Whether he is a god controlling or simply one of his created angels cannot be answered and probably should not be answered. Better to be god from Brevard's perspective, even if a recurring string of 'facts' mitigate against desire.

But for our selective purposes, it is probably sufficient to know that Brevard's obsession with time and events thousands of years in his putative past, his need to model events irrelevant to his time without end, cannot be really understood out of his time. We can only create and substitute a metaphor—in our case, no less than that of the about-to-be-foreclosed JFK, we chose a sexual metaphor—for his driving needs and frustration, needs and frustration which he vents into a fractured reflection of a time when ending is commonplace and death is itself something of a metaphor. A difficult take-down, to be sure: a puerile minimization rather than a deconstruction of the profound.

You may, of course, substitute a metaphor of your own. For our part, we like the (sexual) metaphors of the ancient incidents of the assassination of JFK and 9/11, for they are time tangible and contain a seductiveness which Brevard himself had hoped would mimic the desire which had shaped the creation of his experiment. And we should not forget the still puissant metaphor of sex: the plunge of objects into the unassailable, the assailable, the impermeable, the damned.

THE NEAR AND DISTANT EXPERIENCE OF EVENT

IT'S TIME. PASTS, presents, and futures are all right now, all here at exactly 8:19 on this cobalt blue morning. Reflecting the sunlight like a black mirror, the plum colored Cadillac is now parked just beyond the glass suburbs of the towered city. The city sparkles and flashes and gleams in geodetical splendor. The desert shimmers as night chill meets morning warmth, and the sand swirls into newly shaped dune concretions as if shivering in anticipation (if, indeed, anticipation can even be considered as a state of mind in this interleaved time).

The convertible top is down. Brevard and Zahia Falaise are in the front seat. Leandra Cassiel and Denise de la Calle are holding hands in the back seat.

"Well?" asks one or the other. Leandra and Denise are twins, after all. Their voices, if not their thoughts, identical.

"Shut up and wait for it," Zahia says.

A voice crackles in the sky, loud as a god: "The cockpit is not answering. Somebody's stabbed in business class. And I think there's mace. That we can't breathe. I don't know. I think we're getting hijacked."

"That would be Betty Ong, a flight attendant on American Airlines Flight 11," Zahia continues.

"Ah," says Leandra and Denise in chorus.

But Brevard doesn't move, doesn't say a word. It's as if he's dreaming time, experiencing the events unfolding forward and backwards simultaneously, seeing from the perspective point of himself sitting in the car and from inside the cabin of the Boeing 747 airliner. He sees the airliner arcing out of the blue, another mirror reflecting the blue day, a mirror arcing toward another mirror, or, rather, toward *two* other mirrors: the tallest glass towers in this crystal city, which Brevard has named Eden. (His prerogative, for—according to his lights and purposes, at least—he is god.) "Now we shall return to memory," Brevard said to himself, his reconstructed heart beating like a metronome. "*Now* we shall finally and conclusively acquire sequence and significance."

But Zahia overheard him. She always overheard him. She laughed and said, "Oh, so you think, my dearest darling." She straightened herself, a lascivious look on her face as she touched Brevard, who was already excited. "Wait for it...one...two...three..."

And right on time (?) another voice of the gods crackles across the sky, echoing through all the circles of time. "Something is wrong. We are in rapid descent. We are all over the place. I see buildings. We are flying very low. We are flying way too low. Oh, my God, we are way too low."

"That's not Betty," says Leandra.

"That's must be Betty," says Denise.

"No, that's Amy Sweeney," says Zahia. "I caressed her just before..." Her tone has shifted from the seductive to the satisfied. Meanwhile—

The 747 crashes silently into a glass tower, or, rather, from the vantage of the Cadillac, it looks like the glass tower has swallowed the forward part of the plane; and Brevard and Zahia are now in the aircraft (it's all simply a matter of perspective, after all); they can smell fear, can hear the screaming; and they can't help but cling to life, cling to these very last seconds before oblivion, oblivion, oblivion receding, oblivion turning backwards; and Brevard and Zahia are transported instantly back into the car. There, Zahia naked and glowing in the morning. Zahia touching him as he responds against his will, as he realizes she is right and he is wrong, that the dreadful is happening even as he breathes in ecstasy and exhales misery, for before the second aircraft can strike the second tower, before the first tower can collapse like a million breezeblock dominoes, time reverses.

The 747 is ejected/rejected from the tower and flies backwards into the blue.

Zahia removes her hand from his lap as all their clothes press once again upon their bodies like winding sheets wrapped around corpses. The twins giggle and then descend into a fierce argument about the types of infinities that actually exist. It is when Leandra says something about the impossibility of infinite discrepancies that Brevard glimpses something rising on a dune then disappearing, then rising again: Matthew Murray's train of scientists. Matthew Murray, the other. The antagonist. The usurper. The proof that Brevard isn't god, isn't sleeping, isn't alone. If this is his creation, it has been compromised by those (i.e. Murray) who would reverse everything back to chaos; and there was nothing that Brevard could do but race toward the city and make sure that he reached the Kennedy motorcade in downtown Eden before Murray and company. If he could protect past time and event, if he could prevent Murray from interference, then he might yet—and if Eden is indeed Brevard's creation, if Zahia is wrong and O'Shaugnessey right, then he might yet strengthen memory and sequence enough to encompass chaos and isolate time. If not, then all this would indeed be nothing more than a constructed dream. And so this never would have happened. The World Trade Center would reassemble itself back into its known form, the speeding planes would speed backward to be summarily erased from the sky by the ass-end of an ubiquitous No.2 pencil, otherwise known as the arrow of time. All we (might) know is that somewhere in this abyss between occurrence and possibility Brevard and his companions must work to shape and mold the millennium.

Of course, if Brevard is right—and if he can succeed—then he will have to accept Murray and his scientists as his own creations. His driving will to failure and reversal.

And so he drives. What else is left to him?

After some measure of infinity, Leandra and Denise ask, "Are we there yet?"

"Wait for it..." Zahia answers.

THE BUTTERFLY EFFECT

BUT ALTHOUGH CAUGHT in simultaneity, caught in the constantly expanding waves of the singularity itself, he does *not* wait for it. He drives, drives toward the collapsing towers, drives toward what he cannot help but consider as his destiny—and what an odd and antique analogy that is! Drive on, driving over the imagery of cobalt blue sand, driving along and upon and within this degenerating simulacrum of simulation.

In the back seats, Leandra and Denise giggle and laugh with child-like delight. They stand up, balancing like marionettes on the floorboards, and shout, "Look, the butterflies, can you see them?" And one or the other identicals calls to them, calling them away, calling them to their advancing car, as if insects could be and had been trained like dogs.

Nonplussed, Zahia shouts over the screaming wind-draft of the speeding Cadillac: "They are certainly *not* butterflies."

"They are! They are!" shout the twins, trembling with joy; and whether Brevard has injected his wishes into the tangible reality, or whether butterflies large as pterodactyls are simply part of this time lapsed landscape, you can see for yourself that there are indeed butterflies emerging from the towers.

Brevard presses the accelerator, and the Cadillac spins into overdrive.

He is impatient to reach—and pass through—the emptiness that was the towers, although he can clearly see them (now as after-images or present images or future images) falling slowly toward their majestic crashing slumber. And as he drives across this past present future landscape, ever more butterflies emerge, each one a tiny refraction of light describing wide or smaller arcs from the square footage that was and is and will be the towers, each giant butterfly flirting with some micro-destiny, each one moving with the solemnity of gravity toward some secret ending which must fall away from Brevard's plane of sight. And Brevard, for his part, feels exhilarating duration, feels that he is towering over circumstance; and perhaps he is…perhaps he *is* circumstance. Or perhaps, as we have argued and questioned and surmised, he is just another radioactive bit of the flotsam caught in its tidal force.

Another flirting butterfly.

SUMMARY INTIMATIONS

PASSING THROUGH THE city, driving along streets of constructed metaphor and history, driving through an overlaid, reconstructed map of every city, any city, future city, past city, present city, its specificity dawning like the radioactive blotch of sun pouring its life-and-death giving rays upon Brevard and company...and upon his nemesis Matthew Murray and his clackity-clacking train of scientists, who are out of Brevard's sight, but not out of mind. Brevard can *feel* their imposition.

AND A WORD ABOUT THE MODEL

WHEN BREVARD HAD established this world, this universe, this investigation, it was ostensibly to produce *the* most accurate reality: an ever-shifting floor of forms, ideas, and constructions human and otherwise. A grand reality, the last link of the great chain of being. This then would be the final situation, the final solution that would take the very ethos and pain out of desire. Desire in brackets. Desire as metaphor for mind and causality and progress, the truth of which we readers and writers can never know from our bounded twenty-first century perspective. That was Brevard's goal: a final, summary disaster...a disaster so large, so finally encompassing that Brevard, Murray, Zahia, Leandra, Denise, the assassins, all of them could give up any responsibility for their lives. In the century of flame, all consequence would be equal. But this construction had been compromised by the unprompted arrival of Murray.

Brevard—who had not created Murray, at least not to his knowledge—experienced the selfsame dumb embarrassment that Frankenstein must have felt when his creation began to complain about the laboratory; and a new insight came to Brevard or perhaps it had always been with him masked as old knowledge but now revealed in its terrific force that he could not through creation control: God must have felt the same way when he released Abraham. Ah, well, so much for omniscience, even in this carefully created and contained speck of a universe.

ISLANDS OF TIME

ASSIGNATION+ASSASINATION=TOPOGRAPHY

HE COULD SEE the glistening towers superimposed upon their ruins in the rear-view mirror of the Cadillac de Ville Convertible. In that glancing instant, he could also see Leandra and Denise huddled together as if they'd just been attacked. Their eyes were wide, their thick blond hair whipped around their perfectly symmetrical faces like the snakes of agitated medusas. Brevard redirected his concentration forward. Zahia sat beside him, as still as a statue, a beautifully cold, patient, life-like statue. But whether statue or breathtaking alive and mortal, she was a reflection or rather a refraction of mindfulness itself and understood that the next few seconds would be either/or: she would in the fullness and compression of time have the sour proof that she was in the right and that Brevard and his ghost O'Shaugnessey were, had been, and would be infinitely, iteratively, and forever wrong.

It was baking hot. Not a cloud in the sky. On either side of the road which we shall call Main Street were crowds of people and behind them rows of buildings, some high some low; but these were not the buildings associated with Brevard's City of God, the Eden of crystal towers perfumed with perfect memory. No, these buildings were brick and mortar, and it is 12:27 pm, November the twenty-second, 1963.

Brevard did not turn right on Houston Street along Dealey Plaza and then left onto Elm Street in front of the Texas School Book Depository, but double-parked on Main Street, parallel to Elm. He looked around: if the sun had not turned the windows of the Book Depository into mirrors, he would be able to see directly into them.

"There," he said to Zahia, as a white Ford followed by a 1961 Lincoln Continental convertible turned onto Elm Street, "there's the motorcade, and I"—he scanned the surrounding area—"I can't see or feel or sense Murray's presence."

"Perhaps you're not looking hard enough," Zahia said. "Or were you expecting his train to come crashing through these buildings?" A slight smile played on the corners of her mouth. "Or perhaps it is chug-a-chugging down Elm Street as we speak. The railroad bridge isn't far from here, you know."

Brevard allowed himself to appreciate a sensation akin to happiness; and it was as if that momentary lapse into hope heightened his sensitivity...or, more likely, it was a slight shift of sunlight, a passing cloud, which revealed who was really perched behind the sixth-floor window of the Texas School Book Depository.

Need we tell you? Do you *really* need clarification? Everything to this point has been historic, long frozen in academic replication, devoid of the speculative. Credulity will get you everywhere. The political forces of that ancient century (and all the others) have proven that.

TIME'S BOOMERANG, SUPERPOSITION, AND DECOHERENCE... OR, YOU'RE DEAD!

MATTHEW MURRAY OF Holbeck, Nottinghamshire (and, as previously acknowledged, England, Europe, the planet, the solar system, the mind of God, Matthew himself, et. al.), unappeased and centered, fired the first shot at the President of the United States from that sixth-floor window, and that bullet struck Michael Evreux Brevard like the prick of a sewing needle. It then moved through his body and exited just below his throat, finally ending its jagged journey in Texas Governor John B. Connally's left leg.

And Murray is now about to fire his eight pound Carcano 6.5 millimeter rifle again. The plan is working. He feels little instantaneous flares of satisfaction moving rapidly inside him, moving toward some kind of culmination. He knows full well that this second shot will tear away the President's skull, huge flaps dangling as pendants of the twentieth century. Murray's face—unnoticed of course—bears a rictus of satisfaction as he squints into the sight of the rifle's four-power scope and begins to squeeze the trigger. But he is interrupted, gazumped, swindled, done over. Kennedy is indeed shot a second time, but not by Murray. Who is that shooter, that carrion born interloper on the Grassy Knoll? Murray is stunned, unmanned by this sudden intrusion. What other force, what gangling demon has intervened? Astonished, cheated, Murray hurls his rifle aside and prepares to bolt. Leave it for the keepers. Leave it to larger forces. He always knew, always *should* have known that this would happen. The President's shattered skull is surrounded by a halo of blood. Figures are furiously running away from the Grassy Knoll.

Murray departs. It is easier than he ever would have surmised.

Easier for Murray, but too late for Brevard.

LAST THOUGHTS BEFORE AND AFTER DEATH'S CRUEL CURTAIN

AS JOHN F. Kennedy explodes, his wife Jackie Kennedy screams beside him, screams at Special Agent Roy Kellerman who is in the right front seat, screams at the Connally's, at the broken doll beside her that was Jack, at the street, the buildings, the sun, the shrouded, invisible moon: "I have his brains in my hand!" And a few seconds later, as if encouraged by an invisible prompter, she shouts again, "Jack! Jack! They've killed my husband!" But who were "they?" Who are "they?" If we knew this we might in fact know everything: the great conundrum sealed. Unfortunately we will never know. This will remain the greatest mystery of that ancient ceremony, never to be solved within the myriad conjunctions of real time.

Beside her, holistic fragments of Brevard/Kennedy's shrapnelled brain think distant, numbed thoughts as he, or rather as they realize that time and this very act of passage existed only in his broken head. It was time's own remorseless gunshot that struck him/strikes him dead. It is time's own remorseless gunshot that struck him/strikes him dead. "You win, Zahia," he murmurs, his breath and words corresponding to the extension and contraction of phantom limbs. "You lose O'Shaugnesssy." And not only does Brevard experience phantom thoughts after death, but phantom hopes as well. He hopes that Zahia has been distracted. It also occurs to him as he stares through the halo's surrounding, narrowing circle that for her too this will be a last chance. He hopes, ah hope!, that his calculation was not wrong. He hopes that in her distraction and fear she will find some rudiment of clarity. But it would seem that poor Zahia is only distracted. *Momentarily*—a word we have arbitrarily fixed with meaning—her defenestration is arrested. A frieze of impossibility. A single, singular *demoiselle d'avignon*.

Momentarily…

Ah, moment and sequence: perhaps O'Shaugnessey the superpositional ghost is having a last laugh after all!

AND A FINAL ENTOMOLOGICAL EPIPHANY...

ZAHIA—*DEMOISELLE D'AVIGNON*, TIME'S custodian, time's catamite—watches the great butterflies rising from the ruins of Brevard's construction, the city, desert, sun, and sky their manifold chrysalis. Behind her, the twins rustle in ecstasy and extend their newly-formed wings, Then they, too, rise to join the others. They rise to form the sky. Although Zahia might have been at one time more purposeful than the twins, she accedes to this last iteration. She follows them. But even in this eye-melting sunlight, her irradiated wings glow as if in pure thought. She rises magnificently; and Brevard, ah, Brevard! He lies somewhere below, a desiccated pupa to their imago, an absent god to their absent Abraham now lost to view from the killing floor. What did Abraham know and when did he know it?

What did *any* of them know?

AFTERWORD TO "THE TOWERS OF EDEN"

BARRY N. MALZBERG and I have been collaborating on short fiction since 1981. We've written a handful of stories together, two of which are included in this collection. I enjoy co-authoring short fiction, as can be seen by taking a look at my collaborative short story collection *The Fiction Factory*, which includes collaborations with Gardner Dozois, Susan Casper, Michael Swanwick, Janeen Webb, Jack C. Haldeman II, George Zebrowski, Gregory Frost…and, of course, Barry. And there was a period between 1979 and 1985, my 'Fiction Factory' period, when my collaborative fiction was selling to the slicks, the most difficult magazines to sell in their day, for what was then considered serious money. It was an exhilarating time, a time that felt like something right out of Hemingway's *A Moveable Feast*. That time is well past. Gardner, Susan, and Jay (Jack C. Haldeman) have passed away, turning the universe—my universe, anyway—into a much emptier place. Yet Barry and I still keep producing stories together, stories that are quintessentially different from each other, stories that continue to surprise me, stories that continue to bring me a rare and lustrated kind of joy.

Writing with Barry is a singular experience, as he is an extrodinarily fast writer, who has, in fact, written hundreds of books under his own name and under various pseudonyms. I—on the other hand—am a slow writer, and our correspondence while working on a story usually consists of:

Barry: "Where's the story?"

Me: "I'm working on it."

"The Towers of Eden," our homage to J. G. Ballard's surrealistic *Vermillion Sands* stories originated in a dream. As I wrote Barry:

"This dream had all the precision and reality of a lucid dream, something I haven't experienced to this degree for some twenty-plus years.

"I was flying on a jetliner with my mother, who had risen from the dead. I was dreaming of an elastic alternate timeline where dream grotesqueries are as natural as in our own. Then, inevitably, something went wrong with the engine. But there were only a few seconds in which to be terrified. Although I couldn't 'see' it through the windows, we were flying over a city, flying toward a skyscraper conceived by Shrodinger himself, a tower of glass that dwarfed our own lost Twin Towers; and so we flew toward this 9/11 iteration of oblivion, but oblivion it was not. The pilot landed on the very top of the building, impossible of course, but rationally explained in the dream by a steward who told me that the building was wide enough to be equipped with a catching mechanism such as those used on aircraft carriers, and though it was nigh-on impossible to accomplish, the pilot managed it. As in a film, the dream then cut to me doing an errand on the street below, and I looked up at this vertiginous building and sure enough perched on top of it like a gigantic gargoyle was the plane."

Barry responded:

"Fantastic, there is our story, a Ballardian cesspool, a Ballardian dreamscape, cloud sculptors of Empire landing atop the ruined towers, exiting the wreckage (curiously intact) and wandering through the building as we wander through the landscape of our own failing bodies into which we have landed. It is all there, jewel-like, the facades glinting, all that we need are the aliens clambering on ropes to extract us from the building and take us through its rubble and surfaces to the small and precise rooms of our childhood. Write this. We should write it."

And my response:

"An idea for a title came to me: 'The Towers of Eden'. Don't know if it's any good, but there it is.

"This is what I'm mulling:

"The protagonist has bought a ruined earth, or a part thereof, and has rebuilt it to his liking, has 'reincarnated' those survivors who had stored their 'engrams' electronically for a future re-embodiment, and they are in the position of indentured servants to him. There are but few, and the distances are great a la Ballard. The protagonist has created a city of towers, his version of Augustine's 'City of God', glowing glass spires reaching to the heavens, and he sees, from below, from some French-style boulevard, the great 747 or whatever version of plane we choose, sees it crashing through the top stories of these diamond skyscrapers and then watches it land on the narrow ridge of the largest and longest tower, landing neatly, impossibly.

"He has his chauffeur (?) drive him to the tower and takes the elevator to the roof where he discovers that the pilot and passengers aren't any of those he has reincorporated, but are either aliens or humans who have literally crashed into his space and reality. And as soon as they do, the city/desert/world begins to change, to crystalize, and he and we as writers and readers must discover why. And Just as Ballard had the self-involved Leonora Chanel causing havoc and death...and a satisfying plot resolution, we would we need such antagonists and protagonists..."

And so back and forth we went until we completed the story you've just (theoretically) read, which became the lead story in *Caped Fear: Superhuman Horror Stories*, edited by Steve Proposch, Christopher Sequeira, and Bryce Stevens. A graphic novel of "The Towers of Eden" is under consideration.

THE TRANSFORMATION OF TARG
(WITH PAUL BRANDON)

IT WAS a typically bitter New York morning.

The wind was like a splintery hand across the face, each slap feeling like it left tiny shards of ice embedded in the skin. It chased crumpled balls of old newspaper up the gutters, spinning them around the ankles of the hurrying people. Up between the buildings, rivers of flawless blue could be seen mirroring the avenues of grey, cloudless cold.

Commuters bustled up the streets, heads bowed, turtled into scarves or high collars. Cars and taxis seethed.

Just off Fifth Avenue, down a bleak alleyway made almost impassable by large, overflowing dumpsters and trafficked by rats and scraggy cats, a door opened.

From inside the ally it was no different from any of the other doors; paint-peeled and somewhat bowed, it was utterly unremarkable except for the odd-looking thumb-latch. It appeared to be nothing more than an old back access door to the Starbucks that fronted Fifth.

As it swung silently open, light bloomed out suddenly, then died away. From across the alleyway, two dark figures could be seen standing within; but it wasn't the store room of a coffee shop that they were inside, not by any means.

They stood within a small circular chamber. Black brick walls wept water that bled down across a cobbled floor to gurgle down a grated drain. Bodies hung, a few still alive, in various states of interrupted agony from the walls. Small crackles of blue lightning still arced between the two that were still shrieking, the last remnants of the magic that opened the door.

The two figures that stood just inside were fearsome indeed. Closest to the door was a huge barrel of a man, or at least he would have looked like a man if he'd had a normal head. Great curling horns, polished to an ebony gleam, lifted away from features that more resembled a horse than anything human. His skin was mottled, green and brown like lichen, and he was dressed in formidable-looking armour of interlocking leather plates. In his right hand was an enormous war axe, even more polished than his horns.

But it was the second figure that commanded the eye.

Simply dressed, he wore a long black cape and creaseless black pants tucked into his polished black boots. A leather jerkin, made of blackest leather was stitched across his chest, overlaying a shirt of midnight silk. He wasn't particularly tall, especially standing next to the other; but what he lacked in stature he more than made up for in presence.

His skin was white, the pale, chalky white of bones rather than of purity, and his face could simply be described as cruel. From the top of his left brow (where a shock of white hair flared against the black) a wicked scar traversed his face, gouging a line down across the empty socket of his eye to tug the top of his lip into a permanent sneer.

But it was the other eye that captivated; flat, glassy, like a shark, it seemed to make up for the loss of its twin with an intensity that was little short of terrifying.

The two figures waited patiently while the blue sparks flickered between the last of the hanging men then, with a last shrieking cry that reverberated quite nicely around the small chamber, the hanging men died.

Smiling, the man in black gestured politely to the other, “After you, my dear Sarpent,” who frowned back at him then stepped through the doorway.

The air rippled, as if the space between the frame was water and a stone had been tossed in, and as he passed out into the alley, the Sarpent changed. Gone was the armour, replaced by a pin-striped Italian-cut suit. Instead of the wicked axe, his right hand held a black leather laptop case. All that remained of the equine features was a slightly jutting lower jaw on an otherwise handsome face. His skin was the color of an expensive full-cream latte, the horns replaced by beautiful blond curling locks.

The second man stepped through, and the change was equally startling. His suit was unadorned soft black wool. His hair was still the same; but a mirrored, silver-rimmed monocle covered the vacant eye, a spider thread of gleaming chain tickling down along the ridge of the somehow noble-looking scar. Black Gucci loafers supplanted the leather boots, though nothing could replace his aura of absolute power…deep, dark, sickening power. The only splash of color came from a blood red handkerchief that poked out of his breast pocket.

“You have the address?” he asked in a voice that brought that same reaction as a broken fingernail down a blackboard.

Sarpent nodded, tapped his breast pocket and set off towards the bright bustle of Fifth Avenue. When he realized the other man wasn’t following, he turned, frowning. “My Liege…?”

The Dark Lord was bent down, stroking the ear of a tatty black cat that wove between his legs. Even from half-dozen yards away Sarpent could hear it purring like a little motor. The lord was making little chirping and cooing noises.

Sarpent took a long, deep, steadying breath and muttered, "And you wonder why we're here?"

"What was that?"

"Nothing, oh fearsome and mighty lord."

THE WAITING ROOM was paneled with mahogany and smelled faintly of expensive cigars.

A stunning glass installation the size of a coffee table hung from the wall directly opposite the entrance, its surface laser-etched with a welcome for the visitor to Dr. Hiram Hirsch's Exclusive Evil Consultancy.

Medical certifications in gilded frames were scattered across the other walls like art, interspersed with pictures of a heavy-set, middle aged man (whom Sarpent assumed to be Dr. Hirsch) catching a huge marlin, standing with one foot up on a freshly shot tiger, shaking hands with Saddam Hussein, Oberon, King Drakkor the Black, even a slightly faded one of the good doctor with his arm around a smiling Bin Laden.

There were no chairs, only four Chesterfield sofas, upholstered in solferino-red leather and brass studs. A single door, at the other end of the room, stood closed, next to a desk that fronted a stiff-looking receptionist dressed in finest Ralph Lauren. She lifted her head as they entered, frowned, then subtly pressed a button on the edge of the desk.

As had happened when they had stepped through the portal, the air around Sarpent and his Lord wavered, then like a roller blind snapping back upwards, the suited illusions were lifted away, revealing once again the man in black and his horse-faced guard.

Sarpent growled, a low, guttural sound, but the receptionist simply pointed to a small sign by the door that read in jaunty, self-help letters:

"If you can't be yourself here, then where can you be?"

The Lord laid his hand on Sarpent's arm and said lightly, "I suppose that's very true."

They approached the desk. The receptionist pretended to be busy for a long moment, then looked up. "Name?"

Sarpent bristled, "This is his Mighty Revenant Overlord Targ, Destroyer of Mordane and Ruler of—"

"*First* name, please?"

Sarpent's large mouth clicked shut; he blinked with surprise and turned to face his lord, looking apologetic.

The Overlord cleared his throat and in a small voice said, "Brian."

"Well, Brian," said the receptionist as if she were talking to a small child, "Doctor Hirsch is ready to see you now." She gestured to the closed door. "You," she said to Sarpent with a flick of her wrist towards one of the Chesterfields, "may wait there."

Sarpent looked at his lord, who was just about to knock on the door, then nodded and sat down on the couch. There was a huge outrush of air from the leather cushions of the Chesterfield. Sarpent laid his battleaxe across his knees, picked up a copy of *Vogue*, and settled in to wait for his master.

"OKAY OKAY, NOW where did you *just* go wrong, huh?" A fit-looking older man sat behind a beautiful glass-topped desk.

His head was covered with a thick thatch of perfectly pomaded white hair, although the huge moustache that antlered under his nose was a sooty black. The face itself had a yacht club tan, fierce blue eyes and a somewhat bulbous nose. Thin moist lips, barely visible beneath the overhang of hair, were set in a smile that seemed more rehearsed than genuine. His voice was somewhat nasal, and carried the slightly accusatory-sounding New York cadence well. "Come on, it all starts right here. Right now. What was your first mistake?"

Brian frowned, somewhat bewildered by the sudden questions. "I… err, didn't wipe my feet?"

"No no *no*!" Hirsch said smoothly. "You *knocked*! You're the *Mighty* Revenant Overlord Targ, *Destroyer* of Mordane and *Ruler* of—" he discretely checked his notes, "—Heckinor."

"Hellinor."

"Whatever. Heckinor, Hellinor. Do you see my point? You *never* knock. You march in, you sit down, and if anyone doesn't like it, you order that person's head to be removed immediately. Or something else, you decide. *You're* the Boss." Hirsch stood up and offered his hand, "Hiram Hirsch, Consultant to Evil."

Brian shook the pudgy hand as hard as he could, which was difficult because it was like greeting a jewelry store. "Erm, Brian." They were about the same height, but the sculpted white hair made Hirsch look taller.

"Very pleased to meet you Brian, have a seat," he gestured to the reclining leather chair. "You don't mind me calling you Brian do you? We shouldn't stand on ceremony in here, don't you agree?"

Brian understood the question was rhetorical, but he nodded anyway. Somewhat reluctantly, he lay back. The ceiling was paneled the same way as the walls, and the little squares of wood were somewhat hypnotic.

"Now," Hirsch began, "you were referred here by…let me see now… the ArchWitch Hagspittle. Ahhh how is old Maggie doing?"

"Fine," replied Brian. "She has her Dark Court back under control and is even planning an offensive against the Shining Dawn next season. She speaks very highly of you."

"And well she should. When I first counseled Maggie, she had lost touch with evil to such an extent that she could barely string two spells together. The distances and dimensions my cliental comes to me from never ceases to amaze… But anyway, let's not get sidetracked. This is about you, now, isn't it?"

Almost against his will, Brian found himself nodding.

"Now, you wrote in your initial consult application that you"—Hirsch's voice took on the tone of someone reading—"just don't seem to have the heart for evil any more, that it no longer gives you that shivery black thrill that it used to, and that you'd rather go and raise alpacas in Idaho. Is that true, Brian?" Hirsch sounded terribly disappointed.

"They're a lovely animal, very friendly."

"I meant about losing the will to be evil." Hirsh leaned forwards on his desk. "Have you lost your mojo, Brian?"

Brian swallowed. "Maybe…"

"Why don't you tell me about it?"

So Brian did, from the first hesitant moments when he realized that for no reason he could discern, he had suddenly run out of creative ways to wage war and execute and torture his myriad enemies. Hadn't he botched up his invasion of neighboring Callidan Island by forgetting to requisition and build enough boats, so the invasion had to be called off before they'd even left the shores? The Callidani laughter still rang in his ears. He touched upon his fondness for cats, for jesters and motleys, skipped over his secret plans to implement a better and more fair justice system, and talked briefly (but somewhat fondly) about his aim to one day establish an autonomous government.

When he finished, he felt oddly better, more at peace, at one with the universe.

Then there was silence, broken only by the creaking leather of Hirsch's chair and the occasional clunk of a piece of jewelry against the glass-topped table. Brian resisted the urge to look over, but he could imagine the doctor staring at him, stroking his giant moustache.

"Do you have a mask?"

"Hmm?" (Brian had nearly dozed off) "Yes, of course. I brought it as per your request." He reached inside his jerkin and pulled out a small black square of velvet which he carefully unfolded.

"Put it on please," Hirsch told him.

Brian slipped it over his head. It was a little like a cross between a balaclava and an executioner's mask. Instead of eyeholes, there was a wide slit that just reached his nose. The velvet looked almost wet in the dusty office light.

Hirsch leaned forwards, steepling his fingers, considering. "Hmmm," he said after a long moment's thought. "It's not exactly, well, intimidating, is it."

Brian shrugged. "I do have another one, made from an elf skull."

"Well, *that's* a little more like it!"

"But it's dreadfully heavy and it brings me out in a rash around my ears."

"I see."

More pondering.

"Well Brian, we need to take this one step at a time. Here's what I want you to do. Before our next visit, I want you to find some people, any people, a village, a settlement, some group that's always annoyed you."

"The Do'raki Fenlanders," Brian said, snapping his fingers. "They have never shown proper respect and were late with their taxes this year. Come to think of it, they were a bit late last year, too."

"Whatever." He leaned forwards. "I want you to destroy them."

Brian's eyes blinked out from the slit in the mask. "Destroy them? I'll lose revenue."

"Yes!" said Hirsch feverishly. "Destroy them utterly. Forgo lost revenue. This is more important. Show them no mercy! You're the *Mighty* Revenant Overlord Targ, *Destroyer* of Mordane and *Ruler* of—" he discretely checked his notes again, "—Heckinor."

"Hellinor."

"Yes, that's what I meant. Destroy all Do'hicky Finlanders!"

"Do'raki Fenlanders," Brian mumbled, correcting the doctor before raising a clenched fist, and repeating in a small, somewhat uncertain voice: "Destroy them."

DR. HIRSCH PICKED up the receiver of his antique Princess phone; the numerals of the rotary dial glowed yellow in the darkness.

"Hello?"

The line was crackly and sounded like it traveled across the bottom of the ocean. "Doctor Hirsch? This is Sarpent speaking, General of the Revenant Overlord's Fifty Legions, Commander of the Night Watchers, First Chief of—"

Hirsch waved his hand, "Just what is it with you people and your titles? Sarpent would have done you know. I'm old, not senile."

"Forgive me, honored doctor, but I…I find myself unable to…I don't know quite what to…"

"Take all the time you need. I bill by the minute."

"It's the Overlord sir, he, well, may I ask just exactly what it was you instructed him to do?"

"Well, Sarp, I can't really tell you that, doctor-patient confidentiality being what it is. May I call you Sarp?"

"Yes, doctor, whatever you wish."

Okay, Sarp, then why don't you just tell me what he did, and I'll tell you if he's following my instructions."

"Well, sir, the Lord gathered together the whole second battalion, and we all had high hopes, but he, ah…"

"What?"

"He relocated the Do'raki Fenlanders."

"Well, that's not *exactly* what I had in mind, but displacing is a start—"

"It wasn't exactly displacement," Sarpent said around another bark of static. "More like…sir, the Overlord helped them move."

"He *what*?"

"Well, they live in the fens, and they're always being flooded. The Do'raki are extremely poor, *filthy*, but, on the other hand, they're fierce little fighters and they usually pay their proper taxes to the Overlord."

"All the more reason for them to be wiped out!"

"For paying taxes?" Sarpent asked.

"Don't be literal. You know what I mean," Dr. Hirsh said.

Yes, sir. I agree on general principles that they should be wiped out. But the Overlord, well, ah, he took…*pity*—" he spat the word out like a bitter pip "—on them and had the battalion build them new hovels on higher ground. Sir, he had my men…"

"Sarpent, are you still there? You're breaking up. Are you on a mobile?

More static, "Just a moment sir…"

Hirsch held the phone away from his ear a little, which was fortuitous, as Sarpent suddenly thundered, "*Get the spell together! YOU USELESS NUMBSCULL OF A WIZARD! Now, focus, before I cut off that little beard and stick it where the spells don't shine!*" There was one last yelp of noise that sounded uncannily like a fist striking flesh (or a fish being slapped onto pavement), and then the line cleared remarkably. "There, is that better doctor?" Sarpent asked in a calm voice.

"Much better. Telecommunication problems?"

"Oh, nothing that a good sharp jab with my sword won't fix." The end of the sentence sounded like it was aimed away from whatever Sarpent was using as a phone. "So you did not suggest that my lord help the Do'raki move to a more up-market location."

"I am not presently a real estate consultant."

"Well, what should I do next? Bring my lord back in? I need help here, doctor. He's really not himself. He's becoming a laughing stock for the other emperors and warlords."

"Let me think for a moment, Sarp... Do you have any judgments coming up soon, any judicial trials, anything like that?"

"Well, we don't have courts here, of course. The Overlord just decides their fate. But the criminals are due to be paraded around the hanging square in a fortnight."

"Excellent. I need you to help. The morning before the parade, you will have to talk to your lord, remind him of his notable evil deeds, his past victories, slaughters, all those kind of things. Get him in the mood, give him a few ales at lunch time, then sit at his right hand and prompt him to kill all the criminals as a supreme gesture of His Evil Will to his people. A brief sudden display of malevolence might be just what he needs to jar him back into his nasty ways. And it will be a tonic for the general populace, too."

"I understand. It shall be done sir."

THE STEPS OF Judgment were quite impressive.

They were located to the rear of the castle, where the black Cliff of Despair buttressed against the Obsidian Mountain. Started at ground level, they ascended up towards the Throne of His Glorious Will like a fan, forming an upside down amphitheatre. Originally, the architect had designed and built it the other way around, with the Throne at the bottom, so that even the people who couldn't afford a front row seat could see everything; but the Overlord didn't like people looking down on him, so he had the architect killed and the Steps reversed, stone by stone.

Sarpent's deep laugh boomed as he told the story, refilling the Overlord's gold tankard and stealing a quick glance at his Lord's face. The Overlord had chuckled at the memory, which was a good sign. Sarpent lingered on the part where the Overlord had personally taken the architect apart, fingernails first, then knuckles, then hands and so on, as a demonstration of how annoyed he was at the prospect of dismantling the Steps. He thought the architect had gotten the message, but it was hard to tell between the pitiful screams and pleadings for mercy.

"Mercy," Sarpent said, mouthing the word as if he'd found an old piece of decayed food behind a tooth, "is for the weak, the spineless. Fear…now fear, intimidation, terror…they are the tools of the strong, do you not agree, my Lord?"

Brian nodded absently; he was still thinking back to a rather disconcerting yet pleasurable dream he'd had the night before where he'd freed all the prisoners and everyone had loved him for it. The people had called his name, thrown flowers, cheered…

"Would my Lord care for one last drink?" Sarpent asked, interrupting his thoughts with a wave of an ale bottle. It was a fine brew, strong, but Brian didn't want his head spinning any more. It would be hard to be just if one were pissed. "A lord must be just, mustn't he?" Brian said out loud.

"Wha—?" Sarpent said.

"Of course justice resides in the definition, and it is I who decides all definition, is it not so?"

"Yes, Great Lord, you decide all things."

"As was and shall ever be," Brian said by rote.

"As was and shall ever be," Sarpent dutifully repeated as he made the sign of fealty, which resembled the traditional bird: index finger erect.

But Brian wasn't paying attention; he stroked the ginger cat curled up on his lap. "Did you know it is Mrs. Tinkle's birthday today?"

Sarpent blinked, "Mrs.…Tinkle?"

"That's right isn't it," Brian cooed at the cat, who was kneading his knee with a paw. "You're the little birthday puss."

Sarpent swallowed, fingering a horn nervously. "Another movie then?" he said hurriedly. "We have the time, the serfs won't mind waiting and I'm sure the dead—I mean the accused—aren't going anywhere." Sarpent picked up another of the DVDs that Doctor Hirsh had leant him. "We've watched most of the Steven Segal films, but there's still the early Schwarzenegger and some man called Tarantino that comes highly recommended…"

Brian shook his head. "No, I've seen enough. Disconnect that…thing."

Sarpent nodded and reached over for the plug to the borrowed TV and DVD player, which was inserted into the last socket the original inventors had ever considered as a power supply. The dumpy-looking wizard who had been chanting the spell to create ignescent electricity let out a huge sigh, followed by a yelp as Sarpent's boot helped him out of the room before he'd even had a chance to lower his robe.

"Now," Sarpent continued. "Which mask for today?" the Overlord paused, hand stroking the cat as he considered. Sarpent could see his Lordship's gaze lingering on the soft velvet, so he said, "If I may be so bold, my liege, Doctor Hirsh would probably want you to wear the elf skull today…for therapeutic reasons."

"Yes, I suppose he would," Brian sighed. He put the cat gently on the ground, stood up, and reached for the pale monstrosity, which had once been the treasured possession of King Ulran of Arboria—so treasured in fact that it had taken a sword through the neck to part Ulran from it. Brian slipped it on, hoping that Sarpent wouldn't notice the distaste on his face. It was heavy, ill-fitting and smelled of elves, no matter how many times they boiled it. And Brian hated elves, almost as much as he hated cats.

But he didn't hate cats anymore.

Brian sniffed. Well, maybe it didn't smell so bad, after all.

"Perfect," Sarpent enthused, bowing. "My Lord looks truly fearsome and mighty. The walking dead—I mean accused—will surely soil themselves mightily upon your approach."

Let's hope not, Brian thought, remembering the last time. It had taken his valets days to get the splash marks off his best black boots.

THE SENESCHAL BOOMED his staff on the ground, and in a voice that Brian had now considered too hammy, pronounced, "*RISE* for his highness, The *Mighty* Revenant Overlord Targ, *Destroyer* of Mordane, *Ruler* of Hellinor, *Slayer* of the Venomous *Were*Spider of..."

Brian yawned discreetly under his mask. That was one thing he did like about masks, you could yawn, smile, even doze off, and people never noticed.

He walked slowly past the blood encrusted trap door to the Throne of His Glorious Will (*or should that be My Glorious Will?* he thought absently). Behind him hung Pain, the huge executioner's sword that Sarpent used to dispense the Law. After raising his arms to the cheering crowds (his royal guards were using their whips and bludgeons with great subtlety to encourage them), he turned and removed the sword from its ornamented bracket. He spoke the ceremonial words of opening and handed the sword to Sarpent, who, as always, was the official dispenser of justice. Then he sat down on the throne, careful not to let his robe bunch up under him. The unwashed masses descended away beneath him in a maelstrom of color, cacophony and chaos. People from all walks of life jostled for seats, shouted, argued, stood in line for pies from the vendors. Away to his right was the disheveled row of the accused, their shaven heads bowed, some weeping, other looking passively out over the crowd, grimly resigned to their fate. Children threw stones (fruit was generally saved for eating) and occasionally a prisoner would cry out and try to raise his manacled arms to ward off a missile.

Brian listened patiently while the first prisoner was brought forward and the charges read out by the seneschal. He'd been caught cart-jacking; however, his arrest had gone wrong, and he'd managed to kill a pair of guards. With Hirsh's words echoing in his head, the very sound of conscience, Brian stretched out his arms and turned down his thumbs. Fair was fair. Guards were hard to come by these days and expensive to train, and this man had killed two and lamed a third.

The roar of the crowd surged over him, and Sarpent took but a moment to loosen his shoulders before striking the man's head clean from his body with an almost negligent swipe. The body stood headless for a moment, before the trap door sprung open and it plummeted from sight. With a skillful back heel-kick from one of the ceremonial guards, the head followed.

Now that wasn't so bad, Brian thought. Sarpent was nodding his approval, and the crowd were chanting, "*Overlord...Overlord...*"

The next prisoner was another murderer, though this time the occasion had been a bar brawl. The wiry man had a pockmarked and surly-looking face. He contended that that he'd not started it, that it had all been in self-defense. He then wailed and pleaded, but somehow all of it sounded rehearsed. Brian listened, nodding, as if in agreement. Then he stretched out his arms and turned down his thumbs.

Sarpent was elated. It looked like his Lord was back to his old evil ways. Grinning from ear to ear, he put a little too much effort into his sword swing, and the head went soaring out into the crowd, where the peasants amused themselves by tossing and kicking it around like a beach ball.

Once again the trap door clattered. The next man was brought forward.

This one was just a thief, and Sarpent was a little disappointed to be instructed just to remove a hand; but still, it was all blood and suffering, and the crowd always enjoyed a bit of variety.

Five more thieves followed, and Sarpent felt more like a surgeon than an executioner as he was ordered to remove several ears, a nose, and two fingers.

There was a brief flash of hope as the Lord ordered a rapist castrated, though secretly Sarpent wished he'd just ordered him beheaded. It was far less fiddly.

And then it happened.

A baker accused of short-changing his customers was given a custodial sentence.

"Surely, my Lord," Sarpent whispered, "a hand, at least...thumbs... tongue?"

But Brian was having none of it. He was now determined to imprison, or fine, or even pardon criminals who had committed minor crimes.

The blood on the blade of Pain dried as it hung by Sarpent's side, unused.

After such a promising start, it was all going so terribly wrong. Worse yet, the Overlord actually seemed to be enjoying himself. He questioned each accused and took the time to consider and weigh each crime before dispensing something that looked far more like justice than punishment.

And then it happened.

The Overlord stood before the crowds and raised his arms. A hush fell over all. In a loud and impressive voice, the Overlord declared: "Good people of Hellinor, in honor of a dear friend's birthday, I have just decided that today shall be a day of amnesty. All but the most heinous crimes will be forgiven, and furthermore, I have also decided that it will be a public holiday, with a lifting of the usual dusk curfew." He paused as the crowd let out a huge enthusiastic roar. He ignored Sarpent's groan and continued, "Henceforth, today shall be known as…Tinklefest."

"TINKLEFEST? *TINKLEFEST*? OH Brian, what were you thinking?" Hirsh shook his head, causing the freshly waxed tips of his moustache to bob.

"It seemed like a nice thing to do."

Mrs Tinkles had let out one hiss at the doctor then promptly hid under a cabinet at the far side of the room.

"A *NICE* thing… Oh, Brian, Brian, Brian… I've got to tell you that in all my years of practice I've never, *ever*…" Hirsch just shook his head again.

"You're disappointed in me," Brian said softly, transfixed by Hirsch's exaggeration of a moustache.

"*DISAPPOINTED*?" Hirsch took a deep breath and looked around, counting to ten under his breath to dispel the anger. Brian's study at the top of the Black Tower was small but surprisingly comfortable. He had a large desk (not unlike Hirsch's own, but without the glass protector, *which*, Hirsch thought absently, *he could really do with*, as the blood-stains were ingrained and the edges were rutted with that looked like axe marks). Four huge arched windows looked out over the land to all points of the compass, letting in a nice amount of natural light, and the views were stupendous. *I should build myself one of these in Manhattan.*

Seven…eight…nine…ten. He released a long breath and returned to the task at hand. "Brian," he said, "you do know why Sarpent called me out here."

Brian nodded.

"Well, then why don't we start with you telling me exactly what was going through your mind yesterday? Just take your time. Sarp has already signed a treasury wavier for my call-out fee. You're putting my three grandchildren through college—and I believe little Hiram Junior is going to Harvard. Think long and hard, great lord of Heckinor.

Brian started to say "Hellinor," but gave it up.

I want to know everything," Dr. Hirsch continued. "I want to know exactly when things started to go bad…or rather, good."

Brian smiled, thinking the doctor was making a rather funny joke, but the expression fell from his face when he saw Dr. Hirsch angrily and compulsively biting the edges of his moustache. Brian stroked his smooth chin, wondering if perhaps the secret to evil lay in facial hair. After all, Hiram Hirsch seemed to have no problems thinking up clever and horrid plans…there was the BoneDoctor of Riddel. He was supremely evil *and* he had a huge beard, then of course the ArchWitch Hagspittle had a bit of a moustache herself…and there was Saddam and Adolph, Bin…

Hirsch slapped his hand down on the desk, "Brian!" he shouted, making even Sarpent jump. Another cat hiss came from somewhere behind the cabinet. "You're doing it again."

"What?"

"Procrastinating. Daydreaming. An idle mind leads to idle deeds, and evil is *never* idle."

"Sorry. I'll remember that. Evil is never idle. Would make a good motto, don't you think?"

Hirsch just shook his head again.

"There was a time, sir," Sarpent said, folding his hairy arms across his broad chest with a creak of leather armour, "that you'd have someone's head cut off for speaking to you like that."

Brian sighed and lowered his head into his hands despondently. He tried to focus on his green chakra.

"Okay, let's start simply," Dr. Hirsch said. "What's bothering you right now, at this very moment?"

Brian frowned, stopping himself from voicing the obvious answer. "Well…I'm a bit worried about reports that the Armies of Bil'tha are massing to the south again—" Sarpent grunted, but Hirsch silenced him with an upraised hand, "—the Do'raki ambassador is here, and Mrs Tinkles is off her biscuits."

"That's perfect!"

"Not really, I have them shipped in specially at great cost."

"I meant the ambassador. Is he here now?"

"Waiting in an antechamber on His Overlord's pleasure," said Sarpent, absently using one of his horns to pick some dried blood from under a fingernail.

"What does he want?" Dr. Hirsch asked. "Isn't the land you relocated the Do'raki to upmarket enough?"

Sarpent flicked his fingers. "The ambassador claims they've not had sufficient time to replant crops, and therefore he and his people can't afford to pay their tax this financial year."

Brian said, "Which sounds fair enough, given that—"

"*WHAT?*" Hirsch's moustache was practically curling back on itself. "Am I mistaken or did the word 'FAIR' just leave your lips?"

"Well, I…"

"There will be no buts and no excuses this time. Brian, go out there and strangle the ambassador with your own hands. Right this minute. And then I want you to take your army and kill, maim, torture, rape, and pillage your enemy."

"Right this minute?"

"You heard me."

"I…*can't*," Brian cried. "I *like* Ooblier."

At Hirsch's frown, Sarpent leaned over and whispered, "The Do'raki ambassador's name is Ooblier."

"Oh, charming." He turned back to Brian, who was tracing an intricate whorl in his desk, desperately trying anything to avoid eye contact. "Brian, what on earth is wrong with you? Have I missed something? Is the air not foul enough in your kingdom? Is the water unpolluted? You used to be an Overlord of repute. Now you're behaving like a…a *putz*. Surely your parents taught you that Satan only helps those who help themselves?"

There was a pause.

Despite the wicked scar, the missing eye, the flash of white hair against the black, Brian looked very much like a little boy, and the sneer resembled a crooked smile. "My mother always used to complain that I had a sunny disposition. My mother and father would thrash me and send me to my room to think about things, but it never seemed to help. So they'd burn me with pokers then thrash me again. I started *pretending* to be evil to please them. It worked for quite a while, but I guess I'm finally coming out of the closet."

"Well, you'd better think long and hard about going back into the closet," Hirsch said.

"Why don't *you* do it?" Brian suggested after a moment.

Hirsch was baffled. "Come out of the closet?"

"Sure," said Brian, sitting up a little. "You always seem to have the best ideas about how to be evil. And we're about the same height, build. You can be me. After all, nobody would recognize you. You'd be wearing a mask."

"The Overlord is supposed to always wear a mask," Sarpent quickly pointed out to Hirsch.

"Well I don't know. I'm a doctor, not a dark lord." But Hirsch stroked his moustache, obviously considering Brian's suggestion.

"What if I watched you, from one of the secret spyholes? Perhaps if I could see evil working again, maybe I'd be…inspired?"

The doctor was still curling hairs around his fingers, and Brian could see by the excited gleam in his eyes that he had him. Brian's eyes narrowed slyly.

"This is all *highly* irregular…"

"Think of it as a new kind of therapy," Brian said. *I could get the hang of this therapy thing*, he thought as he rose from his desk, crossed over to the mask stand, and picked up one of the soft velvet masks.

"Do you…do you think I could have that one?" Hirsch said almost shyly, pointing at the big elf skull.

THE NEW CAREER was going well.

He had the office redecorated in eggshell white with classic cream carpets and friendly vases of fresh flowers everywhere. He kept the Chesterfield sofas, but had them reupholstered in the finest beige calfskins. The bragging photos were gone, replaced by small paintings by Cezanne and Durer etchings; the cool, lush sounds of the Modern Jazz Quartet drifted out of a pair of matching white Bose speakers above the receptionist's desk.

Even the self-help sign had been changed. It now read:

"Be the person your cat thinks you are."

Behind the desk, above the receptionist's beautifully coiffured head, was the glass installation that welcomed the visitor to The Tinkle Studio: An Ethical Executive Consultancy.

Brian opened his office door and stepped out into the waiting room. Dressed in a soft Armani linen suit and Gucci loafers, he looked more like a yachtsman than a therapist; but that was the idea. His eye patch was exactly the same colour as his pocket square, something which, for some reason, had set the New York fashion scene alight.

Even after a year, Brian still marveled at how everything had turned out. Hirsch had so enjoyed being Overlord that he offered to buy him out right there and then. Sarpent hadn't minded—he just wanted to serve evil, and if not Brian, then Hirsch would do just as well. The negotiations had been relatively simple, and though Hirsch had come off much better (though the price of a Kingdom compared to Upper West Side real estate wasn't really that different), Brian didn't mind. He had the New York practice, a reasonably immense fortune stashed away in a place called the Cayman Islands, and a brand new alpaca farm in Idaho.

Brian discovered that he had a natural talent for steering people back towards the light. Kings, seers, sages, presidents, ministers, and all manner of monsters and piebald creatures from across the breadth and width of the ninety-nine dimensions sought his sage advice when they found themselves succumbing to their darker desires.

"Your three-thirty is here, Doctor," the receptionist said politely, handing Brian a manila folder. A single, sad-looking elf sat enveloped in one of the Chesterfields, hands held stiffly in his lap. Brian smiled, remembering how he'd felt when he'd sat there waiting for Hirsch. He opened the folder, glancing quickly at the front page. *Having decimated the world Kah in error, the LightLord of Quaa'lar, First Seeker of the Justice of Marlorr, Luminescent Silverhand of...* Brian skipped down.

His first name was Simon.

Well it seemed Simon continued to stray somewhat from the light after his administrative mistake and had taken a blue orc for a mistress and murdered her prankster in a jealous fit. Nothing that couldn't be put right. Well, the prankster might be a problem, but he could probably be resurrected, or at the least, reincarnated.

Brian motioned the elf through with a smile and a soft welcoming word.

This should be a walk in the park.

And he would certainly be finished in time to hop a plane to Idaho for the weekend.

AFTERWORD TO "THE TRANSFORMATION OF TARG"

WELL, THERE ARE times when deadlines are…not met. This rather passive equivocation of a sentence just goes to show that I am not comfortable with the idea of missing deadlines, something I rarely do. Sometimes—rarely, admittedly—the result of a missed deadline can have a felicitious ending: such was the case with the story you just read.

In 2005 Russell Davis asked me to contribute to an anthology he was editing with Marty Greenberg. This was the brief:

Title: *If I were an Evil Overlord.*

"If you've been alive and involved in science fiction or fantasy in the last decade, you've probably heard of the Evil Overlord checklist—a widely circulated and highly variable list of things an Evil Overlord should follow if he/she wishes to succeed where so many other Evil Overlord's have failed. This anthology of original sf and fantasy stories will take the checklist to new heights, inviting authors to spin a story based on one or more of the numerous creeds an Evil Overlord *should* follow (or by inventing one of their own), such as never saying, 'No! This cannot be! I am invincible!' or 'Once my power is secure, I will destroy all those pesky time travel devices.' Stories can (and probably will) be humorous for the most part, though a serious tale would also be welcomed."

The idea of writing a humorous fantasy story promised to be a refreshing change from the novel and anthologies that I was currently working on; and so when I was doing a gig in Brisbane and spending some time with my pal Paul Brandon, I brought up the idea of a collaboration. I can still remember sitting together on Paul's porch and plotting out the story amidst much giggling and hyperbolic evil overlord cackling.

Once I was back home, we continued our collaboration long distance; but events (i.e., life!) intervened. Conferences, including a guest-of-honor gig at the huge Dragoncon convention in Atlanta; shitstorms of deadlines...and a death in the family. Although the story was just about there, we simply weren't going to make Russell and Marty's deadline.** So we politely bowed out. Actually, we weren't too worried, as this was a funny romp of a story; and we were confident that it would find a home...which it did. Enter that most perspicacious award-winning editor Jonathan Strahan, who included it in the first volume of his *Eclipse* anthology series!

* Mea culpa on this one. Paul was constant and on time. *I* was the laggard!

THE CARBON DREAMER

1.

IT HAD been snowing for the past four hours. The water was unusually quiet, at least it seemed so to Fleitman, who was standing in the sand behind the breaker rocks. The foam splashed over the rocks and drooled into puddles in the brown slush. The water blended into the sky, a white canvas turned grey with dust. The snow enveloped Fleitman as he watched the ocean.

The girl nearby continued to scream. A thread of blood tinted the eddies swirling around her trapped ankle. Her knit coat was pulled behind her shoulders, hiding her ribboned pony tails. Her crinoline dress was torn and folded back, revealing a tent of skin, goosebumped and grey. A man, his overcoat open, crawled over her, muffled her mouth with his palm while neatly spreading his coat over the rocks. Only two faces now, expressions much the same, turning and stabbing at each other. The little girl fainted and the man continued, spasmodically bringing himself to completion. He remained on top of her, stretching his coat over the rocks.

It had stopped snowing. The man stood up, wrapped his coat around himself, and slipping on the ice covered rocks, reached the sand.

Fleitman was hidden by the rocks. He watched the man leave and waited for the tide to come in. It would soon be suppertime. The wind was stabbing at his face, catching the wrinkles and blowing through the microscopic crags and mountains of his skin.

The man turned around and stared at Fleitman. Fleitman noticed that the rocks no longer gave him cover; the man had walked a diagonal. And then he disappeared.

She was still screaming. But she had fainted, Fleitman thought.

Fleitman had left out the middle. He had pieced together the beginning and the end. She had not stopped screaming. Her tiny voice cut into the chill air; she was still scratching at her attacker. Fleitman knew that she was twelve, but he did not dwell on it: the tide would be in soon.

Patiently, feeling like a patriarch, a wizened father, Fleitman waited for the tide. It was past suppertime. The shore lost an inch. That was enough, leave, she'll freeze, but you can't remember; you've got to give a piano lesson. Was the man still looking? The piano was couched in the corner of the room, under an old oil painting. It was warm in here; the wind could slice through the building, but not through this room.

The ocean, rocks, sky merged into walls and over-used carpet. He fell asleep in the cold, dreaming of warmth, as the sand disappeared. He awakened a second later, waved his hands in the air, and began home.

He had forgotten something very important.

2.

HE SAT ON the piano stool, his back against the piano. It was dusk and the breakers pounding on the beach seemed to grow louder. She should be here ... *now*, he thought as he watched the door, waiting for the glass knob to move. Now, the door is open. Come in. A draft from the window tickled his shoulder. He gazed out the window. The sea mist—a monochrome of grey streaked with an occasional daub of white—shrouded the reconverted summer house, pressed against the uncaulked timbers, chilled the unheated rooms.

It began to snow again, slowly at first, and then in great sticky drops. The grey snowflakes silently crashed against the windows and then settled on the sill: a grey melting latticework. The constant rumble of waves falling on the rocks became a distant hum, overshadowed by the wind wheezing past the house.

Fleitman stared into the mist, unfocused his eyes, permitted the motes and particles outside to grow into giant balloons glowing with color. He still had his coat on. He buried his face in the collar. The chill consoled him. As he fell asleep, the gray dissolved into azure and appeared again as cylinders of vermillion stacked side by side. Numbness tickled his fingers, pushed through his arms, and languished before passing into the thickness of his body. Rotted, rotted old man. Sleep. Wagon wheels driving tracks into the snow, into the grey sand.

He yawned and the night seemed to merge with his dream of the beach, the same dream he had every night. It would only take a few seconds.

It is evening. Fleitman stands in the sand beside an abandoned beach house. The house smells the same: rotted wood, smell of chicken somewhere. The basement windows are covered with sand. The stars are pressed judiciously against the sky, and the calm water reflects the icy pinpoints. The water splashes against the wharf before him. Out of the corner of his eye he sees an old woman standing in the shadow of the house. She holds an orange shawl against her face to conceal blue climbing veins. She stares at him as they walk toward the wharf…

"Hello Fleitman." A large hand clasped his wooden shoulder. "Didn't mean to just walk in. Come on. Shit, it's only Paddy … Beer?" he asked as he sat down on the bed. "Goddamn building's without heat again.

Sandy's in bed with the youngest just to keep warm. Here, take a beer." He took a can from his six-pack and handed it to Fleitman. "Come on, take it. I just came to see if little Suzy was up here to play your piano. She has one of your lessons today, doesn't she?"

Fleitman took a sip of beer. She had never missed a lesson before. "Your wife is alright, isn't she? Suzy should be here. She's never missed a lesson. You get your check today?"

"No. Look, if Suzy comes up or you see her, let me know. I'll be in the rec room. Sandy's really worried. Enjoy your beer."

Fleitman turned to the window as the door clicked shut. Paddy was neat, even in his filth, he thought. His stains were somehow purposeful—an emblem of his manhood. Fleitman would have wanted him in his youth. He had that swollen appearance that Fleitman used to seek, a decadent beauty that grew in revulsion. Dream Fleitman. Right yourself. It's over. He let the dream resume.

The wharf is silhouetted against the black water. The old lady walks faster. She runs along the rotted, wooden planks. Fleitman crawls along the sand. She is now at the end of the wharf, the black water and sky merging behind her. Her long white. hair clings to her shoulders. She is smiling. Bending over, she clutches her ankles and pulls herself inside out. Her reversible skin is a map of crawling blue veins and arteries. But Fleitman must get to the water. He waits for her to move. She will stop him.

"Paddy was looking for you. You see him?" asked Eva Pedon, a dark Puerto Rican woman who lived across the hall from Fleitman.

Fleitman was now hunched over a table in the rec room. His coat was unbuttoned. His head was lolling over his right shoulder. He was sweating.

He often walked in his dreams; he merged them with reality.

"Come on, old man. Wake up."

It was warm in the rec room. Fleitman enjoyed a few more seconds of the dream. The old lady was speaking to him: *I love you for yourself, bravo.* Frank, a tall lanky man playing the pinball machine, shouted at Paddy who had just walked in. Paddy was slapping at the snow on his coat. His wife walked in behind him.

"I don't know where the hell she could be," Paddy said as he sat down beside Fleitman. "Still sleeping, hey?" he asked Fleitman. "We've been looking everywhere. Any heat in the rooms yet?"

"No," Eva replied. "And stop staring at me," she whispered to Paddy. "When is George going to fix the boiler?"

"He's not," Frank said, leaving the pinball machine and sitting down at the table. "Right, George?" he shouted.

The manager appeared behind the food counter. "The thing's cracked too bad for me to fix. The soonest I can get someone over to fix it is tomorrow. So we'll just have to suffer."

"Sonovabitch," Paddy said.

Walking past the wharf, the damp sand sticking to his legs, he can hear the wheezing of the squall rippling the water. He walks along the pier, his head down, watching the sand bunched up in the cracks of the wharf. A little further, the elevation increases; he can see the rills of sand through the wooden slats, and then the cold dead water below him. The old lady is at the end of the pier. She sidesteps to meet him. She fences him off before he can reach the end ...

Fleitman rippled the pages of the old Schuam book. He did not know why he had taken it. He thought about taking a walk. It was cold, he told himself. But he took a walk every evening.

3.

HE OPENED THE rusted latch and let the door fly open, relishing the onrush of cold wind against his face. He heard Paddy screaming, "Shut the goddamn door," but the sharp wind melted his words into the wheezing of the trees. She had missed her piano lesson. That was the first time. He watched the ground as he walked. He carried the Schuam book, full of happy memories interlocked with the simple chords and arpeggios, under his arm. Somehow, he felt that it was protecting him.

The beach was different at night. At night the shadows became lords of their objects. The cold white sand and snow would darken and merge with the sky, leaving only the luminescent seawater to crash on the rocks. But tonight the snow was a neon roadmap of light and shadow—a bright heap of sand here, a well of shadow there. Magnifying itself through the clouds, the full moon illuminated the crashing foam and silver rocks. Fleitman felt a chill as he passed through the open gate. He lost sight of the painted backdrop of houses and streets as he walked toward the shore

He overlays his dream on the hard surface of his surroundings. He hears the screams of the old woman, but he pushes them back into his sleep. He remains awake, following an unconscious impulse to see the rocks before he returns home to his bed.

The rocks stood out pale white against the background of black churning water. A glistening layer of freezing rain had smoothed out their harsh angular contours. The rain acted as a fixative for the snow. It had stopped raining in time for Fleitman's walk. Soon it would start snowing again, Fleitman thought. It would probably snow all night. He shivered and continued his evening walk: it pushed his dreams a little farther away.

He watched the waves splashing between the rocks. He stepped carefully over a small ridge The little body was nestled between the rocks before him, submerged under a thin layer of ice and snow. Fleitman did not want to look. Her stiff coat, pulled behind her shoulders, disappeared into the sand. Her face was white; the snow did not blanket the dainty features etched into the mask of ice. And she screamed. Fleitman saw the tiny bubbles at the corners of her mouth. He waited for the scream to pass through the ice.

The ice cracked and the screams, trapped for hours under the ice, escaped with one concentrated shriek. Fleitman held his hands to his ears, but the sound was already in his head. He joined it with a scream of his own and pushed himself intothe rocks. The hard edges and shards of rock broke the skin, pulling warmth deep inside him to the surface. As he closed his eyes, he retained the retinal image of blood streaming from her trapped foot. That too was suspended under the ice, he thought. He dreamed of joining it, but the old dream of the quay returns.

The old woman has beaten him again. He turns away as she tears off protruding organs and throws them at him. He cannot reach the sea. She will grow new parts to throw. A glistening white fin cuts through the water behind her.

In his dream Fleitman is only an observer. He could not completely forget the rocks and the rain. If he did, he would freeze to death—no one would find him for days. The dream receded and Fleitman stiffened with cold. He did not move, and the numbness returned with the dream; but the dream was a blur and Fleitman was too far above to make out the tiny details. It began to snow again.

Standing up, he felt the shock of cold, recognized the numbness radiating from his hands and feet. A flap of coagulated blood hung from his cheek. He did not touch it. His trousers were torn and stained. His awareness brought more pain. Stumbling over the rocks, he reached the sand. Its softness brought on a sympathetic wave of nausea. She shouldn't have gone outside, he told himself. She should have stayed inside until her piano lesson was over. He felt for his Schuam book, but he had left it on the rocks. Hurrying past the gate, he walked on the grass beside the sidewalk to avoid slipping. The snow swirled around him, pressing him to dream, drawing off his consciousness.

As Fleitman approached the apartment house, the images of his dream covered everything with a warm glow. As he opened the front door, everything began to blur. There was no one in the office. Blowing streamers of icy smoke through his nose, he edged along the wall to the rec room. The hall was strewn with newspapers. Fleitman felt a tightness in his stomach and watched amazed as he vomited against the rec room door.

He screamed as he fell to his knees, pushing the door open. "She's in the ice, in the rocks. I left my book there." As he listened to himself, he felt embarrassed. The cold floor felt good in contrast to the overheated room. No suspicion, he thought as he heaved again. She's already frozen. I couldn't do it. I gave her piano lessons. They know.

Paddy had his palm behind Fleitman's neck. Fleitman chuckled as his perception suddenly cleared, but he gagged before he could verbalize it.

"Fleitman, where is she? Where on the rocks, you crazy sonovabitch?"

Fleitman waited, enjoying Paddy's warm breath on his face. It smelled pleasantly of beer and brought back memories of laughter and young girls. He contemplated feigning unconsciousness for a few more minutes. The dreams returned, stronger than before.

It is very warm. In the nineties. Fleitman has all the windows open, but the air is stagnant—there is not the slightest breeze. Fleitman leans out the window. He can smell chicken frying upstairs Or is it chicken soup? But it is so hot. The fire escape is cool to the touch …

"On the rocks, Paddy. Near the wire fence. Near the old World War Two cement bunker. The one that the Eaton kid fell off of last summer."

"You sonovabitch."

"I feel sick."

"What were you doing out there, you goddamn old pervert?"

"On the rocks. I always take a walk." He knows that, Fleitman thought. He knows, but he's upset. She missed her piano lesson. And the Schuam book.

"Come on, Paddy," Sandy said. "I want my baby."

Eva Pedon pushed a damp cloth against Fleitman's face. Fleitman could smell his vomit. He opened his eyes and shut them. Eva was pretty, but her features were too coarse, too leathery. She would have been good—at one time. Fleitman mused over the prospect of making love, but his dreams contained more reality.

"Get a doctor," Eva said. "He's an old man. Christ, he's probably already got pneumonia."

Paddy ran out of the room, followed by everyone except Eva and a woman behind the counter. Eva left the cloth on his face and called for a doctor.

She returned, rested her hand on his forehead, and talked to him. But he could not understand Spanish. He tried to remember how he had felt when his body was hard enough to be touched. He could remember only by trick of reason, by sterile imagination. His past had been excreted with the growing of new skin, withered grey skin, dropped in folds under dim eyes that barely perceived the brown girl sitting beside him, pitying him.

He sank back into his dreams, and the little girl wiping his forehead shrank into a little brown cockroach pedaling across the floor.

Up the fire escape. It is the apartment above him. Fleitman loves the old lady cooking the chicken, although he has never seen her. It is chicken soup, Fleitman is sure. He pulls himself out the window and begins to climb. He is very hungry, He is in love ...

4.

FLEITMAN DID NOT pay any attention to the doctor prodding his chest with a stethoscope. The sheets of his bed were cold, reminding him of pieces of ice that would melt in his hand. He savored the cold trickle of sweat that ran off his palm. He did not move his fingers. He could hear the rattle of the electric heater that Eva had brought in, and he could smell gas. The oven was turned on to heat the room.

"No, he's awake, aren't you Mr. Fleitman? Those cuts and bruises look worse than they are. The main thing is to keep warm. Have him take these pills. I've given him a sedative. I'll look in on him tomorrow. He should be all right; he seems to be in good health. Don't get out of bed, Mr. Fleitman. And take these pills. And keep warm."

The doctor left. Fleitman was hungry. He waited for the soup. Doctor said you're healthy, Fleitman thought. You take walks, every day. Yes, she missed her piano lesson.

Sometimes, in his dreams, Fleitman can smell colors.

As he climbs he smells yellow. It is always the same color. He remembers as he dreams. The steps are smooth from wear, the ground is magnified below him. Fleitman closes one eye and looks between the slats. He is not very high. But he has been climbing for hours. He can see yellow clouds wafting out of her window …

It was chicken soup. Fleitman finished it, placed it on the floor next to his bed, and pulled the covers over his head. It grew warm as he inhaled his own breath. He shivered. The fire escape was cold.

5.

SOMEONE WAS TRYING to open the door. It rattled. Fleitman looked out the window, hoping for light. It would be morning soon. He was perspiring; the oven was still on, and the electric heater was coughing. The knob did not turn. Not so soon, Fleitman thought. He would not be here so soon. They would get him. Fleitman could not remember his face, but he remembered that he was a neat man: he had left the little girl in order under the ice.

Fleitman counted for the morning. The sound of the water and the predawn grey made him shiver. He was coughing, spitting gobs of phlegm into tissues. Throwing the tissues at the garbage can and missing. Fleitman covered his chest with his arms; he stopped shaking. He took another pill. The alarm wasn't set; he would sleep.

He tried to resume the dream. He could feel the warmth of a summer day, the coolness of the fire escape. But the yellow smell of chicken revolted him. He thought about fat boys and shuddered. He spat into the tissue. The dream would have to end, but he could not do it now. The man kept pushing at the door, but Fleitman wasn't worried: it was too early.

FLEITMAN DID NOT remember the next day. He took his pills and the doctor saw him again. But Fleitman had stopped dreaming: there was nothing to hold onto. He did not change his pajamas. It was still grey outside and the streets had turned into brown slush.

But you remember him. No I don't, Fleitman said to himself. He sat up in the bed, his skin shiny from accumulated oil. The man was about thirty. No he wasn't. Remember Fleitman? He was older.

Fleitman looked out the window. His eyes were wet; everything blurred. He squinted. It was sunny. Fleitman pretended it was summer. The oven was still on, although the heat was now working. Fleitman refused to shut it off. He would not blink his eyes. They began to sting, and Fleitman could almost see the rainbow hued gas puddles shining in the gutter and the plastic umbrellas held aloft as protection from the rain-heavy leaves that shook and turned in the fitful breeze. And he could see the young girls pacing to the beach gate, carrying boom boxes and dark stained army blankets, waiting for the sun to seep through the clouds and turn them into nut brown Cinderellas. The young boys followed, cigarette packs tucked and rolled in the short sleeves of their snow-white tee shirts.

Fleitman shivered. But the cold was leaving his body.

In the distance the water, dotted by ships defining make-believe horizons, merged into the grey sky. The foam breakers wafted soap bubbles and tar smears onto the matted beach. A blanket was already pinioned in the sand; books, shoes, purse, and a bottle of suntan lotion held the corners in place. A young girl tiptoed into the water, unnoticed by the crowd that would soon form.

Fleitman, you're dreaming.

He leaned against the headboard, head propped up on pillows, covers drawn over his chest. Fleitman whispered to himself: do it right. Dream it. Dream it first.

You can do it later.

Fleitman walks along the beach. The hot white sand doesn't burn the soles of his feet—they are calloused. Past the swimmers, past the sitters and the show-offs, Fleitman walks toward the rocks. The water is green; it could easily have been blue. Fleitman skirts the rocks and notices a Schuam book, suntan lotion, and a paperback novel lying in the wet sand.

The girl nearby continues to scream. A thread of blood tints the eddies swirling around her trapped ankle. Her knit coat is pulled behind her shoulders, hiding her ribboned ponytails. Her crinoline dress is torn and folded back, revealing a tent of skin, goosebumped and grey. A man, his overcoat open crawls over her, muffles her mouth with his palm, while neatly spreading his coat over the rocks.

Fleitman steps over a puddle of water and sits down in the wet sand. He remembers that the man is neat. Fleitman will have to wait. He thinks about the fire escape and the old lady, but there is no time for that now. Fleitman picks up the paperback and studies its red and green cover. He remembers reading it. He turns the pages. Not much time. You should be done. Hurry. Fleitman is beginning to wake up.

The man leaves. He turns around and stares at Fleitman. Fleitman is still thumbing through the book. He looks up in time to catch a glimpse of the man before he turns around and runs.

He has grey hair, bleaching to white, like you, Fleitman. He is fifty-five or sixty, Fleitman thinks. His eyes are deep set like mine and he is frightened. But why a little girl? Fleitman was bending the paperback. As he begins to understand, the book crumbles, the beach turns grey with snow, and Fleitman has no chance to walk home before he awakens.

FLEITMAN WAS HUNGRY. Eva should have brought him something by now. It was almost one o'clock. Exactly right. A knock at the door.

"Come in," Fleitman said. "The door is not locked."

Of course it's not locked.

How did the man comb his hair? Fleitman wondered. Was it parted down the middle like mine, or did he part it on the side to cover a bald spot? You should have run after him. You haven't touched the piano. Fleitman reached for his pills on the night table—the bottle was almost empty. But you saw him twice.

Fleitman giggled at the detective pulling a chair next to his bed. Eva was there—he could smell food. "These men have to see you about little Suzy," Eva said as she laid a tray of soup and cold fish on the night table. Too fat, Fleitman thought as he watched the detective sitting beside him. And he had a tic in his eye, a tiny insect crawling under his skin.

"You take a walk every day, don't you, Mr. Fleitman?"

A uniformed policeman stood in front of the bed. He was much younger than the detective. He loosened his tie and took off his hat, revealing short-cropped hair. Fleitman once had a brush cut. He remembered how it used to scratch his palm when he combed it. You're old, Fleitman told himself. That's a good enough reason. He's sure to come for me, he thought. Tell them. He's sixty or so. I'll be seventy-five.

"Did you see anyone else on the beach?"

She had probably been dead for hours, Fleitman thought.

He answered the questions as he dreamed. He curled inside himself. He didn't listen to his answers.

He pauses for breath. How many steps has he climbed? Everything has turned to specks below him. He looks out at the ocean. He can see the curve of the horizon. It is tinted slightly yellow. Watch the water, Fleitman. It will still change its shape, flow and ebb. Only a little more fluid than the metal handrail you're leaning on, already dead, slowly decaying into something else, to ferment and build new fermenting shapes. All shape, Fleitman. All illusion. There, it moves again. Subtly changing into air, adding an atom to the jellyfish glistening on the hot sand. Keep your eyes on the slippery foam; it's a thousandfold reflection of your insides—it's dying and rebuilding and separating and decaying. And so are you—but you have the illusion of consciousness. Fleitman looks up and the steps shiver under him. He remembers something important and forgets it again …

Fleitman wanted to tell them something. He was in danger. But from what?

The detective had finished asking questions. Fleitman wondered if he had answered them correctly. Had he forgotten anything? He ate his soup and tried to remember. He tried to remember the scratching at the door, but he was too tired. He thought about the man's age. Say sixty. I'll be seventy-five, he thought. And he's sure to come for me. He looked right at me. Fleitman was still a bit chilled. He would remember what he wanted to tell the detective tomorrow.

6.

A BLINK, THE shudder of an eyelid, an ill-timed glance at a coat billowing in the wind, and the world might end and instantaneously build itself again upon the excretion of the old. Fleitman had missed many endings. As he stood before his window facing the storm fed sea, he counted the possibilities. Each death and rebirth changed his world subtly, pushed him back a moment in time, changed the curve of his path slightly. Dimmed his vision softly. But he was too young to be senile. He was here at the window, basking in the winter sun, soon to bury itself in the waves of the horizon.

How old are you really, Fleitman? Fleitman felt a subtle change as the world built itself again on the sand-corpse of the last, a little dimmer, a little more complicated.

Eva told him all she knew about the incident. Fleitman compared her gossip with what he saw and his dreams. He felt better, relieved. He could not tell the police anything. He could not tell them now that he had seen it all. Could he tell them he had forgotten? That he was dreaming at the time? Things had become clearer lately. And that shouldn't be, Fleitman thought. Yet, everything had also become more complicated.

He would not reveal his secret, even though he was in danger.

"Paddy's been drunk since it happened," Eva said. "Sonovabitch made another pass at me this morning. Sandy just cries. Poor baby. But there's nothing to do for her."

Fleitman gurgled for effect. Her blouse was always half unbuttoned, he thought. It felt good to watch her.

"You heard what the doctor said. You can start getting around now. No more food—and you owe me some money. Your check came in today." She opened another button. Fleitman turned to the wall.

"Well, the rest of the meals you get yourself. And here's your goddamn check."

AFTER SHE LEFT Fleitman made himself some tea and turned on the radio. The music was loud and didn't make much sense to him. That's why he did it, Fleitman thought. *Because* he was old. Overcompensation. Then why don't you take Eva? Because you're afraid you couldn't do it. That would be worse than knowing. But a little girl … Even if you couldn't make it, it would be an act of love. Fleitman felt a slight sympathy for the man. But how could he continue when she screamed? And he left her, a crumpled rag doll.

But you left her, too, he told himself. But I was dreaming. That doesn't count. And Fleitman dreams.

Imagine the wharf, the old worm ridden wharf extending into the puddle sea. Imagine the quiet evening and the house in the sand. The same wood, the same hour labors under the weight of the little woman on the quay. She steps aside. Fleitman can walk to the water now, but he doesn't move. This dream is over. He should not have returned again.

"HELLO, MR. FLEITMAN. Can I come in?"

Lenny Thompson stood in the doorway with a sheaf of music under his arm. "I'm supposed to have a lesson. It's Friday. You want to change it? Ma wasn't sure if I should come. You know, with all that stuff that happened."

Fleitman put his teacup in the saucer, spilling tea on his trousers. It was sticky and Fleitman was immediately uncomfortable. He would try not to move his leg. The wet spot was suctioned against his skin. "Yes, come in, Lenny. We'll have a lesson."

The spot turns cool, then cold. It is a shiny icicle impaled in his leg. Fleitman dreams of ice, large shimmering cubes heaped on the floor. Budding stalagmites press against the blocks. They will soon support the ceiling, growing heavy with sister stalactites. Fleitman touches the large blocks, careful not to break the pointed buds beside them. He finds room to sleep ...

"They had a fight about you."

"Who did? Fleitman asked.

"Mom and Dad. You know, because ..."

"Well, let's forget about that for now. What exercises did you prepare?"

"Which book?"

"The Hanon." Fleitman took a notebook from the top of the piano. "Sit down, Lenny." He pushed back the fallboard. The keys were badly yellowed. One day, he thought, he would have it tuned. "E" and "A" were flat, and High "C" responded very slowly. "You were supposed to prepare Exercise Number Twenty-three. Did you do that one?"

"I don't know that one very well. I haven't had much time to practice. There's been too much noise."

"Well, begin."

He sucks in his cheek and begins. When he stumbles, he goes back to the beginning and plays the piece over again. Fleitman doesn't stop him. Fleitman understands that he must finish the piece perfectly. Once the boy made a mistake, there was no sense in going on.

"You're not using the right fingering," Fleitman said. "It's five-four-three-four-five in the left hand. You're starting with your fourth finger."

Fleitman listened as the boy ground his fingers into the keys, pushing and stabbing at the music like a baker kneading bread. Children are so small, Fleitman thought. He felt the man on the rocks crying. But once she started screaming, it was too late. That ruined it, broke the container. Fleitman watched the man cry, the tears trapped in the hollows of his eyes. He should not have tried to scrub himself with the child.

Lenny played the exercise over and over again. And then he played the next one, stumbling and beginning again. Fleitman waited until the required time had passed and then stopped him. "That's not bad, Lenny—for not practicing very much." He leafed through the pages of Lenny's books quickly—he felt another dream forming. He fought it.

"Move over, I'll play this for you. This is your next assignment. It's difficult."

Fleitman had always liked Schubert. And "The Erl-King" had been one of his favorite pieces when he was a child.

"See, it's *presto agitato*, that's very fast." He began playing. He did not need the music. "Can you hear the horse's hoofs pouncing? And now very soft, and loud for the Father's Theme. He is riding home with his sick child. He is racing with death. And now the Erl-King's theme, at first very soft. And louder, then the child. Notice the pedaling. The key changes. It is faster, death is gaining. And *lento* and the last chords were *forte*. Did you watch the pedaling?"

Lenny nodded his head.

"Well, it's marked. Be very careful with the pedaling. Did your mother give you any money?"

"No, I'll bring It the next time."

As Fleitman watches Lenny leave, he discovers a small piece of ice in his palm. Bands of ice are wrapped around his legs: he is frozen to the chair. The little piece of ice in his hand traps his fingers. He leans his head against the wall—it freezes in a comfortable position. As Fleitman falls asleep, he remembers that it is Friday. He always has dinner with his nephew on Fridays …

7.

HE WILL PROBABLY do it again, Fleitman thought. He already has little Suzy's mouth. That one screams louder than most. Maybe the next time will be better for him. He will certainly try again. And if the next one goes bad, he will have another mouth to yell and scream inside his head. Surely, it could not be much louder than Suzy's. He probably collects them: each little girl leaves him a little charm.

Fleitman could hear Suzy's screams, but he had become used to them. He had collected a mouth himself. Probably by mere proximity, he thought. He could examine her little white teeth. They were slightly uneven. She was so small. How many other tiny malformations and potential diseases did her body contain? How long would she have fermented before they matured? Fleitman listened to her teeth chatter while he thought about her.

The man would eventually fill his head with those little mouths and become deaf. They would scream until his eyes watered. But there was nobility in those gross movements. Maybe the rocks lent charm to the man from Brooklyn. The man's image became clearer after Fleitman had given him a residence.

And he probably was from Brooklyn, anyway.

FLEITMAN DRESSED AND took a subway to Manhattan. His nephew lived in the West Village, on McDougal Street. He had moved in after

Fleitman's brother had died. Like father like son, Fleitman thought. The streets were crowded. Fleitman pushed his way though tourists wearing heavy fur coats, week-end hippies in Friday night outfits, businessmen who had lingered for a drink after work, office workers browsing, children playing in the crowd, chased by their mothers. The old locals were here somewhere, Fleitman thought, but he could not see any.

A group of boys pushed past him. They all wore jeans and carried guitars. Fleitman smiled: one of the boys wore his beard Van Dyke fashion. As a youth, Fleitman had sported a beard. He remembered combing and trimming it, contrasting beard and sideburns, skin and hair. Then short hair. Brush cuts became stylish. The man on the rocks wore a brush cut, Fleitman thought. He kept it a little longer than Fleitman thought proper, but then Fleitman had let his hair grow out once too.

There were twelve and thirteen-year-olds all over the streets. They were purposely scruffy. A few of them smiled as they passed Fleitman. He paid no attention to them. He concentrated on watching the clothes waving past him. Coats thrown open to reveal orange shirts, blue waistbands tied around leather jackets. An azure tee-shirt contrasted with grey skin.

Fleitman pretended that colored sailboats were racing past him. He did not look down at legs; that would break the illusion. The coats and open jackets glided along the cement. Children were the hardest to control: they were too little. Every time Fleitman looked down at them, the tangle of legs surrounded him.

All these children, Fleitman thought. All running around, bumping into each other, getting lost, stoned, laid. They were all anonymous. They were all little mouths surrounded by flesh. All screaming and laughing, tasting and mashing. They were so unlike little Suzy. He could still hear Suzy yelping, her little mouth popping in and out. This is where the man should be. Suzy could certainly scream louder than these ragamuffins.

Fleitman looked for his nephew. He usually waited in front of his building. Fleitman walked the five flights slowly. A young girl standing in the hall mumbled something to herself. Fleitman stepped over a plastic garbage bag. The super would find it. He kicked it down the stairs.

Before Fleitman could knock, Stuart, his nephew, opened the door. "Hello, Uncle Jake. Cold as hell outside, isn't it." It was a very small apartment. Fleitman gave Stuart's children a kiss and five dollars each and then sat down in his favorite easy chair in the living room. Stuart's wife Fran waved hello from the hallway as she called the children into the kitchen.

That's better, Fleitman thought. He could sense the fire escape, almost see a wavering image. He talked with his nephew until Stuart's wife called them to dinner. He listened to mother and daughter talking, preparing for grace. The little girl acted very grown up—she copied her mother. "One more year," Aileen said, "'and I'll be in the same school as Stephen." Her brother didn't seem to notice. He just stared at his plate.

Aileen was Suzy's age. Fleitman looked away from her mouth, which was constantly moving. He watched his hands as he ate, watched his fingers curling to hold his fork, arching to push his knife, pinching together around a falling napkin. As he concentrated on style of movement, on tilting his wrist at the proper angle, his movements became jerky. He cut himself.

Stuart and Fran fluttered around him; the children continued eating, looking up once in a while. As Stuart wrapped a bandage around Fleitman's finger, Fleitman noticed that his nephew's eyes just seemed to stare in whatever direction he turned his heed. They had no life of their own.

"There," Stuart said. "It could have been a lot worse. You have to be careful. Let's have a smoke."

They sat down in the living room while Fran and the children picked up the dishes. Fleitman didn't usually smoke, but he took a cigarette.

He didn't want to disappoint his nephew. Stuart lit Fleitman's cigarette. Fleitman waited for his eyes to blink.

"What's the matter, Uncle Jake? Honey, bring the dessert in here. And send the kids in, too."

Stuart was like the children outside. He was anonymous. The glazed eyes and bent nose were for effect. Like the man on the rocks used nobility to good effect. His eyes still did not blink. It could just as well have been Stuart on top of Suzy. But Stuart had no reason, Fleitman. He is young.

Stephen came into the living room holding a metal tray. "Strawberry shortcake," he said. "Ma says you can put the whipped cream on yourself." Fleitman noticed that one of Stephen's eyes was glazed.

"I have to take him to the doctor. He's having trouble with that left eye again. The drops helped some, but then the same thing happened again."

Fleitman nodded. "Yes, you'd better take him back."

When Fleitman finished his desert, Aileen sat down on his his lap. "Is your finger alright now?" she asked.

"Just like new," Fleitman said, bouncing her up and down. She was not at all like Suzy. She would not have screamed. She would just whimper and die. Fleitman felt sorry for her; she was like her father. She would have no reason to kick and scream; she would have no identity to hang on to. Fleitman bounced her a few more times. She was too soft; she had no bones. This could not provide love. This would be no challenge. And Suzy was lost. How could anyone find chastity in this? She was no more chaste than a piece of chewing gum. Fleitman thought he understood something, but he quickly forgot. He wanted to leave: there was no reason to stay any longer.

"The steak was very good," he shouted to Fran. Aileen was holding on to his belt. Fleitman lifted her from his lap, swung her around, and sat her down on the couch. She was laughing and gurgling. Her little body seemed to bulge around his hands—he quickly let go.

Fleitman promised to come again next Friday. He waved good-by to Aileen; Stephen had disappeared. Fleitman hurried to his subway station. The streets were too crowded. All those faces painted and accentuated for effect. All the same person. The tiny distinctions were affectations. But there were real people scattered about. They would never smile or nod to Fleitman as they passed. But Fleitman could tell they were real. He tipped his hat to an old lady walking a Pekingese. She was real. She quickly picked up her dog and cradled it in her arms. He also found a real beggar and gave him a quarter.

It was quiet in the subway station. A train had just pulled in. Fleitman walked down the platform until he found an empty car. He sat down next to a window and watched his reflection in the glass.

The steak has bloated his stomach and he rests, dreaming about the ice pillars growing in his room. They are growing over him, fusing into a lattice of prisms, Crystalline trees hang upside down from the ceiling , breaking the sun into rainbows. The room is petrified. Fleitman watches the crystal splinters grow along a crack in the far wall, vitrifying into a gilt design. The furniture is covered with a glacé sheath. Fleitman is chilled. The food in his stomach is freezing. His organs grow transparent. Fleitman slowly turns to glass. He dreams about Suzy. She is warm. She contains everything he has lost. But she is lost, too, Fleitman.

THE CONDUCTOR WOKE him up. It was the last stop. Fleitman took a bus from the station. He would take a walk on the beach before going home. It took him a few minutes to get used to the darkness. Trees blotted out the lights. He could hear the waves splashing on the rocks and the scrunching of his new patent leather shoes in the sand. He would have to clean his shoes when he got home—they would be covered with tar slick.

Fleitman could make out the outlines of the beach. In the distance the rocks were grey, intermittently covered with black water. Fleitman could hear voices, then discern faces. They all looked unfamiliar.

"I don't know exactly where it happened," said a girl wearing jeans and a navy pea-coat. "Maybe where that ledge is." She passed her cigarette to a tall boy standing beside her. He inhaled loudly.

"Hey man," he said, "you know where that little kid got molested?"

Fleitman quickly walked past them. They were all laughing. Another boy tried to say something, but he could not stop giggling.

"Hey, fucking child molester," said the girl. "Come back and show us where you did it."

Fleitman walked along the water. There was another exit further along the beach. They were still yelling and laughing, but Fleitman couldn't hear them. He could only hear Suzy screaming. It grew louder. She was biting her tongue inside his head. As he passed the rocks, the voice became a whisper and then died. Fleitman's hands were cold.

The tall boy could have done it, Fleitman told himself as he walked toward the gate. Or even the other one. They were real. But you saw who did it, Fleitman. He was an old man. But why couldn't he be young, Fleitman? Because I saw him. But he could have been anybody. It could even be Stuart. And he isn't even real. Fleitman could have seen anybody. He stopped at the gate: it was locked. He thought he saw somebody. He would let it be one of the kids for a while. They were available, at least.

Fleitman skirted the fence. If he could find a tear in the wire mesh, he could reach the avenue through someone's back yard. He didn't want to walk back to the other gate—the kids might still be on the beach. Fleitman found a spot where the fence was loose. He lifted the wire as best he could and crawled under. He hurried across the yard.

Two drunks were arguing under a street lamp. Fleitman would have to wait until they left, before he could step into the street. He crouched behind the bushes that fronted the yard and listened.

It could have been one of them, Fleitman thought. That's no stretch of the imagination. Fleitman could feel the presence of the man that did it. He could smell the strong, musty odor of the man. But it was the screaming that convinced Fleitman. He could hear all those little mouths screaming and wheezing. So the man did have a collection of them. But you could be wrong, Fleitman. Suzy's screams were loud enough to make up for five or six little girls. Fleitman was sure of it: only Suzy was screaming. Her little mouth was an orchestra.

Fleitman was breathing heavily. He held his mouth. The man must not find him. He controlled his breathing. He was shivering with cold. His legs ached from crouching. He kept his eyes closed until the drunks left the vicinity of the streetlight. He knew what the man looked like: he had seen him on the rocks. Fleitman didn't want to look at him again; his nearness had been too overpowering.

FLEITMAN DID NOT relax until he reached his apartment. He bolted the chain lock and wedged a chair against the door. He was not sure if the chair was positioned correctly; he had only seen it done in the movies. The presence of the piano made him feel better. He left the lights on and lay down on the bed. Suzy was screaming very softly.

Fleitman heard footsteps in the hall. He didn't move. They stopped in front of his door. It could have been Eva or even Paddy, he told himself. The door creaked. Someone was pushing against it. Then Fleitman listened to footsteps hurrying away.

He turned toward the wall for security. The man would be back, Fleitman thought. He would wait for the right time. But Fleitman understood. He tried not to fall asleep: he would wait.

The sun has disappeared behind a puff of cloud. It is suddenly cooler. Fleitman is climbing, two steps at a time. But the steps are creaking. The fire escape is shaking. A shard of metal hits Fleitman. on the shoulder. He hangs onto the handrail for support. He can see the ground undulating below him. He will hold on and wai…

8.

FLEITMAN HAD CHANGED his habits. He would stay awake all night and sleep in the day. Fleitman had learned to enjoy sleeping in the day. He could watch the clouds scudding past his window as they changed into familiar shapes. Sometimes, as he watched the dust drifting in a band of sunlight, he felt as if he were swimming underwater without a mask.

At night Fleitman waited for the man. But lately he had begun to doubt the man's existence. But he must exist, Fleitman. Someone had to do it. But Fleitman didn't care. He was no longer afraid to stay up at night. The shadows, the noises, the groaning of settling wood were comforting. It was a private show, and Fleitman was the only one awake to enjoy it. He could watch the world build itself and then scratch and crumble into something different. Everything changed many times at night, even Fleitman. Sometimes Fleitman was aware of the changes and he would count them. But Fleitman did not know that every time *he* changed, he had to start again.

And Suzy was his orchestra. He had been correct: she could easily scream loud enough to make up for five or six little girls. He had become used to the screams; he learned to filter them when he played his radio. Fleitman found that his tastes in music were changing: Suzy preferred Cage to Haydn, Joe Cocker to Gianni Poggi. He could feel her little mouth pucker up, move into a more comfortable space in his head. She would snarl quietly as he listened to his radio.

When Fleitman tired of the radio, he would try to make words out of Suzy's screams. Sometimes, he thought he could hear *no*. Lately she scolded him. She often grumbled. Fleitman isolated *choose*; he could hear it over and over again. But usually it was a voice and nothing more, sound without sense.

Fleitman could not understand why the man did not come. Because I chose not to believe he would. Fleitman felt at ease. He chose to keep Suzy for himself. You've stolen everything, Fleitman; her mouth hangs only in your head. He studied the crack in the door-stile and waited for an answer.

None came.

Well, I'll stop thinking about him now, Fleitman told himself. Why? He killed little Suzy. But you don't care, Fleitman. You've stopped feeling sorry for him. Why? Because you've stolen his girl?

Fleitman left his apartment and went for a walk. It was late. Everything seemed muted: the crashing of the waves was dulled, the splashing water seemed to drift in the air, removed from Fleitman's arbitrary time sense. Only you can hear her screams, he thought. They were too concentrated to be spread between two people.

Fleitman walked slowly, letting his heels drop into the sand. The snow glistened on his boots. The screaming had stopped. Why didn't he notice before? Fleitman tried to bring the screams back.

He hurried home. He was afraid again. He did not want to think about her; her little mouth was a grotesquerie. He knocked on Eva Pedon's door. There was no answer. Could she be with a man? Fleitman asked himself. He knocked again, harder. He heard a groan.

"Who Is it? Paddy, if that's you, get the hell out of here."

"No. It's only Fleitman."

She opened the door slightly. "It's four o'clock in the morning. What do you want?" She rubbed her eyes. The hollows under them were grey. Fleitman looked at the floor. He could leave now, bolt and run. But she was already laughing, her beautiful olive pit face was cracking. "We'll since it's you, Fleitman. Come on. But I only do it because you're old. As a favor. For very little."

Fleitman sat down in a chair and watched her take off her nightgown. She was slightly flabby, her hips were too fleshy. It's no good, Fleitman thought. She's like me.

"Remember, Fleitman. You don't tell anybody."

She's ugly, Fleitman. He tried to wrap himself up in a dream, but he had stopped dreaming. Why hadn't he remembered? He could not let her touch him; he would have to pull away.

She curled up on the bed. "Come on. Let's do it."

Fleitman could taste saliva, then vomit. She's so ugly, he thought. She's turning grey. Her skin is sliding off the bed.

He vomited and bolted for the door. He had trouble opening it. She had used the chain lock. He turned the key and the chain dropped free.

"Why you sonovabitch." She jumped out of bed and slipped on the vomit. She kicked at him, but he was already in the hall "You faggot sonovabitch." Tears slid over her cheeks, each taking a different path. Her face was too smooth and coated with oil. She was almost a little girl, Fleitman thought as he fumbled for his key. As she cried, he could hear a whispering inside his head. But her skin is falling off. She is flaccid like you. She grows jowls. Her hair is white. "You sonovabitch."

Fleitman closed his door. The whisper grew louder, turned to table talk, then a scream. The little mouth inside him opened up, curled its lips over uneven teeth, and screamed. Fleitman leaned against the wall, allowed the screams to pass through him. He thought he could hear Eva, but Suzy would not permit that.

ISLANDS OF TIME

It was getting light. It would be a dull dawn, he thought. The cold grey water would splash against the rocks and coagulate into ice in secret hollows. There were too many changes that night, but it was not quite day—there was still time. It was still damp. The hoarfrost on the window sparkled.

It would be a very cold day.

Fleitman was very tired, but he could not sleep. At first the screaming demanded all his attention; then, as he became used to it again, it calmed. It left him time to think. He didn't want that. He played with the radio, turning the selector knob. Country Joe and the Fish. The screaming became louder. He changed channels. Prokofieff's *Cinderella*. He could picture the dancers quarreling over the shawl they were embroidering. The two sisters, Khudyshka and Kubyshka, depart, leaving Cinderella alone on the stage. The screaming grows louder. Fleitman does not have to think. He listens. The screams become a roar. A shout interrupts the Portrait Scene. Fleitman can also hear a news program crackling in the background.

And then the screams stop. Fleitman is alone. You could not have done it, he told himself. You picked the little girl, like the man did. No, Fleitman thought. The man will come. Even your nephew could have done it—and he had that dead eye. Remember the bushes, Fleitman? Of course, one of those men did it. Because you were listening. It follows you, Fleitman.

Of course it followed, Fleitman thought. He turned the radio off—the screams returned. Fleitman could feel the little mouth wedged inside his head. It goes wherever I go. And he remembers. He sinks into his chair and dreams. It is very bright outside; the light permeates his closed eyelids and provides a damask background.

The girl screams. A thread of blood tints the eddies swirling around her trapped ankle. Fleitman tries to pull off her coat, but she fights him. He pulls it behind her shoulders. He gropes for her dress; it tears and he folds it back, revealing a tent of skin, goosebumped and gray. Fleitman opens up his overcoat and crawls over her. He muffles her mouth with his palm.

Make it up, Fleitman. Fill in the spaces. He cannot remember. But that was the best part, Fleitman. You scared her. You took away her littleness. Now she's bones, a receptacle for insects. Like you, Fleitman. Except you're aware of your decomposition.

Someone slapped his door. "You sonovabitch. I hope you drop dead," It was Eva Pedon's voice. He listened to her footsteps click down the hall. He could feel Suzy's mouth moving inside his head. He felt a sharp pain.

She was chewing on him, biting him with her uneven teeth.

Don't worry, Fleitman. It won't be long. Her teeth will crumble.

It had been snowing for the past four hours. The water was unusually quiet, at least it seemed so to Fleitman, who was standing in the sand behind the breaker rocks. The foam splashed over the rooks and drooled into puddles in the brown slush. The water blended into the sky, a white canvas turned grey with dust. The snow enveloped Fleitman as he watched the ocean.

Fleitman felt faint. he tried to sleep, but Suzy began to cry. And then she screamed; long needles of pain gently passed through his skull. Whimpering, she clicked her teeth together and tore his flesh. She chewed it carefully. Took another bite.

Then continued to scream.

AFTERWORD TO
"THE CARBON DREAMER"

OF ALL THE stories I've written over the years, "The Carbon Dreamer" takes the prize for length of time between creation and publication: over forty years!

Richard Chizmar, who is the publisher of this collection, included the story in his *Shivers* anthology series. As I wrote to Richard in 2016:

"Would you believe, this is the story I sold to Harlan Ellison for *The Last Dangerous Visions* way back in the day. I didn't pull the story before because Harlan and I are dear pals**, and I'm loyal; but I know that his *LDV* will never come out...and I must be the very last *LDV* contributor in this universe to pull his story. When I scanned and tidied it, I was quite surprised: "The Carbon Dreamer" really *is* a dangerous vision; it's about as horrific and surreal a horror story as I've ever written. And although every reader will have to make up his or her own mind, *I* don't believe the protagonist did it!"

* Harlan passed away in 2018, and I miss him every damn day!

THE FIRE-EATER'S TALE (WITH JANEEN WEBB)

FIRE. IT was always fire…

Gron was almost an elemental himself, slipping between the worlds at will.

They'd been afraid of his deformity, the filthy, stinking raiders who had swept down from the mountains to rape and murder his miserable family, to gorge on the meagre food of his pitiful village. Their superstition had saved his life, if not his body. 'Demon', they had called him, passing him back and forth between them as they abused him. It amused them that the demon-child wept and screamed at their torture, these men more hideous than any demon of the priest's imagining. But they dared not kill him outright. So they hurt him past his enduring, then left him, unconscious, face down and naked and bleeding in the smouldering ashes of his home. And they moved on.

But still he did not die. The fire that melted his face and smeared his skin across his misshapen bones showed its secrets to the dying child. Halfway between this world and the next, Gron had seen them—the salamanders, the firedrakes, the elementals. And, fleeing from his pain, his spirit had loved them, loved them with his child's simplicity, for their wildness and their fierce joy, for themselves. And so they touched him, marked him for their own.

When the circus folk found him, this charred phoenix-child annealed in the ashes, they felt the luck on him. Adopted him. And Gron was home. In the weird family of the sideshow troupe, he fit right in. A freak among freaks, his vestigial extra head was of no particular consequence. Nestled in the hairy bosom of his bearded adoptive mother, his sobs subsided. His healing was slow, but safe. Cocooned from the prying eyes of the world, Gron lived.

Now, when he swallowed the fire and spat it back into the night, the elementals danced for him. And those with eyes to see watched in wonder.

THE SHOW WAS about to begin in Madison Square Garden.

"This Show of Shows," this *Olympiad* of circuses, this *city* of carnivals included troupes from all over Europe and Asia and South America—over a thousand circuses and sideshows had been brought together to perform in and around New York's concrete version of the Crystal Palace. But Gron and his company were nowhere near the glittering center rings inside the protected walls of the Garden. Like hundreds of other troupes and companies, they were relegated to the parks and streets that had been cordoned off from traffic. Gron's troupe had been cast from the light, thrown almost into the sea, for they were to perform on the grounds of the 79th Street Boat Basin. The park seemed to glow in the night, fairy lights netted over trees, lamps casting baleful yellow-eyed illumination and deep, stationary shadows; and gimcracked arc lamps burned into the very sky itself, announcing that even here in this little park by the river, the circus would play, clowns would dance, horses would prance, acrobats would build fleshy, almost geometric forms and then collapse, tumbling past gleeful children and their watchful parents, a Ferris Wheel would revolve, arcade hucksters would shout at passers-by in Bosnian and broken English, and black tents would hide the traditional and universal grotesqueries, which sometimes included Gron, the two-headed boy, the demon who could also eat coals, inhale fire, and exhale the spirits of the dark like fine streamers.

"Precious boy, come out," Drakulic—the owner of the circus—cried into a microphone; and his high-pitched voice boomed through the sound system provided by the City of New York. Drakulic, who was tall and broad-shouldered, stood on the matted, muddied grass that functioned as the center ring. High above him a huge canvas blotted out the moon and dim stars like a ceiling.

Gron was in one of the small tents beside Slavenka, who had become his mother after his family had been killed. She, not Drakulic, had found him, and he was no more than a little child then, and he had cried at the sight of her; he had thought she was some sort of an animal, or a werewolf, or a man who looked like a woman; but she wasn't a spirit, or a ghost of the dead, as perhaps he was; she was human and fleshy and smelled of sweat and animal. Now, sitting beside her in the cage which protected them from the onlookers who shouted and laughed and joked and tried to get their attention, Gron could imagine that he was back home. Anything would be better than this place they had come to. He inhaled Slavenka's odour and glanced at her: she was tall and thin, and her eyes were deep and piercing. She could kill you with her look Drakulic would say. She was beautiful; her face was delicate and high-boned, but you had to see through the curly black hair that grew on her cheeks and neck and chin…on her arms, and her breasts, which Drakulic said were God's perfect shapes. Young men who had paid their five dollars to see her said things Gron could not understand, but he knew they were bad; just as he knew that they hated him for the vestigial head that grew out of the hollow of his neck like a fat radish out of dirt.

"Go now," Slavenka said to him as she stared grimly at those who watched her. "Do as your father asks." She stood up and danced flirtatiously and stuck her tongue out at the men making obscene gestures at her.

"I could kill them," Gron said.

Slavenka rolled her hips and laughed. "They are only boys and men. If they can break the bars, they can have me. But they can't. They do not have gifts as you do. But you cannot have me because I am your mother." She laughed, her voice like bells and paper rattling. Now go to your father." Just as Slavenka had become his mother, so Drakulic called himself his father.

"I am afraid."

She turned away from their audience. "Afraid of the fire?"

Gron nodded.

"Then you must not eat it. But *you* must tell your father."

"AND HERE HE is, ladies and men, my son, who has been burned and befriended by the fire."

As Drakulic spoke into the microphone, so did a small, dark-haired woman, translating his words into English. It sounded to Gron like an echo, or like the terrible sounds one remembers from dreams. Gron stood before Drakulic, head bowed, waiting for the proper moment to speak. Drakulic went on, telling Gron's story, but out of respect, he did not mention the small head, which was nothing more than a lump of scar tissue, a sort of goitre, cracked and blackened, as if by fire. Those who had seats close to the grassy ring could see Gron's scarred lump, but those higher and farther away could not.

"Ladies and men," shouted Drakulic, "if you watch carefully, you will see something you have never seen before. You will see the demons of fire, you will see them wrap themselves around my son like snakes, you will see..."

And then Gron was alone, surrounded by the crowds.

It was too late to be afraid of the fire.

THE SALAMANDERS CAME at his call, and they danced for him when he spoke to them, here in this strange, raw country across the ocean. But their game was rough, dangerous, menacing. Here, they were not used to being summoned, and they took it ill that he could command them at all. They challenged him, running with their sinuous lizard forms along the length of his body, their claws catching in his circus finery that was designed to expose his chest and shoulders, their small, sharp teeth seeking purchase on his ears, his nose, his fingers—on every inch of exposed skin. Gron felt the tiny trickles of his blood, but, in the throes of his fire-ecstasy, it was of no matter. He filled his lungs, took the flames into his throat, and exhaled them high into the night. He became the creature of fire that the crowds had come to see, blazing like a human bonfire in the dark centre of the ring. The salamanders covered him, their long tails whipping through the blaze of his hair, their fiery lizard tongues darting, licking his blood and sweat, tasting him, taking his measure. They felt his love for them, and they fed from it. Gron staggered in their embrace, and still they sucked at him.

The show went on, the onlookers unaware of the struggle they were witnessing. Gron almost made it through his routine. On his last, spectacular fiery exhalation, his control slipped, just for an instant. It was enough: the crowd gasped as a huge lizard-shape, gorged on Gron's life, and escaped shining and glowing into the night, swimming with a peculiar crocodile-gait into the darkness, disappearing into the parkland and streets beyond. The applause was rapturous, unafraid.

Gron's father helped him from the ring, hoping the audience would mistake his son's limpness for a deep bow, bowing and smiling himself.

The torches guttered.

The show was over.

And in the trailer, Gron lay like the dead and dreamed with the eyes of fire.

He rode the fire-lizard that was gaining its life from him, that was growing stronger while Gron grew weaker. Gron felt himself slipping inside the fire-lizard, becoming the testing, inconstant shape of fire, and he crawled along the pavement of Riverside Drive, spun through the air on Amsterdam Avenue as he licked and tasted this world of cement and dirt, this world of endless flesh and scurrying insects. He was fire swirling through the streets and buildings until they exploded into flames…into searing heat and fiery light…into life, his life; but it was the fire-lizard, not Gron.

Not Gron.

For Gron was lying cold and shivering in dream-sweat in Slavenka and Drakulic's trailer.

IT WAS LATE next day when the trance left him.

He awoke from his nightmares of conflagration to find his body crisscrossed with razor fine cuts, bruised with the love-bites of lizards. These things he could understand. But his muscles were inexplicably sore from running, and the sweat of his exertions was dried and stinking in the armpits of his nightshirt. And more alarming than any of these things, his vestigial head had grown. Gron touched it as one would touch a newly-discovered boil or tumour. It felt larger indeed, no longer cracked and rubbery. There would be the eye hollows, and the bridge of a nose, and the high ridge of cheekbone and—he pulled his hand away reflexively, as if he had been suddenly bitten, or burned; and he heard, or thought he heard, a voice that was not his own.

It spoke to him alone with the terrible sound of dreams.

"What it is, my precious boy?" Slavenka asked. She sat beside him on her bed, tending and nursing him, just as she had all night. She dipped a rag into a basin of water and herbs, then rolled the rag between her hands and placed it over his forehead. "Your body has been marked. It is a miracle. You, my son, are a miracle. Jesus' miracle. His own. You will rest until your skin is smooth." She touched his vestigial head, as if with longing, as if she were adoring it and not him, talking to it…not him.

Praying to him, as if he was the Saviour himself.

Gron, for his part, couldn't speak; yet he heard a voice that was his.

"No, my darling son," Slavenka said, "you are far too weak to get up. Your fever will break soon, and then I will feed you."

And indeed Gron's fever did break.

He shivered and drank some of Slavenka's medicine, even while his head-shaped goitre burned with the heat of a firedrake's birthing; and while he shivered and drank and burned, fires burned all over New York.

It was as if arsonists had been working in concert.

The first floor of the Empire State Building was blackened, yet unharmed, but one block away Macy's and the A&S Plaza had become six-alarm fires. The Whitney Museum had caught fire, curiously, impossibly, for the exterior was unharmed; but the fire destroyed everything inside, including Alexander Calder's magnificent circus sculpture in the lobby. A hundred years of art turned to charcoal and ashes.

At 200th Street and Southern Boulevard, the forty-five acre forest in the Botanical Gardens was in flames, and thousands of butterflies took to the air like bats, escaping, as if they were the firedrakes transformed.

GRON FELT A little stronger as the day wore on and the nightmares receded, but there was no escaping the insistent heat emanating from his neck. Necks. He yearned to be alone. And in the peace of the twilight, in the little space when the daylight had died and the fairy-lights were not yet lit, when the fairground was not yet open for business, Gron crept away from the caravan and went where he always went when he wanted to be alone. The Ferris Wheel turned slowly for its solitary rider, its lamps unlit, its music-box silent. He swung high into the purple air, the garish little metal car creaking in the soft, damp breeze that tasted of salt from the ocean, air that was cold against his burning skin. At the top of the arc, Gron could see the reddish glow of spot-fires still smouldering in the distance, could identify the bitter back-taste of smoke in the salty air. The old Gron was afraid, afraid for himself, afraid for his family.

The new Gron-head exalted.

THAT NIGHT GRON performed for a huge audience that had spread throughout the grounds surrounding the main tent—word had spread of his "trick" of turning fire into a great golden lizard that ran into the night, flaming like a fireworks display. Although Slavenka was worried and begged him to rest, Drakulic thought the enormous crowds more of a miracle than the miraculous marks on Gron's body. Or the disturbing changes in Gron's vestigial head.

Slavenka worshipped it.

Drakulic ignored it.

And Gron...he was being choked by it. It had grown larger, defining itself in the exact image of Gron—a perfect likeness that was the size of a cantaloupe. It had taken Gron's voice and his will. It had taken *him*. Now *he* was the shrunken, lumpish head that had no will or desire. He could but watch and listen and think his thoughts, which were nightmares, as if he had dreamed his life and this head with its white teeth and smooth skin and phlegm-yellow eyes...as if he had dreamed his mother and father and the men who had killed them—who had raped his mother and forced him and his father to watch before they killed his father, and then raped and tortured Gron himself—it was all dreams, dreams, dreams, only the firedrakes had seemed real; and now, they, too, were dreams, even as Gron watched himself perform, as he...

Ate a coil of burning, tar-dipped "link"

Devoured a plate of lit sulphur with a fork

Then burning wax and exploding gunpowder, all the traditional feats that had been passed from fire-eater to fire-eater through the generations.

Gron felt dead as he watched, but then he—his other self who was in control—poured lighter-fluid over himself and danced in the flames, and suddenly the salamanders, the firedrakes, the elementals were dancing all over him, pricking, stabbing with clawed feet, with flashing yellow mouths distorted by the heat from their fiery bodies, and he could hear the audience shriek and shout and cheer as his clothes burned away from his body, revealing his other head, this one now alert and exultant, the grinning phoenix aflame—ah, what a good trick, what a perfect trick; and the elementals wreathed the small head aborning, burned it into spirit, into essence, into themselves; and Gron was on fire, in agony, dying now, dying as he should have years ago when the raiders murdered his family—and murdered him; but the pain was so great, so overwhelming that it became ecstasy, even as his father and other men in the troupe were pouring water over him, trying to douse the elemental fire, trying to save his flesh. But he was no longer flesh, and he performed his last trick, the trick the audience had come to see: he turned into a great golden lizard that ran into the night, flaming, burning, illuminating; and now, now he was free, he could move, he could shout, and the nightmare that was his voice…

Was the crackling and hissing of fire.

He took the shape of the boy with two heads, but he was of one mind.

One mind…

Now he could look through the eyes of fire, though the eyes of dream; and he could see Drakulic and Slavenka standing over the remains of his flesh. Slavenka was screaming, as if at Gron, as if he had deceived her, which he had. She touched the place where his vestigial head had been. It had been burned away, all burned away, and she kneeled, praying and mumbling, "My son, the fire will save you, but do not let it take you… do not let it take you." Her palms were black, burned from touching Gron…what had once been Gron.

Drakulic pulled her away, and then he beat his chest and his face, for he had brought Gron back to the fire, had asked him to perform, had begged him.

But all that was dream.

There was a new, burning world before him.

A city…

THE GREAT FIRE of New York had begun. The greatest city on earth was burning, burning as Carthage burned, as Rome burned, as London had burned before it. The city was aflame, a conflagration, a pyre of souls burning into the dead, flat sky; and Gron was the sweeping fire, the pneuma, the very soul of the eternally changing devouring element. He was the fire-maker and the fire; he was the lambent flame, the sleeping fire, the cheerful fire, the cosy fire, the raging, killing fire. His hot soul coursed through the elementals. He was death's bright angel, and with every inhalation and exhalation, he burned the city, wreathing Manhattan and Harlem and Brooklyn and Queens in white heat, melting skyscrapers and boiling the ocean; and he could see…he could see without pain, without memory—which were one and the same. The world had turned red and white, the mandrakes and creatures of high temperature danced and made love, changing, interposing, breathing in all the oxygen, boiling, scourging. And Gron drifted in the flames, slept in the fire, awoke recreated in his own incandescent image—

To behold, through the knives of fire and veils of smoke, a vision beautiful and terrible, terrible and eternal. The Ferris Wheel, rotating in the char and dust that had been the park on 79th Street, told his story. Outlined against a molten sky, the great wheel of fire revolved, its spokes and tower smoke and heat; and there were Slavenka and Drakulic in their fiery gondola seats, and the men who had killed his mother and father in the swinging gondolas above them; and as the wheel slowly turned, he could see his life turning, rolling before him, and he wished it gone.

Wished it into the white-hot flames of dreams and death.

And still the city burned.

AFTERWORD TO "THE FIRE-EATERS TALE"

THE CO-AUTHOR OF this story is a fabulous writer…and also my partner.

I realize that the reader could accuse me of some slight favorable prejudice. My response would be: "Read any of her novels or short fiction and then come back and talk to me." She carried this story. I was pleased just to be allowed into the engine room.

This story appeared in the limited edition anthology *Lisa Snellings' Strange Attraction.* The email solicitation contained the following description:

"The concept for *Strange Attraction* comes from the kinetic sculpture called 'Crowded After Hours' by Lisa Snellings. The sculpture is of a carnival big wheel, peopled with odd and often haunting individuals, each marked by his or her own history. The wheel is quite crowded, in fact. Aside from those riding in the wheel's cars are those balanced between its spokes, hanging from its supports and twined in and about its bone-like frame.

"Each of these characters is at least a step removed from humanity. Some only to a small degree, others to the extent that one must wonder if any part of them was ever human. How did they come to be here, swaying on this ancient, creaking wheel that materializes in the mists each night when the booths are dark? As midnight approaches, and the Joeys sleep restless in traces of their grease-painted grins, its thin music grows stronger, the bone-joints of its frame more solid, and it begins to move, its turning somehow out of phaze, dizzying.

"There is no stopping to momentarily tease and dangle the topmost riders. None get off. No new riders climb on. But occasionally, on darker midnights, a new soul finds a place on the wheel. Did it wander there accidently? Or by some ill-fated scheme of its own doing? Or was it lured there by some inexplicable, strange attraction? The wheel turns, creaking. The carnival whispers with faint echoes of screams lost in the long ago."

And *that* was the brief.

TRAINSPOTTING IN WINESBURG

WE WAS watching the trains as we always do, even though it was so hot that our armpits smelled like dogshit; but it never mattered whether it was cold or hot or in-between, since we didnt have no school never more, we always came here. Its our favorite place, even though you cant actually get down the gradient and into the trainstay, no, you got to keep well enough away from the blueprick station guards and the Race and Settlement Corps soldiers who they must grow in a special tank cause theys so friggin big, bigger than a pancake as my mother used to say, God bless her perfect soul and all that shit.

So, anyway, just as I was telling you, we always come here; and we come here because its the only place where you can really see the trains cause they got them high cement and wire bunkers everywhere else all along the tracks. And the reason we get away with it and dont get shot or electrocuted or sumpthin is cause we know a secret place like a tunnel that goes right under the wires and comes up behind a treecopse on the west side of the trainstays embankment. It haint perfect for trainspotting, but at least we can see what goes by; in fact, we can see pretty good with the Zeiss binocs that we stole from B. J. Kleins Megashit store in Leongatha, which, in case your a dumb-ass and dont know geography, is in South Gippsland, which is in the Federal Protectorate of Australia. And just for the record—as you can plain see this whole thing is a record—my name is Jamie Peretz and Im a writer, and dont let my age put you back cause I might not know all the nasty bits of the Koran or the *Ethics of the Fathers* Jewbook, but I know shit. A slice with a working battery is all you kneed if you kneed to quote sumpthin from the good old King James Bible to keep the district officers happy. They all think its incumbent upon them (see, I told you I was a writer) to take me to every fucking Friday prayermeet. Just because I dont got a mum no more, and your probly wondering where the hell my father is: well, when you find out, you can let me know. He ran away after Mum—

I dont want to think about any of that right now.

Right now Im living with my Aunt Kate, who gets sumpthin called a stipend from the district for keeping me, even though shes not really my aunt and even though she couldnt give a rats ass whether Im here, there, or anywhere, except (however) when she wants what she calls a baby shag. Shes fat, old, dirty, and probly thirty or sumpthin, but I just close my eyes and pretend shes Kathy Robunson.

Sorry. Okay, back to what this memorandum (which is sort of like a diary, you can look up the word) is about, which is trains, which is what me and Sam and Stink and Morton and Charlie and Palomar the Mountain and Kathy Robunston (the only girl) come here every day to see. We count trains, and I can probly tell you we know more about what makes em chug than anybody in Winesburg, except, of course, the specialists in the barracks (which technically haint in Winesburg; they got their own special shire) and the mayor and officers and regulation officials who live in them big houses with porticoes and stuff way up on Snobs Hill, which is restricted, so you cant go up there, anyway. You just have to take my word for it, and my word is good as my bond, ask anyone; and because me and Stink and the Mountain, we snuck through and seen everything for ourselves when everybody was watching the Prime Minister on the community hol in Sugar Park.

—Stand up Australians. See and be seen.

—Thats what keeps you safe.

Yeah, and elephants have scales.

Sorry, again, but Kathy—and shes probly right—tells me that Im all over the place; and if Im supposed to be a writer, then I should be able to concentrate and focus and all that crap; but she dont got no space to talk from cause she haint never read anything but King James holy shit (Oh, God forgive me, for Im a sinner), and *Ive* read James Joyce and Jack Kerouac and L. Ron Hubbard.

So, okay, okay, we saw two trains, each going the opposite ways; and I wondered whos in which train, whether its taking officials to Melbourne—thats probly the one train heading away to our left—or the other which was probly carrying caskets or terrorists or boat sneaks to the work malls. Now, I should tell you that Winesburg haint such a big Federation trackstop, but special trains usually stop here. However and but, we got a problem. What you might call a vision problem. You see theres these tall water tanks and a shed thing that covers the ingress and egress (you see, fuck you, Kathy, I know words) around the station, so from our particular vantage we can see what trains goes in and what trains goes out, but we cant see any of the important shit that happens when the trains stop. And we cant very well just wander around to get a better view unless we want to get caught out and get a bullet in the eye or sumpthin.

Okay, look there.

Well *that* fooled us.

See, the Vulcan Foundry locomotive going northwest to Melbourne, that one kept going, but the big black Baldwin Consolidated, that one just stopped. We saw a few guards right there on the edge of the shed thing. And then after a while, maybe five minutes later we heard rifles popping, that clickclickclick noise followed by a sort of a crash noise, and there was funny wailing begging noises, and it sounded high-pitched like a girl, and then somebody shouted sumpthin in Strang, and then there was a different clickclickclick noise, the kind that comes just before the engines start, and then the train started moving, the locomotive building up its head, and all the stockcars that we could see, they was all green with a yellow stripe painted over their slats, disappeared around a hill that was green as the paint in Kathy Robunstons bedroom.

—Well, you gotta keep clean, Morton said. And then he said, Thats what my Da always says.

I should tell you that Mortons a crip cause hes only got one lung and only three fingers on his left hand. None of that stops him much, slows him down a little, the lung, you know, but not so youd really notice unless you knew him like we do.

—Yeah, my Da say the same, Stink said.

—Yeah, said Charlie, too. Charlies hair is white as an old mans, and he dont have any eyebrows, none at all. You should know that Charlie always agrees with Stink, although it beats me why since they hates each others guts. Go figure it out cause I, sorry, cant.

—Your so full of shit your brown, I said because I dont necessarily believe that listening to guns shootin has anything at all to do with being clean and racial.

Well, Morton really got mad about that.

—Dont ever call me that, he said. You call my Da shit? You think he dont got an eyeflap or sumpthin?

—No, I wouldnt say nothing bad about your Da. Hes clean, just like you and your mum, I wouldnt say nothing on your family like that.

—Well, you called *me* shit, just then, right? He looked over at Stink for approval.

—He did, yeah, Stink said. Stink was always looking for some kind of trouble whether it was for himself or someone else like me. And of course Charlie couldn't help himself:

—He did, yeah, Charlie said.

Well, there werent much of a choice for me here: I could either get my ass kicked cause one lung or not, three fingers or not, Morton werent normal when he got irked, and he was strong as a bastard. Stink told me that Morton got pissed off at one of his cousins once and killed him dead. Or I could make some moo sounds and calm Morton down. After all, he was my best friend, so I did what I always did when I didnt want to fight with Stink: I sang this poem Id read in a real book published in the year of our lord amen 1916 by a guy called Jonathan Cape. It went like this:

Pull out your eyes,
Apologize,
Apologize,
Pull out your eyes.

Morton smiled and nodded. Just as long as I sang apologize he was all right again.

—They was probly just obeyin the Palmer Laws like theys supposed to, Morton said, giving me the eyeball and trying to ingratiate me now that I apologized.

—But every damn time we hear a bullet pop you get all knotted up about being clean, Morton continued to tell me. He just couldn't help himself, so he went on like this: It dont matter if nobody says one friggin word about being clean, you still get all fired up. Anyway, they was probly just shooting some birka girls, right Kathy?

Kathy had curly red hair, which was sort of straggly so as you couldnt really tell whether it was clean or dirty. But, you know, I didnt care because she had tits and would let me feel her up so long as I touched her just right between her legs and so long as I kept doing it until she shook all over and said okay, thanks. Then she usually put her face down on me, and whether thats love or not I dont know, but I certainly try to make sure she keeps liking me. I dont know if she does that with anybody else, but when I asked her once, she told me it werent my business.

—I dont ask who else puts their face on you, she said.

Well, that seemed fair enough to me.

—Right, Kathy? Morton asked again because Kathy was distracted and looking at me in that way that would make wet seaweed hard, and I was looking at her as if I could see her tits right through her teesark.

—Yeah, Coulda been birka girls, Kathy said. Sounded a little like girls shouting.

—Whats a birka? asked Kathys little sister Pam who had a teeny-tiny whiney voice and didnt even have a monthly yet. I shouldve told you this before: although everybody Ive been mentioning are all transpotters, sometimes Kathy babysits her sister. Like now. And so she dont got no choice but to bring her sister along. You might look slant eyed at us because sometimes we had to bring Pam up here when we was watching trains; but Pam, shes a quiet little thing, and worse come to worse we could gag her mouth if there was any trouble.

So, anyway, back to where we was…

Kathy laughed at Pams question about whats a birka, but softly: everything we did up here was softly, even if it was a punchup. That happened once, when Morton cracked Palomars jaw, but nobody heard and Palomar had to wear a plaster and eat through a tube for two weeks.

—Birkas are sort of like hats for girls, stupid, Kathy said to Pam; but even when she called her sister stupid, she said it gently without no malice. But only shitskin illegals wear them, she said, clarifying. Sluts like them we seen in the alley behind the conditioner factory, remember?

—But Mama said we shouldn't never go there, Pam said. She waited a while, thinking, before saying in a whisper:

—Mama said they…died, which was good. Why was that good, Kathy?

Kathy put her hand over her sisters mouth and held it there while she wriggled around like a worm.

Then Morton all of a sudden slapped me on the shoulder.

—You comin over for dinner? Weer having rice with curry.

—No, thanks, I said, even though I love rice with curry.

He looked at me funny, then shook his head like he always did when he was looking at the time or somethin else in his peripherals.

—Well, its late. We gotta go *now.* Then he looked at the others like he was daring them to disagree: if Morton said we gotta go now, then they was all sure as hell going.

—So you comin or not? Morton asked me. (He gets impatient fast like my father used to.) Or you going to stand here till the alarms come on?

—Im going to stand right the fuck here till the alarms come on, I said.

Remember I said how Morton looked at me funny before? Well, he had that same look again, only more so.

—You haint got much time afore curfew, he said, puzzled. You wanna be here after cutoff?

—Theres sumpthin I need to do…alone.

I knew that Morton wouldnt ask me what that sumpthin was lest he lose his face in front of the others, and he wouldnt never do that in a million years. And the others, they couldnt ask either, leastwise not in front of Morton. But tomorrow—if I was even going to have a tomorrow—you can bet round money that Morton will get to me private and ask what the fuck.

And for just one instant I could see his eyes suddenly got wide with respect and then he said:

TRAINSPOTTING IN WINESBURG

—You really intending to miss cutoff, aintcha? Aintcha…
Yeah, if I got nothin else, I certainly got intention.

NOW I KNEW the trains came at night like clockwork, and although they didnt always stop during the day, it was different at night. Everybody knows that. You just have to listen and you can hear the trains clatter-clacking back and forth, and if you know your trains you can see em in your mind and count em and name each and every one. I can hear them from Aunt Kates livingroom. (Just to keep the record right, I live in the livingroom cause Aunt Kate rents the bedroom out most nights, except Friday, of course, when the district sends somebody over from the church.) Anyway, one night I counted two Kurandas, three Ingalls Centipedes, an Indian-Baldwin, and five (I think it was five) Sydney Super-Ds. I can differentiate (!) em by their individual clatterclacks and thunderheads.

So once Morton left with the rest of the trainspotters (and Kathy's sister Pam), I got a move on. Now I should tell you that just moving around, just walking around—and I mean during the daytime: anytime—just doing pretty much of anything inside the prohibited zone is dangerous; and I know for a fact that Ambert Johansson (what kind of a name is that?) got caught in the zone and he was never seen again. Like I said, never seen again, and, worse, nobody ever even talked about it.

Just like with my mum.

Anyway, I didnt want to get caught out cause once curfew was sounded Id have to stay put wherever I was and pretend I was a bush or somethin cause once curfews called and the darkness descends (!) well then the trainstay lights up like Christmas, and the foggy light just rises up into the sky and looks just like the light around the moon on a cloudy night. You've seen that, right? Of course, if your stupid enough to walk in after curfew then youll surely get wired or shot, and like I told you before, if you get in you never get out.

Thats all true, or I think its true, anyway.

But I figure this way: I haint goin in, Im *already* in and my plans to stay the night into morning when curfews lifted, and even then Ill just sit my ass where I plant it just in case. Because one way or another I just have to see where my mum went or what happened to her or fucking *something*!

Look, I really love trains just like Morton or Palomar or Kathy or Stink. (I dont know about Charlie; hes mostly a hanger-on.) But like youve probly already guessed, it haint just about trains for me. I didnt become a trainspotter just because I have a hard-on for locomotives. I became a trainspotter because I got an agenda.

Aunt Kate told me once (when she was stoned and right off her face and talkin out of turn) that since Mum wasnt entirely clean (bullshit!), she had to get refreshed or sumpthin like that, and that then she would come back for me. That didnt explain about my father. He werent a drunk or a shitshooter or anything like that.

—Nothin but a coward. Thats what Aunt Kate told me. Nothin but a coward. And he wouldnt even need an operation to make him clean like he was before he married my mum. But I knew. I knew that was bullshit. They dont take citizens born here. Blacks and chinks and Allahs, thats different.

WELL, I GOT to tell you that I moved down and along the gradient so slowly that I still got memorized in my head every copse, line of dirt, twig and leaf, and I guess I was lucky cause nothin blew me up, nobody shot me, nothing went blink; in fact, I didnt see no metal or electrics nowhere, just stones and twigs like I said and the hummus smell, dark and thick and sour. I went round and back of the station, then up a little until I had a panoramic (!) view past the shed, which was all corrugated, and there was a cement thing like a pier except there was no water; but that pier was pretty big, anyway; and you and probly fifty men could stand on it and look down from a safe vantage at the yards around the tracks. And sumpthin else which made me feel like I had flies in my stomach: there was two Valtion machine gun emplacements one on each side of the pier. You know the guns: they got that circle sight on a little black rail thing. We found one once, well part of one, anyway, in Mister Freylanders paddock over by Stockyard Creek. They was used by RSC soldiers after the Melbourne Shutdown before everyone got registered and cleaned. It was all twisted and black like it had been in an explosion.

Anyway, I should probably also tell you that there was a dogwire pen on the east side of the pier, too. No way we coulda seen that from our usual trainspotting position on the other side of the gradient.

So…nothin to do now but wait, and I waited and those flies in my stomach seemed to be silently buzzing around in there, and my feet got restless, fidgety, like they were itchy but without the itch; and I counted my breaths and waited and time seemed to slow down like it always does when you got nothin to do, when you dont even got a book or a slice to read. And I should tell you that you cant just go round showing off books (or even a slice, for that matter), or readin em right out in the open. Not that it haint legal to do so. We even got a library, its just that you got to make sure you haint readin the wrong material, which I figure is most everything thats interesting. (I haint got time now to go into how I get them, books and downloads, you know.) Anyway, Im keeping focused, whatever Kathy says or thinks about me being all over the place notwithstanding.

Finally it got dusk, then dark, and, pop!, the kliegs snapped on like eyes opening all over the station and the air was glowy and you could see the dust swirlin around like flies, and like I said, the light rose right up into the sky, and then you could feel some somethin rumble right deep in the ground; and although there was no whistle, you could hear the trains clatterclack just slightly, a rumblin that used to make me feel comfortable before Mum left and Dad left, and then I could see dim headlights and ditchlights coming in from the northwest, but I could tell from their arrangement that they belonged to a Sydney Super-D, even from this distance; and sure as shit I was correct cause in came that choo choo tamping its brakes and hissing like a goose until it stopped.

That wasnt half of what was happenin, though, cause silent as night that entire yard and the pier, too, filled up with blueprícks. They was manning the guns and they had their own rifles and pistols, all unstrapped; and right there in the center of it all was Pastor Lamphire of the Egalitarian Church on Kaffir Hill Road where I went (like I told you) to pray and listen to his lectures about white Australia every Friday night; and, bastard, if he werent dressed in a blueprick uniform, golden epaulets and all; and they all just stood like statues when the train pulled up and then the doors of the first stockcar slid open and psalms and music started comin out of loudspeakers and people was standin in the doorway of that first stockcar and the pastor was waving em out and the bluepricks was helping em out of the train and they was screaming like a radio, but the bluepricks helped em line up before the pastor who was probly blessin em cause he was wavin one to the right and another to the left and it didn matter if they was man or women or girl or boy, no, the bluepricks herded the ones on the left into the shed while the others was herded through a wire door into that pen I was telling you about on the east side of the pier.

And right then and there, Im telling you, right there on that pier the bluepricks manning the Valtions shot them brown and black and yellow and white men and women and girls and boys that was herded into the dogwire pen until they was all dead. Them Valtions must have been fitted with silencers cause it was just a popping, maybe just a little louder than what we all heard earlier in the day, but quick and efficient; and then the train moved forward a little and the next stockcar was pulled into position. Two bluepricks sprayed the dead people in the pen and the whole business started all over again: Pastor Lamphire was blessin everybody and choosin who was to go to God and who was to go into the shed; and to tell the truth, it didnt take long to get through that entire train, and not but an hour later another train arrived—I could tell from its lights it was a Baldwin—and the same business happened again. A bunch of Allahs tried to get away, of course, but the bluepricks just shot them and left them where they were on the tarmac. I guess there would be cleaners comin along later on.

I looked to see what was happenin to the people chosen for the shed cause they couldnt just keep jammin people in there, but it seemed thats exactly what the pastor and the bluepricks had in mind. Eventually (!) another Baldwin came into the station from the other direction, and the bluepricks emptied everyone—well, almost everyone: Ill tell you about that in a minute—out of the shed and into the Baldwins stockcars. Those stockcars were just like the ones with yellow slats that I told you about earlier. Anyway, in they went, all screamin and cryin, and pleadin for mercy just like youd imagine; and I dunno, I mustve been just sittin there like I was asleep with my eyes open or sumpthin cause all of a sudden I was justabout jumpin our of my skin, cept I didnt move, I didnt blink. Hell, I hardly breathed cause somebody—had to be one of the blueprick or RSC officers or maybe just a regulation official—was draggin a girl or a woman through the bush not too far behind me and to my right. I couldnt see them, but I knows it was a female on account of her cryin and screamin; and then her voice got muffled and there was a lot of gruntin…then nothin until the officer or whatever got up and made noise crunchin through the bush; and me, I was all worked up inside and though it made me feel guilty somewhat I figured all that time that I was pretty safe cause if I couldnt see him then he probly couldnt see me.

I just looked strait ahead, watchin trains come and go in the klieg-lit dark until there was a shift change or sompthin cause Pastor Lamphire stopped blessin and separating the birkas and Allahs and sluts and darks, and one of the blueprick officers took over the job (maybe he was a pastor, too, who the hell knows? He was just as fat as old Pastor Lamphire); but he was fast, faster than the Pastor, maybe cause he didnt have to be blessin everybody:

—You in the dogpen, you in the shed, you in the dogpen, you in the shed, and he waved everybody this way and that way faster than I could even say it, and it was just after that when I saw what I saw that made me so sick I justabout pissed myself:

It was when the train moved a little forward again, bringin the next yellow stripe stockcar into position and the doors of the stockcar slid open and psalms and music started comin out of loudspeakers and people was standin in the doorway of that first stockcar and the blueprick officer was waving em out and the bluepricks was helping em out of the train and they was screaming like a radio. (I dont mind repeatin my prose: no sense makin it up all over again or pasting it up in a different configuration (!); thats what I think, anyway.)

So I was watchin that and thinking about the locomotive, which was a Calumet Ivory, one of my favorites, and just tryin to get through the night and wonderin when Id try to get back through the wires to civilization, if you can call Winesburg civilization, and wonderin if, in fact,

Id get out at all or maybe theyd catch me and put me in the dogpen and shoot me with the sluts and Allahs; and *thats* when I saw a kid dressed just like me lookin right up in my direction to where I was.

Like he had x-ray vision (!) superpower or something and could see through trees and walls and watertowers and sheds.

Well sonovabitch and fuck me blind…it was *me*!

(Well, he sure as hell looked like me, anyway.)

And his mum was beside him, right beside him—but only for a minute cause the officer who took the pastors place pointed for him to go into the shed and for her to go into the dogwire pen.

The *her* coulda been my mum. She was just standin there lookin scared in her dress with the blue flowers all over it, cept the dress was dirty an stained bloody; and I wanted to shout to myself and shout to my mum, but I just sat where I was lookin, sat where I was like I was dreaming everything up, like I was probably eating rice with curry with Crocker and his folks in their house on Toora Road, but, no, I was here; and then like in the time it takes to blink dirt outa your eye, the Valtions were poppin and me and Mum—the me and Mum I seen down there—was gone and the kliegs was getting dimmer and there was pink and gray streaks in the sky.

I stayed there where I was for a long time. You know, just lookin strait ahead. And the sun got high in the sky before I left and got through the wire and back to Aunt Kates who didnt even know Id been gone; but I got to tell you somethin: even though Im safe and sound, even though Im back in the livingroom while Aunt Kates doin who knows what with some asshole in the bedroom, I somehow feel like Im still on that gradient and lookin down at the trains. And it feels all the time like its dark like it was then. Like I said, I still feel like Im still there.

ISLANDS OF TIME

WELL, THAT'S THE end of this memorandum.

Cept to tell you that I never went back trainspotting with Sam and Stink and Morton and Charlie and Palomar the Mountain and Kathy Robunston.

And I never told them nothin.

What was I supposed to say?

That Mums dead? And Im in the shed?

OH, YEAH: I should also tell you that I dont think about trains no more. Not even when I hear them from Aunt Kates livingroom.

AFTERWORD TO "TRAINSPOTTING IN WINESBURG"

THIS STORY FIRST appeared in *Concentration*, my collection of Holocaust stories. Although it is perhaps the most 'Australian' of the stories in this volume, it is part of my small oeuvre of stories that attempt to "testify", to remember the irreal horrors of the Holocaust. As the philosopher George Santayana wrote, "Those who cannot remember the past are condemned to repeat it." In her introduction to *Concentration*, author and scholar Marleen S. Barr addressed the issue of my use of fantasy tropes to depict the Holocaust by quoting the historian Hayden White: "This is not to suggest that we will give up the effort to represent the Holocaust realistically but rather that our notion of what constitutes realistic representation must be revised to take account of experiences that are unique to our century and for which older modes of representation have proven inadequate."

I went out on a stylistic limb with this story—echoes of James Joyce's *Portrait of the Artist as a Young Man*—to try to tear even the narrative away from the expected and the traditional. I figure it's the author's job to pillage and steal from giants and icons...and, as referenced in a previous afterword, to stand on the shoulders of the aforementioned giants and to risk falling flat on our authorial asses!

And, yes, the title is an ironic reference to Sherwood Anderson's *Winesburg, Ohio.*

SUMMER

ADAPTATION TO COOLING WOULD NOT BE AS SIMPLE AS ADAPTATION TO WARMING.

—S. FRED SINGER

1.

THE SAND is down there, down down down there, hard-packed and crusty under the snow and layers of translucent green ice; and somehow that gives you comfort, albeit cold comfort to be sure. Even the ironies, the metaphors and similes, freeze; the whole fucking world is frozen. Everything is frozen, and you—you came down here to Florida to get warm, to get away from the snow and the forever grayness of northern Michigan.

You'll think about Michigan later.

It's too dangerous to think about the past.

2.

BUT YOU CAN'T help yourself, can you? Memory is everything, and you stand and dream on the ice and snow that is—or was—New Smyrna

Beach, "THE SAFEST BEACH IN THE WORLD," or so said the sign. But that sign was there eons ago, millennia ago.

Forty years ago. That's when it was, and it's all frozen, all the seconds, minutes, and hours are now unchangeable, impermeable. So you look out at the gunmetal gray purling sea, and you select a few perfect moments. Yes, life is a pack of cards. Now that's a warm, palpable metaphor. Pick a card Laura. You've got a billion of 'em.

3.

YOU REMEMBER...YOU REMEMBER when the sun was warm, when the sand would clot under your bare feet, crusting between your toes. (Remember when you could *breathe*...when you could walk and not run out of breath?) The ocean would be a warm roaring, as if you'd put a conch shell to your ear, and your body was like new clothes. But you were proud of that body, ordinary as it was.

There you are, melting back into the past, standing right here, right on this very spot, and you're practically naked. You've got small breasts, but they're good enough to fill out a bikini.

There's a couple sitting on a blanket a few feet away from you, and you can *feel* the man staring at you. You can feel that he wants to touch you.

How does that make you feel?

4.

YOU TOUCH YOURSELF, right here, right on this spot, right in public, although there is no public. There is no one here but you and the snow and ice and sea. The snow is beautiful. How many times have you told yourself that? How beautiful is a snowflake?

You've thickened in the hips and thinned in the lips. But it's more than that, isn't it? Everything has fallen. But you're there, like the sand under the ice. Your hair is gray. You gave up and stopped dying it. Your breasts are good, though. Small breasts don't sag so much. But when you look into the mirror, you're not the same person anymore. Some rouged, prune-wrinkled, rather nice-looking old lady has grown over you, submerged you, subsumed you. She's pleasant enough looking, isn't she?

That's all you were ever going to be…you know that. You knew that.

You should have had more sex, but there was so much disease, wasn't there?

You should have stayed with Harold.

You shouldn't have gotten cancer.

(Ah, yes, why you? Why not him? *He* was the smoker.)

If you hadn't had cancer, you wouldn't have left Harold, you wouldn't have—

Don't think about that. Don't think about any of that. You've only lost the lower lobe of a lung. You've still got your breasts. They still look pretty.

(Stop coughing!)

But as you look out at the glacial blue divide of sea and sky, you imagine that you're looking into the mirror. You're deep inside that mirror.

The real you the warm you the beautiful you.

5.

YOU IMAGINE THAT you can see the glint of one of the huge orbital mirrors in the sky, but you can't. You see a frozen, cloud-clogged sky that merges with the sea. Sea and sky united in…anger. Yes, that's it. Anger. The mirrors aren't working, of course, aren't warming the world enough, but they were a technological feat. One of the last, hey?

You're late for school. You have an idea where to begin your lecture about Winter, which is a pleasant enough euphemism for Ice Age.

Eiszeit.

But German won't help you now. The world has become larger, rather than smaller. When were you last in Frankfurt? You laugh, for it was long before Winter.

You could open your lecture with the Little Winter that began in the fourteenth century and lasted—on and off—until the nineteenth century.

What caused that, class?

They won't know. But *you* know that Little Winter was caused (in part, not entirely—don't get carried away) by the felling of forests during the Middle Ages. Tell them that. Tell them that forests reflect between ten to twenty percent of the sunlight while snowfields reflect up to ninety percent. Explain albeido. (Ah, were it libido, but you couldn't explain that anymore, could you? Could you?)

Tell them that their ancestors helped make/made their very own Little Winter.

Did you make yours?

Did we make ours?

6.

YOU LOOK UP and see the smeary blotch in the cloud cover (the sun), and then you leave the ice flows of your sacred beach and march to school.

You're dressed like an Eskimo.

You're a twentieth century locomotive breathing steam. (Stop coughing!)

And you're still cold.

So much for modern technology.

7.

THERE ARE ALWAYS enough students, and lecture hall #7 of the Chrysanthemum Heights School of Higher Education is packed with alert, motivated, bright, interesting students. The cream of the crop. (You can do better than that, Laura. You wanted to be a writer, remember? Choose a proper metaphor.)

You hate them. You love them. They are your life, or, rather, would be your life, if you had a life.

How many people are left in the world? you ask yourself. You should know the answer. You're an educator.

You've questioned the students about the migration plagues and their ramifications. Hands are still raised and waving, which makes you think of wheat fields. The cream of the crop (cream as metaphor being transformed into the plural) have a great need to respond, even if there is no question. You accommodate them with a question.

"Who was Genevieve Woillard?"

"She was a twentieth century Belgian botanist who examined the pollen in peat in France and discovered that the pollen vanished," shouts a tall, skinny boy without waiting to be called, without raising his hand. His head seems too large for his body. He'll grow into it. It isn't a bad looking head. Thin features marred by pimples. He isn't wearing enough protection, even though it's cold enough to see your breath. Most of the other children are bundled up, as are you. Perhaps Mr. Clive Marsten—that's his name, you know all their names—is the New Man, the survivor who needs no clothes.

"Mr. Marsten, this class really isn't interested in the fractured response of a show-off. I might not be able to compel you to dress appropriately, but you *will* wait your turn."

"I humbly apologize, Ms. Fuchs."

There is always a whispered titter, as if you're a failure because your name sounds like the makings of sex, as if someone who's past it should give up the name and credentials.

"Apology accepted. Now perhaps someone else can enlighten us as to *why* Ms. Woillard is important and exactly what she was doing in the Alsace region of France?"

As if any of it is important.

There is a show of hands to choose from, and you listen as one Rita Byrne tries to answer the question. Sandy haired Rita looks like you—like you used to look—doesn't she? No, she's prettier than you were. Maybe not. As smart, though. And a tomboy. Yes, that.

"112,000 years ago—during the last interglacial epoch—the climate changed from temperate to frigid within a twenty-year span."

"And what," you ask, "does that tell us about our own Winter?"

"Well, isn't that obvious, Ms. Fuchs."

8.

YOU DAYDREAM, AND the students try to answer your detailed questions; but you aren't there. You've left, and you daydream and dreamdream and like a ghost, you breathe and cough and whisper yourself through the storm covered windows.

ISLANDS OF TIME

9.

WHISPER YOURSELF BACK home.

Oh, no, not your old home in Clarewood, Michigan, which you imagine is preserved without flaw or tear below the translucent blue-green depths of the glacier. Like Pompeii in amber.

No no no.

You can dream perfectly round and perfect dreams, but you know with the certainty of late maturity that your past—both geographically and reflectively—is tundra. Snowfields. Your stucco house (in Clarewood) on Saginaw Street (corner of Owosso and Blind River Drive, to be precise) is probably no more than a stone foundation.

If that.

No, you daydream—sweet sweetbreads of memory—of your present home right here in New Smyrna Beach, your dream home, your repro Conch house with gingerbread wooden grillwork, classic-cream double-decker verandas, shutters, a sloped blue-gray roof, and roof hatches (called scuttles). That's the daydream. That's the house of memory, but it's real. The roof has deteriorated and the verandas have become catchments for snow and ice, permanent snow and ice. The grillwork is long gone and the paint is scabbed, as if the house itself had acne like your preemptive student Mr. Clive Marsten.

The house is broken.

Snow swept

Ice capped.

Buried.

That's the reality.

But still, even now, in Winter Winter Winter (of course, you reflexively think winter *of your life*, but that's too obvious, isn't it?), you live there in the house that Harold built.

SUMMER

10.

YOUR HONEYMOON HOUSE.

Your classic-cream conch shell honeymoon house.

Listen to the memories: summer, Florida summer, before Winter, when the sun on your arms smells like baked bread, when the beaches are tanned bikinied leggy bodies: television shots of adolescents laughing; volleyball; hot dog vendors; lifeguards (on elevated chairs) watching children wading into the safe shallow ocean; the ocean bubbling, like champagne; but that's such a lousy simile, and you know it.

You can hear the children from your bedroom in your new Conch house. You concentrate on every sound. Ah, memory, Laura, you can remember, *we* can remember: lying in bed all those summers ago (summer now just another metaphor for ice). Remember the pain, the numbing wheezing crawling pain? Remember lying there in your bed under the red linen sheets, lying in the selfsame bed you share(d) with Harold?

The chemotherapy induces constant nausea, infinities of nausea, and where are you Harold, you sonovabitch bastard?

Bring me a Maxolon.

Rub my back.

Rub my shoulders.

Harold, where are you…?

11.

OH, HAROLD HAD excuses, so many excuses, so many charming excuses. His father died, Harold had to be with him, too, you know; and he had to work. That's the best one, isn't it? He had to work to earn money. Who could argue with that? Certainly not his dear pals who loved him, his world of friends and supporters.

Everyone loved Harold.

You whisper (to him? to yourself?) "You could have been with me a little bit. You weren't working every night. You could have faced the truth, that I'm sick, that I might die." But he declaims (ah, what a word!) that he *is* there for you, that it's not his fault, that he has always been there for you, even as he leaves you, even as he hides away from you, from what you might become (from what you have become), and when you tell him to leave…

When you close up, shut up, lock up the pretty pale blue shutters that are your (you just can't resist another metaphor, can you?) eyes and ears and mouth (ears and mouths aren't blue!), Harold is honestly—

Surprised.

12.

BUT NOT AS surprised as you, Helen, lovely, blue-eyed, shutter-eyed conch shelled Helen; not half as surprised as you.

He left, as per your request/demand, disappeared into what became the cold Winter, and you missed him, loved him, wanted him back.

But you were…shuttered, weren't you, Laura. Frozen. "Incapable of any more humiliation." You weren't the same person that you were.

None of us is the same person that we were.

Don't try to diagram that sentence. Listen to me. I'm smarter than you, and I *know* you. And so you laugh, knowing that your narrator can't be your older self. Certainly not your younger, callow, gullible self.

"Who are you?" you ask. Talking to yourself.

Finally figuring it out.

Seeing yourself completely.

In and out of your history.
Such a small, such a profound epiphany.

13.

THE BELL RINGS, class is finished, the last class, and you wait while the cream of the crop pour through the high, metal double doors; and you mark their spot tests and leave them in a neat pile on the upper right hand corner of your desk, which will be accessible to the students when they arrive tomorrow morning; and you attend a staff meeting, everyone keeping warm in the cold, yet heated conference room; and then you leave for the last time.

14.

YOU HAVEN'T EVEN the slightest urge to return home, to take one last look. You go directly to the beach. It's low tide, and the beach is two hundred yards wide, as slick and smooth as a skating rink. But not for long.

Not for long.

You sit down on the ice flow—it takes time for the chill to reach into your thighs and buttocks and the balls of your feet—and dream.

Goodbye, Harold, you bastard. I'm sorry. You're sorry. Everyone's sorry. But I'm too young to waste my life. Too young too young too young, and as you chant your incantation to a Beach boys' melody, you can feel the rising heat. The delicious smell of the sun and sea-salt humidity.

The ice is melting in the sun, and the ice turns to cool asphalt and then to yielding, smooth sand, scratchy and granular; and you pick up handfuls of it and throw it into the air. It tastes...warm, dry, like choking.

You stretch out, breathe deeply, and let the warmth in, even while you watch yourself simultaneously getting up and walking to the sea.

(Ah, the conundrum, which you is you? The narrator *you* or the you *you*? Let the narrator *you* be *me*.)

15.

WATCH ME, DEAR, sweet glacial Laura.

Queen mother of ice and dreams and broken conch.

Watch me slip out to the sea.

AFTERWORD TO "SUMMER"

IN 2002 I received the following email from Mike Resnick[**]:

"So I say to myself, who's *messhuginah*[**]* enough to give me a story in the first person of a woman on three weeks notice, and I say, Nobody on *this* continent, that's for sure.

"Hi, boychick. You wanna write me a short story for an anthology called *Men Writing SF As Women*? All it has to be is SF or fantasy in the first person of a woman—and if changing her name from Victoria to Victor doesn't invalidate the story, then you done did it wrong.

"Three to four weeks. Under 7500 words. Friendly editor. What more could you want?"

Although I considered the fundamental MacGuffinesque idea for this anthology to be somehow…wrong, off-center, or perhaps silly, I could not help but think that anger, grief, hope, and resilience are not gender specific. And it seemed to me that writers worth their pens or computers (or both) should be able to write from multifarious points-of-view… So I leave it to you, dear reader, to determine whether or not the concept for Mike's anthology was ill-conceived—and whether the story you've just read might have been better left in the proverbial drawer.

(*I* vote against the drawer!)

---

* Mike was a colleague and a pal. Sadly, he passed away in 2020. He was a prolific author and anthologist, accumulating many awards and accolades, including five Hugo Awards and a Nebula. He was also the editor of *Galaxy's Edge* magazine and executive editor of the now defunct *Jim Baen's Universe.*

** For those of you who aren't Jewish or do not live in New York City, *meshugge* means crazy in Yiddish. As opposed to a *draykop*—who is someone who looks at you funny and maybe can't quite focus—a meshuggener is the sort of person who hits you over the head with a Q-tip!

A PERFECT SUMMER FOR BASEBALL, TENTACLES, MUTANTS, AND LOVE

(WITH BARRY N. MALZBERG)

OUT OF THE MOUTH OF GORLOTH

ALL OF us members of the West Side Central Gang were still excited about last week's Marichal vs Spahn pitching duel in Candlestick Park. And in case you came from Mars or the Moon or somewhere, after four hours and sixteen innings, there was no score—nothing!—until Willie Mays homered and finally won the game for the Giants. That's all we talked about mostly, except, of course, when Mr. Gorloth picked us up from school in his rickety, rusted-out Volkswagen van. We called him 'the Mouth of Gorloth'—not to his face, of course—because his stories were more interesting than anything in the entire universe. I mean even more interesting than Marichal and Spahn.

And I should probably tell you right now that the West Side Central Gang wasn't *really* a gang like in *Rebel Without a Cause* or like that; but we were still pretty tough, and we were the all-time high-scorers of the Triplet's Little League Baseball Club, which until this year, 1963, was the farm league for the Yankees. And Mr. Gorloth was our coach, but he was way, way more than that. He knew everything about everything, not only baseball; and, man, could he tell stories! He certainly knew everything about the adventures of Satchel and his gang of superpower mutants. (In fact, I've got a sneaking suspicion that Mr. Gorloth *is* the real, honest-to-goodness Satchel!) Those stories were so scary that they kept all of us up at night. Well, fighting the unspeakably horrible, evil monster gods that are even now secretly taking over the world is pretty scary.

We were the only kids in the world that Mr. Gorloth confided in; and, day or night, we were ready to hear about the adventures of Satchel and his mutants.

Like right now at 3:37 pm on our way to Homestead Field behind the Carvel ice cream shop on Riverside Drive...

5:15 PM: IN THE PARKING LOT AFTER IN-FIELD THROWING DRILLS, From the Mutants With All Dark Splendor

NOW EVERY TIME Mr. Gorloth was about to give us the next breathtaking episode of what happened after Satchel and his gang of superpower mutants saved the world by vanquishing the invading kangaroo-legged Ghasts and the green, oozing, shapeshifting Uleths (and a few other malevolent servants of the spider god Atlach-Nacha), he would explain that neither the mutants nor the slavering monsters were really real.

"I want to emphasize that, guys. These are just stories. They're what's called 'imaginative', and I don't want you going home and telling your parents or brothers and sisters that they're true. You'll just get yourselves into trouble...and get me fired! Is that clear?"

We would all nod.

"Promise?"

We would all nod again, impatient to get through all this so we could hear the next installment. But Mr. Gorloth wouldn't be satisfied that easily, and he'd explain (as if we couldn't remember anything from one day to another) about how the mutants had come to Earth a long time ago, but until very recently they had been in disguise, had been in a kind of costume to look just like us because their real appearance was so 'disturbing'. If they were to show themselves as they really were, they would get into a lot of trouble and probably get locked up by the government and experimented on. But if they could 'slide into the normal scenery of civilization', they would be more or less undetected.

After about the millionth time Mr. Gorloth told us about that, I raised my hand (I was sitting with Keith Kadariak in the very back of the bus) and asked, "Mr. Gorloth, then your mutants—"

"How many times do I have to tell you to call me Danny? Only my mother calls me Mr. Gorloth." He chuckled at that, and I couldn't for the life of me understand why his mother would call him that or why he would think it was funny, but I said. "Yessir, er, Danny."

"And they're not *my* mutants," he continued. "They aren't Satchel's mutants either. They don't belong to anybody but themselves, and they follow Satchel into danger and sometimes into the very bowels of hell because they believe in him. And they believe in him because he is the only person in the universe who can save the earth from the gods that inhabit this universe and other universes. Is that clear, Franklin?"

Although I prefer being called Chip, I said, "Yessir...Danny."

"So...now what was your question?"

"Well, you said that the mutants had to hide their appearance. Sounds like they're shapeshifters just like the Uleths."

Mr. Gorloth smiled. It was what my friend Keith called his conspiratorial smile. I should probably tell you that Keith is a genius, at least that's what our homeroom teacher Mrs. Killick told my mother. I figure

Keith is a sort of junior Mr. Gorloth. He seems to know something about everything. Except Keith is fat, or big boned as he calls it. Mr. Gorloth, on the other hand, is skinny as a rail—that's what my mother said the first time she met him. He's tall and skinny and wears these thick black-framed glasses (except when he's coaching), and his face is always red and blotchy. I guess old guys get acne, just like my older brother Charlie. Except Charlie's fifteen, and Mr. Gorloch is way, way older than that.

Anyway, after Mr. Gorloth made his conspiratorial smile, he explained that the green, oozing alien Uleths learned how to shapeshift from Satchel's mutants; and I've got to tell you that some of the guys actually gasped when he told us that the mutants started off bad, really bad. They were as bad as any of the gods with tentacles or glowing eyes!

"Satchel saved the entire mutant species from extinction," Mr. Gorloth said, smiling again, but this time with just his mouth, not with his eyes. "After that, the strongest and smartest and most talented and decorated of the entire mutant race, swore eternal allegiance to Satchel. And they swore on their wrinkled foreheads that they'd fight on the side of right for ever more." Mr. Gorloth paused, as if he was considering very carefully what he was going to say next. "All that is a story for another day. But I'll tell you this much now: the mutants were the ones who were given the assignment by the Great Old Ones themselves to open the way."

I think all of us wanted to know what the 'open the way' business was all about, but we didn't want to interrupt him because he might just say "Wait for the next installment" and take us back to the drop-off site in front of C. Fred Johnson Elementary School.

"I'm not saying that I know exactly what the Great Old Ones had planned," he continued, "or exactly how opening the way would work: the mutants only tell me as much as they want me to know. They say we are not ready for the entire truth and won't be for a while."

Then with a knowing nod Mr. Gorloth turned away from us, turned the key in the ignition, and the van shuddered into life.

"You see, Chip," Keith whispered to me at we rattled along on the highway, "Gorloth keeps giving himself away, no matter how much he tells us that Satchel and his mutants aren't real. *He's* Satchel!"

I was about to laugh off Keith's comments, but just then, at that very moment, I saw something that would keep me awake all night. I only saw it for a second. Maybe it was the sunlight reflecting off the windshield or something like that. But…

"Chip, hey, Earth calling to Chip, you all right?" Keith asked, grasping my arm.

"Yeah, I'm okay. Why shouldn't I be?"

But I felt as if I was suddenly in some sort of a fog.

I know I saw *something*!

I *know* I saw a tentacle with bluish suckers crawling right into Mr. Gorloth's ear.

BACKWARD AND FORWARD IN TIME: PRELUDE TO A NOCTURNE AT THE RED APPLE REST

BEFORE I TELL you any more about that tentacle with the bluish suckers, I should tell you about Lydia because you need to understand about her if you're going to understand anything about what happened to Mr. Gorloth, me, all the guys in the gang, and the entire universe, for that matter. So I'm telling you this from the future, which I managed to alter a little bit just like Mr. Gorloth taught me. He used to say (or rather will say) "In order for you stupid idiots to really understand what happened or what's going to happen, you must know the story backwards and forwards. Only then will you have even the most infinitesimal hope of altering the time scheme."

Anyway, the first time we met Lydia in what I think of as her human personification was in the last short weeks of summer in 1963 (or perhaps it might have been 2063 if you're using an alternate time scheme).

We were on our way to Camp Hat-i-Notha in Mr. Gorloth's old rusted out bus.

Camp Hat-i-Notha is in the Catskills, which for some reason was called the Borsht Belt by my parents who wouldn't know a borsht from bacon. And it was because Mr. Gorloth was a senior camp counselor and staff advisor that the whole West Side Central Gang, except for our best pitcher Carl 'Baby' Ruth, had signed up for three weeks baseball practice and 'amazing adventures'. Even though Mr. Gorloth used his influence to get Baby a special Hat-i-Notha's assistance award (and offered to pay the difference out of his own pocket!), Baby's parents weren't going to take charity from "a goddamn Jew phony."

Mr. Gorloth said "in retrospect" that Baby's absence was probably a good thing because Baby could have had an accident or died or something. I don't know about any of that, but it sort of shows you the unintended consequences of altering time schemes because Baby died of leukemia in 1965.

I should probably also tell you something from the perspective of one of my future selves. I know it can get complicated, but I sometimes interrupt myself because once in a while (like right now!) my consciousness jumps back and forth in time. I can't help that; it just happens. Anyway, me and my gang member friend Keith Kadariak—he's the one I always sit with in Mr. Gorloth's bus—well, we are the miscreants who discovered that consequence isn't a causal determination kind of thing, that time is much more than a complex collection of Roveillian layers...and that time can also be interpreted as consciousness itself. Our equilibrium paradox won us a Nobel Prize in 1987, although Keith lost a lot of weight and most of his hair after that...assuming you still believe in the concept of 'after'!

And I'll always feel guilty about getting an award for probably killing Baby.

I WASN'T REALLY thinking about guilt or what I'd learn about my future selves when we were on our way to Camp Hat-i-Notha. Mr. Gorloth told us Hat-i-Notha had something to do with an Iroquois word for singing, or something like that; and so I figured that they probably do a lot of singing at that camp. There were girls there, too, he told us, although to be honest, right now most of us were more interested in who was going to cover for Baby. Davy Brown was a good catcher. He was the richest kid in our gang—his father had invented elevator music or something like that—but for some reason he was too shy to perform well in an actual game. So I figured that I would be the best bet to replace Baby because I was probably the best over-all catcher; and, like Baby, I could throw a pretty good split-finger fastball. But Winky Minoso thought *he* was the best pitcher, better than me, better than Davy, better even than Baby, which was pure bullshit, of course; and I told him so. He stood up in the bus like he was going to come after me, but Hank Rickey tripped him. I guess I stood up too, but good old Keith pulled me back into my seat.

Now the weird thing was that during all this commotion Mr. Gorloth didn't say a damn thing. Didn't even shout at us, and I should tell you something else: he'd been acting weird since we started this trip, like he was happy and distracted all at the same time. But he still had the power: he was, after all, 'the Mouth of Gorloth'. So when he finally stopped humming and whistling and tapping his ring on the steering wheel and asked us if we wanted to hear about Satchel and his mutants, we all shut the hell up and stopped worrying about who'd be pitching when we got to the camp.

"I don't think I ever told you about what attracts mutants, did I?" Mr. Gorloth asked. But he didn't wait for an answer. "You probably figure that Satchel's gang of mutants were all males, right?" Again he didn't wait for an answer. "Well, let me tell you: sometimes they're male and sometimes they're female, and sometimes they're both at the same time. You see, it all depends on their mood and what they're doing, or need to do. Now when they're one sex or the other, they call themselves by different names, just as they use different names when they're both sexes at the same time. And it's also the same for those mutants who are also part alien—you know, mutants who are, say, part Hyperborean Voormi or Martian Aihais; or who are part god, you know, like part Karakal or Lobon. That's why sometimes I seem to be talking about a mutant horde when I'm really only talking about Satchel's gang of fifty, give or take a thousand or so close relatives." He laughed out loud at that. "But usually Satchel is with his trusted confidents, the 'Satchel Eleven', as I call them. And out of the Eleven, only Gooney, Kah, and Spitroneh are part god or alien.

"And you wanna know something else?" he continued. "Mutants can fall in love with themselves, as well as each other. Hell, they're really quite loveable. Now I'll bet you didn't know *that* about them, hey?"

Well, none of us knew what to say. Mr. Gorloth seemed to be going sideways or something. We were waiting to hear the next installment of how Satchel and his mutants planned on stopping the Great Old Ones from opening the way...and we were still waiting to find out what opening the way meant, anyway. We surmised—that's Mr. Gorloth's word—that it meant "the utter destruction of Earth by either the minions of the 300,000 year old Deep One, Pth'thya-L'yt (who I later found out had detachable tentacles that could move around and attack on their own); the tentacle whiskered Y'nathogguans; or the enormous army of the octopoidal goddess Ayi'ig.

But none of us were interested in the love life of Satchel's mutants. Not even a little! None of that mattered to Mr. Gorloth, though, because he just went on and on about how mutants fall in love and how they make babies and all sorts of disgusting stuff like that. And then he finally said something interesting. He said we were going to stop at The Red Apple Rest for lunch. Everybody shouted and waved their arms when he said that because who wouldn't want to go to The Red Apple Rest where you can get the best hot dogs and hamburgers in the universe, lox and bagels (whatever the hell lox was), milkshakes, malteds, soda, knishes (I like those), cakes, pies, any sort of candy you can think of, and chicken soup with these matzo ball dumplings that actually taste pretty good. And we all shouted again when we came to the first billboard with a huge picture of a big red apple:

RED APPLE REST—FOUR MILES.

CAFETERIA. BUSSES WELCOME.

"And I want you guys to be on your best behavior. You know why?"

Nobody knew why.

"Because we're going to meet a friend of mine at the cafeteria. She's going to the camp with us. And if anybody says anything stupid or off-limits to her...or swears or anything like that, I'll knock your ears flat. Understood?"

We all said we understood, although we really didn't know why he was getting upset with us before we even did anything wrong. We certainly didn't like the idea of having a girl on the bus, messing everything up; but I sure as hell wasn't going to tell him that. So everybody just looked around at everybody else like "what the hell's going on?"

"Okay then," Mr. Gorloth said and that was that. He didn't talk any more about the mutants and their personal stuff, didn't tell us about Satchel or who he thought should fill in for Babe as pitcher. Didn't talk about the girl we were going to meet. No, in fact, he just kept tapping his ring on the steering wheel and whistled tunelessly all the way to the Red Apple Rest, which, I should tell you, has this enormous wooden apple sitting right on its roof.

Anyway, it was sort of like Mr. Gorloth had suddenly turned stupid or something.

Keith, who always sat next to me in the back of the bus and like I told you before was a genius, said girls can make you act like that. According to him, Mr. Gorloth was obviously madly in love; and because of that, he wasn't going to be interested in us or baseball or anything else for as long as she was around. "Just wait, you'll see."

"So maybe we should just ignore her," I said. "Maybe she'll take the hint and just leave Mr. Gorloth and everybody alone."

Keith thought that was pretty funny. He said, "Nope, that'll never happen, believe me. And did you know there are girl counselors at the camp? She's probably one of those. So she'll definitely be there for the whole three weeks. But who knows? Maybe she's a good pitcher."

I didn't think that was nearly as funny as Keith did.

I did have this uncomfortable thought, though, when we finally got to The Red Apple Rest and Mr. Gorloth drove us into the parking lot right beside the cafeteria and told us he'd get food coupons for each of us and that if we wanted something more expensive, we'd just have to pay for it out of our own pockets. But all I could think of when he was talking was that time at baseball practice when I had seen that tentacle with blue suckers crawl right into his ear.

And I wondered if tentacles and love had anything to do with each other.

I guess I was getting as stupid as Mr. Gorloth, and I wasn't even in love.

Or at least not yet…

ISLANDS OF TIME

OH LYDIA, OH LYDIA, OH HOW LOVE DEVOURS
OH MY, OH SAY, HAVE YOU EVER MET A LYDIA

OKAY, ABOUT LYDIA, who I was supposed to tell you about in the last chapter, remember? Well, it turns out that Lydia lived just off Route Seventeen right in the Southfields section of Tuxedo, which is only about a five-minute walk from The Red Apple Rest. Besides working part time at the restaurant and being a dancer and gymnast and everything else, she was also a cashier and singer at the Concord Resort, which was supposed to be a big deal. Of course, as I found out later, none of that was really true (in this time scheme, at least). But she could make you believe anything.

Anyway, while we were running around from counter to counter in the cafeteria and using our coupons and allowance money to order hot dogs, hamburgers, milkshakes, creamsicles, and lots of candy for snacks—Wax Lips, Zagnuts, Sky Bars, Astro Pops, Rolos, Kitkats, all that—Mr. Gorloth disappeared, which wasn't like him. He was usually watching us like a hawk, as my mother would say. It was Hank Rickey who finally discovered where he was, and he was so excited that he lost his coupons and had to explain to the manager what happened. But he rounded us up like he was Mr. Gorloth himself, telling us we had to see Mr. Gorloth's girl, that she and Mr. Gorloth were at one of the outdoor tables in front of the washroom sign painted on the white wall of the restaurant and that we really had to see her and that he was going back there right now.

By the time Keith and I got to the table—we both had to pee after ordering our food—the gang was all there waiting for the food to arrive and looking at Mr. Gorloth's friend the way that I guess a group of adolescent boys without experience but a hell of a lot of impulse would look at a girl like this.

Well, she wasn't just any kind of a girl. She was a full-blown woman. She was…extraordinary. She was younger than Mr. Gorloth, who looked like he had just won an election or something, but she was way older than us, maybe twenty. And she just looked so beautiful that I felt a funny sort of heat in my privates. There was something shivery and wavery about her, and just looking at her was like eating candy and wanking at the same time. She looked sort of like Jayne Mansfield, only with black hair; but then when you looked at her again, she looked shiny and skinny and sort of slippery like she had her own sunlight and didn't need the noonday sun to make her visible. And she looked at Mr. Gorloth like he was the most fascinating person in the world; and he kept looking away from her, as if he was staring into the sun and it was burning his eyes.

Lydia enthralled (another one of Mr. Gorloth's words) everyone; in fact, two waiters who were working inside came out to ask us if we needed anything; or, rather, to ask Lydia if she needed anything. Lydia would just laugh, look slyly at Mr. Gorloth who looked somehow weak and rubbery sitting beside her, and say, "No, I've got everything I need right here." And she'd look at Mr. Gorloth again with her green eyes that could have probably contained the entire ocean. She also talked to us, asking "How do you like camp? Are you first-timers or have you been going here before? What's your favorite part?" and then she asked us about baseball and everybody started talking to her at once; and although she looked at everybody like she looked at Mr. Gorloth (whose hand she was holding), I could see that she wasn't really interested in anybody except Mr. Gorloth…and me.

Yeah, I know that sounds really crazy, but as beautiful and smart and slippery shiny as she was, I wasn't enjoying any of this. In fact, I felt sick, like when you wake up from a really scary dream only to discover that the dream isn't over, even though you're awake. Or think you're awake.

Lydia kept looking at me. Oh, she was looking moon-eyed at Mr. Gorloth and at all the other guys; but when she looked at me, I could hear her like she was talking inside my head; and her voice wasn't like the one she used when she was talking out loud. The voice I heard was echoey like wind blasting into a cavern or something, and it sounded like some huge animal roaring like when it jumped on its prey. Even though this probably doesn't make much sense, I don't know a better way to describe how I heard her inside me head. So it went sort of like this:

Keith, who was acting as dumb as everyone else, asked her if she'd played baseball; and she told him she knew everything about the game and was as good on offense as defense; and then he asked her if she was a decent pitcher. Mr. Gorloth gave Keith a really nasty look and told him not to be impertinent. "Well," Lydia said, "I'm okay. I suppose I can pitch as good as Sandy Koufax in a pinch."

Everybody laughed at that, but even though she wasn't looking at me, I knew that she was *looking* at me...and talking to me.

"Who do you think 'guides' the best pitchers? Do you think Marichal, Koufax, or Gibson could have won all those games without me talking inside their heads like I'm talking to you? I helped them see around corners, just like I'm helping you right now."

But I didn't want to be helped. And I didn't want to see what I was seeing...what nobody else at the table or outside or inside the cafeteria could see. First of all, I could see that almost everyone sitting around us weren't human. The gang was, and so was Mr. Gorloth; but I could see someone—or, rather, something—that looked like a blob of green jello with a human head. It was covered with purple tentacled suckers and sitting at a table right next to us with a woman dressed like she was Jacquie Kennedy. She was talking to it like there was nothing wrong while it had one of its tentacles stuffed right down her throat and was making gulping noises like it was drinking her blood or something. And there was someone else that had a fanged beak instead of a mouth, and someone else with giant wings flapping like that's what he had to do to keep his balance on the bench he was sitting on. And there were mutants all over the place. I knew they were mutants because of the stories Mr. Gorloth told about them. But I also knew that if these were part of Satchel's Gang of Fifty, there weren't the good guys. Just looking at them made me even more queasy and scared me even more than the things with wings and tentacles.

I knew I had to be dreaming because it felt like there was a fog shifting and swimming in my head, but I knew I was awake. That was the worst part of it all. And Lydia was still cooing at Mr. Gorloth and chatting with the gang at our table. And still talking to me…

"And I'm a better pitcher than Marichal, Koufax, and Gibson put together. After all, you should know by now that women will dominate this future time scheme. But they won't be able to prevent us from opening the way. They won't be able to stop my Danny here." She used a long, polished fingernail to scrape a tentacle out of his ear. I was sure it was the tentacle I had seen before. And then she popped it into her mouth like it was a candy snake. She smiled at Mr. Gorloth and said (to me), *"You saw me put it into his ear, remember? Oh, sorry, you saw my little tentacle, but you didn't see* me. *You weren't ready to see me…or I wasn't ready for you to see me. But now I am. Would you like a tentacle?. It will clear everything up. You'll see."* She giggled, and everyone at the table laughed, too, although they didn't hear a word she said to me.

"If you and Danny are going to help me open the way, you'll need all the help you can get," she continued.

I could hear her even though I had stuck my fingers into my ears, and I could feel something wriggling inside my head, and I should tell you now while I can that Lydia didn't look like what everybody saw.

I could see her now, really see her. She wasn't a human, a mutant, or an alien monster. She or he or them or all other combinations of genders fail when used to describe a true god, this god: the three hundred-thousand-year-old Deep One, *Pth'thya-L'yt.* So I guess I was in love with Lydia, the Deep One, because all I wanted to do was close my eyes, or gouge them out.

Then I heard Mr. Gorloth say to Lydia or me or the gang, "You cannot tell in this season. Anything can happen"; and as we all got back on the bus, I wondered what baseball could have to do with the end of the world.

BASEBALL AND MEMORY AND LOVE AND MAYBE THE END OF THE WORLD AND, OF COURSE, AH, FAIR LYDIA

SO THERE ARE actually two stories I could tell you. One is about what happened during our three weeks of baseball training at Camp Hat-i-Notha, how I came down with Strep and had a fever and was probably hallucinating before Mr. Gorloth and Lydia took me to the infirmary, where I met Mary Goldstein and told her (after we swore never to tell any of the secrets we shared) that I was in love with Lydia.

"How can you be in love with somebody you only met one time?" Mary asked. She sneaked over to the boy's side of the infirmary every five minutes it seemed, and she had blond hair and a red face because her skin was peeling from sunburn. I just thought of her as a boy with long hair. Even though she had breasts, she was nothing like Lydia.

"Well…?" asked Mary, who was very persistent about everything; and, believe it or not, she was a better catcher than Davy Brown. (He's the rich kid.) Hell, for that matter, she was probably a better catcher than me!

"Well, what?" I asked.

"How can you be in love with somebody you don't even know. I'll bet you don't even know her last name."

Mary was right. I didn't. But that didn't make any difference.

What did make a difference was that I just couldn't stop thinking about Lydia. I thought about her almost every second, even after I got out of the infirmary. Hell, I was thinking about her when I explained to my parents over the phone that I was just fine, and they didn't have to drive up to the camp to take me home. I told them I was playing some of the best ball I'd ever played, not that that would make any difference to them. My mother thinks sports are a waste of time, and Dad didn't care about any sport except football. But since he was a a lawyer and a judge and had to get elected every once in a while, he would take me to all the local Triplets games because it was good for business or something like that.

Anyway, since I seem to be writing this from two perspectives—the 'me' who's here right now and the other me who lives in the future of this particular time scheme—I'll tell you that I married Mary back in 1983, that she became an appellate court judge, was and is way smarter than me, and we haven't gotten a divorce yet (although we separated twice)!

Meanwhile, Mr. Gorloth coached our team every day and spent some time with us in our dormitory, but he was reluctant to tell us any more stories about Satchel and his gang of mutants, especially if Lydia was around...and she was around almost all the time. She claimed that she really, really wanted to hear the stories, too; but Mr. Gorloth would say that his heart wasn't in it, and then they'd both say good-night and leave us to tell our own stories about them having sex in the woods behind the baseball diamond. But mostly we'd talk about baseball after lights-out, and I'd dream about what Lydia would look like naked.

ISLANDS OF TIME

I SHOULD TELL you that I didn't talk about the crazy stuff I saw when we were at The Red Apple Rest because the guys would probably tell Mr. Gorloth who would call my parents to take me back home; and I would probably end up seeing a psychiatrist or be packed away to Rockland State Hospital, which was where my Uncle Harry went to after his last breakdown. Of course, all my Red Apple Rest symptoms could be attributed to my strep throat, so I probably wouldn't have to go to the nuthouse for that.

So to bell the cat, or whatever the hell my mother would say to finish up a story, not much happened at camp after I got over the strep. Mr. Gorloth mooned around with Lydia, who was counselor to a bunch of her own girls, and we played baseball every day and groused about how Lydia had shut the Mouth of Gorloth; and what went unsaid was that we'd lost respect for Mr. Gorloth and finally got sick of Lydia...even I was sick of it all. (I think that was just about the time I started seeing Mary as a girl with breasts.)

And then camp was over, and we had to pack and attend the last sing-along, and on a rainy Friday morning, we all piled into the bus along with Lydia, who wore a pink sun dress and wasn't speaking to Mr. Gorloth. They'd had a fight, and she told us all right there on the bus and in front of Mr. Gorloth that it was over and we'd better make sure that we don't become lying bastards like our coach. She didn't even say goodbye to him—or to us, for that matter—when we stopped again at The Red Apple Rest.

We never found out what Mr. Gorloth lied about. In fact, once he dropped us all off at our respective homes with our suitcases and knapsacks, we never heard hide nor hair of him again. It was like he just disappeared in a puff of smoke or something; and since Lydia didn't live near us, we never heard anything more from her either. We never found out what happened to Satchel and his band of mutants, just like we never found out what happened to Mr. Gorloth.

A PERFECT SUMMER FOR BASEBALL, TENTACLES, MUTANTS, AND LOVE

Truth to tell, as I try to remember the long hot summers of my childhood, I can't really be sure if I even went to Camp Hat-i-Notha that year.

MORE BASEBALL AND MEMORY AND LOVE AND MAYBE THE END OF THE WORLD AND, OF COURSE, AH, FAIR LYDIA

THE OTHER STORY, *this* other story, is what really happened, whom it happened to, and who made it happen. The one I just told you was about baseball and a superficial accounting of adolescent infatuation and the initial iteration of true love. This story is about baseball, loss, grief, circumvolution, and the difficulties of distinguishing Satchel and his band of heroic mutants from the inescapable exaggerations of myth and legend.

So, just like I told you in the other story, I got strep, went to the infirmary, met Mary (ah, poor Mary, she didn't survive what happened before Lydia opened the way), was released from the infirmary, and convinced my parents to let me stay on at the camp. But it wasn't because of a high fever that I was seeing monsters and mutants and hearing Lydia's voice inside my head...it was because the monsters and mutants and the voice inside my head were real. And although I could see Lydia in her true form as Pth'thya-L'yt, although I could now see the tentacles that extended and fell from her face and body like long maggots shaken loose from dead flesh, I couldn't help myself: I was still in love with her.

Her voice spoke to me all the time, echoed around my brain, explained life, death, and the universe, taught me to throw a fast ball no one on the team could see, much less hit; and as she whispered to me in echoey gutturals, as she manipulated time and even space for me, as she pointed out which mutants and humans I was to kill when the time came, and as she allowed me to 'see' the breathtaking beauty and ecstasy that opening the way would bring, so did I begin to understand that Lydia was truly a major god, and Mr. Gorloth and I were only the smallest little players in the destruction of earth and the universe and the restoration of Lydia's monstrous alien deities known as the Old Ones.

But I, Daniel 'Chip' Clayton Carpenter, Jr., had been chosen by a god to help open the gates of hell!

I guess it was like I was hypnotized or something because I didn't think much about what I was seeing, especially all the aliens and monsters that were arriving and starting to take up a lot of space in the camp. I was in love with Lydia, tentacles and all; and I loved listening to her voice and obeying her capricious commands (such as strangling Mary in the woods behind the girls' dormitory). Pretty soon, we'd kill everybody; and then we'd be killed. It was all foretold and determined, according to Lydia, which meant it was right.

Yeah, I was hypnotized, all right, as I supposed Mr. Gorloth was, too; and one bright, Saturday morning before we played our first inning of the day, Mr. Gorloth pulled me aside for a 'man-to-man' talk.

Only it wasn't Mr. Gorloth.

It was Gooney, one of Satchel's wrinkled-faced, shapeshifting mutants who was impersonating Mr. Gorloth; and once we were behind the makeshift dugout and out of sight, he shapeshifted into his natural self and slapped me hard in the face. Only I didn't feel a thing. I just... woke up. Lydia wasn't inside my head. And I suddenly started crying like a baby because now I could remember the terrible things I had done under her influence. But then Gooney stuck me again, and I guess he could do the hypnosis thing, too, because I became as calm as the cloudless blue sky above.

"We don't have time for regrets," he said, "Not in this *fakakta* time scheme," and then he explained that Mr. Gorloth really was Satchel and that Lydia had killed him dead because she could see that he was playing her just as she was playing him; and what everybody thought was Mr. Gorloth was simply a bunch of Lydia's snakes moving around inside his corpse and Lydia was sort of like a ventriloquist who could make him talk even when she wasn't with him. I thought it was strange that he didn't smell bad—I just figured that a corpse was supposed to smell bad—but I didn't interrupt Gooney about it. Although Gooney had tried his best, he couldn't save Mr. Gorloth. He did, however, manage to 'wake up' most of the other mutants who were under Lydia's influence; and he did it "under the wire" as he called it, so that Lydia still doesn't realize what he did. Well, that explained why I thought that the mutants were monsters when I saw them at The Red Apple Rest: they were the ones who had already fallen under Lydia's influence.

So to cut to the chase, which is something my father would sometimes say, Gooney told me that preparations were being made among all the mutants universe-wide and all the enemies of the gods—Lydia, fair Pth'thya-L'yt, was just one of many, many malevolent gods and deities and aliens wishing to eliminate this universe and all its timelines. "And your job is to monitor Pth'thya-L'yt."

That was pretty heavy stuff to lay on a kid who wasn't even born when Mickey Owen had dropped that third strike, which led to a humiliating loss. It was as if tentacles and a smiling face had suddenly appeared in front of Ralph Branca before the second pitch in the 1951, shaking him into throwing that curve that Thomson hit to short left field but not short enough.

"Me?" I asked. "Why me? You've got professional mutants to do jobs like that. I'm just a kid."

Gooney grinned: seeing a mutant grin can be a disconcerting experience. "No, they have to be passive entities. Under the wire, like I said because she'd catch them out, just as she caught out your Mr. Gorloth." A soft, wistfulness seemed to radiate from him like the sun was setting or something, and he said, "Your Mr. Gorloth, and our Satchel." But his mood changed in an instant. He grinned again, as if that hideous mutant grin was pasted onto his wide, squashed face and said, "Ah, Pth'thya-L'yt really seems to enjoy her Lydia identity, and she likes you. I mean she really likes you, Chip."

(I liked it that he called me Chip.)

"You see, even though you know who and what she is, even though her true octopoidal aspect sickens you right into your guts, you're still in love with Lydia, and your infatuation is her delight. And her Achilles' heel."

"Her what?"

"Never mind." Gooney said, then asked, "Well, will you do it? When you learn that she and her minions are about to open the way, you let us know; and that will be the signal for us to act."

"How would I let you know?"

"We'll be around."

"But what can you do against gods?" I asked.

"Not much," he said sadly. "But we've got some game. We've got some ideas. We've got some plans. We've..."

I could tell that closing the way or whatever the hell they planned to do was pretty hopeless. But I said okay, anyway; and I also said, "Camp is almost over, though. She'll be going back to where she lives. Near The Red Apple Rest."

"She lives everywhere," Gooney said, tapping his bald, wrinkled head, "and she'll remain inside your head. She'll defile you, she'll ruin you. Are you still willing to..."

Another sentence he didn't finish.

I nodded, already feeling like I had soiled myself or something. But just thinking about Lydia, the Lydia without the tentacles, made me feel warm and itchy in my privates again.

"So what do we do in the meantime?" I asked.

"We just keep playing baseball, that's what we do. You don't think the Dodgers team is made up of humans, do you?"

THE LAST SUMMER OF LOVE
NEXT TIME IS ALL TIME:

THE DODGERS HAD it easy that summer, all the way through to the World Series which they had every right to win but they ran into Don Larsen and fate in the fifth game and in the seventh Don Newcome ran into the Yankees, got yanked in the sixth inning, left early and beat up a parking attendant who expressed a low opinion in a low way and in between, in the sixth game, winning 1-0 had proven something Jackie Robinson said to the reporters in the locker room after the seventh game:

"If you only score one run in three games, mathematically, you have to lose two."

Losing that Series was not the end of the world, but Lydia—oh, fair Lydia in all her dark splendor, Lydia from whom love devours—was now whispering something to me that might just involve the end of the world.

AFTERWORD TO "A PERFECT SUMMER FOR BASEBALL, TENTACLES, MUTANTS, AND LOVE"

AND THEN THERE is that odd and rare story that is an absolute joy to write.

"A Perfect Summer For Baseball, Tentacles, Mutants, and Love" fits that particular bill. First of all, it was a collaboration with a dear friend, which meant I wouldn't be facing down the blank screen of my laptop alone. Except in rare—and unfortunately short—instances, the joy of writing, of creating, is a subsequent emotion, one that washes over me *after* a period of good work is finished. The actual business of sitting with the pen or laptop and trying to make the vagueries of dream and intent real is ninety-nine percent difficult, time-consuming, frustrating, solitary work. The muse can indeed be generous, but such generosity is usually short-term and the hapless writer is then left alone to complete the arduous task of turning what is essentially a Rube Goldberg structure into a cohesive, structured, realistic, believable, compelling story. However, when one is *collaborating* on a story, the miscreant (and crafty) collaborator can shift the blame, work, and ideation onto the other party.

For instance: "Here's a paragraph to get us started, Barry. What do you think?"

And miraculously via email a rough-draft story opening appears complete with plot, dialogue, and characterization. All I have to do is 'edit', which, however, may involve adding, interpolating another five thousand words or so.

Of course that's not *writing*. Not really.

That's just editing...or so I tell myself.

THE HANGING

I CAN'T WORK or read on the Melbourne to Los Angeles run. It's the quintessential red-eye special; seventeen hours sitting in cattle class; knees pressed practically to your chin; bad, recirculated air; execrable food; two movies and assorted short features; and jetlagged flight attendants. It's like being a child once again, staring out into the darkness, praying for sleep's oblivion and daylight and freedom.

The cabin was dim, the window a black oval reflecting my face. Beside me a young couple read and whispered and slept. And below, all those thousands of feet below, the jet-black sea waited patiently to receive us all. I'm afraid of height, and deep water, and the dark; but this flight is outside of time, outside of the reality of waking up and going to work and going to sleep. It's somehow oddly relaxing. No one can reach you here, at least not without difficulty; and I've only once ever had the urge to slide my credit card into the skyphone reception slot. Business class would certainly be easier than flying on the cheap. But if you're self employed, you fly cattle class. If you're on a writer's income, even cattle class is a financial strain.

Although I would go to New York City and make the obligatory pilgrimage to my editors' offices, this wasn't a business trip. I had nothing to sell. I should be in Melbourne writing my novel, which was already past deadline. Instead, I was going back to my home town.

Back to grieve with an old friend.

MARTY DEIGHTON.

He had started a very successful construction company in Merrick, Long Island, and then, when he thought he had everything dicked, as he used to say, he discovered that his company was being used as a Mafia front. He testified, and then disappeared. The Witness Protection Program gave him a new life and identity. In Seattle. Two years later, hollow-eyed and underweight, as if he was just coming off a long binge, he drove up to my door and said he was through with the bullshit and would I help him settle down in Johnson City.

"What's wrong with Seattle?" I asked. "I hear it's a lovely town, and safe, everyone knows CPR and it's warm." We talked in his car, a '67 Gold Impala Caprice convertible that he called a classic, but had rusted through from the inside and would cost a fortune to salvage. Ever since college, we had always talked in cars. It was private, and there was something about being on the road at night, chain-smoking cigarettes, discussing problems we wouldn't tell anyone else, seeing the world as flat shadows, and talking about the old times, always the old times. Then we'd stop in a bar, never at home, for after being private we always felt the need to be around people, perhaps to affirm that life was indeed still going-on, even if we were fucking it up royally.

"There's nothing wrong with Seattle," Marty said, "except if I stay there I have to be Michael Kissler, and I fucking hate being Michael Kissler. I'm sick of working for somebody else, sick of living in a suckhole apartment, sick of pretending I'm somebody else. I'm sick of Seattle. It rains all the time."

"It rains all the time here," I said, but Marty didn't seem to hear me.

"I still don't know my way around there, it would never be home."

We'd been driving down Route Seventeen, past luminous strip malls, endless fast food emporiums, and downmarket chain restaurants such as *Ponderosa*, *Yesterdays*, and *Stew's Chicken House*. Beyond the highway glitz were hazy constellations of streets and avenues arrayed upon the hills. Binghamton and Endicott and Vestal and Johnson City had a population of almost 100,000 people; this was "The Valley of Opportunity," home of IBM and Singer-Link. Finally the lights were mercifully behind us, the world once again flat black shadows as we approached Appalachian, which had become a hick suburb of Binghamton; then we drove west to Owego, into deer and beer country. It was a hot summer night, and we rode with the top down and the radio tuned to WKOP, the AM classic rock channel. "Isn't it dangerous for you to come back east?" I asked.

Marty laughed. "It was all a fucking masquerade: changing my name, moving, the FBI, all of it. Christ, it's all forgotten. I don't even think the wiseguys remember any of it. They wouldn't give three shits about me now, anyway. I was small potatoes...the whole fucking operation was small potatoes. It was a rinky-dink operation from the getgo, nobody important got hurt, the Feds got to look great in the newspapers, and everybody but me made money."

"But why Johnson City, for Chrissakes?" I asked. "There's nothing here but farmers and tract housing."

"You're here. And country suits me fine. Even if it has all turned into a giant fucking mall." He grinned. He'd been visiting me here in upstate New York since we were kids in private school. My folks had even considered adopting him.

"And how you gonna eat?"

"I got enough to start small, do some contracting. Hell, there's enough industry here to keep me going. And money to be made..."

"So what can I do to help?"

"Say you don't mind me moving into your town."

"I don't mind…"

"You'll hardly know I'm here," Marty said, and he was right. We saw each other over the next few years. Marty got married and moved to Greene, New York, a lovely one-horse town that was idyllic and rustic and too far out for tourists to find, yet was only twenty miles north of Binghamton on Route 7. His business never quite seemed to get off the ground, but Cynthia, who had been one of twelve Barbizon-trained beauticians working for *Hair Unlimited* when Marty met her, became a country judge. I suppose stranger things have happened; and you don't need a law degree to become a justice of the peace and hand out traffic fines.

But you couldn't take that away from Cynthia; she was smart.

Two kids later she found someone else. A country doctor with three children of his own.

Then she talked Marty into letting her new husband adopt the children.

That was ten years ago.

ALTHOUGH I DON'T read on the plane, I always take books I'm *supposed* to be reading for research. I brought the requisite number of heavy hardback research books as an act of masochism, but I also brought Marty's book. He didn't write it—the author was one Hannah Hamilton—but he'd certainly lived it. Any writer will tell you it's definitely not the same thing; nevertheless this was Marty's book. He had inscribed it to me as if it was his own: "To John, my best friend in life." On the face of it, the inscription was silly. To "my best friend" would have been fine. But to "my best friend in life?" Perhaps he thought we would be best friends in some film-noire version of a Homeric afterlife.

I was being snide, perhaps out of embarrassment.

Marty didn't believe in God or organized religion. He was a poet, and I was his best friend in life, just as surely as that awkward, poignant line of his was dragging me back home.

THE LAST TIME I was in the States, Marty waited patiently as I autographed books for a small crowd of fans in a local bookstore.

As always, he seemed happy for me, for my success. I had left the country without telling him. I hadn't had a chance to explain what had happened to Helen and me, what had gone wrong with two people he'd known for half a lifetime, how against all the odds I had met someone at a conference in San Francisco not two months after my divorce, was immediately smitten, and found myself living in Australia three months later.

I had turned gray, but Marty's shock of red hair was now white; it was thick, in marked contrast to mine, and fell to his shoulders. He now wore a full, closely trimmed beard, and his eyebrows, which had always been white, still looked as if they had been pasted onto his ruddy face. He wore jeans and a striped workshirt; I wore a suit: the image of the writer as businessman.

We both had new lives now.

After most of my friends and acquaintances and old teachers and friends of my parents had left, Marty and I had a few minutes together.

That's when he gave me his book.

"It's all here," he said, "what I've been looking for all these years."

I turned the pages. The book was about an orphanage in Canada that sold babies. According to the cover copy, the story was about to be made into a television movie of the week. Marty had been one of

Windhaven's lucky charges who was adopted by a wealthy family. When he was twelve, he found his adopted mother blue and bloated in her car in the garage with the engine still running. His adopted father died of cancer eight months later. Marty was willed to his dad's best friend, who immediately put him in a military school. The Manlius Military Academy. "Manners Maketh Man." I met him there and roomed with him and then we went to university together. Marty had always been obsessed with finding his parents. He still spent his vacations in Canada because he was certain that's where he'd find his parents.

"So you were definitely in this orphanage?" I asked.

"Yeah, they have me in the records."

"And your parents?"

Marty shrugged. "We don't know yet, but there's a chance…"

I nodded.

"I have one of the caskets."

A few friends were lingering at the door, trying to get my attention; we were all supposed to go out for a late snack. "What?" I asked.

"It's all in there." He tapped the book I held, then tapped my hand, a small gesture of love. "The orphanage used old wooden milk boxes as caskets for the dead babies. The babies they couldn't sell, they killed."

"Could've been you."

"Yeah."

I asked Marty to come out to dinner, but as expected, he made excuses. I gave him one of the cards I had run off on my laser printer. "It's got the phone numbers, and all the country codes. Just dial all the numbers and you'll get through. No problem." We hugged each other, and I told him how bad I felt that time was so tight and that we wouldn't be able to get together. Next time. Call me.

I knew he wouldn't call.

I was wrong.

ISLANDS OF TIME

MARTY PICKED ME up at the Edward A. Link Broome County Airport and took me to my mother's home in Johnson City. I didn't feel the effects of being jetlagged; the exhaustion and sleepless anxiety would come later. Right now I was wired, and nostalgic; and it seemed for all the world that I had never left Binghamton, that my Mother hadn't died three years ago, that I was sixteen and not fifty and still lived at 87 Union Street in this big white empty stucco house with the green door.

I kept the house. Somehow, I couldn't bear to sell it.

We sat in the living room on Mother's purple velvet couch, staring at the artificial fireplace on the opposite wall. The rotor made a chink-achinkachink noise as it spun around a red electric light bulb behind the grate, simulating flames. "How long have we got?" I asked.

Marty looked at his watch. "A couple of hours, it doesn't start until two."

"We cut it pretty close," I said. If I'd've known it was today and not tomorrow, I probably wouldn't have come." As soon as I said that, I regretted it. "Ah, I would have come anyway."

"Yeah." Then silence, ticking, dark silence even though it was late morning and sunny. A sunny day in Binghamton was a rarity, especially in winter. But the streets were clear. There hadn't been a blizzard for two weeks, just ordinary snow.

"You wanna get to the church early?"

"No, I want to get there when we're supposed to," Marty said.

I nodded and waited for Marty to talk, but he couldn't. What the hell did I expect?

His eldest son had just hanged himself.

So we stared at the fake fireplace and listened to the rotor make its noise while old ghosts flickered through the rooms of the old house. I was waiting for my mother to look into the living room and ask us if we wanted coffee, I was waiting for the phone to ring. Helen would surely want me for something. She always did. But Helen was living in Philadelphia, our son was married and working for a lumber company in New Hampshire, and Mother's remains were in the family plot on Riverside Drive.

I wondered where would I be buried. Here or in Melbourne?

"You gonna sell this place?" Marty asked. He wore an open shirt and a wide-lapeled, single-breasted suit. He had trimmed his beard, but his white hair was still long. He looked awkward, uncomfortable, even here in this house that we both thought of as home.

"In this market? With Link and GE gone, and IBM threatening to leave? Johnson City is already a ghost town, every other house is on the market. So what would I get? Forty thousand? Maybe fifty on a good day? It's worth at least a hundred."

Marty nodded. "Would you ever sell it?"

"No," I said, although I had meant to say *yes.*

Of course I was going to sell it. Eventually.

I HAD ONLY met Marty's son Stephen once, and that was just after the divorce. He was only five years old and had Cynthia's baby fat and Marty's red hair and freckled complexion. He crawled all over me like a cat trying to find a comfortable position on a sofa. That's all I remember. But I could easily imagine him as a young teenager. I had only to remember Marty at that age. It's odd what came to mind, for I could see Marty in my mind's eye as he was at fifteen. His face was thin and heavily freckled, and he had a pop-eyed, innocent expression that endeared him to adults. Although nothing had ever seemed to surprise Marty in those years, he always looked surprised. His hair was styled in a flat-top, which was just a variation of a buzz-cut; his collar was open and his tie loosened; and his dress-blue uniform blouse was too tight around his shoulders, a reminder that he had been in that school too long. It was Saturday morning at Manlius, and we were preparing for a full white-glove inspection. As if I were peering through a telescope that blacked out everything but one tiny circle, I could see his desk and small table, each neatly covered with a decorative towel. Marty had been determined to make that small, austere room we shared his home.

I tried to imagine him hanging from a rafter in an old barn.

I glanced at his face in profile, but could no longer see the boy in there.

WE WERE DRIVING to the church. As we passed my old house, an 1860's vintage Greek Revival that fronted Route 7, neither one of us spoke or even looked at it. We had both been trying to ignore the recent past, as if only our mutual past of private school and university could be safely exposed. So we talked about the old times, about Manlius, always Manlius, and Hofstra; the stoned out nights in East Meadow and Hempstead, Long Island; and the college bars: *Zoli's* and *Doctor's* and *The Reef*, all the places we closed without scoring; and now, once again, counting down the women, always beginning with the toothless girl in the skating rink in the Skyland Amusement Park and always including Mrs. Fritch, our landlady, who would not allow any women in our attic apartment...except for her granddaughters.

About five miles outside of Greene, Marty broke down. He didn't cry, he just talked quietly, trying to work it out for himself. "To think that I allowed Stephen and Marty Junior to be adopted out, it's so fucking stupid, absolutely fucking stupid, but I felt at the time, I felt it was the best thing for them, Christ, my business was down the tubes. Nothing seemed to fucking work." He smiled, then nodded. "Only time it worked, I got busted, remember?"

I nodded, although he really wasn't speaking to me; and the question was rhetorical. The road had become slushy, and the hills and houses and fields were covered with soft snow, the kind of snow that shapes and rounds, that connects houses and yards and trees and power lines with its floury filigree, molding the heavy, dead, leaf-brown world below into a cloudscape of the cleanest white.

"Cynthia's old man seemed all right," Marty continued. "Actually, he is all right. It was Cynthia's doing, Sam wouldn't have the neck to go against her. Anyway, Cynthia made what seemed at the time like a good case for adoption. Sam really wanted the kids, he could put them through college properly, give them all the shit I couldn't. And she was right. He did. It just never fucking ever in a million years occurred to me that she wouldn't allow me to see them."

I knew the story, although neither one of us had ever figured out why Cynthia had cut Marty off from the kids. Who knows, perhaps there was something Marty wasn't telling me…would never tell me. I had always sympathized with Marty, but stayed out of it. I hadn't talked to Cynthia since their divorce. "What about Marty Junior?" I asked, figuring it was better for Marty to talk. We'd be there in a few minutes anyway. Perhaps that's why he was talking, to let me in before we went in.

Marty shrugged. "He and Stephen called me once last year. On Marty Junior's birthday. I haven't heard anything since…until this. And I only found that out from the newspaper."

When Marty had called me in Melbourne, he said that Stephen had been cremated. Now I asked him if he knew why.

Marty's knuckles were white; he held onto the steering wheel as if it was the safety bar of a roller coaster car. "Don't know. Cynthia probably wanted to have it over with before I knew what was happening. Who the fuck knows what she thought, or thinks."

"She must have realized you'd be at the service," I said. "Same thing."

"No. She made the decision. It's over now, done. She wouldn't even give me that much, to let me...ah, fuck it, it's over."

We drove into Greene, passing a few stores, a bank, two churches, a clinic, and a dozen clapboard houses with tar paper roofs and open porches. Cynthia's church was on the far side of town. It was an old, imposing stone building. Marty parked in the lot, and we watched people in their Sunday best going into a side entrance. I was about to open the car door when Marty said, "I read up on hangings. How maybe he could have strangled instead of breaking his neck, how he would've gotten a—" Marty just stopped then and shook his head, as if he could shake away whatever terrible image had come before his mind's eye. It had stopped snowing, but gusty winds turned the air white with the dry, powdery snow that blew around the buildings and pavement like sand. Marty laughed and said, "You know, I don't know how many times I read the piece in the paper, but I can't remember what it said now for the life of me." Then he pulled his keys from the ignition and followed the others into the church.

I caught up with him, and he just nodded, as if acknowledging that he had forgotten about me. We passed the rec rooms and the minister's office. His door was open, and I recognized Cynthia standing with a man who must have been Sam. Marty Junior wasn't with them. Cynthia's hair was streaked with gray, and she had gone to fat. I remembered her as earthy, smelling of cigarettes and a particularly sweet perfume. Marty paused, but when Cynthia did not acknowledge him, he just walked on. I nodded to Cynthia, then followed Marty up the stairs.

Without signing the register, we took our seats in the last pew.

The organist played something dissonant and funereal; Cynthia and Sam walked down the center aisle and ignored us as they passed; and the minister followed, looking down at the carpet. He was a tall, lanky man in his middle fifties; his gray suit was wrinkled and shiny, his hair was combed over to one side to hide his bald spot; but his voice was deep and resonant and rich. He paced back and forth before the congregants, and he would pause often, as if testing and tasting every word. He wasn't nervous, just uncertain.

I found myself holding Marty's hand.

But I was afraid to look at him.

I watched the minister. Whenever he paused to consider his next sentence and take a breath, the room would become too quiet. Every cough, rustle, and sneeze was an embarrassing explosion; and there were the sweet-sour human smells, the heat that was turned up too high, the motes of dust dancing in the gray light, the distant familiarity of it all. I heard only bits and pieces of his eulogy, how difficult it was to contemplate the death of a child, how it shakes the foundations of the entire community, then break, stop, silence, and he was eulogizing the family, Cynthia, Sam, Marty Junior, what could have caused a boy to end his life, what terrible grief and pain and frustration we'll never know, but not the fault of his loving family; and time stretched and contracted, every sound and movement and thought a ticking, and Marty beside me, his hand cold and gently pressing mine, and we breathed in and out and in and out until we had to stand up and sing and sit down for more words, for closure; and it was all mundane, minute to minute. Although people were crying and sniffing and whispering all around us, Marty just sat stiffly beside me; and finally it was over and we watched the minister lead Cynthia and Sam out of the church. Cynthia was crying, but she walked on her own, as if trying to escape her husband's attempts to support her.

Everyone filed out of the church and onto the street.

I sat with Marty in the empty church. After a few minutes, I asked, "Are you ready?"

"Yeah, let's get out of here."

We headed directly for the car, but the minister caught us just outside the church and introduced himself. "Thank you both for coming, are you friends of the family? Forgive me for asking, but Stephen had so many friends, he was such a lovely boy, and I still haven't met half of Sam's and Cynthia's family, even after all these years." He smiled and looked hopeful.

"I'm…I was Stephen's father," Marty said.

"I'm so sorry. Cynthia never mentioned…I—"

He stepped back, nodding, as if he now understood everything; and we walked past him like two thieves leaving the scene of our crime. The temperature had dropped, and the sky was as white as the snow-covered hills in the distance. A sharp, gusting wind numbed our faces, even as we walked the few steps to the car. I had forgotten how claustrophobic I used to feel when I lived in Johnson City. The sky was too close. A great, gray weight. As we drove out of the driveway behind a line of very slow cars, we passed Cynthia. She was alone, waiting, shivering. She looked at Marty as we passed, as if she needed his attention, as if she had something to tell him; but he looked straight ahead.

A long moment, as if we were once again in the church.

And then we were on the road, picking up speed, then stopping for the only red light on Main Street, which became Route 7. Driving through the swirling, powdery snow. Time and event and memory merged into the whiteness of snow and atmosphere. Houses and farms and small factories grew large and then were swallowed behind us. We were still in the church. We were still in my Mother's house. We were still twenty years old and driving fast down the Long Island Expressway, our hair long, not yet gray.

We would party now for we would surely be dead by thirty-five.

Surely…

THE HANGING

I SAW MY editors in New York, stayed at my old hotel, The Algonquin, which had been restored to its former glory, but was no longer a home away from home and certainly no longer a writer's hotel. It now specialized in package tours. Most of the guests were Brazilians, and the bellmen were unhappy that the old crowd had stopped coming. I commiserated with them and did business over drinks and tea in the Victorian style lobby with its small tables and waiters in livery. I saw dear old friends, talked about the old times, and then I was in a Cadillac limousine driving to JFK, and then I was in LAX Airport waiting at another ticket counter while a young man in a buzz-cut stared into a computer and told me that all the exit row seats had already been pledged, and walking along slidewalks, and drinking stale coffee, and waiting in the huge lounge to board a white and gray jumbo jet at 10:00 PM, watching my soon-to-be fellow passengers, who looked exhausted before the trip had even begun, all the same tick-ticking dream, bits and pieces contracting and expanding, all slipping smoothly, quickly into memory, bits and pieces, flashes, and…

Familiar darkness and the reassuring pressure of the safety belt and the same old safety video ticking away on all the screens, safety and sleep and the hours ticking, dreams, chewing over old memories, and I wondered why Cynthia and Sam hadn't brought Marty Junior to the church, and I remembered that Marty had said he'd heard from him on his birthday. The stewardess asked me if I'd like a drink as we flew over the black Pacific; the oval portholes were dark mirrors reflecting the world inside the cabin. I can't remember when it occurred to me to call Marty. I'd never used the skyphone. It would have to be an important deal at $8.00 a minute, or however much it was. Nevertheless I slid my credit card down the slot in the seat in front of me and called Marty.

I asked him if he wanted to live in the house, in Mother's house. Hell, it was empty and furnished and beat the hell out of where he was living now.

He said he'd think about it.

Later, I dreamed that Marty and I were in church for a High Episcopalian service. We were wearing our dress blues. Pete Pfeiffer was sitting behind us, a chaw of tobacco in his mouth. He would get through the entire hour without spitting. He just swallowed the sweet acid from that prune plug. And Fat Kayata was sitting beside him. The rest of A Company was a blur, but I knew that everyone was there. It was a cool, brilliantly bright Sunday. I held Marty's hand. He just stared straight ahead, listening to the sermon with that pop-eyed, surprised look of his.

The look he would have had just before he hanged himself.

I asked him why he was going to hang himself, but woke up sweaty and cotton-mouthed in the air-conditioned darkness before he could answer.

AFTERWORD TO "THE HANGING"

AS YOU HAVE probably surmised, this story cuts close to the bone; and as I reread it now in a city that is some ten thousand miles away from my home town, it has the resonance and tincture of a just remembered dream.

Way back in 1994, when I was living in Johnson City, New York, I wrote a short autobiography for *Contemporary Authors.* The following excerpt partly explains my motivation for setting this story there:

"Although I've spent quite a bit of time away from this area, it has always been my home; and I returned for the kinds of emotional layering and correspondences that I find only here. It is as if there is a corresponding map of Johnson City and Binghamton in my mind, only this map is one of space and time—a grid, so to speak. I remember this same building where I now have my office as it was when I was a child—the building hasn't changed, but as I have, I see it differently now. And yet I have that visceral sensation that the other 'me's' caught in those beads of time that I perceive as the past, are still here. And I remember, or rather see, the world as I saw it then. In a way, it's like living in an excavation, and one's life becomes an archaeological dig.

"In the course of a day, I pass by old buildings where I used to live and places where I used to play. I see ghosts everywhere as I pass back and forth through the years, and many of those ghosts are myself. I remember walking up and down Main Street with Gardner Dozois, one of my closest friends, and experience once again that sensation of compacted experience, of being alive in an open-ended way: the time of the twenties when, as Harlan Ellison might say, we live at the top of our lungs...

"I feel a strong sympathy for the way Andrew Wyeth painted Kuerner's farm in Pennsylvania for twenty years, going back to the same place over and over again, and always finding the new in the old, a world in microcosm. That is somewhat the way I feel about the whole Binghamton area, and upstate New York in general. Ray Lafferty once wrote that certain parts of the country, the old lands, have ghosts, the layering of generations. (He wrote this as fiction, of course, and as memory isn't strong on this, I may be garbling what he wrote.)

"For me, this land has its ghosts and layerings."

And I must admit that even after all these years, those ghosts and distant lands still inhabit my dreams and memory.

UNDER THE SHADOW OF JONAH

A sadder monster, or more cruel plague so fell,
Or vengeance of the gods, ne'er came from Styx or hell
—Robert Burton

AND SO did the rich merchants, guildsmen, landowners, money-lenders, ambassadors, courtesans, the archbishop and his retinue, well-to-do churchmen of the variant faiths, courtiers, the priors of the Chancery, and the ruling families flee the shadowed palaces, villas, and cathedrals of the greatest city in the world. Not that it would do any of them any good, for the many-eyed monster that blocked out God's own sun in His sky above could see them all—would find them all—at least according to the hellfire preaching of Father Savonarola.

The monk stood on the perron steps of the great Cathedral of Saint Maria del Fiore and told the kneeling crowds of penitents that there would soon be dying and great hunger, flames and sacking and a scourging of the pious and profane alike, that the churches would be ruined and the priests dispersed, that two thousand devils were to be unleashed from the great object darkening the sky over the city, that this dark, hovering imminence was the Devil's own form, and the sparkling iridescences that flickered in the poisoned sky were indeed his manifold eyes.

Just as the Lord God was omniscient, so could His enemy direct igneous rays of unholy, poisonous light to see into our darkened souls. Pico Della Mirandola, physician to Lorenzo the Magnificent and the greatest philosopher since Democritus, had already predicted that the igneous rays of demons could cause earthquakes and burn all flesh and material with cold melancholic vapor.

And so in the manure stinking streets and alleys around the Via De Servi, did buildings began to shake and collapse and burn with a cold fire.

LUCIAN HELIOGABALUS SAT atop the high banks of the newly built canal that connected the mighty Arno River with the sea and watched the high-masted ships being pulled toward the light of day by a seemingly endless procession of horses and mules straining against the leather webbing of their towlines. The ships were all sailing away from the burning city. Although it was midday, the sky above was dark, covered with Savonarola's cloud of devils; yet far away and in all directions, the sun was unbearably bright and poured its golden rays upon distant fortunate lands. Only Florence and its green hills seemed to be under interdiction, but that was probably illusion. Although Florence was a large, encompassing country, the light of day, which appeared to be a hot, narrow, circular band, was many stadia away.

Lucian looked up into the darkness, looked up at the creature—or was it some great ship or edifice of angels?—and tried to make out the textures of its surface. He took notes, scribbling in his own shorthand Cyrillic, and made sketches in the margins. The flickering, coruscating lights reminded him of fireflies, yet the dark massive thing was shadowed, wrinkled and pocked like skin. Perhaps Savonarola was right;

perhaps it was the devil, a cloud...a mass of devils, Satan's own shape. He preached that the many was in the one, that one thing different was another thing the same. The priest was, of course, crazy.

Or perhaps not.

The truth would be known soon, for even as Lucian gazed upwards and sketched, the floating beast continued to descend; in just hours it would touch the earth, scorch it, perhaps destroy it; and Lucian, this Greek Jew who had been accused of murder, simony, and usury in his native land, who had taught the children of Florentine burghers, craftsmen, and the lower clergy the exquisite delights of natural science, mathematics, and the three categories of philosophy, would take notes until the end of the world.

He had been considered no better than a slave in Venice, Naples, and Genoa; but in Florence he was respected as a Bookman and able to earn enough to survive. Hadn't Lorenzo the Magnificent praised him in a speech to the Signoria and referred to him as a revenant Socrates? But Lorenzo had fled the city, leaving it to Savonarola and his followers. The great and faithful Leonardo da Vinci accompanied Lorenzo, while his dear friend and fellow artist Sandro Botticelli remained with the priest and was no doubt praying for miracles right now. Leonardo, however, would not be praying; like Lucian, he would be watching the sky, wondering, reasoning, taking notes, sketching.

What else could a scientific man do when confronted with devils and miracles?

Church bells rang, and Lucian could also hear a distant moaning: the citizens of Florence praying, screaming, begging for forgiveness. Or perhaps it was just the earth groaning in self-pity. The object above was now almost touching the great copper cupola of the Cathedral of Saint Maria del Fiore. Lucian's eyes squinted as he tried to make out more details. Indeed, it looked like some foul, live thing come to crush everything beneath it; it seemed to be covered with some sort of mottled flesh, rather than a capping of bronze or wood or iron; and a smell of sulfur permeated the air, drying the mucous of his nose and throat and burning his eyes. He coughed and wheezed and could not resist the urge to run. But there would be no place to run. All he could do was slide down the steep embankment and pray that would give him some protective distance from whatever was descending upon the earth.

As he moved to the embankment's edge and looked for the safest way down, the thing above extruded huge shoots. These roots, if that is what they could be called, were the size of tree boles, and their glittering striated surfaces looked suspiciously like bark. Bole after bole shot downwards, each one hitting the earth with a hollow, drum like sound; and then, a moment later, the boles lifted their bottom edges from the earth.

Lucian pushed himself over the crest of the embankment, slid over rocks and roots that tore his clothes and his skin, and landed right beside a bole that seemed to hover like a live, percipient thing beside the fast-moving water flowing through the canal. It was as if the bole had known Lucian's path of escape and had positioned itself accordingly. Reflexively, he looked for his satchel and notebooks, as if the feel of leather and paper could somehow remove his fear and panic. His breathing was ragged, his heart beating fast; blood pounded in his throat, yet he was fascinated. He looked this way and that, and saw what could only be described as an inverted forest, the huge trunk-like extrusions above and around him; they seemed to cover the world, but, of course, his field of vision was very limited. He reached out and touched the bole beside him. It felt warm, satiny. He shivered, revolted.

No, not satiny...slippery, slimy.

The sky above was the creature; the suffusing light was alien; it came from the boles and from above, a grayish, blue-tinged twilight, which was somehow satisfying to Lucian, for it mirrored the time of day when the world turned blue for a few moments before dark; and Lucian was sure that this thing would indeed bring some endless night. Nevertheless, he was a man of learning and perhaps there was some wisdom to be learned from all this before the world ended in fire and ash and suffocation. In fact, he wondered if the boles could be burned like trees. He stepped under the extruded bole, bowing his head, for he was taller than the average Florentine man. He smelled something metallic, the familiar tingling odor that always occurred before storms; and, yes, there was also a slight sulfurous smell. Not quite sulfur, but neither was it the good smell of God's incense. It was also cold under the bole, and dark, pitch dark...and it was only the sudden vertiginous sensation in his stomach and a subtle change in the density of the air around him that hinted at ascension.

Lucian was rising.

He could feel a chill on his face, could feel the subtle and quick motion, yet his feet were heavy, as if his boots were still standing on the loamy earth beside the flowing water of the canal. Only now the water was flowing upwards...and it wasn't water anymore. It was air, and he was rising through the tenebrous black air of the pit, of unholy places.

He tried to move, to shift his balance, but he was caught, as the proverbial fly in amber. And then he was not.

WHEN LUCIAN CAME to rest in the body of the beast, he looked around him; but it was as if he was blind. He could see blackness and a few gauzy red and green retinal afterimages, which he considered to be visions that couldn't quite be made out. He shouted, but his words were swallowed in the thick cold darkness. There were no echoes in this place, or in this being. Careful not to fall, he took a step, and then another. It was like walking on ice. He wondered if there was endless empty space around him, or whether he was imprisoned in a small room, or some sort of horrid, stone-cold intestine. He stood still, listening, trying to peer out of his blindness; then he carefully kneeled and sat down. He felt the surface of the floor, which was smooth and cold, slippery to the touch—perhaps it *was* ice or wet glass—and he could feel soft vibration.

Suddenly he felt dizzy, as if he was tumbling, sliding across the floor; and he could not tell which direction was up, or which was down; and as he was about to scream in sheer terror—as if fear had finally found him, revealed itself to him—he discovered that he could make out faint objects, lines of perspective. It was as if he were looking at a etching, only the silverpoint was silvery darkness superposed over a deeper darkness. But there was depth created by the lines and edges, and although Lucian could have no knowledge of photography, he grasped that he was staring into negative spaces. He could make out a geography on a grand scale: hills and rivers, ravines and mountains, paddocks, but nothing that breathed, no living thing as he knew it, just an impossible country that rose and fell as far as his eyes could gaze, a country of black and silver. Could these shapes be the outlines of the organs of an impossible creature? Could they be some dark reflection, some dark twin of his own world below? As if to get a better perspective on this dark domain, he stood up. He called out again into the massing darkness, and he was answered, but not with words, not with breath, but with pure intelligence.

Then the hard, cold surface he was standing on suddenly gave way, parting like wounded flesh, and he fell backward. He flailed his arms and screamed, for surely he was falling to his death…into his own dark epiphany.

His screams now echoed through the vast body of the beast, magnified into what Lucian could only believe to be the music of the spheres, the synesthetic sounds and shapes of pure mathematics itself. As he fell, or as he imagined he was falling, he felt something being taken from him. Something that resided in his mind and heart, something that connected his flesh and blood and organs with the ectoplasmic *pneuma* that was the living stuff of his spirit, something pure and vital had been siphoned out of him.

And now he lay on the ground, the real ground comprised of dirt and stone and rotting branch, beside the rushing, gurgling, whistling water of the canal. Now he looked up into the bole above, but the world entire had shifted.

The bole was still there, but it was merely an outline, a shadow. Similarly, the beast above was now nothing but a faint outline of itself, bleached and rendered faint by the warm sun.

As Lucian stared up into the now transparent belly of the beast, he *knew* it was somehow alive and intelligent. He could not yet speak to it, could not yet see into it, but he was part of it, every bit an extension of its own foul pneuma as the bole floating above him. Fearful that his blasphemous thoughts could release the bole from the beast to crush him, Lucian rolled away from it and climbed up the bank of the canal to where he had been sitting and writing earlier. The sun warmed his face, but he felt cold. He looked at the disappearing constructions of beast and bole superimposed on what was now a beautiful June afternoon and tried to think his way back into the creature.

Tried to imagine what he had lost in the silvery darkness above.

The beast, however, was closed to him. He could still barely make out the sparkling iridescences in its ghostly superstructure above. They were its eyes, watching him; and Lucian now had a strong desire to be in the city, to be among people, to talk and to touch. He mistrusted those feelings, but could not repress them.

He desperately needed time to think, to consider.

But he felt a cold, numbing darkness welling in him like joy.

THE BEAST WAS now all but invisible.

As Lucian walked through hilly meadows and grassy fields, past copses of pine and chestnut and the shimmering leaves of olive trees, he felt like he was walking out of a bad dream and into the literal, all-encompassing light of day. The Tuscan light was soft and scented as a courtesan's perfume. He gazed out over the red tiles of a farmstead roof, looking for the beast that had swallowed and expelled him; but, try as he might, he couldn't see it. The world had been cleansed. Yet he felt hollowed out, and cold, even with the sun warm on his face; and as he walked, he noticed that he did not perspire.

He could hear bells ringing as if it was matins and compline combined; all of Florence's churches and cathedrals reaching into the clear, blue sky, rejoicing. Lucian continued along the dirt road, rutted by ox carts and pack trains. It was as if he were being drawn to the city for some contrary purpose he could not comprehend.

THREE PEASANT CUTPURSES, their bare arms calloused and dirt-encrusted, stood on the stone path, blocking Lucian's way. They were all shorter than he was, but all were stocky and well-muscled; Lucian was tall, a long drink of water, as his blessed mother used to call him; but he was skinny, frail as the stereotypically poor, peripatetic scholar.

The oldest peasant, a man in his forties, his head and face shaved clean as an egg, stood behind while the two younger men came toward Lucian, one to his right, the other to his left. The cutpurse to his right had greasy, sandy hair; the one to his left was overweight and as bald as the older man, who was probably his father.

Cutting around the boy on his right, Lucian made a dash toward a winding line of mulberry trees. Beyond were dense woods. Lucian had an unerring sense of direction and would easily find his way out; but the overweight cut-purse was deceptively fast and caught Lucian, pinning his arms, pulling him up short, squeezing the life out of his lungs. Then, as if burned or scalded, the boy suddenly let go and stumbled backward. He let out a soft cry, more a sigh; and Lucian turned toward him, breathing deeply, inhaling the cutpurse's *pneuma*, inhaling his spirit, his life. He stared at the boy and tasted blood, but he knew immediately that he wasn't tasting blood, but the subtle vapors of the boy's soul. He felt the shock of inverted sight, of seeing into the boy's dark, silvery thoughts and humours. He could also taste the cold black bile that poisoned the boy's organs and spirit; yet Lucian was nourished by it...by all of it. He felt full, as if after eating a heavy, unhealthy meal, and strong, and connected to the invisible, negative presence above. He also felt cold.

Then he reached out to the cutpurse with the greasy, sandy hair, who was kneeling beside his brother.

"Poppa, Piero is dead."

But Piero wasn't dead. Lucian could see him as a dark shape superimposed on the silvery darkness that seconds ago was sun-drenched grass beside the stone trail.

Lucian was seeing with the eyes of the beast now.

He tasted blood and vapor again, as he breathed in the soul of Piero's brother. Then he turned to the boys' father, and, full to bursting, inhaled his spirit.

Thus did Lucian discover exactly what he had lost to the imminence above.

UNDER THE SHADOW OF JONAH

PICO DELLA MIRANDOLA, the young theurgist and philosopher to the court of the Medici, traveled back to Florence from Lorenzo the Magnificent's villa in Careggi alone. Since the mad priest Savonarola now had control of the city and the hearts and minds of its citizens, it would be too dangerous for Lorenzo and his advisors to return. So they sent Pico back to the anathematized, excommunicated city as a spy, for he claimed he could see things other men could not. Niccolo Machiavelli had offered to accompany him, but Mirandola told him the city was poisoned and that the humours in which Machiavelli's soul dwelled were too cold to give him protection.

"But you can protect me," Machiavelli said, as they stood on the great purple-colored perron steps of the villa.

"No, Niccolo, I cannot."

"And your humours, they are not cold?"

"They are as hot as your temper, Niccolo."

"How do you know that *you* will be protected?"

Mirandola glanced knowingly at his patron, Lorenzo, and said, "I had a dream, an intuition last night. I dreamed that the Black Reaper was walking the streets of Florence again. I also dreamed of his companion, the hag Lachesis, who is thought to follow after him, weaving her tapestry of death. Only in this dream the hag had taken the dark, celestial form of the cloud that lingered over the city, and her black thread extended from the cloud that was her form to the Black Reaper like an umbilicus."

"Then it *is* plague," Machiavelli said, secretly making the sign of the cross.

"Of a sort. But I know this Reaper."

"As we all do."

"No, Mirandola said, I know him. He's a true acquaintance of mine..."

ISLANDS OF TIME

ONCE IN FLORENCE, Pico Della Mirandola—the only magician who had ever unlocked the secrets of the Jews' Cabbala, sorted and catalogued the myriad of supraterrestrial beings, and discovered the single great secret of demons—searched the streets for the Reaper.

It was a pellucid afternoon. The sky was pale and cloudless, and the edges of villas, churches, ramshackle houses, streets, courtyards, and piazzas were soft, as if slightly out of focus. Mirandola could smell dampness and the acrid odor of ash, ozone, sulfur, and smoke; and, indeed, as he walked down claustrophobically narrow streets darkened and cooled by arches and overhanging walls, he could discern those who had been touched by the Reaper. He had learned to see the pneumatic soul-stuff that flowed around all men; he could read the ordinarily invisible networks of rays emitted from the celestial stars and from every bit of matter, living or not, that comprised the city and its surrounds.

He passed through the artisan's quarters, past the stalls of blacksmiths and furriers and vegetable vendors. Soulless wraiths crossed his path: peasants, vendors, merchants, cutpurses, beggars, and those from great families. They looked like ordinary men, women, and children, but they were hollow, emptied, and silent. They had the aspect of shadows and nightshades, dark, inferior forms silhouetted against the white-hot radiations that flowed between the higher beings and the world. But what of those who still had their hearts and souls? They talked and shouted, bargained and bought and sold; were intent, as always, on commerce, comfort, time, and habit; and were oblivious to the wraiths searching for something they could not know they had lost.

But the theurgist was beginning to understand what was happening: He could see through the air around and above him, could see that it was choked with the usual multiform spirits; with archangels and angels radiating their characteristic soft, ocher light; beneficent demons always eager to interact with men, their tenuous pneumatic bodies so dim as to be practically invisible; and he could also see the dusting of malevolent demons who are invisible and utilize cold passion to cause violent and permanent destruction.

He could also sense (rather than see) the bloated spirit or creature made of eyes that still floated in the heavens above the city...the creature that had become invisible to other men after it extruded a forest of tentacular boles that hung only meters from the earth and were now also invisible. The monster did not fit into any of the celestial categories, nor could it belong to those sublunary demons who feast and fast in the cleansing fire found only above the highest regions of air.

No, this demon, if it could be called that, must be a stranger to God's perfectly wrought cosmos, an invader, an enemy of everything that Christ had built in the world and the heavens above.

MIRANDOLA WAS NOW in the goldsmiths' and jewelers' district. The smells of smoke and burning were overwhelming. He passed Andrea Verrochio's scorched and gutted three-story workshop in the Via dell'Agnolo. It was here that he found the tiles and walls of the closely-built houses and bottegas splattered with molten gold. Exploded shards of glass and crystal were strewn about in the twisted, broken alleyways. And something else: transfigured gems that would have once been smooth and faceted now lay in thin sheets, broken mirrors of sapphire and amethyst and beryl impossibly reflecting the poisonous wan light of the cobblestone streets. Ahead, along the route leading to the great cathedral of Santa Maria del Fiore, was desolation: burned out buildings, collapsed arcades, ash floating like mist in the air. Fire still played in the empty streets, fire that had wrecked and burned, but it was no ordinary fire. This fire was cold...the fire glimpsed only in gemstones such as sapphire and amethyst and beryl...gemstones of affinity...gemstones that could mirror the soul and attract celestial presences.

Mirandola picked up a shard—for that was what it was—of sapphire from the cobbled alleyway. It was thin as parchment and light as frost on a pane of glass. But its affinities were not with the cold and dark humours; the blood purple wafer attracted heat and light as a furnace drew air. He looked upon its dark, mirrored surface and let his mind rest while his eyes projected the invisible white-hot light of igneous rays onto the wafer. He called upon Saturn's angel Oriphiel, who was his intermediary, to help him locate the Black Reaper. But concentrate as he might, Mirandola could not feel the familiar hot presence of the angel. Still, he continued to gaze into the wafer, conjuring images, phantasms of the imagination that correlated to the sensory world.

But the only image that reoccurred in the purple depths of the gem was that of the nearby cathedral of Santa Maria del Fiore.

Perhaps Mirandola's angel *was* present, for he could hear the faint yet bombastic voice of the priest Savonarola calling.

LIKE IRON FILINGS being pulled and ordered by a great magnet, all of Florence was being drawn to the wounded cathedral. Its sweet sounding bells had flowed like water, as had the great, bronze palla that topped its dome. Its stained glass windows had dissolved into crystal tears; and the very stones of the cathedral, the foundation that contained all of God's prayers, had melted into grotesque new shapes.

Lucian, too, was being drawn to the cathedral because the cold, jittering intelligence—the poisonous soul, the phantasm that had replaced his own soul—needed to devour and consume this swirling soul mass of cold energy.

Cold drawn to cold, Lucian thought, aware of the irony that warm flesh and hearts pumping warm blood could have such affinity with cold humours...and with the beast watching and feeding above. Lucian, for his part, was aware and yet trapped by his irresistible compulsion to feed on others, to taste the silky bitterness of their souls and their sad, poignant memories, to feel the twinkling brightness of their intelligence and the heated, coarser stuff of their emotions. He needed ever more souls to fill the aching void of his own loss; he needed to be satiated with souls, and satiated as he would be, he would then be emptied, evacuated by the many-eyed creature above. The cold, alien intelligence that commanded him had not and would not speak to him; it remained as a subtle but painful presence that informed his every movement and desire. It dampened his emotions and cleansed any untoward, independent thoughts that might be dangerous to its existence and unrelenting need. And Lucian, who was replete with souls one moment, would be empty and benumbed the next. Would remember and grieve for the loss of his own mirrored soul.

The Lord giveth, and the Lord taketh away.

But absolution and surfeit were once again at hand.

LUCIAN STRODE INTO the crowd. Extending his arms, he brushed against beggars and guildsmen; passed liveried retainers and processions of brigand riders that represented the great competing families: the Neroni, Pandolfini, Acciaiuoli, Alberti, and Rucellai. He pushed past priests, priors, nuns, and the hated Dominican *inquisitore* who were also known as Companions of the Night. The brigands were outfitted in armor and livery of red velvet and gold; and their horses were clad in the same cloth as their riders. The clergy wore black robes, and, indeed, appeared to be manifestations of death themselves; but as Lucian feathered past them, he stole and inhaled their tepid souls, tasted their yearnings, frustrations, petty grudges, and small, whimpering lusts. The souls of the *inquisitore* were devoured in like fashion, as were those of merchants, guildsmen, prostitutes, beggars, children, and brigand riders. The children's souls were incandescent, as if made of the same stuff as the cold fire that had devoured brick, stone, and mortar; and as Lucian tasted each small, bright soul—like a supplicant standing before the altar and accepting the body of Christ as a wafer—he felt brighter, colder, less hollow and more complete. He didn't even need to touch the riders high on their armor studded horses; he merely needed to imagine them being captured by the vapors and radiations that poured out of him.

In moments, he was glutted with them. His weakening heart, which had once translated vital information from his senses into messages only his soul could understand, pumped and fibrillated to bear the invasions of these captured spirits. But no amount of rich, pure blood could fill the hollow where his soul had once rested. His mortal body would not cope for long with these transfusions and infusions of foreign souls and spirits.

Full to bursting, he walked toward the cathedral. But now he was the magnet; the cathedral mere destination. He could hear bells, but there were no bells ringing at Santa Maria del Fiore. He was hearing the thoughts of the many-eyed beast, hearing its exultation. Lucian looked up into the slippery dark mouth of one of the many tentacular boles that hung over Florence...the inverted forest of the many eyed beast. The extruded boles were invisible to all but him. He imagined that he was staring into a conduit created out of darkness itself; and he was suddenly, traumatically emptied.

As a multitude of souls made their ascension through the invisible bole, Lucian was left once again empty and exhausted. Finished.

And so he would remain until he could find enough strength to press forward.

His mortal heart made a hurried descent from his throat to its rightful place in his chest…and as his heart slowed, so did his intoxicating hunger quicken.

He heard music, but it wasn't the chromatic music of the spheres vibrating his senses; it was the antiphonal voice of the priest Savonarola. The voice was as dark and cold as the priest's soul, a soul that was colder than any of the souls Lucian had stolen; and the intelligence above wanted to feel the texture of its thickening chill.

It *wanted* the crystalline jewel that was Savonarola's soul.

PICO DELLA MIRANDOLA held the shard of sapphire tightly as he hurried to the cathedral. The stone absorbed some of his body heat, as if tasting it; then it returned the damp energy as hot humours that kindled him, focused him…and would make him as dangerous as the quarry he was seeking. The stone was a living presence, purple as the darkest, coldest, and most melancholy of humours, yet hot as a stoking iron. Although it would not *physically* damage his fleshy palm and long, feminine fingers, he knew that he would not be able to able to draw or press the strings of his lyre for a long, long time. The jewel wafer—along with Mirandola's incantations, prayers, and the ingestion of a purifying herb—had indeed lured the mediating angel, temporarily trapped it within in the stone.

Mirandola closed his fist even tighter over the gem.

The angel whispered its council to him. It penetrated his deepest thoughts, luxuriated in his fears and yearnings and secrets; but didn't manifest itself as an occultation in the network of invisible rays that vibrated and oscillated around him.

He had tricked the angel and forced it into submission.

Now he would have to trust it.

The angel directed Mirandola through the huge crowd that had gathered around the black-outlined steps of the cathedral to hear the celebrated friar Savonarola, who stood with his back to the great carved doors, which were wide open; inside, in the magnificent, shadowed confines of the cathedral, the wealthy families and high clergy stood cheek to jowl, separated from the rabble and the castigating friar. Savonarola had a powerful, yet intimate voice, and he could be heard across the piazza, or so Mirandola assumed...perhaps the angel was whispering Savonarola's words into Mirandola's ear, perhaps the theurgist was too far away to hear clearly the words of the black robed, asthenic-looking prophet.

"People of Florence, you have been granted a reprieve from the darkness of the many-eyed beast that wished to swallow you. Christ has vanquished your enemy, and all he asks in return is your fidelity. He is your champion, but he has a just grievance against you. He has worn himself out calling out to you. He has made his voice hoarse, for all day long he cries through the mouths of his prophets, yet no one hears. Well, those who turn back to their avarice and usury..."

Mirandola could clearly see the boles that had descended from the sky; they appeared like striated, crystal columns floating over the piazza. The boles had also penetrated the great dome of the cathedral to hang unseen over altars, naves, and chancels. Mirandola could also see pneumatic mist rising through one of the boles: souls that the Black Reaper had stolen; and there, with the help of his intermediary, the trapped angel Oriphiel, he could see the icy pneumatic thread that connected his old acquaintance Lucian Heliogabalus with the many-eyed beast that had invaded the heavens above Florence.

Mirandola made his way through the crowd to the Reaper, who was standing still and exhausted under a crystalline bole; and when Lucian raised his arm, greedy to touch him, Mirandola pressed the sapphire wafer into his open palm.

LUCIAN SHIVERED, AS if the gem pressed into his palm was burning hot… or burning cold. He stepped back and uttered a soft mournful cry. Then, slowly and painfully, like an old man trying to spread arthritic fingers, he opened his hand and let the stone drop.

Mirandola caught it before it could shatter on the cobbles of the piazza.

"What do you want?" Lucian asked, but his eyes weren't focused on Mirandola. He extended his arms and inhaled deeply. He inhaled the frost-frigid souls of the penitents standing near him, gained temporary strength and succor, and for a split-second, he filled the empty cavity where his own soul once resided.

"Lucian, look at me," Mirandola said, as he watched a wisp of smoke or dusty light curl into the soul stealer's eyes. He could see this transiting soul as plainly as he could see angels. The theurgist tried once again to touch his friend with the gemstone wafer, but Lucian stepped quickly out of reach. Before he could disappear into the crowd, Mirandola said, "Wait, you must hear me, or you will remain cold and empty."

"I am far from empty," Lucian said.

"But you will be soon, won't you. The thing above will empty you like a draught."

"Pico, you can't help them"—meaning the soulless crowd around him—"or me." Lucian stared hard at Mirandola, as if he had suddenly found sight and memory and perhaps humanity. "No one can."

"*You* can," Mirandola said, extending his hand to Lucian. "Take the stone."

"I can't, Pico, nor can I stand here without breathing in those around me...including you."

"Don't concern yourself with me. Just take the stone."

Lucian shook his head. "It burns me."

"I can *see* the thread that binds you. The sapphire will disconnect you from the beast...at least for a moment."

"And what will that gain me?"

"Clarity."

Lucian accepted the gem. As he held it, he grimaced in pain and breathed heavily. Choking. "It is so very hot."

"Just a bit warmer than your own frigid humours...and that of the beast. That's the gem's affinity."

Lucian nodded. He looked at those around him, those who were now like him, bereft of their souls. Again he choked. "I can't exhale their souls," he told Mirandola. "I can't—"

"Tell me what you know of the beast.

"Nothing, except that it is cold and empty, and has a plan."

"Tell me of its plan," Mirandola asked.

Lucian looked at his friend with hollow eyes, then shook his head. "I can sense its intelligence, hear its music of pure mathematics, feel its hunger...my hunger now." His face looked like stretched parchment, as if all warmth and moisture had been leached away from him. Tasting the word, he whispered it again.

"Hunger..."

Lucian reached out to Mirandola, who stepped back.

"Get away from me while you can," Lucian said, his face contorted in pain.

"Try to concentrate on the jewel in your hand, Lucian. Tell me more about the beast."

"It is a world like ours, only dark and empty. Our shadow." Lucian laughed and said, "But soon the beast will be full, and we will be the shadow." Suddenly flushed with strength, overwhelmed and washed clean with cold darkness, Lucian crushed the sapphire wafer in his hand, crushed it to powder; and feeling what could only be described as God's power flowing like cold black bile through the aetheric umbilicus that connected him to the beast, he flung himself at Mirandola.

Crushing him in viselike arms.

Shuddering as he inhaled Mirandola's white-hot soul.

Feeling the quake and convulsion of Mirandola's hummingbird heart.

INHALING MIRANDOLA'S SOUL was like breathing fire. Lucian coughed, vomited, tried to exhale it; but it caught in his throat, in his lungs, liver, and spleen. It burned him, seared him. Lucian cried for the beast to take his friend's soul. He stood under one of the beast's myriad crystalline boles and felt a momentary shadowed coolness, but the burden would not be lifted.

Mirandola's soul burned so very hot and painfully inside the Reaper.

There was but one way to quench the fire: Reach the priest and inhale his cold essence. The many-eyed beast above would not help him. On the contrary, it would let him burn until it got what it wanted: Savonarola.

Lucian made his way across the crowded piazza toward the priest. He inhaled every soul around him, but they were tepid; not nearly cold enough to absorb the heat of his friend's soul. The closer he got to Savonarola, the hotter the soul fire in his chest. It was exhausting him, taking him down. He wanted to pray to the One God, but that in itself would be blasphemy.

"*Pico, for the love of God, leave me,*" he pleaded. "*Tell me how can I expel you…?*"

And in that last instant—as he rushed up the black-edged perron steps of the Cathedral of Saint Maria del Fiore and embraced the priest Savonarola, the priest who was the coldest of currents, whose soul was ice and snow and silvery darkness, whose spirit was so like the silvery negation of the beast above—Lucian realized that he had inhaled much more than the white-hot spirit of Mirandola.

In that last instant—when the Reaper embraced the angry, excommunicated priest who tried to step away from him...when the Reaper finally inhaled Savonarola's ice-shard of a soul—Mirandola's angel exploded inside him.

Oriphiel...

MIRANDOLA, WHO WAS across the piazza, felt the impact.

He staggered backwards, just as he had when Lucian had ripped his soul away from him. Once again he felt bereft, felt the aching, empty-hollow pain, as if his own pounding, flesh-bloody heart was being pulled right out of his chest cavity.

Once again he screamed, screamed for his angel.

Oriphiel...

And in that ratcheting telescoped instant, he realized that he had never actually seen his intermediary. He had only felt it as a white-hot presence, heard it as the soft voice of reason and loneliness, the voice that had spoken to him from inside his head when he was a child.

Oriphiel...

The voice that spoke to him now, spoke to him from the proximity of his chest, where his restored soul once again resided.

WHEN LUCIAN CRUSHED the turquoise wafer, the angel Oriphiel was released...and when Lucian inhaled Mirandola's hot coal of a soul, Oriphiel insinuated itself into Lucian's cloudy *pneuma* and soul-poisoned flesh. The angel had no *need* to reside in crystal; it could reside in itself, in any matter, or any flesh.

And in that last instant of Lucian's bookish and perhaps noble life, when he inhaled Savonarola's icy soul like a beast ravenous for oxygen, his already weakened heart exploded.

No mortal could long withstand the reaction of Savonarola's icy spirit with the searing fires of Oriphiel and the still-burning soul of Mirandola.

As Lucian fell dying to his knees, cracking his bones, Saturn's angel Oriphiel carried the displaced souls from the dying bookman to the theurgist Mirandola on the other side of the piazza.

MIRANDOLA: *ORIPHIEL...*

Yes? answered the angel.

What have you done?

Returned your soul. Animarum venator.

What?

Was it not you who discovered the divine secret of demons and higher beings?

To hunt souls.

No, young theurgist, you forget yourself...it is to place souls into earthly bodies. And so I did.

Oriphiel, I am so cold...and hot. I am burning and freezing. With what have you infected me?

With the souls that your friend contained.

And my friend, is he—?

He is dead, as you might soon be, theurgist.

You murdered him.

One without a soul cannot be murdered, but, yes, I did. To stop him, to collect the soul of the priest, and to save you.

Save me?

For a purpose, theurgist. Now you and the cold soul of Savonarola are the lures…and now you must leave this place. Can you not hear the beast? You are being called.

MIRANDOLA COULD INDEED hear the beast, but it was not words that entangled and captured him; it was music and mathematics, elegant equations perfectly balanced, enough harmony, measure, and mathematics to fill a cosmos, to fill all vacuums and all eternities. Mirandola was the lure and the lured…fascinator and fascinated; and he was enraptured by the geometrical music and ratiocination of the beast, by its inductive need, by its calculus of the void, its dark Boolean choruses of emptiness filling emptiness with ever more hungry emptiness: equations of cold agony and filament hot pain.

Cold fire…

The music of the spheres.

The music of the beast.

Mirandola could feel the connection with the beast, could feel the aetheric thread that had once connected his friend Lucian to the many-eyed monster. It knew that Mirandola contained the souls it desired. Mirandola was the angel Oriphiel's cloak and disguise; and if they could fool the monster, perhaps they could foil it. Perhaps the angel could save the myriad of souls Lucian had stolen for the beast. But whatever

Oriphiel did, Mirandola would have to release the souls trapped inside him, or he would certainly die. He could see the ghostly boles hanging above the piazza, a crystalline forest that extended past the cathedral, where a soulless Savonarola gaped at the crowd; and behind the priest, in the cathedral, the scions of Florence were also lost, were also quiet. The world had come to silence.

Paused...

Mirandola stepped under the nearest inverted bole to release the trapped souls and save himself; but Oriphiel carried him upwards, as if he, Mirandola, was as light as his soul, as all the souls he carried combined; and up up up into darkness and chill, up up up into the belly of the beast, into the country of the beast; and the beast, all mathematical need and godforsaken emptiness, was the vacuum sucking theurgist, angel, and souls upward into itself, through its barked membranes, into the silverpoint blackness of its negative spaces...into its country... its world...itself...its soul.

Mirandola: *Oriphiel...*

Do not speak. Give the beast what it wishes.

Mirandola tried to stand upright, but the glassy surface upon which he stood was dangerously slippery. He fell and spun on the fleshy ice, on the innards of the creature that might be beast, country, and world combined. When he came to rest, he tasted bile and smelled sulfur—or was it his own sweat?—and desperately wished to retch, to release the poison inside him, to flood the glacial darkness with fire. But he choked instead. He strained to breathe, but his lungs were stone; and he felt shackled, shackled to the slithery, slightly undulating floor, which was as cold as time itself. As he stared fixedly into the vertiginous depths before him, shapes resolved, as did color and light; and as Oriphiel whispered to him, he could see that the souls the beast had stolen were now germinating this shadowed country, this cold reflecting terrain, this place that was a reflection—or would soon be a reflection—of all that was below. And when this world became bright and visible and alive, the world below, the earth and its local heavens populated by the hypercelestial gods, archangels, angels, demons, principalities, and human disembodied souls would cease, would be emptied.

Now, Oriphiel whispered. *Now. Give the beast its due. Give up your insides to its insides*; and Oriphiel did so command Mirandola's mind and nervous system that the theurgist could do nothing but comply.

He retched ectoplasmic streams of the good father Savonarola, cold riverun streams of Savonarola's ice-caressed soul...Savonarola the pious and unforgiving, the desired familiar of the many-eyed beast.

And as the young theurgist collapsed and died, releasing blood, shit, piss, more captive souls, the angel revealed itself in all its white-hot strength and burning beauty. With a breath, it shattered the cold glass reality of the beast and its intended familiar Savonarola. With a glance, it boiled the silverpoint mountains and burned through the very being of the beast.

The many eyes of the beast darkened, became the dead portals through which the trapped souls of the Florentines escaped. The souls feathered down to earth, seemingly from the eggshell empty sky. They were swept along invisible networks of vibrating and oscillating rays of air and spirit. They swirled earthward and settled like thick fog drifting into morning green valleys, souls searching for the flesh in which they had once inhered.

LUCIAN LAY ON the steps of the cathedral where he had died. His kneecaps broken, his skull cracked and bleeding, he stared upwards into the clear Florentine sky. His eyes—the waiting windows of the soul—had long glazed over; yet even as the bile and humours thickened in his stilled body, as his blood coagulated and flies crawled into his nose and mouth, he could glimpse a pneumatic wisp of soul-stuff settle upon his face like the lightest of autumn leaves. It passed through his eyes, penetrated him, and then snaked back in the aether.

As Lucian gazed mutely into the dissolving atmosphere above, he could see the myriads of angels, spirits, demons, and released souls that inhabited the stellar light and airy regions; and as the eternal darkness descended, his last, splintered thoughts were of his mother and father, his youngest sister who had died as a slave, his friend Mirandola, and the demons whose celestial task was to place souls into earthy bodies and, in turn, free them.

Oriphiel…

AFTERWORD TO "UNDER THE SHADOW OF JONAH"

THE IDEA FOR an alien encounter story using authentic Renaissance magic as practiced by Marsilio Ficino, Giordano Bruno, and Pico Della Mirandola came to me sometime in 2006; and as I couldn't shake this story out of my head by ignoring it, I had no choice but to write it. Over the course of my career I've discovered that ideas can be as persistent as door-to-door salespeople. And once ideas take charge, they determine the how and when and where the story will be written. The writer's role becomes nothing more than mere apparatus.

"Under the Shadow of Jonah" evokes the Renaissance universe of *The Memory Cathedral*, my novel about Leonardo da Vinci, and foreshadows (pardon the pun) many of the ideas that later found their way into my most recent novel *Shadows in the Stone*.

I suppose it could be suggested that writers are thieves and vandals: not only do they steal from other writers...they also steal from themselves with wild abandon.

EDEN

Homage to Damon Knight...

THE OBJECT hit the dam at Guyra just after at 2:43 AM on Monday, December 6th. It was a needle the size of a football field, and it slipped into the water like a coin being dropped edge-first. The spacecraft disappeared; only the three spiney rods of its terraforming unit pierced the surface of the quiet water.

If you put your head to the ground, you could hear a slight humming. It made the thrub-thrubbing sound of a dishwashing machine. And if you looked carefully, and the light was exactly right, you would be able to see the tips of the alien ship's terraforming rods.

The alien machine was working, purring away underwater.

It would only take a few more days to reach critical.

At 5:15 PM on Thursday, December 9th, five divers went into the dam to prove that the object was debris from a satellite.

None of them ever surfaced.

The EPA, EOC, and the army laid down a perimeter around the area before dawn on Friday. No one was allowed into—or out of—Guyra. Although Emergency Operations claimed that there was no danger to the town's 2,000 residents, they were in quarantine. A robot submersible was lowered into the water later that afternoon. It disappeared, as did the boat, which had gotten too close to the alien craft's spiney rods.

By midnight, the weather became suddenly hot and humid, and steam seemed to be boiling over the surface of the water. Rainforest began to grow at an astonishing rate, but the shapes and textures were completely alien to anything ever seen before. Guyra and the area around the dam were developing their own clammy climate, and their own flora and fauna.

The contamination spread.

"Hey, this stuff tastes good," one of the residents told an ABC television news reporter, and he stood there eating what looked for all the world like a green donut. The tree behind him had sprouted them. "It's a freakin' doughnut tree is what it is," he said.

That was the last ABC transmission.

Six hours later, the Prime Minister ordered in the army.

Not a man or woman returned.

The United Nations became involved. Surveillance and fighter planes flew over the area…and disappeared.

Missiles were launched…and disappeared.

The infected area now covered the length and breath of New South Wales.

No man, woman, or child outside of New South Wales area would know the answer…until it was too late.

A COMPOSER AND pianist who had accompanied the first ABC reporter to disappear knew the answer, however.

ISLANDS OF TIME

THE COMPOSER MADE his way to the edge of the water…and was there when the glittering shaft of the alien craft rose from the water and extruded walkways. A huge ten-foot-high cockroach, presumably the captain, walked toward the composer, who, frozen with fear, stood his ground.

"Hallo," said the extraterrestrial cockroach in an enormous, booming voice.

"Hello," said the composer.

"Do you like the changes?" asked the cockroach.

"What are you doing here?" asked the composer.

"Creating a salad."

"What!"

"Yeah, all the greens. Don't you like salad?"

The composer just blinked at the cockroach swaying over him. Then he said, "You came all this way to make a salad?"

"That's right. We're civilized, after all. We *always* have a salad before our main course." And with that, the cockroach pulled a green doughnut from the tree, chewed noisily, and then grabbed the composer.

The cockroach swallowed the composer in one gulp.

Then he belched, and said, "I just *love* bipeds."

AFTERWORD TO "EDEN"

I WAS ASKED to write a story for the ABC in Australia after a meteroite fell into a damn in Guyra, New South Wales in December 1999. I remember asking when the network would need the story.

"We need it *today*."

So much for a generous deadline. But at the time, the ABC didn't know exactly what had happened and had reporters in Guyra reporting live at the scene.[**]

"Can you do it?"

"Of course I can," I said, forgetting that real life deadlines are different from the time-shifting vagueries of fiction.

A few hours later I called the ABC to tell them that I had indeed finished the story and was told, "Great. Can you be ready to read it in an hour?"

Huh?

I had assumed the story would be read by one of their professional narrators.

My unprepared yet canned response: "Of course I can."

"Eden" is a homage to Damon Knight's famous short story "To Serve Man". Damon's story was wryly satirical; mine is about as subtle as an Abbot and Costello routine.

"So, nu?" one alien asks the other. "Who's on first?"

---

* Thus the 'human' in the story is depicted as an ABC reporter.

SPIRIT DOG

MY NEPHEW Edmund McDowell came to live with us on June 6, 1862, which, coincidentally, is the same day his hero General Turner Ashby died in battle. My dear wife Rebecca Cowles McDowell and I will be eternally grateful to the Reverend Doctor A. A. H. Boyd, pastor of the Presbyterian church on Loudoun Street in Winchester, who recognised Edmund when he was found at the site of the second fire at my late brother's farm. It is due in large part to Doctor Boyd's bold efforts that Edmund was reunited with his family. He also tried to help us locate the servant Hanna, of whom Mundy seemed to be so fond. Our efforts, alas, were unsuccessful in that regard. We will always be grateful to this man of the cloth who believed so fervently in a cause diametrically opposed to our own.

But it is with extreme sadness and disappointment that I must report that Edmund left us the summer after he completed this diary. We have exhausted our resources trying to locate our nephew, to no avail—May the Lord God in His mercy protect him.

Edmund left us only the following note inserted in his diary:

"Can't wait any more. Gone back to find the spirit dog."

SPIRIT DOG

—Lieut. Col Randolph Estes McDowell (Ret)
September 29, 1865
Scranton, Pennsylvania

IT WAS AROUND the time I saw the spirit dog and became invisible that I forgot how to talk. I can think the words in my head and write them down on paper (well, you can see that!), but when I open my mouth to try to talk, I just seem to choke. Doctor Keys had a word for it, but I forget what it was. Naming it seemed to make everybody feel better, though. That's more than I've seen most doctors do anyway—except to cut the arms and legs off soldiers. I sure as hell saw a lot of that! I think those goddamn doctors killed more soldiers than all the guns and artillery put together. But I'm getting ahead of myself here. Uncle Randolph says I'm always getting ahead of myself, but I'll tell you the whole story for whatever it's worth.

I could start anywhere, I suppose, but that would take too long, so I'll start right out on March 23rd, 1862. It was a Sunday, cold and miserable and cloudy.

Come to think of it, though, the only real *sunny* day I can remember around then was ten days before General Jackson pulled our army out of Winchester because General Banks had brought his Federals down from Harper's Ferry to invade us. Not even him and Colonel Ashby's "Six Hundred" could've held out against Banks' blue-ass bucktails. Seemed like there was a million of them. And, boy, was there a commotion in Winchester! Poppa took me to town to see General Jackson, although I met him later on my own and wished I didn't. As our army started off toward the Valley Pike, all the girls and old ladies were crying and wailing that they were being left to godless tyrants, and some of the soldiers were even crying, just like their mothers, and then suddenly, the soldiers just starting singing "Yes, in the sweet by and by," and pretty soon everybody was singing it, until they left. Then the town was quiet as death, I can tell you. Well, maybe not *that* quiet, but pretty close to it. Nobody wanted to talk. Everybody just felt like crying, I guess.

But there I go digressin' away from my story...

Anyway, on the Sunday I originally started off talking about, the people in Winchester had damned good reason to be caterwauling and crying because that was what they now call the battle of Kernstown, which you all know about. It was when Jackson came right back up the Pike to fight the Federals who outnumbered him two to one. And it was bad! But I'm going to write about it, no matter how much it hurts me.

Now Poppa used to insist on going to church every Sunday morning. Although he never had a church of his own, he was still a proper minister. Usually Episcopalian. And as we also had the farm and the day school, we made do well enough. We'd usually go to country churches and prayer meetings at people's houses, where Poppa could preach the skin off the snakes, as Mother used to say when he wanted her to do something. But Poppa had friends in Winchester, too, and was invited by Mr. Williams (he was the rector) to preach at the Episcopal Church on Kent Street. Mother was all excited because she loved going into town and seeing everybody, especially Mrs. McSherry, who was her best friend, but I never did like Mrs. McSherry's boys. Not much, anyhow.

Of course, I wasn't going to church with them on account of the ringworm. I had the 'ruption all over my scalp, and it itched like a sonovabitch. My father attributed my malady to hanging around with the nigger kids—he would never say "nigger," even though we had two of our own before they ran away to the Federals. He only allowed us to call them "colored people" or "darkies" or "servants." Like everybody else, I called the old ones aunts and uncles, just like I did my real aunt and uncle, those I knew like family, anyway. I never understood him about that. Christ, the niggers called themselves niggers. So he thought I caught the eruption from the niggers who lived on the next farm—we'd borrow them sometimes to help with the farm work—but I reckon that I got it from David Steward's dog. David was one of Poppa's students, and his half-dead Irish Setter had a terrible case of the mange, but I felt sorry for the damned thing and petted it. David had the ringworm too, so it had to be the dog. Course so did the niggers. Seemed like everyone but Mother and Poppa had it that season.

Mother didn't care how I'd caught it. She'd been doing her best to cure it by rubbing my head with silver nitrate medication that burned like fire and another potion she'd made up by dropping a copper penny into vinegar; and part of my hair fell out because of it, and hasn't grown back even yet. And as a further humiliation, I had to wear a turban around my head "so as not to scratch the worms and infect everybody else."

"I can't go out like this," I said to Poppa when he called me out of my room, expecting me to be all shined up and dressed for church. I was in my night drawers, and I left my turban off. My hair was mussed and greasy and itchy. Poppa was wearing his best black suit and a shiny cravat, and Mother was wearing her Sunday dress and a brooch and a bonnet with a white bow.

He turned to Mother and said, "If you were conspiring with him to stay home on the Lord's Day, you could have at least told me. I would have made provisions. We could have borrowed Eliza from Arthur Allen. She'd look after him while we're gone and make sure he had a decent bible lesson." Poppa shook his head, as if he was telling somebody "No," and said, "At least his darkies didn't run off to the Yankees."

"You *know* why ours left," Mother said sharply. That stopped Poppa pretty cold, and then she looked at me and said, "And how do you suppose we'd look taking Mundy with his head looking all encrustated like that? Mr. McDowell, sometimes I wonder about—" Mother would always get started and then stop just like that. Now *she* was the one looking guilty. She talked low now, as if she was being introduced to someone important. "Mundy will be fine here alone. I've prepared his Bible lessons to study while we're at church. Everything's all laid out on your desk. You might want to approve it, of course. And we can stop at Mr. Allen's farm on the way to church. I'm sure he won't mind sending one of the servants over to look after Mundy." She looked at me and nodded, as if to say "I told you so."

But I knew they wouldn't do any such thing. They always used to threaten me with Eliza. All she ever did though was tell me to read the "Raising of Lazarus" or "Daniel in the Lion's Den" and then she would put on all of Mom's dresses and bonnets and jewellery and twirl around like she was at a ball. But she never did steal anything.

I heard a real good blast of cannonading in the distance; and Mother got the funny look on her face that she always gets when she's concerned and said, "Perhaps we should all stay here with Mundy."

But Poppa said, "It's just the usual annoyance of the enemy," and that was that.

He limped out onto the porch to listen, though. I should have probably told you that Poppa had served in the militia as a chaplain until he got an inflammation in the bone of his leg. He almost died from the blood poisoning and brain fever, and he had to use a cane after that, and sometimes his words would get all mixed up—but never when he was preaching the skin off the snakes.

"It's just skirmishing, like yesterday, and the day before that," he said, sniffing, as if he could smell the noise. He used to do that in the school house back behind the barn, lift up his head and take a sniff, and then he'd take the switch to whoever was passing notes or whispering or not paying proper attention. "But it might just come to something. Your

Colonel Ashby, God bless him, must be biting off General Shields' toes again. And I hear that Jackson's coming north. But that's all gossip. I hear the same thing most every day." He sniffed again, and sure enough the cracking of musket started, then died, and it seemed like it would just be an ordinary Sunday, except I wouldn't have to go to church.

Mother finally came out on the porch and said, "I do fear leaving Mundy alone."

"Well, I gave my solemn promise to Mr. Williams that I'd deliver a sermon, and a man's word is his bond. You can come with me or stay, as you will."

You see, Mother would always turn everything around on Poppa. And there just wasn't any way she was going to stay with me and not go to town, even if she would have to worry about me a little. We were used to the cannonading and the skirmishing. It was, nothing more, I suppose, than having thunderstorms every day. Only that wasn't true. Everybody was fearful, just nobody cared to show it.

I watched my folks go off in their carriage, but I didn't know that I was only going to see them once more in my life. Or that Sunday was going to bring more than thunder.

It was going to bring the dogs right out of hell.

I LISTENED FOR a while to the cannon volleys and musket fire echoing across the hills and waited for them to stop. They always did. But then they'd start right up again like rain falling hard on a tin roof. I knew something more than skirmishing was going to happen—I could *feel* it, and I knew that Mother might talk Poppa into turning the carriage around, so I went out beyond the old corn house that had burned down. I went past the garden and lumber house by the edge of the woods to check the gums, which was what Poppa called our rabbit traps. I don't know why we called them that. I'd asked Poppa about it once, and he just said that's what they're called. We used boxes about two feet long baited with pieces of apple, and they worked better than noose snares, that's for sure. Poppa wasn't much with a rifle and never had time for it, so we ate a lot of rabbit during the winter. I'd catch fifty, maybe more before summer, and that was more than enough to fill out what we had of bacon, sausage, pigs' feet, and ham. It was against the rules to kill rabbits on the Sabbath, but I usually did anyway. I'd leave them hanging in the smoke house because it wasn't fair to leave them in the gums until Monday.

I knew I was fooling myself with all this business of going out to the woods to check the gums. I knew I was going to see about the skirmishing, but I just felt better fooling myself. Maybe I might change my mind and go back to the house and study the bible.

I found only one rabbit; it was in the gum by our stone fence. It was a big one with brown spots; and as I grabbed its hind legs with my left hand, it shook like it was vibrating. I know how to kill rabbits quickly and efficiently, just hit it sharp on the back of the neck and drop it before it dies. Bad luck if it dies in your hands. Aunt Hanna, she was our servant who ran away to be with Uncle Isaac, told me that if an animal dies in your hands, it's bad luck and you'll surely die before your next birthday. So I always dropped them quick.

Anyway I was ready to hack this fat rabbit right behind the ears and drop it next to the gum when something strange came over me, and instead of killing it, I threw it right over the stone fence and let it escape into the woods. To this day I don't know why I did that. It wasn't like I felt sorry for the rabbit. Maybe it was because I knew I was going to break my word to Poppa and go out to watch the skirmishing. Maybe I didn't want to commit two sins right after the other. Angry with myself for being so stupid, I climbed over the fence and left the farm. But, you know, something felt different, not right, as if just then something had changed; and yet I couldn't tell you what.

It wasn't difficult to figure where the fighting was. I just had to follow my ears, which, of course, led me just about to Mr. Joseph Barton's farm. I knew this country pretty well and cut through the woods and over Sandy Ridge. No sense walking big as life through the fields and getting your foolish ass shot off. The woods were empty because the fighting was concentrated pretty much along the Pike, and it was just skirmishing, nothing much more than that from what I could tell. But I couldn't see anything much, not even from the Ridge, which is pretty high and starts to the west of Winchester and runs some six miles down to the Opequon Creek. The Pike's not far and runs along to the side of it.

I guessed that the Yankee guns were firing somewhere around Pritchard's Hill, and that our own were returning fire from Hodge Run or maybe below. If General Jackson and his army were around, they certainly weren't *here*.

Course, soon as I figured that, I heard twigs snapping all over. Then I heard what seemed like a thousand muskets firing all around me, and there seemed to be a whirlwind of balls suddenly flying around and hissing just like snakes. I could almost feel the whomp of a minié ball as it hit a tree trunk to my right. Somebody shouted and I heard the thud of a ball hitting something soft and a noise, such like someone just had his breath knocked out of him. And then I heard a heartbreaking wailing like a mother who'd just lost her son. "Come on, boys," someone shouted in a bluebelly dialect, and more twigs cracked as men ran through the woods.

I stayed close to the ground. It was cold and damp, and I could smell the moss on the birch and, I swear, I could also smell the sour apple sweat of the soldiers even though I couldn't see much of them. I did see several men through the trees, and I thought they might have been our own, but I couldn't tell; they could just as easily have been Yankees. I crouched even harder against that birch tree as if I could squeeze myself right into the bark when the muskets started firing again. It was hard to tell where the balls were coming from. It didn't seem like there could be that many soldiers out here. Most of the Yanks were at least a half-mile away. Then I heard someone stepping through the woods near me calling and crying over and over in the most plaintive voice you ever heard, "Whey is my boys? Whey is my marsters?" And that voice sounded just like Jimmadasin, the McSherry's house servant. You couldn't miss it; he had a voice that was so high and reedy, it sounded just like a woman's. But I always thought he was having it up on all of us because when he sang his voice would suddenly get deep and full. He was responsible for minding Harry and Allan McSherry, who were twelve and fourteen respectively. (I told you about them before; their mother Cornelia was my Mother's best friend.)

Well, the shooting stopped, and someone said, "Get the hell outa here, you crazy nigger. Yer gonna get yourself killed." That sounded like one of our boys, but I guess it didn't much matter to the nigger who it was because he just kept on walking until he was right beside me.

And just as I'd thought, it *was* Jimmadasin right there in the flesh. He was wearing the filthy felt hat he always wore, pulled down right on his forehead, and though he was old, he was no bigger than me. His face was wrinkled up like a dried prune with bushy white eyebrows, and he was shaking like he was going to have a convulsion. But he wasn't hiding or ducking down to get out of the way of those minié balls. "Lord, please, dey just chillen, bofh a dem," he whined, spreading out his arms like a preacher calling to God. "Please, marsters, don' kill dem." Then he turned and saw me, and his head nearly cracked backward with surprise. "Lord Lord, yes indeed I foun' one a my boys, see? It's a miracle."

I didn't make a sound. I wasn't going to say a thing to this crazy nigger who seemed determined to get himself—and me—killed. But no one was paying any attention to us. Someone shouted "Forward." There was another explosion of musket shot that just about shook the trees. There was shouting and crying and then it was just quiet except for cannon being fired near the Pike. I suddenly realised how scared I was, and I was probably shaking as much as Jimmadasin because he suddenly started hugging me and cooing like a bird and saying, "Dem soldiers gone, young marster's safe wid me," and I suppose we just sat there against the tree, rocking each other like babies until the shaking stopped and I realised that I was humiliating myself. But Jimmadasin must have read my mind, or was just thinking the same thing, because he let go of me gently and stood up, slapping at his legs, as if he was cold, and looking around, as if he were suddenly curious and impatient. "We godda get goin', more soldiers gonna be comin'."

"What're you doing here?" I asked like I had just woke up and found him standing over me, his face big as the moon.

"I thought for da minute you'se young Harry," he said, extending his hand out for me to take hold. "'Das da h'nest truth. Come on now, id's dangerous here."

I let him pull me up, but before we went running off to safety, I wanted my question answered to my satisfaction. And I know this sounds crazy, what with musket exploding and soldiers running around all over here just seconds before, yet I felt safe here in the woods. There weren't any birds singing, and there were cannon and muskets firing, but right here felt sacred or something. I told you it didn't make any sense. "I ain't going noplace," I told him, "until you give me an explanation of what you're doing here."

"Whad *you* doin' here?"

"I asked *you*," I said.

"You ain' mah marster, but I'll tell you again jes like I tol' dem soldiers, I'se lookin' for mah marsters, mah chillen, an' mah mistress is jus 'bout half crazy wid worry."

"Then Mrs. McSherry sent you," I said, and, believe me, it didn't escape my notice that he was talking in a low, deep voice now that almost was scaring me.

"*I* sen' me," Jimmadasin said and started pulling me away, but I wanted to investigate because I heard moaning not far off. "I gotta find mah marsters, an' you're goin' to help me. "I goin' to save you for your folk, 'n you ain't goin' to fight me or pull away to sneak 'round dose dead n' dyin' soldjers."

"And what are you going to do if I do," I said, feeling the humiliation burn around my ears."

"Wahmp your fuckin' arse is what I gonna do," Jimmadasin said, and when he said that in a low rumble full of meanness and menace, I felt like I was six years old again. I probably didn't mention this before, but when I was a baby, Poppa used to threaten me by saying that if I didn't do what Mother asked me to, he'd call Mrs. McSherry and have her send Jimmadasin over with his stealin' bag to steal me away and get me out of her hair. I'd seen Jimmadasin walking home once with a bag slung over his shoulder, so I knew it was true. Anyway, Poppa had turned him into the bogey monster, and I used to have dreams that Jimmadasin was coming right through my window, even though it was on the second floor, to throw me into his bag. Then he'd take me somewhere dark and dirty and when he'd pull me out of that bag, I'd be somehow turned into a girl. And I'd wake up screaming. I didn't find out until later that his real name was James Madison, after the old President. But when he talked in that low voice I'd heard him use when singing, I knew he'd do just what he said. He was my size, but everyone knew how strong he was. So I went along with him until I could escape. We kept inside the woods for a while, then went across a field with broken stone walls here and there. We were between the Cedar Creek Road and the Middle Road, and way up ahead was the toll gate and the white tents of the Yankee camp and, of course, Winchester town. The sky looked gray like it was promising to rain, and I suddenly felt the cold, maybe because I wasn't wearing any shoes, but unless there was snow on the ground that would freeze your toes off, I didn't usually wear them. I had so many calluses that I could step on stones and briars just like I was wearing shoes. I was wearing a short coat, though, which was warm enough.

Then out of the blue, after not talking, just walking, Jimmadasin said, "I 'pologize for bein' harsh. I wasn't goin' to whump ya, just potectin' ya." His voice was still soft and low and grumbly.

"I know," I said.

He nodded and said, "Den show me whey is my marsters."

"How would I know where they are?"

"You know."

"No, I don't."

"You plays wid dem."

"Only once in a while, not today."

He looked down at the ground. I could see he was disappointed. "Den I'm taking you home to be safe, an I'll find 'em myself. Don' stop here, we godda keep walkin'. The solders behin' us, we just saw a few a dem, but der's an army comin'." And he whispered, like under his breath, but so as I could hear, "A 'ntire fuckin' army."

"Whose?" I asked.

"Gen'l Jackson."

"Did you see him?"

"I jus' know, dat's all, now are you gonna tell me whey is my marsters, or am I gonna take you home? I should prob'ly do dat anyhow."

He took hold of my arm, gently but tight, and I figured I'd better appease him, so I said, "I'll take you to the places I know, but it's gonna be like finding a needle in a haystack."

"We can do dat."

And so I really did try; I took him to all the places I knew around here that Harry and Allan liked best. As they always got everything they wanted, and had their own muskets, I used to go hunting with them. (Of course, their muskets overshot everything, but once you got used to them, you'd have a fair chance at hitting something.) Sometimes they'd let me shoot wild pigeons or doves or partridges, and I used to like their dogs that would always go along. So I took old Jimmadasin to Neil's Dam and to the woods where we always had good luck and a few other places with pretty good views, where they'd probably be if they were anywhere; and Jimmadasin started getting nervous, as he thought we were getting too close to danger, and started to talk to himself in a tiny, high voice like he was his own mother scolding him.

I asked him about that.

"You think I'se a dumb nigger fuck, don' you, but I ain't. You'se white an' don't got to worry 'bout nuthin'. If you was colored, you'd understan' quick, believe me." He laughed, but he was talking mean and quiet. "An' you also thought I mus' be a dumb, crazy fuck, Marster Mundy, whan I was lookin' for my boys in the woods. But dem solders ain't goin' to shoot what dey think is a dumb nigger wid a mamma's voice, now ain't dey? Nidder da 'Federate or da Yankee solder. I 'ready proves 'dat to you. If I was hidin', an' dey caught me, dey'd shoot Jimmadasin's ass dead. An' maybe shoot you wid me just for good measure or by mistake."

I owned that was possible.

"So maybe come a time when Marster Mundy learn dis nigger's tricks," Jimmadasin said, and we both started laughing because now we knew something nobody else did. And as we walked all over hell looking for Harry and Allan McSherry, the fighting got worse and worse, and we had to back off and keep going up toward Cedar Creek Road near where it meets the Valley Turnpike by the tollgate, which was near Abraham's Creek. I knew the creek, and so did Harry and Allan, but

I knew that if they were here, they wouldn't be that far away from the fighting, which was behind us in the woods and fields between Cedar Creek Road—the lower part—and the Valley Pike near the Opequon Church. Damned if Jimmadasin wasn't right; we saw our 'Federate boys marching across from the Pike along two routes. We were above it, but this wasn't no skirmishing; it was war. We could hear so many volleys of cannon that it just turned into one continuous roll, like the kind of thunder that seems to keep going on and getting louder after each flash of lightning. Seemed that now there were soldiers all around us, Yankee soldiers, and without saying a word we just ran, and I must admit I was glad to have Jimmadasin holding onto my hand. Everything seemed to go fast and slow at the same time. I know that sounds crazy, but that's how it was. Everything was happening inside of a second, yet it was slow too. Ah, I don't know, that's just how it was. There was smoke everywhere like there was a fire, and I could smell powder, it was sharp and hurt my nose like I had breathed in pepper and iron filings, and there was an explosion nearby that nearly knocked us down and pieces of metal and trees were flying through the air, and Jesus Christ I thought I saw a bloody hand falling with all the dirt and debris; and there were men screaming for help and calling for their mothers and then sonovabitch if another shell didn't explode like lightning striking the same place twice, and clots of earth and leaves and branches were flying, it was like the whole world was flying up in the air, and there were more screams, probably our own, too, and I stepped on something that seemed to burst under my foot. It was part of somebody because my foot was bloody and sticky, and I remember screaming then, I don't know why because in a way I wasn't scared, it was like I was off to the distance watching Jimmadasin and myself running like fools, and everything got dark and cloudy and everyone was shouting and shooting, and Jimmadasin was pulling me along and we were both shouting, and then suddenly it was over and we just sat in a field together breathing heavy and I was so exhausted that I upchucked a little before I could even catch my breath. I could still feel whatever it was that I had stepped on, and I rubbed off what I could of the blood with dirt and leaves. "Get the hell outa here, boy," shouted a Yank soldier up ahead of us, and I couldn't tell if he was yelling at me or Jimmadasin, and behind him ran a standard bearer, who didn't look like he was much older than me. I should have been fighting the Yanks, but Poppa wouldn't have none of that, and maybe I should have run away to join the militia, but I figured he would have stopped it anyway. Mother would cry that I was a baby every time I brought it up. I was old enough to be a drummer, at least. You could be twelve and be a drummer, and fourteen and be a soldier. "Move it out," someone shouted, and again, I didn't know if he was talking to the soldiers or to us, but Jimmadasin and I moved. More Yanks were moving down to meet our boys, thousands it looked like, marching down a mud road that wasn't much more than a path; and they were moving everything, including cannon. I thought we were safe hereabouts, but then we came upon a bluebelly who looked like he was asleep against a tree. One leg was stretched out straight and the other one was pulled up to his chest, which was a good comfortable way to sleep. Except he had a mess on his lap that looked like sausages.

"'Testines," Jim said, pulling me along. "Musta been from dis mornin' 'cause dey so swollen. Big guns do dat, just 'splode all over like we seen."

I was feeling a little sick, but once we walked right through the Yankee ranks, as if we were passing them on the street in town, I felt relieved and ashamed. Relieved because I could see town people around here on the hills who came to watch General Jackson shoot the asses off these Yankee invaders. Ashamed because now we were behind Yankee lines, under the protection of General Shields, who was the enemy, and I figured that was only a coward's reason to be comfortable.

I can't remember how long we remained just standing around, as if we were lost and trying to get our direction back, but it seems that it must have been a while because I was hungry, which was probably what was making me sick all along. Still, the sound of cannon and musket echoing around the hills was a continuous roll, and I thought then that there must be thousands getting shot and blown up and killed. It wasn't that many, but I learned quick that once you've been right there with all the dead and dying soldiers, Confederate or Yank, you feel the same if it's two or two hundred. I didn't know that, then, though. I was jittery-nervous, like I was in a dream where one minute you're here and then one minute you're somewhere else, and I had a metal taste that sometimes almost choked me whenever I swallowed; and something else. Everything seemed pressed together somehow, and maybe because it was exciting, but even with all the dying and screaming I felt a strange and horrible sort of happiness.

Once I saw those people from Winchester standing around, people who I'd seen before but didn't really know like Mr. Rosenberger, who was on the town council and knew Poppa, and Doctor Baldwin, and the dentist who's name I can't remember, I knew where we'd probably find the McSherry boys. The fighting was all going on in the woods and fields on and around Sandy Ridge, mostly where we'd been, and I pointed out some likely places to Jimmadasin. Most of them were taken up by spectators trying to get a good view, but Harry and Allan were nowhere to be found. I told Jimmadasin we had to go back down a ways closer to the fighting if we were going to find them. He said no, but went anyway—he sure as hell loved those two boys—but he scolded himself in his high, scared voice all the way back. I didn't expect to find them; I just wanted to get close to where I could see and get away from the other spectators, but we found them anyway sitting on a stone fence with a near perfect view of the Federal regiments.

"Hey, Mundy, you come to the right place to see the fight," Harry McSherry said, ignoring Jimmadasin, but looking uncomfortable nevertheless.

Jimmadasin screamed for them to come down from there because of how dangerous it was. He ran right up to both of them, pulled them down from the stone fence, nearly breaking their bones, and hugged them. They tried to escape, but, as I said, old Jimmadasin was strong; and it didn't seem that he'd ever let go of them again.

"Yo' Mamma's sick wid worry o're you, both of you."

"Lemme go," Harry said. His brother Allen didn't struggle; he just looked scared of everything. He was eleven, more than a year younger than Harry and me. "Momma knows we're watching the battle," Harry said. "We went early this morning. She gave us permission, you ken go an' ask her."

"I don' hafta ask nobody, 'cause she tole' me to bring you home safe 'n soun', dat's 'xactly what she say. An' dat's what I'm goin' to do right now." Jimmadasin started marching them around the side of the fence and turned to me, expecting me to follow, but Harry begged to stay just for a few minutes more and explained that it was safe here and Jimmadasin could see that, for there were no dead bodies here or nothing.

Jimmadasin allowed five minutes.

We could see the Federals hiding behind stone fences, and between them and General Jackson's army were trees and small brush and more fences. There were woods down a ways to the right and a ravine, but there was nothing straight ahead beyond that stone fence but empty field, and our Confederates throwing everything they had at the line of Federal soldiers. The Federals were shooting back, of course, mostly cannon somewhere off to our left, but mostly they were getting shot at and shelled. It was loud, and much of the time that we all sat there together on the fence, we couldn't hear ourselves talk. Harry was wrong about one thing, though: there were dead soldiers all around here. I could see them when I looked hard. They were covered with dirt and filth and blood that looked black, and they blended right into the ground and woods and brush, which were all torn up anyhow. Even though I don't care a wet shit about Federal soldiers, it half made me sick to see them dead and lying around all over. Course I just figured they were Yanks. They could've been our own men...

Well, then all hell broke lose, and we almost got killed by our own 'Federate shells, which exploded in the trees right behind us; and it suddenly seemed that you couldn't be safe nowhere. A head torn right off at the neck rolled right in front of Allan's foot, as if it was a pumpkin or something; and Allan screamed. Course, I don't blame him for that, especially since I could swear that the lips moved. Jimmadasin made some sort of a sacred sign with his hands, then there was another explosion, and Jimmadasin and Harry and Allan McSherry were gone.

It was like I woke up and they were gone, but I remembered what happened only afterward. Jimmadasin had grabbed Harry and Allan with those big hands of his and tried to do the same with me, but I was running before I could even think about it, not necessarily away from Jimmadasin, but running just the same, and I didn't stop until I was in a little grove of brush and young trees. There was noise all around me, and I could hear men groaning and breathing and reloading their muskets. I got to know the rattle a ramrod makes when it's pushed down into the barrel.

I had run the wrong way, and I didn't dare move, and how I wished that Jimmadasin had grabbed me, damn him, because I was right in the thick of the fighting. I could see pretty good, too, and then even more bluebellies came running into the battle, replacing the Federals who had been killed—and they were lying everywhere, like it was a game and couldn't be real, and when I didn't see pieces of flesh and smears of blood, that's the way I was thinking it was. The fire from both sides was devastating. Not even the stone wall could protect the Federals from that terrible hail of shot and shell, and I imagine our own boys were dying just the same on the other side of the wall. There were more Federals to my left, and I could see that they were the Eighty-fourth Pennsylvania. One of their officers waved his sword and shouted like he was giving a speech, "Hold your ground; stand solid; keep cool; remember your homes, and your country; don't waste your powder," and the damn fool was standing right out there in front of his men, leading them forward until someone called him to fall back because he was exposing himself unnecessarily. But he didn't pay any attention and advanced with his men right into the fire of our boys. More bluebellies were falling than advancing, it seemed; but when I saw that officer fall, even though I felt sorry for the poor bastard, I thought right then that, yes, we were going to win, that General Jackson was going to kill so many Yanks that General Banks would have to retire back to where he came from and get the hell out of Winchester for good.

I crawled forward, emboldened by the killing, I guess, although I wasn't being smart, just curious, and I've leaned better since then.

Now I could see our army down below what was a hill or maybe more like a ravine, and the bluebellies were charging right down there through galling fire; and you had to hand it to the Yankees, they were determined. I watched two of their color bearers fall, and saw the flag lifted up again each time. But our guns were too much for them, and the right side of what looked like a thousand Yanks just gave way, and the Bluebellies were running right back in the direction they came, but like flies around honey, more soldiers just seemed to swarm in, then the Yanks let out a terrific shout, something like a wolf howl; and Yankee and Reb were killing each other with bayonet and fighting hand to hand and getting all mixed up with each other. But the Yankees got past the stone fence, and sonova*bitch* if they didn't turn our own boys, route them, and I remember saying to myself that this was only one little tiny piece of the fight, that our boys were pushing the Yankee soldiers back everywhere else, but I could feel that wasn't true. I just felt sick and sort of paralysed, and suddenly I wanted to get home, even though I would be in big trouble. If you want the truth, and I'm ashamed to admit this, but I wanted my mother. I wanted to smell rabbit stew and all the fixings. I wanted to feel the warmth of the hearth and all that. And all this would just be sort of like a dream I would forget, or just remember like you remember a good story.

I could tell by where the sun was, or the smear that was the sun behind the clouds, that it must be close to twilight. As I probably said already, everything seemed to be going fast and slow at the same time, even though I know that's impossible; and somehow the whole day had gotten swallowed up in a few minutes. But I was going home, that's all I knew; and so I just walked in the opposite direction of the fighting, back up toward where Jimmadasin and I had gone to get out danger before. I didn't know better then, but I thought that nothing could be worse than seeing all those dead and wounded soldiers laying all around like they were dolls or something. I had to keep my eyes open and be alert, but I found I could ignore seeing the dead soldiers and the wounded ones too; only thing I couldn't ignore was their cries, and so I gave some of them water, which they all begged for; and even now that I think of it I'm ashamed I didn't try to do more for them. But I just left them.

Well, I couldn't have done anything much for them anyway, except keep them company when they cried for their mothers and give them a little water.

I should've stayed with them.

But I wanted *my* mother.

So I pretended it was all going to be all right and took the straightest route home, not even thinking that I might step into more fighting. I just figured if I ran straight ahead, big as life like old Jimmadasin taught me, I'd get home safe and sound. Which I did. It was just before dusk when everything looks blueish and pretty, and the fields and woods were all shadowy like they were sunk in dark pools of water or something, but if you looked out at the mountains you could sometimes see parts that were sunlit, and you could sometimes see rays coming right out of the sky like a painting in the bible. That's how it looked when I reached our farm; but even before I could see the family house, I knew something was wrong because I could smell burning and hear terrible screaming and crying, and I could tell my Mother's voice, and Poppa's. Poppa was screaming more than anyone, and then he stopped and there were other voices I didn't recognise. I ran right through the woods to get to the front yard of "the Big House," as we called it, as if we had a hundred slaves like the Barton's from Springdale, who Poppa knew. But that doesn't matter, and I'm just keeping away from telling you what happened.

But I'm going to…

Anyway, there was our house with its big chimney and porch with columns and the red sandstone flags that made a pavement through the lawn between the shade trees and stopped by the board fence that Poppa and I had whitewashed. And there was the sunlight just going over the mountains. And the smell of smoke. The entire farm except for the big house seemed like it was on fire, the barn and lumber house and school house. I was behind a big tree, and I could see every little detail of everything it seemed, and even though I wish I couldn't, I remember it all—I remember the rotten trunk of a cherry tree that was just beside me, I remember the white fungus growing on its grey bark; and I remember the smell of the woods and the smell of the smoke, and the screaming, although as I think about it I still want to close my eyes, but I didn't, although I wish I did because two men came riding out from the back of the house; and they were hooting and shouting and laughing like they were drunk or probably crazy; and they were both wearing cheap butternut coats and pants and those funny-looking Federal hats that had enough fittings on them to make a copper kettle. One had a pine torch, and he was leaning low on the side of his horse, almost falling out of his saddle, to touch that torch to everything he fancied. The other was just riding behind him, pulling along two other horses.

"C'mon outa there," shouted the one with the torch. "Gonna get hot, an' it's our turn, ya greedy fucks."

And the house started smoking. He had started the fire in the back of the house, and suddenly I could see flames licking the roof, and I could hear terrible cracking noises like bones were being broken or something, and then someone ran out of the house and shot the horse right out from under the soldier with the torch, and someone else came out of the house, and he was pulling Mother, and she was naked and full of blood, and I wondered where was Poppa, where was Poppa, I remember thinking that over and over like a song, and I was watching when I should have been running right out there and killing them, burning them and shooting those sonovabitches, but then the soldier that had been pulling Mother just dropped her outside the door on the porch. She wasn't making any noise, but I saw her move, and then the soldier whose horse was shot out from under him ran over to the porch, and all the men started fighting with each other, and they fell right over Mother, and I heard a keening, a noise like Jimmadasin would've made, and I realised I was hearing myself, hearing the inside of my head, and I blinked, that's all it was, I blinked, and then one of the men must have dragged Mother off the porch and onto pavement, and he was on top of her and his pants were down, and another one, another one was

Looking straight at me. I know he saw me. He must've. He just looked right at me, and I didn't move, and I didn't breathe, and then he looked away like he never saw me, and I remember thinking then that I was invisible like air or like a tree in a huge forest.

And then he was gone, as if *he* had disappeared, and so had the other men, but maybe it was me, maybe I just went blind or something because all I remember from then on, for I don't know how long I was watching that man hurting my mother, I was remembering nice things and terrible things, as if I had escaped from that tree and the time and what I was seeing and was only seeing things in my mind.

I had to go in and save Mother I had to find Father, for the house was burning, burning, catching fire in a hundred places, and I could feel the heat, but I was thinking remembering couldn't move touching the bark, feeling the slimy moss remembering remembering how at the start of spring Poppa and I always made piles of brush and dead leaves and vegetation anything else burnable that we could gather in our fields. Then Poppa would check that the wind was just right, so that the fire didn't get out of control, and then with a pine torch he'd light those piles, poking them here and there with a long pole, going from one pile to another, while I ran around gathering everything that would burn to keep the hungry fires going and I remembered and remembered so well I could see it right before me, so well that I could blank out what was happening right in front of me, and I saw me and Ishrael Moble and three of his darkie children that Poppa had borrowed from Arthur Allen who owned the next farm down the road from us, and Ishrael was ploughing a furrow around our field of broom sedge, and when he was done Poppa would light the sedge on the windward side, and it would blaze like a sonovabitch, and Ishrael and his kids and me and Poppa would beat out the fire with green cedar branches whenever it escaped over the furrow, and once it did and we lost a rail fence and burned a field and—

They were gone.

SPIRIT DOG

I found myself standing on the edge of the woods, holding my breath, being invisible, looking at the house burning, feeling the heat on my face like waves coming over me, and I had seen everything, I knew that I had seen what the men did, what they did to my mother, and I could see mother there yet, lying on the red sandstone flags, and I just ran across the lawn to her. It was as if I had just gotten here. Like I hadn't been watching, hadn't been invisible, hadn't held my breath for...how long? Five minutes? Ten minutes? Uncle Randolph says it's impossible to hold your breath longer than a minute, but I know I could have held it forever that day.

I heard that keening and knew I was making strange noises and sobbing and crying, but as soon as I knelt beside Mother I saw that she was staring off and not blinking. But it wasn't even so much that. It was like she had been turned into a doll or something. She looked like porcelain, like all the stuff had gone out of her, and I knew she was dead.

Poppa...

I tried to go into the house, but the fire was bad inside, and so I came out and dragged Mother away from the house, but I saw that it was hopeless, that everything was hopeless because I knew that Poppa had been in the house and was killed too.

It was when I was guarding Mother that I saw the dog. It came running from the direction of the meat house, where I figured it had gotten in. It was the biggest dog I ever saw, more like the size of a horse, and its coat was as black and sleek and shiny as the big crow perched on top of the smoking ruins of the Big House. That dog smelled terrible of dampness and burning, and it was running right toward me with its mouth open. Its eyes were on fire. They were big as saucers and looked like balls of fire.

No one is ever going to tell me that dog wasn't real, because I saw it, and like before, when the men burned down the house, I became invisible. I kneeled there beside Mother like I was frozen. I didn't breathe. I didn't make a sound. And that dog stopped so near to me that I could smell its sour-rotten breath and its damp, sweaty fur. And I could feel the heat of it, and it seemed to just fill me up the same way Mother did when she'd pull the covers up to my chin and kiss me good-night and talk about Jesus.

It sniffed at Mother, looked at me a real long time like it was putting thoughts in my head, and then it ran off to the edge of the woods where it watched me with its eyes that were burning in the dark because it had gotten dark while I had been sitting there with Mother. It kept watching me and waiting to see what I was going to do, and I stayed with Mother while the house burned. I held her hand, which was like ice, and I felt something fill me up again like I was a bucket and hot lard was being poured into it, and I wasn't angry or sad any more because all at once everything seemed right and perfect, and I knew exactly what I had to do. It was like I was having one of those visions Aunt Hanna was always telling me about because it came to me all of a sudden that it was up to me to kill everybody who'd killed Mother and Poppa, and that it didn't make much difference who it was. It was the spirit dog that put that thought in my head, I swear, 'cause I could feel the spirit inside me, breathing right inside my chest until I understood it all; and then when I turned around the spirit dog was still there, watching me with those burning eyes and calling me to him with my own thoughts.

Calling me to go back to Kernstown field, which was filled with muskets and caps and cartridges.

I'd gather them up to do my own killing.

For Mother.

For Poppa.

For everyone.

Until the spirit dog and me had evened things up, and then we'd just probably

Disappear.

AFTERWORD TO "SPIRIT DOG"

A FEW OF my novels have been referred to as 'fixups'. In the *Encyclpedia of Science Fiction* John Clute and David Langford defined a fixup as "A term first used by A E van Vogt to describe a book made up of previously published stories fitted together—usually with the addition of newly written or published cementing material—so that they read as a novel." Actually, my process is the exact opposite of a fixup! I write the novel and then, should the opportunity or creative need arise, I excerpt a section of the book and rework/revise/recast it as its own stand-alone story. Such was the case with "Spirit Dog," a story that takes place in the same universe as my Civil War novel *The Silent.*

The Silent was a critical success. The aforementioned John Clute referred to it as "*The Painted Bird* as told by *Huckleberry Finn*." *Kirkus Reviews* called it "A ferocious portrait of the Civil War's human toll"; and *Library Journal* wrote, "This is narrative storytelling at its best—so highly charged emotionally as to constitute a kind of poetry from hell. Most emphatically recommended."

Being humble and rather egoless—two characteristics that define most of us who toil in the lancinating vineyards of fiction—I only mention these reviews in case you enjoyed or were moved by "Spirit Dog" and might want to be made aware of the existence of a larger edition. Translation: give *The Silent* a read!

THE LAST MASKIL

Know this, you who would cling to the Truth and avert annihilation. Remember this, for it is your sole ember of hope:

Remember that the incarnation and embodiment of both fire and light is the two-winged angel Gabriel. Know that he is the First of the seraphs.

Know that his place is beside the diamond throne of the Invisible One, the True God. Remember that his element and substance is sapphire, which is his seal, sigil, and soul.

Know that he may select you to receive the serpent...
Remember that he may select you to receive his sapphire sigil, which will pierce your flesh like an arrow.

—Charred fragment translated from the Ethiopic; thought to be a lost scroll from The Gospel of the Damned

'Trismegistus, who will the angel Gabriel choose to be his dark companion?'

THE LAST MASKIL

'The angel has selected the last *maskil*
to do God's will, Rheginus.'

'Listen to me, Trismegistus. Why would he choose a boy to walk beside him in the final struggle against the demiurge and his demons?'

'Ah, Rheginus...Rheginus. Gabriel does not choose.
He is enjoined to follow God's will.
Would you contradict His choice?'

'No, Trismegistus, I would not. But—'

'Yes, Rheginus?'

'But why do we refer to him as Gabriel's dark companion?'

'Because of the great darkness that will engulf
and violate him—if he survives.'
—Excerpt from the Preliminary Discourse
22,17-11

YESTERDAY, WHEN Lucian ben Hananiah had climbed the sheer precipice that overlooked the yellow, sulfurous expanse of the Dead Sea, he was a boy of twelve. Today he was a man who had reached his majority. Today he was allowed the singular privilege of praying and studying inside the innermost sanctuary of *Merh Fl'awr*, the Cave of Light, the highest and most sacred repository in all the fortified settlement of *Khirbet Qumran*. But as he sat before a natural outcrop that had been used for centuries as a reading plinth, his back against a wall of smooth, worn stone, he did not feel the joy of privilege. He felt trapped, alone, and humiliated, for other boys were not allowed to take the oath of the Covenant until they had reached their eighteenth year and were considered learned enough in the *Book of Meditation* to be recognized by the Council and the twelve priests as a 'son of light'. And only the *maskil* and his chosen priests were allowed to enter the Cave of Light.

However, other boys weren't the firstborn son of Hananiah ben-Yohanan the Zadokite, the hereditary leader of the community. Other boys couldn't trace their lineage back to God's chosen *maskil*: the first master and guardian of the sacred scrolls. Other boys had to *earn* the privileges of entering the Covenant.

Lucian had felt the force of their hatred and disdain—and the hatred and disdain of their white robed fathers as they accompanied him to the foot of the cliff face; and even after his father and the twelve priests blessed him, even after his father blessed and thanked the standing congregation—none of them remained to watch the newest member of the Covenant navigate the dangerously stepped handholds and footholds called the stairs. Only his father remained to guard, fast, and pray on the heat-shimmering stones and marl below.

Lucian gazed out at the dusty light of the cave's narrow twilight zone, shook his head as if to clear it of unworthy thoughts, and then looked back down at the copper scroll before him. It shone like burnished gold in the flickering light of the oil lamps. His father called it the golden scroll and swore Lucian to secrecy before speaking of it in tones of awe. Older than the mountains, as old as the moon, it was God's terrible and puzzling warning to the chosen. No one else in the community, not even the twelve priests, knew of its existence or whereabouts. But the future *maskil* needed to know; and now, until the waxen moon rose full above the cliffs and crown of the settlement, Lucian would have the priceless artifact to himself.

The scroll was pitted, creased, and wrinkled. A section at the end had been cut or torn away, and some of the ancient proto-Hebrew script was impossible to read: words and entire lines looked like they had been scratched or pounded out. He touched the indented script and filled in the missing or indecipherable words as best he could:

Listen to me now, sweet, vulnerable children of light, listen to me, you who are worthy but will not see until the shadows of the tree of death are upon you. Until its twisted vines are already emptying your souls into the darkness. Yea, even as they devour the angels sent by the Lord of Hosts to protect and nourish you.

He memorized as he read, as he would be expected to discuss the scroll in detail with his father, for it was unlikely that he would be allowed to return to this place until he reached his physical majority in another seven years.

The demiurge who is the shadow of a shadow that your fathers and mothers and brothers and sisters mistakenly worship and offer sacrifice to as the true Lord of Hosts awakens with intention. He will make certain that the angels and demons he created with his own seed are not disturbed or turned by the creatures of light. And his faithful servant Belias who rules the darkness will make certain that his intention is their intention.

Blasphemy, he thought. But, no, that could not be. It *must* be God's truth or his father—and all the *maskils* who guarded and kept the scroll secret before him—would not revere it so. He continued reading; but try as he might, he could not make out the words that were partially scratched away.

And what is the intention of the demiurge, the one I will call Yaldabaoth, vulnerable children? It is to end the age of life, destroy your souls and mine, and humiliate and destroy the True Father of us all in His heaven above all angels and thrones. It is written that such calamity shall come to pass unless you can save the last

And there the scroll ended.

Feeling perplexed—and somehow soiled—he searched for answers:

Last what? Maskil?

And who will end the age of life?

The Lord of Hosts?

No, the Lord God in Heaven, Holy be His Name, could not be the Adversary.

Satan is the Adversary.

But Father will know, he consoled himself. *Father always knows.*

The cave's depths seemed to be closing in on him, as if the dusty darkness had weight. He felt the need for light and air, for the bright sunlight that baked even the sea to salt and the air that was as soft as hair. As Lucian began to pull himself away from the scroll—it was a tight squeeze between the plinth and sitting stone: there were no fat scholars in *Khirbet Qumran*—he heard a rasping noise that sounded like wind blowing. But it was not the wind. As he leaped away from the sound, he felt something strike his bare foot; then felt a searing, burning pain like the touch of red-hot iron. And he saw a rock snake side-slip across the floor, its smooth scales glittering like cut sapphires in the flickering lamplight. Its rasping coils sounded like wind pushing through stone chimneys.

fh-fh-fhh-fff fh-fh-fhh-fff fh-fh-fhh-fff.

Fh: the Egyptian name for viper.

It slowly side-slipped back and forth toward Lucian as if it were now stalking him, or herding him. Lucian backed away and would have cried out in terror, but for the burning numbness that struck him like icy-sharp shards of hail. Lunging for his neck, the snake struck again. Then it simply disappeared...disappeared into his flesh.

He felt as if he was filled with light, as if he was burning with it.

It's the venom, the poison, he told himself as he staggered toward the mouth of the cave. But venom was coursing through his arteries like Greek fire. He was dizzy, and his legs were numb. Soon they would be useless.

If I can just get far enough to call down to Father keeping vigil below. If I can just…

His labored breathing sounded like the rasping coils of the sapphire snake. His vision blurred; and as he fell, he heard the droughty, fricative *fh-fh-fhh-fff.* But it was not the hollow sound of his own breathing echoing in his ears. He turned his head toward the rasping…and saw an angel hovering before him.

It was bathed in pure white light, and its great feathered wings were partly furled, as the cave walls were too narrow to contain them. The beautiful apparition seemed to shift in and out of sight.

Lucian took a deep, dying breath.

fh-fh-fhh-fff fh-fh-fhh-fff fh-fh-fhh-fff.

And the sweet uplifting scent of cinnamon perfumed the air.

"AM I DEAD?" Lucian asked the angel, blinking.

The angel smiled at the skinny, gangly, and frightened thirteen-year-old and settled to the ground. He wore purple robes and a white circlet around his head. His features were sharp as etched glass. Handsome and beautiful he was, heroically masculine, yet gracefully feminine…he was translucent as vapor, and as substantial as the cave itself.

"No, young maskil. *Today is a day of learning and forgetting. Your tomorrows will be for remembering."*

"The snake that bit me, that—"

"Yes?"

"Was it…real?"

"Do you still feel the pain of its bites?"

"Yes," Lucian said. His neck still ached and burned. He propped himself against the cave wall and looked at his leg, which was red and swollen.

"But you mean to ask if I *am real or a vision, a phantasm."*

"Yes," Lucian said again. His head seemed to clear, the pain suddenly abated, and he felt comforted by the soft brume of warmth and light that radiated from the angel. "Who are you, and why have you come to me here…and now? And…"

"What else would you have?"

Lucian felt the angel's laughter, although he could not hear it. "If you are an angel, as you seem to appear, can you not draw away the poison that sickens me?"

"A poultice of physalis somnifera *and onion would serve as well."*

"But as you can see, angel," he said impatiently, "I don't have such a poultice."

"Would you speak in such a manner to your father?"

Searing, pulsing pain and dizziness returned.

Lucian groaned and said, "No, I would not. Please forgive me, Holy One."

Now Lucian felt the angel's amusement.

"You may call me Gabriel, and I am both real and a phantasm. Like the snake that bit you. But even when you forget, as you surely will, you must try to remember that although both the snake and the vine will seek you out, only the snake will sustain you."

"But how can I both remember and forget?"

"Your heart will remember, and your heart is yoked to your soul."

"Why must I forget?"

"So that you may grow into your great soul and discover how to fulfill your destiny."

"Can you not just tell me…or show me?"

The angel laughed, a swirling lightness of cinnamon and joy, and said, *"I could easier teach you to fly. And if I did—if I could and would—you would become as loathsome as the twisting shadows that seek you out."*

"What shadows? What you said before: the vines? Or the snake? Why would such things seek *me* out?"

"The snake is my own. My gift to you. It is my sigil, my seal: my soul, if you like. But the vines…they are the creatures of another: They belong to Belias, the dark angel described in the scripture your father sent you here to study. Belias is bound to Yaldabaoth, the demiurge you call Jehovah. It is he who created you and all your kind. And now he is ready to destroy all creation, all that has been, is, and will be."

"But why would the Lord of Hosts wish to—?"

"The demiurge is not *the Lord of Hosts…any more than I am. He is the dark angel created by the Lord's beloved Sophia, Queen of Angels."*

Lucian could feel the angel's controlled wrath; and for an instant his chest froze, and he couldn't breathe. Then, with a gasp, he inhaled the cloying smell of cinnamon sweetness and tasted the tongue-searing bitterness of ash.

"Sophia wanted to bring forth another luminary like herself," Gabriel continued, *"but she did so without the consent of her creator; and her miscreant desire produced an imperfect, misshapen thing. When she tried to hide her shame from the Lord of Hosts, her creation overwhelmed her, stole her power, and created his own realm of angels and authorities and seraphim. In his arrogance, the demiurge exults himself over all. He cannot admit to being consequent, to being other than the One. And his intention, young* maskil, *is to destroy the Lord of Hosts."*

Lucian was still shivering; whether from abyssal fear or the snake's flesh-swelling poison, he could not know.

"Now you understand the warning of the scroll," the angel said, reading him like writing on parchment. His voice was soft and lyrical, a tangible

manifestation of a profound, sympathetic sadness. *"If the demiurge is to prevail, he must destroy everything, including himself and his minions. His very success depends upon his own annihilation."*

"But how can he become the One if he destroys the world and the heavens and himself? And surely no one—or no thing—can prevail over the Lord of Hosts."

"By possessing and destroying every single soul, he denies—and destroys—the Lord of Hosts. And all that would remain is—"

"Himself," Lucian said, overwhelmed by the angel's radiating grief.

"Yes, childe, for one eternal instant the demiurge would become the One, the only one."

Lucian shook his head, as if he could deny by force of will what the angel had just told him. The angel gentled the boy's hair, soothing him as if he was a startled animal and then said softly, *"Even now one of Yaldabaoth's servants approaches...even now you are in danger."*

"But why? I am nothing, I—"

"He seeks you because of what I have given you...and because of what you have the potential to become."

"And what would that be?"

"Perhaps the last maskil,*"* the angel said, looking sadly at the boy.

"IF THE LORD of Hosts awakens his angels to destroy us, what can *I* do?" Lucian asked the angel. "You should be speaking to my father, not to me. He knows...he knows..."

"I'm right here, Lucian."

Lucian stared hard at the angel, whose robes were no longer purple, but were striped black and white linen. "Father...?" he asked earnestly, grasping his father's linen sleeve in recognition and twisting his hand inside the fold as he did when he was a child. "I'm very glad to see you. But why did you come to find me? Is everything all right?"

His father nodded, touching Lucian's forehead gently with his free hand.

"When you did not come down from the cave at sunset, I became worried. I found you in high fever and dared not move you until you awakened. It will soon be light…and thanks be to God who delivers us from all distress, your fever has broken."

Lucian shivered and looked around the cave. The oil lamp on the opposite wall was guttering, and there was no twilight zone around the cave opening. "Did you find the snake?"

His father looked at him quizzically.

"The snake that bit me."

"No snake has ever been found up here," his father said. His eyes looked deep and shadowed in the flickering lamplight. "I fear that my rashness has made you ill. I have asked too much of you too soon, worked you to exhaustion, but—"

Lucian tentatively touched his neck and examined his leg, but could find no swelling or puncture marks. There had been no need of a poultice. There had been no snake. No angel. Just fevered imaginings brought on by a sudden ague. Relieved, he drank deeply from the water skin his father proffered. He wiped his mouth, which felt cottony and swollen, and asked, "But what, Father?"

"You have accomplished the tasks I set before you, and you have made me proud," the older man said softly. He stared into the cave entrance, stared at the halo of dawn's first light as if he were trying to see through time itself. "Did you commit the words of the Golden Scroll to memory?"

"Yes, Father."

"Every one of them? Even the excision marks?"

"Yes, Father. Do you wish to test me?"

He turned to Lucian and embraced him. "No, my son. You have already been burned deeply enough by God's words. Your fever was proof enough." His father still held him close.

"Are you cold, Father?"

The *maskil* released his son and said, "No, I am perfectly fine."

"But you're trembling."

His father smiled indulgently. "I am old. Old men tremble. Now ask me the questions that must be still burning inside you, and then we will climb down the stairs together. Surely you must be hungry, and I promise not to exhaust you with study again. Your mother will take a long time forgiving me."

"Does she know why you readied me to take the oath and enter the sanctuary?"

"She knows that you are the future *maskil*."

"You are the *maskil*, father. My time is many years away."

His father looked at him, touched his forehead again, and nodded.

"But you are worried that something bad is going to happen, aren't you?" He leaned closer to his father. "That something will happen to you."

"I just need you to be ready. If you read the tablet with understanding, you know that the age of life might come to an end at any moment."

Lucian nodded.

"Are you strong enough to climb down the stairs?" his father asked, meaning the footholds and handholds that were cut into the cliff face.

"Yes, father, I will try."

"Try? No, you rest here. I will—"

The piercing trills of distant rams' horns echoed across the Dead Sea, which magnified sound like a crystal focusing heat.

"Father…?"

Lucian's father sighed and said, "They have found their way to us sooner than I expected."

"Who, Father?"

"The Christian Knights of the Temple. Their grand master inquisitor leads them. They've made no secret that they seek our scrolls." He smiled ruefully. "To protect them, of course, as they do all holy relics."

"We must not let them—"

"No, we must welcome them, as we would any other honored guest." Lucian's father caressed his son's hand. "We might succeed with brigands, but our swords and numbers are no match for these sons of Cain." He tapped his forehead and his chest, indicating wisdom and guile, and said, "But we are not entirely without resources." Then he stood up and adjusted his robes for climbing. "Now I must go down and oversee what must be done. Are you strong enough to climb?"

"Yes, Father, but what can we do?"

"We will do what we have always done: We will pay Caesar his tribute…but we will give him brass instead of silver." He nodded, as if trying to convince himself. "You will see, my son, I promise, you will see."

HIDDEN ATOP AN ancient *birkeh* tower that was no longer used for smelting, Lucian watched the company of armored, black-tunicked riders approach the main gate of the settlement on their sweat-steaming warhorses. Then he flicked his gaze down to the delegation of elders and priests waiting to greet the Christian knights in the cooling shade of the stately palm trees that lined the public *mikveh*. The immersion pool was fed by an aqueduct that was as old as the settlement's square watchtowers and tumbledown fortification walls…and by God's own miracle, it magnified sounds toward the heavens. His father, dressed in his finest white, turned away from the priests and his fellow elders and looked up in Lucian's direction. Only for an instant, and then he stepped ahead of the others to greet the Grand Master *inquisitore*, who alone wore a white surcoat emblazoned with a crimson cross. The inquisitor dismounted and then signaled his guard of brown-mantled knights to do the same. The rest of the soldiers—hard-faced lances, alert and a hundred strong—remained in saddle. He bowed to Lucian's father who said, "*Salam*. May peace be upon you and all those in your favor."

Lucian could hear his father's voice clearly, and he could make out the features of the inquisitor who had soft, kindly eyes and an aquiline noise that did not seem to be in harmony with his full, generous mouth and slight double chin.

"Please, refresh yourself," Lucian's father said, gesturing toward the immersion pool and long tables covered in linen and set with earthenware bowls, cups, and plates. Slaves appeared, bustling back and forth from nearby pantries and kitchens with pitchers of sour milk, loaves of freshly baked bread, terrines of soup, platters of meat and wild greens, pitchers of wine and green olive oil, dipping dishes, and pomegranates, olives, dates, honeycombs, grapes, cucumbers, and cakes of pressed figs. One of the slaves was Lucian's childhood playmate and only friend: dark-skinned Orpha, the daughter of Jerobaal who removed ash from the ovens. She was two years older than Lucian and already a woman.

The inquisitor washed his hands and face perfunctorily in the pool, then after handing back the towel proffered by young Orpha, he politely took a date and said, "My officers and I eat what the Lord provides. Thank you, but we are sufficient." The men in saddle did not even look at the pool or the food; but for the horses that had to be kept under tight rein, these soldiers of the cross might have been sculpted out of stone.

Lucian's father nodded and said, "Then how may we be of service to the Knights of the Temple?"

His father's back was turned to the *birkeh*, so Lucian could not see his face; but he could see the inquisitor smile indulgently.

"You very well know what we've come for, *maskil.* Although we've not met before, I know you well. My…predecessor told me that he had visited you some time ago. In vain."

"I hardly think it was in vain," said Josephus, the high priest. He was a tall, imposing man, his hair black as a youth's; only his beard was flecked with gray. "Your crossed knights pillaged our sacred scrolls and—"

Lucian's father stepped forward, cutting off the impetuous high priest; and the inquisitor smiled and said, "I do not expect to impose on the generosity of your community for very long, *maskil.*" He smiled again and bowed: one man of knowledge and power addressing another. "I am Bartolomeo Falce…Bartolomeo. And you are Hananiah ben-Yohanan."

Lucian's father bowed, but said nothing.

"We are all sons of Abraham," continued the inquisitor.

"No, *we* are not," said the high priest, shouldering past the *maskil.* "*You* are the seed of—"

Without hesitation, the inquisitor snapped a blade out of his sleeve and slit the high priest's throat. In a trice his guards were all around him, swords unsheathed, and leveled at the priests and elders. A few of the slaves and servants tending the tables and the pool panicked and ran off; but the rest kept to their places, their heads bowed.

Lucian watched in shock as his father and one of the elders caught the dying priest and gently laid him to rest on the ground. Although he was terrified for his father at the hands of this executioner with the kindly face; there was nothing he could do, except obey his father's orders to remain hidden on the tower roof.

This certainly wasn't what Father had in mind. This—

After Lucian's father blessed the dead priest and stood up, the inquisitor continued as if nothing had happened. "As I was saying, Hananiah ben-Yohanan, we are *all* sons of Abraham. We both wish to protect

God's word and holy relics. We both seek the knowledge hidden in the sacred scrolls. You and your community have born the burden of caring for God's words"—with that he nodded to the other priests and elders, who stood stock-still in fear—"and for that we honor you."

"By killing our leader?" Lucian's father asked.

"*You* are their leader," the inquisitor said, "and I seek but two sacred artifacts. Return what belongs by divine right to the church, good *maskil* Hananiah, and we will leave your community in peace forever more. On that you have my word."

None of the other priests or elders responded.

"You have little to lose, and everything to gain," he continued. "Surely you have memorized the contents of at least one of the relics we seek."

"What artifacts might that be?" asked Lucian's father.

"The golden scroll, as you call it, and…the sapphire seal." The inquisitor looked at the *maskil* benevolently.

"I am not aware of these artifacts," Lucian's father said.

"I don't believe you," said the inquisitor. "But I can see you are a man of honor and would not carelessly reveal what you know…even if I executed every one of these holy and learned men who stand beside you. Is that not so?"

The *maskil* was silent.

The inquisitor looked past the *maskil* as if he were surveying the brick and stone buildings and the cliffs beyond. Lucian felt something wet and cold spray inside his chest: for an instant, he felt that the inquisitor was looking directly at *him*.

"My spies tell me that you have sent your women, children, and most of your able-bodied men away."

"Your spies?" asked the *maskil*.

"Oh, don't be so surprised, *maskil* Hananiah. We all must do what we can to gain knowledge and power, is that not so?"

The *maskil* said something, but in a voice so low that Lucian could not hear it.

"Sending the flower of your community away was a wise strategy," the inquisitor continued. He gazed at the priests and then nodded approvingly to the *maskil*. "And I see that your most learned mnemonists are not here to greet us—I must congratulate you: you've certainly done your best to ensure that your community and its precious knowledge survive. But I, too, have prepared, *maskil* Hananiah. Turn around and look there."

The inquisitor pointed to the *birkeh* tower…

"Look up at the roof."

LUCIAN HEARD SOFT rustling behind him, but too late. Before he could even turn, he was overpowered by three men wearing the rough, white bleached robes of the sectaries. Lucian struggled as they tied and gagged him. He heard his father's scream, followed by the inquisitor's modulated voice: "Hiding that which you love in open sight. Another good strategy. However, a better strategy would have been to expunge those who are dissatisfied with your society…"

As the men carried him down the cracked and crumbling inside stairwell—they seemed to be familiar with every crevasse and loose stone—all outside sounds became muted. There was only the guttural rasp of breath, the rustle of fabric, the plash of leather on gravel…and later, after all the horrors of the day were past, he would still smell the thickening stink of their sweat.

ISLANDS OF TIME

THE INQUISITOR'S LANCES had insinuated themselves into the town and the surrounding arid countryside. They gathered the wives and children of the sectaries of importance—the elders, intermediates, priests, councilors, judges, and scholars—and marched them to a plain that overlooked *Reĉhes Shell N'eshah.*

The Ridge of Punishment.

There, up close, on high, and under guard, they could watch the proceedings.

"You must not do this," Lucian begged the inquisitor. He strained against the two burly guards who held him fast. They were deep in a glen at the bottom of *Reĉhes Shell N'eshah.* No vegetation grew here, not even scrub. Above were cracked towers of stone and broken mountains of yellow marl. Beside him, cowed and ashen-faced, stood the community's elders and priests...blades at their throats. A few yards away from him were his mother and father. They stood upon makeshift platforms beneath a stone overhang. Their hands were tied behind their backs, and rough-fibered ropes pulled tightly around their necks: the inquisitor's knights had used the stone outcrop above as a gibbet.

"Look away from us, Lucian," his father said. "You must not—"

The inquisitor turned away from Lucian, frowned at the *maskil*, and then slapped Lucian's mother hard in the face. "Silence, *maskil* Hananiah, or I will give her—and your son—to pleasure my men." Then he turned back to Lucian and said, "You are soft enough to be a woman, are you not?"

Lucian's mother groaned.

With a nod from the inquisitor, one of the knights stepped onto the platform, ripped apart her linen gown, slapped her stomach, and squeezed her breast. Exposed and humiliated, she bit her lip so hard that blood dribbled down her chin. But she did not scream.

"Well, young *maskil*-to-be," said the inquisitor, "tell me—"

It was Lucian who screamed; and in that red-limned instant of fear and wrath, in that instant of adrenal strength, he managed a wild kick at one of his captors, unintentionally breaking the guard's shin, and pulled himself away from the sweaty grip of the other astonished knight. As he leaped toward his mother, the inquisitor barked "*Goccia di lei*!"

Drop her!

Before Lucian could reach her, the guard who had torn his mother's dress stepped back and kicked the platform out from under her feet...and he heard his mother's neck snap heard his father scream heard groaning and shrieking from those watching from the plain above and he smelled feces and death and heard thunder inside his head and then he was back in the custody of the inquisitor's guards. He called out to his father, even as one of the guards was gagging the *maskil.* He could *see* the desperate warning in his eyes. As if the igneous rays of sight could be transformed into words.

Remember the covenant. Tell them nothing.

Then the inquisitor was upon him. His face was so close to his that he could taste his breath as if it were uncooked liver. Lucian tried to turn his head, tried to look toward his father, but the inquisitor held him close. His small, pudgy hands were like cold iron clamps clasping his face. His sad, brown eyes were like tunnels; and Lucian suddenly felt dizzy, as if he were falling, spinning into a pit.

"Tell me what I need to know now, or your father is next to drop. And then every single one of your priests and elders will hang."

Lucian heard one of the priests or elders gasp, but no one spoke.

"I have only reached majority," Lucian said, sobbing, unable to catch his breath, choking on the bitter bile of fear and hatred. "How...how would I know where the holiest of holies are kept?"

The inquisitor sighed and released Lucian. After gently patting the boy's face he said, "I will count to three, young *maskil.* Your rash actions have cost your mother her life. Now you must decide whether you will also murder your father."

"It is not I who—" Lucian caught himself. *Yes, it was my fault. Mother is dead because of me, because...*he wanted to look to his father, needed help from his father; but he couldn't raise his head. How could he look again in the direction of his mother? Not after what he did. How could he reveal the secrets the community promised to protect? Death and torture were far preferable to apostasy.

"One...

"Two..."

"I—I only know—"

One of the priest's beside him tried to speak, but was cut off with a gasp. Lucian dared not look, lest he falter and kill his father as he had his mother.

He intoned the Psalm of Forgiveness—

Blessed art Thou, oh Lord,

Who pardons rebellion and unfaithfulness,

Who forgives transgression and iniquity,

Who casts away our sin and purifies our hearts

That we may inherit the glory of Adam.

—and then said, "I speak the truth to save my father. The golden scroll is...it is in the Cave of Light."

The priests beside him wailed and tore their tunics, then chanted the prayer for the dead, which was echoed by those standing on the plain that overlooked the Ridge of Punishment. "*Yis'gadal v'yis'kadash sh'mei raba...*"

But they were not praying for the soul of his mother...they were pronouncing *him*—Lucian—dead. Excluding him. Excising him. Humiliating him. He looked to his father, pleading, but the *maskil* turned away from his son.

"He will forgive you...in time," the inquisitor said; but Lucian knew that was a lie. "Now, young *maskil*, save your father and your people and tell me exactly where the scrolls can be found in this cave of yours.

"I am not the *maskil*!" Lucian said angrily. "My father is the chosen one."

"Be that as it may, if you wish to save his life, you must tell me what I need to know."

Lucian gave him the exact location, and the inquisitor sent a contingent of his guards to retrieve it. When they returned with the scroll—and after he examined it carefully—the inquisitor said, "Very good, young *maskil*. Now...you only need to tell me where I can find the seal that the angel gave you."

"How did you know about—?" Lucian recovered himself...too late.

"Tell me the name of the angel."

"I—"

Once again the inquisitor clasped Lucian's face in his hands. "Tell me!"

Lucian slurred the word "Gabriel."

The inquisitor released him. "Very good. Now tell me where you hid his gift of living sapphire."

Lucian looked toward his father. But his father gazed right through him: the *maskil*'s son was dead, no matter how many times he might draw breath. As Lucian turned back to the inquisitor to plead for his father, he heard thunder behind his temples and his eyes blurred with tears. "I've told you everything I know. Now please—"

The inquisitor lifted his arm, and before Lucian could even take a breath, he heard the scraping of the platform being kicked out from under his father's feet. Saw his father drop. Heard the cracking of bone, the twang of the rope. Smelled ordure. Screamed and kicked and...

Found himself standing on a platform in his father's place.

He remembered being struck by the inquisitor. His head ached; an angry, purple bruise had spread over the right side of his face. He was weak and nauseated. He could barely swallow, for the noose around his neck was tight. His hands were tied behind his back. His arms throbbed. He looked around wildly, trying to shake away the pain that blurred his vision; but the inquisitor and his men were gone, as were his father and mother and the priests and elders and all those who had been watching from the plain above. He tried to swallow, tried to breathe and felt hands around his neck adjusting the noose.

"I have been selected by the priests because I am...unclean," said a hairless slave whose upper lip was curled into a perpetual smile by a scar that extended to what had once been his right eye.

Lucian took a deep, wheezing breath.

Although he had never spoken to this slave, he knew he had been brought to the *Khirbet Qumran* community only last year. Lucian had once caught him embracing Jerobaal, the mother of his playmate Orpha, in the storage cave behind the ovens. But he never spoke of that with anyone, especially Orpha, lest they be stoned for fornicating.

"No one is allowed to look upon you, except for the new high priest and *maskil*," the slave continued.

"You must be born into the lineage," Lucian said, his voice thick. "You cannot be elected. It is not like the priesthood." He could hear himself speak, but it was as if he were somewhere else, somewhere far away, somewhere past the eternal darkness that surrounds the heavens, a small, secret place where time and event are not allowed.

"Well, the one who betrayed the community is now priest and *maskil*, and he watches. So I must get on with this."

"But who—?"

The slave adjusted the noose again.

"Do not shake so, young *maskil*," I have experience with this, for I was once a torturer. You will feel but an instant of pain; and when you awaken, you will see the fine grave I have dug for you." The torturer stood in front of Lucian, perhaps to hide him from the eyes of the new rabbi's spies, and pushed a bitter-tasting herb into his mouth. "Do not spit it out! It will ease your way."

Then the slave stepped off the platform and kicked it out from under Lucian's feet.

LUCIAN AWAKENED FROM a drugged coma to the claustrophobic weight of earthen walls, the acrid smell of dirt and sweat and sulfur. He could see an angry, cloud-covered moonlit sky above him and feel a burning circlet around his neck. He tried to sit up. He grasped at the walls, which were friable; clots of dirt and sand dropped onto him. He tried to scream, but couldn't breathe. A hand covered his mouth. Another cradled his neck. He moaned in pain and tried to make out the slight but strong figure leaning over him.

"It's all right, Lucian," whispered a familiar voice from above—from the edge of the grave pit—"but we must be quiet, lest someone in the refectory hear us. You know how sound can travel. Now rest a moment, gain your bearings, and I will help you out of—"

"Uhfffrrhahh?" Lucian asked, his voice almost completely muffled.

"Yes, dear Lucian, it's me," Orpha said, releasing one hand from his mouth, but still cradling the back of his neck with the other.

"This…is *this* my grave? Are you, are you dead, too?"

The girl smiled. "No, you are not dead and neither am I." With her help, Lucian sat up. Chilled and suddenly overwhelmed with the horror of memory, he panicked.

"I have to get out of here, I—"

Orpha pulled him out of the shallow grave, and breathing heavily, as if sobbing, he lay on the cool, stony marl and thought of his mother. He called to her, as he did as a child, and then caught himself, embarrassed. Orpha held on to him, as if it were she who had suffered the loss. She stroked him and whispered to him in the baby-talk language they had used since they were children. He touched the linen bandage that was wrapped around his neck. He could feel the damp of blood still oozing. "Leave it be," Orpha said. "Mother said not to remove it for three days. She has soaked it in healing salves."

"Mother?"

"Yes, she sneaked away to tend you. She was a healer before..."

"You never said."

"She smiled sadly, her scarred face beautiful in the moonlight. "I am a slave, you are a—"

"I am nothing now." Lucian felt suddenly calm. It was over. Everything was over. He raised himself on this arm and gazed across the stony terrace with its rows of graves...a thousand graves. Graveyard's end was a deep cliff; and beyond that were more limestone cliffs, more crowns of stone and hidden caves, dry stream beds, and the ghostly expanse of the Dead Sea reflecting the silver of the moon. Behind him, blocking easy views from the settlement, were the remains of what had once been a fortified wall. The large stones were corpse white and shadowed in the moonlight.

"My father says—"

"Your father?" Lucian asked.

"Yes, my father, Lucian. Your mother and mine schemed to have him brought here, but they could not acknowledge that he was her husband

and my father. That would not be allowed. It was my father who hanged you and saved your life. My father who brought you here. He dug these graves…"

Lucian saw seven graves neatly dug in a row, the excavated dirt piled beside them, ready to be shoveled over the corpses. Beside him was a grave, freshly filled and smoothed; but there were no stones piled atop the dirt.

"That grave," Orpha continued, motioning, "is empty. It's supposed to be yours. The other graves await your mother and father and the priests and elders killed by the Knights of Cain." She spat, then murmured a prayer. "They will all be buried according to ceremony."

"But I was to be buried as…an animal."

"No, Lucian, they have to bury you on hallowed ground. You are a *maskil*.

Lucian smiled cruelly. "Yes, the angel was right: the last *maskil*."

Orpha retrieved a sac she had secreted under two stones that might have been an ancient dolmen. "Clothes, water, and food, a few *dirhams* and—" she pulled out a curved knife—"this. It belonged to one of the traitors. If you can make it to Jerusalem and avoid slavers, you should be…you will be safe. But you must leave. Now."

Lucian took the gifts and asked, "What about you? Will you be safe?"

"I will stay outside until it is safe to return." Then she embraced Lucian and said, "I'm so sorry." Although he wanted to cry, he felt suddenly and embarrassingly excited. They had never embraced before, not like this. He tried to pull away, but she held him close. "My father believes that one day you will return. An angel told him that you would die and then live. He said you will be the last—and the first—*maskil*."

"An angel told him that?"

"That is what he dreamed," Orpha said, reluctantly releasing him. "I pray for your safety…and your return. And I—" Choking back whatever she wanted to say, she quickly turned away from him and hurried west through the graveyard.

Lucian wanted to call to her, but all he could do was watch her until she disappeared behind a still-standing section of a ruined fortification wall. Then he, too, turned and made his way into the moon-bleached desert: he would have plenty of time to think of love, betrayal, death, and angels.

AFTERWORD TO "THE LAST MASKIL"

LIKE THE PREVIOUS story, "The Last Maskil" is an anti-fixup. I excerpted parts of my novel *Shadows in the Stone* and molded them into a new, stand-alone story. So in my now familiar authorial voice I say unto you: "Ditto what I wrote in my afterword for "Spirit Dog".

And I emphatically reject the accusation that this afterword is a cop-out!

WAITING FOR MEDUSA

Homage à Harlan...

The most reliable way to make the immortal jellyfish age in reverse...is to mutilate it.
—Nathaniel Rich

One:
A Few Tips from the Flash-Fire Manual of Good Manners

I HAVE A routine I always follow before I die.

I take a good long piss, evacuate my bowels, check and recheck food supplies; then check and recheck every inch of my earth bunker to make sure that no hungry home-boy mutation will be able to smash his way in or burn me out; and *then*, when I'm satisfied that all is as it should be, I just lie down and wait for it. I don't eat. I don't drink. I just starve myself and wait for the medusa. Suffice it to say that I get so god-damn bored and hungry-aching that I finally just fall into a coma and drop dead.

It takes about a week for me to become an ugly-smelling gelatinous blob.

WAITING FOR MEDUSA

My stem cells just keep degenerating—for the record, I should tell you that I'm *all* stem cells—until my microRNA's kick in and start my regeneration from blob to pup. Yeah, I regenerate just like a Turritopsis medusa. In case some uneducated asshole home-boy carnivore is reading this, that's a jellyfish. And in case some *educated* asshole home-boy carnivore is reading this...aside from having two genome duplications, *you* look like a jellyfish, too!

And, yes, for the record, I'm a dog and proud of it.

Okay, let's get this out of the way right now: My name is Teviot Flash Fire 8703898, and my complete pedigree name is as long as your arm (providing you have arms). I'm a classic blackback: brown and white with a jet black saddle; and if the wind is right, I can smell man-stink ten miles away. I'm three feet tall, weigh forty pounds (all muscle!), and have opposable thumbs on my front paws—you can blame the Sprague Dawley Company, the Scientific Procedures Act of 2051, AUSDA, DARPA, and the US Australia Homeland Security Amendment for that! But that's all old news, four hundred year-old old news. Christ, *I'm* two hundred and eighty-eight years old, which isn't bad considering that the natural life of my breed is sixteen years.

Yeah, I've died eighteen times, and I'm not due to kick the bucket again for another ten years. I'm talking here about natural death, of course, which is something one can plan and make provisions for. I've had only two unnatural deaths, both in the killing fields; and both times I was lucky: I wasn't eaten or left to fertilize God's good soil with an arrow in my heart. So here's a free bit of gastronomical enlightenment for all you starving, snaggle-toothed, rot-brained, dog-eating killers out there: eat me and we *both* turn into unregenerationable blobs of flesh-fester.

ISLANDS OF TIME

Two:
Homeboys and Bimbos

AN ARROW GRAZED my dewlap.

A hail of shot almost tore off my right ear.

I felt hot stings across my withers and back; and as I leapt for cover, it felt like a swarm of bees was stinging the hell out of me.

A laser sliced through the air where I had been.

I moved, again and again; and I moved quickly, resting only when I found a temporary vantage point behind (and partly inside) a rotting, vine-strangled tree trunk.

And, yes, it was my own stupid, fucking fault that a bunch of starving, snaggle-toothed, rot-brained, dog-eating killers had managed to catch me unawares.

I WAS FORAGING in South Gippsland hill country, which, aside from the odd mutant and florid green flat-leaf flora, should have been safe as houses. It had been radioed, which turned humans and most of the wildlife into radioactive compost for hungry plants. The place was still hot as Melbourne, Sydney, New York, London, or Bangalore. There shouldn't have been *anybody* here.

I guess it just goes to show that experience, a heightened olfactory sensorium, and augmented intelligence ain't what they're cracked up to be because a rover pack of dangle-armed, hump-backed, anthropophagous mutes had been tracking me for hours. Well, they weren't tracking me, exactly.

They were tracking the crazy bimbo that was—

I'll get to that by the by.

Anyway, by the time I got my first whiff of the mutes' gland-stink presence, it was too late. The wind had blown their smell north, and the acid odor of pelting rain had muddled my olfactory discrimination. I'm not meaty enough to be more than a snack for two or three, but there you are: I suppose the homeboy mutes will just have to fight over who gets what parts of me…and, of course, the bimbo.

I shouldn't call her that, but I'm a dog for Crissakes; and one could reasonably argue that, augmented or not, I'm by definition sexist right down to my brisket and gonads. That I use the term "bimbo" as an expression of affection is, of course, no excuse. Her name is Crash—at least that's what she calls herself: she doesn't give away much information—and she was tracking *me.* Now that's a trick-and-a-half because I should have smelled her.

I should have smelled her when I finally smelled the nose-clogging pong of the mutants…except she's got no signature spoor; at least none that *I* could detect.

Nothing.

As far as I could tell, she was just…green. Green as the air. Green as the refreshing, actinic smell of radiation: that's what fresh air smells like to me.

Obviously mutant snouts could detect her because they were tracking her. Maybe they could smell her sex, although if they could, I *certainly* should have been able to. Whatever. One certainty: if they catch her, they'll screw her to death and then have a finger-lickin' feast on her snow-white flesh.

She is an albino. Big teats (but only two—like most humans) under a torn, close-fitting camouflage suit; thick white hair that cascaded over her face and down her back like long fur; huge oval eyes that were so blue they made you thirsty; a thin nose (nostrils so damn narrow, I often wonder how she breathes through them); and full, pinkish lips. I could see all that as she jumped away from a clearing into the bush. (Yes, my eyesight has also been augmented: I can see in the infrared, too, for all the good it didn't do me.)

She jumped and the clearing exploded...as did the copse of color-shifting spider grevillea that she jumped into.

The shooter was using an ancient Israeli Tavor, which shoots saboted sub-caliber tungsten darts and grenades. The stupid bastard had fired *everything* at her; and once I got a whiff of the rifle's gas signature, I directed one clean shot into his chest. (Yet another authorial intrusion: Of course, I can handle weapons. I've got opposable thumbs, remember? I carry an old reliable Swiss Canton G97 in a bandolier, and I drop to the ground to use it. You don't need any more details than that. What's important is that *I* know.)

That single shot brought the wrath of God down on me. I drew all kinds of fire from what seemed like every direction. Buttress roots, phosphorous bark, and wood exploded into shards and slime around me.

I ran, once again overcome by the ancient blood rhythms of gland, instinct, and reflex; and, as my name implies, I'm fast as a tornado firestorm feeding on dry scrub.

And before I even knew how the hell I had got there, my eyes were adjusting to the cool deep darkness of blackwood. I ploughed through thick and thin forest undergrowth; and as I inhaled its rich purple and sharp forest green in great hungry gasps, I wondered where the hell the woman had got to...and whether she was still alive: I couldn't smell any new blood, except for the mute's—which, although attenuated by distance, still smelled like clay—but, then, I couldn't smell anything that had to do with Crash. Anyway, I didn't have time to wonder for long because shots exploded all around me.

I leaped into a foul-smelling ditch.

It was crawling with moss that would soon start rotting my skin if I lingered too long; but for the moment it gave me the cover I desperately needed. But 'cover' was a bit misleading in this instance, as the mutes were using their rifles to sight me through the blackwood.

(And there was no way I could eliminate my heat signature, short of dropping-dead and falling into an ice bath.) I caught their scents as they started moving in, so I could 'see' their line of action—a pincer; but then they got smart and camouflaged themselves with something that smelled like plastic and was as thick as a rolling front of lewisite. I sniffed, but all I could hear was an occasional soft crunch of twig or fern.

The homeboys could certainly track; I'd have to give them credit for that.

Time to move again.

But too late…again.

A frag grenade sang into the ditch…

Three:
Meet Unnatural Death #3

OKAY, TWO THINGS: (1) either the grenade was a Thales frag, which had a reputation for faulty detonation, or (2) it was a decent Gorhsen pineapple with a degraded fuze system—twelve lifetimes worth of radiation and slime rot can tank even the best can of metal. It detonated all right, but only after a few seconds.

A few precious seconds.

Enough time for me to take a flying leap and roll into a contiguous moss pit; but not before a curl of boomerang shrapnel blew off my muzzle, my nose, and my left rear leg from the second thigh down.

This wasn't good. Two hundred and eighty-eight years ago, the science lab boys fucked up their experiment (me!) because unless I'm practically pounded into pulp, I can't recover/regenerate from a mortal wound (or from being eaten). So much for my anticipated natural death…so much for my mortal coil uncoiling to the sounds of harps and sublime visions of tail-wagging angels with noisome buttocks.

I could smell blood, my own blood (pungent as iron filings and ozone); but that was just phantom sensoria. Although I was sanguineous and pain-shocked, I fired back round after round: by this lifetime, that was an autonomic response.

But for all intents and purposes, I was firing blind.

Sonovabitch!

I was going to become lunch for those murderous bastards; and, just to add sublimity to sublimity, my skin was itching like crabs feasting in pubic hair: that moss I'd been reclining in was particularly pernicious. When the homeboys were so close that I could see them, smell them (or *think* I could smell them), and leap upon them—there had to be thirty of them, at the least—the whole goddamn landscape turned into crack and fire.

My first impression was that I'd been hit again, which was probably true, or that I my adrenals were exaggerating the throaty plosives of my rifle; but, no, it was Crash.

In that red time, which was either an eternity or a heartbeat, I took out, all up, about eight of the mutes. But Crash managed to get around and through them. She'd already taken out six or seven by stealth without making a sound: somehow, she used the mutes' camouflage cloud against them.

And then in a red breath, in a red heartbeat, she blew the hell out of the rainforest.

I imagined the perfumed fragrances of napalm, and then—

All was sensory deprivation quiet; and like a sudden whiff of rain, I heard breathing. I felt cool hands stroke the wetness that had been my muzzle.

"Poor thing."

Her voice was like rain, like wind soughing through shadow-green forest. As she stroked me again, I imagined myself getting a hard-on. (More about the sex-life of the unregenerate dog later.)

Although the proverbial lights were going out for me, I tried to focus my eyes on her albino whiteness, on her sweat-sheened face. That alone took great strength of will; but maybe, just maybe she could help me.

If I could just stay conscious long enough to communicate…

I tried to speak, then realized that I was just thinking at her.

Get your act together, dogshit. Wake-up. Focus. Words. Tongue. Gullet. Voicebox. I managed to say, "Your knife," but my voice sounded like a bark. I started to choke on my own phelgm. I tried again: "Your knife."

She leaned her head close to mine, so close that I couldn't see her face anymore; but I could feel the dangly softness of her hair sliding like wind—like sleep—over me. I tried to speak (I can speak, you know, although I've always sounded like gravel thrown at a wall), but sleep, pain, numbness, blessed cold air-conditioned menthol numbness wrapped me in its silk cocoon and—

"*Let me in.*"

I heard *that* inside my head.

Louder than my own thoughts.

I've honed, developed, multiplied, and habituated into reflexivity my defenses against telepathic intrusion; but somehow she managed to push herself inside me. And even lying there in my own blood and smell, lacking face and limbs, trying not to die for the last time, I wondered how fucking long she had been inside me, monitoring me…

It was akin to being raped while unconscious.

Intrusive, insinuating, illegitimate, misbegotten, deviant mutated bitch!

"*No, no, no,*" she seemed to whisper. "*I've been keeping track of you for a while, but…I can't read all your thoughts. Only the ones that—*"

"*Ones that what...?*" I thought back at her.

"*Only the ones that leak past your siege defenses. The unimportant, stray thoughts. I could track you, but that's about all...until now.*"

Because now I'm weak and dying.

But there was more to it—more to Crash the albino than that.

I hadn't been able to smell her, detect her because she'd been blocking me from the inside out. But didn't matter a bean now. I was passing into cold stillness, numbness, and my unforeseen unplanned unnatural—and final—death.

I felt Crash's proximity, her intrusive warmth, sexuality, sensitivity, uncertainty, and—strange as it sounds and feels—her love.

I *must* be dying!

"*Is there anything I can do to help you regenerate?*"

That woke me up!

"*How do you know about...?*" Didn't matter. I had just enough strength and consciousness to think, "*Your knife. Stab me...and keep stabbing me until I'm dead. If I die now, like this, I won't transdifferentiate. Kill me dead, and then, if you've no prior engagements, stay with me until stolons start to push their way out of—*"

I felt a thud, heard an enormous cracking as knife scratched against bone—

That female was as powerful as a dog.

—and then nothing, no blackness, no falling down endless abysses, no cold, heat, pain, or regret. Just nothingness.

Four:
Ah, the Sweet Green Smells of Love and Duplicity

DYING UNNATURALLY ISN'T so bad once the medusa takes hold of me.

I degenerate and regenerate; and after a few days, I begin to resemble a collapsed soufflé. You don't even want to know what I look like—or smell like—after a week. Ever see a dead human boiling with maggots? Okay, now imagine a wet, rotting, pulsating carcass wreathed with fur. By the end of week #2, I'm a gelatinous mass of programmed stoloniferous growth as my cells begin to multiply and remember what they were and where they belong. In the true physical sense, I'm just a manifestation of memory and experience.

Viva T. Denisovich Lysenko.

By week #3, I start to look like a dog; and I start remembering. First come the ancestral, racial memories—a synesthesia of smells sable sweet and strong and fecal—and then my own: there I am at five (for the first time), there's my second bunker where I died with my companion Leila: no, I won't think about that…ever. And there I am getting laid (for the first time). Not much of anything. Was over before I could figure out what the hell had happened. (Yes, it was with a dog, but just an ordinary unenhanced bitch, part kelpie and dingo…and that, I can tell you, was the last time I screwed one of my kind who wasn't jacked-up mentally. I might as well have made love to a chicken.)

And there I am seeing the Dead Territories for the first time.

And running from a cull.

And dragging my first kill to—

Enough of the *memento mori* crap.

I died, and I regenerated.

And Crash stayed with me…cared for me. I hadn't expected that; but, then, I hadn't expected her to be able to pierce my veil, so to speak, and eavesdrop on my raw, establishing memories. By the time my defenses kicked in, she had gnawed on the marrow of my psyche long enough to mirror my thoughts. I realize now that I had felt her presence early on, during my embryonic dream state. She whispered to me, but I couldn't understand speech. I heard it as soft barking, I heard the green smell of her; only later did I experience the discomfort of being laid bare, examined, probed.

My first words to her after I regenerated were, "*Stay the fuck out of me.*"

She giggled because I thought them at her rather than spoke. "*You needed someone to watch over you, protect you from predators.*"

"What are *you* if not a predator?" That spoken, or rather barked. Even though I meant what I said, I felt immediate regret; I felt her pain as if it were my own. "*Get out of me, now*!"

"*I'm trying to, but—*"

For the first time in this new, discomforting incarnation, I opened my eyes.

I looked around and saw that she was standing well away from me. I could smell her fear. Where the hell were we? I wrinkled my nose: I could smell blood and human ordure. This place was dark and damp, stone damp and smoky; and Crash was but a pale, diaphanous shadow. I heard water dripping, tap-smack, tap-smack, tap-smack, like a heart beating in a huge chest.

"*Some of your thoughts...most of your thoughts just appear in my head. As if they're my own.*"

She shook her head, and her hair looked electric in the dim light.

"*And we're in a cave*, she continued. *I found this subterranean system of linked caves and burned out the occupying fauna.*"

Indeed she had. I saw a tidied pile of charred human remains on a ledge that might once have been used as an altar.

"*You're as bad as the mutes.*"

"*I* am *a mute. And I needed sustenance...and the rover pack is still out there. There were more of them than I'd anticipated.*"

"*Anticipated...?*"

Although she thought something back at me, I couldn't hear her. Biology being stronger than will, I'd fallen into a deep, exhausted sleep. But once I awakened, I would be completely regenerated.

And my first adrenaline-fueled thought would be: safety.

With a fucking great big capital 'S'.

SHE WAS RUNNING her fingers along the swell of my back when I woke up. I pulled away reflexively, although I must admit I felt—and desired—her warmth and closeness. Nevertheless I tried to shake her out of me, but that was a sham effort; and we both knew it. Neither did I try to vocalize. Like it or not, we were as one.

And a tumbling array of images took up my thoughts...a myriad of images.

"*Stop it,*" I said. "*Whatever it is you're doing...thinking.*"

She pulled away from me; and against all my finely-honed instincts of preservation, I wished for her closeness. "*I'm sorry,*" she said, shaking her head. Her white nimbus of hair tickled me. "*I'll try to stay out. Really, I will. But you'll need to close up a bit, too.*"

"*Give me a break, I just regenerated. You should have kept away—*"

She nodded, and I turned away from her. I felt redness, embarrassment, humiliation. She had taken advantage of my situation...but on some deep instinctual level, I allowed her to. I could rationalize that I was unprepared because thought intrusion was a rare occurrence and talent (one I didn't possess). I could rationalize until the cows come home, but I *know* what happened: my dog-mind said "mate" and cracked open like a piñata.

"*My fault. Stupid. Fucking. Idiot. Lame—*"

"*Stop it. We took advantage of each other.*" She caressed me, drawing her palm lightly down the nap of my fur. "*What you heard...I was thinking of home.*"

Safety...

"*You call your home Safety?*"

"*Yes...we call it that.*"

"*We?*"

"*My people, my family. It's a village—*"

I looked through my mind's eye and shivered. "*I can see it. It's big, and it's dark.*" And then I felt warmth and familiarity as I looked through *her* mind's eyes.

"*No, you can see that it's cool and bright.*"

"*Unnatural.*"

"*Everything's unnatural. It's safe and deep and—*"

"*I would have heard of it.*"

She leaned in closer and mischievously grazed her cheek against my muzzle. "*Just as you could smell me when I was following you?*"

"*What do you want?*"

She closed up. Darkness. Separation.

I drew a deep breath and mirrored her psychic walls, covering every chink and peering out like an archer situated behind the crenellations of a keep. But she lay down beside me. I allowed her to pull me close, I was walled up in protective darkness; and she was huge and furless, full and milky-smelling, like a human baby. Although her morphology was hominid and vertical, I'm canid and horizontal by nature: sturdy and steady as a table.

Nevertheless, I felt a distant, albeit slight fecal arousal.

"*You're not a dog,*" I said. A weak and shallow protest.

"*Neither are you...not completely.*" She breathed into my fur, stroked my stomach, and opened herself to me. Seeing myself through Crash was disorienting. I know my true size, weight, and form; but my deep-rooted self-image is altogether different: I'm tiger sized, fast and silky... not cute, cuddly, and small as an extinct koala. I looked into Crash.

I smelled her blond-white milkiness, but I couldn't get past her soft warmth and adrenal pleasure.

I couldn't penetrate her true self.

But I would...I would.

"*Yes...you will,*" she said.

Jarred, I drew into myself.

"*I like dogs,*" Crash said capriciously.

"*What the hell is that supposed to mean?*"

I didn't need an explanation: I could smell her green, mischievous smile.

Five:
The Trouble With Truth...

IS THAT YOU can't control when you'll discover it.

I looked into the blue ocean that was Crash's eyes and asked, "*Why... why did you track me? And why did you stay with me.*"

As she stroked me, I watched her teats swaying slightly and wondered why anything more than a bulge and a nipple would be necessary for suckling. Although her camouflage suit bound them tight (when she was wearing it), the evolution of such appendage-like masses did not seem to be conducive to flight and fight. She did not seem concerned that I periodically sniffed and licked them. Why, then, did she become agitated when I ingratiated myself near her rectilinear expansion? Humans seem to be abnormally fecal-phobic.

She ignored my post-coital musings and said, "*I stayed to protect you.*"

"*That's not the answer.*"

"*You mean it's not the entire answer.*" She smiled, but I couldn't sense any mirth. "*We need you.*"

"*We...?*"

"*Safety.*"

"*And why would they need me and—*"

"*Why would they send* me?" Crash asked, watching me carefully.

For an instant her ice-blue eyes revealed the predator, then softened. My defenses were up and so were Crash's, yet...humans are so fucking antinomic. They are perpendicular even when horizontal...and they are open even when they're closed. Although she had blanked herself out like the genitalia in a re-education videotect, I could feel her fear, hesitation, and—yes, once again—her love. Impossible, I know, especially the implausible depth of her affection. But there you have it.

I could also sense "wrongness".

Difficult to put a word to it: it's a dog thing.

"*I've been sent to bring you home,*" Crash said.

"*Cut the bullshit.*"

"*A place where you'll be safe...and in return you can help us.*"

"*How?*"

"*We're dying.*

"*From what?*"

Crash shrugged. It took me an instant to translate the gesture into color and smell. "*We don't know, but we're aging earlier.*"

"*And dying earlier.*"

She nodded. "*In three years I'll be an old lady. In another two, I'll—*"

"*How old are you?*"

"*Nineteen...going on twenty.*"

Being a dog, I thought that was a ripe old age for a single lifetime. But a moron could see where she was going; and, not being without resources of my own, I had glimpsed the dark edges of her motives when we were, shall we say, experimenting with inter-species rapprochement. "*And so you think a little vivisection might help you out.*"

I was completely unprepared for her immediate, visceral reaction.

She opened herself completely to me, and—truth be told—I'm the guilty one, for I tore her open as surely as if I was wielding a serrated knife; and she flooded me, overwhelmed me, with a tsunami of memory and emotion. In that blinding, storm-forced instant, I saw her whole and complete; remembered as if we were one and the same being; knew her mother and father—both dead; knew her small joys and early awkwardness, her pubescent dreams, adolescent fantasies, and adult fears; I felt her horror of killing and eating (for she was, when necessary, a cannibal); and I saw as she saw :: her first "pet", an grey-bellied Alsatian that bled-out on her lap after a well planned and executed raid on her village :: her first lover, a towering stick of a boy who forced her mouth upon his member—I saw her refracted memories, her repressed memories, and with that terrible, instantaneous knowledge, my hackles lifted in abject, sweaty fear until I, too, repressed her memories—and I heard as she heard :: her shadow-master whispering, whispering, whispering to her in her sleep :: the echoes of her footsteps in well-lit, narrow and safe corridors :: echoes :: whispers :: artificial light :: echoes :: death :: whispers :: dog :: love :: hope :: me.

I comforted her as best I could as she squeezed and petted me and tried to catch her breath; but even after that onrush of emotions, even after I saw into her inner vaults, even after she had turned herself into glass for me, I couldn't shake the sense of wrongness. And although I allowed Crash in, although I allowed her to nestle into my fond memories, I sequestered a tiny node in my spinal cord where I could ratiocinate in private. (Again, it's a dog thing; but when a dog tells you he's of two minds...he means it!) She would never know, of course; and it was in there—in that tiny node complete with its own psyche, anima, smell sensorium, and a memory palace as large as the Hazaduri Palace in Murshidabad—that I could sort clues and explore the fractal connections that she had unwittingly revealed to me.

Such as why the mutes were trying to kill her.

Six: Q & A Doggy Style

"*I'M SORRY.*"

"*About what?*" I asked.

"*About…what just happened.*"

"*You mean bestial copulation with a species of the canine persuasion?*"

She didn't smile, but neither did she turn away from me. (Although dogs don't smile, I've learned to recognize this odd human expression of mirth, pain, and acceptance.)

"*I'm sorry I exposed myself so completely,*" she said. "*I didn't mean to damage your psyche, but I was taken by surprise.*" Then, her thoughts raddled with anger, "*How could you ever imagine that I would have any part in hurting you? How could you…?*"

"*I don't necessarily think* you *would hurt me, or allow me to be hurt,*" I said. "*But perhaps you could be manipulated by those who would.*"

"*No,*" she said, "*not in Safety. It's not that kind of place. We're not that kind of people. Any of us.*"

"*But I've only met* you," I said as I tried to calm and placate her with soft images of acceptance and understanding.

"*And if I had intentions to hurt you, or if my shadow-masters had any intentions to hurt you, we wouldn't be having this conversation. And I wouldn't have done what I did with you.*"

Ocherous smells of intercourse and satiation.

"*And if Safety had such intentions, they wouldn't have sent me to bring you home. They would have—*"

"*Would have what?*"

She just shook her head.

"*But why would you seek intimacy with me?*"

She seemed genuinely surprised: surprise mixed with hurt, anger, and spite. "*Why…? Our kinds have been intimate companions for millennia.*"

"*Not that way.*"

"*Are you so sure?*" she asked, finally smiling: her defenses firmly back in place.

But my attention was suddenly directed elsewhere.

I could smell the faraway hint of rust, rust red and smooth as a beetle's carapace, the now-familiar sanguineous smell of the rover pack. Could the mutes have lost Crash's smell so completely…and for so long? Or had they retreated to base to care for their wounded and regroup?

"*I thought we'd lost them for good,*" Crash said, reading me. "*How far away are they…how much time do we have?*"

"*We have to leave now,*" I said, "*or defend ourselves here.*"

She shook her head. "*I scanned you as best I could when you were regenerating, but I couldn't learn enough to—*"

"*You knew enough to be able to save my life and comfort me. The caves offered the best protection…for what I had to do.*"

And then it happened.

Her final ligation.

The last straw.

The straw that broke the camel's back.

(Ah, how I love human apothegms and tautologies!)

She flooded me with warmth, compassion, and pleasure, as she had done so many times before. She radiated possibility, hope, and trust; but this time I felt an overwhelming cycloramic freshening of memory and experience, an awakening, an apotheosis; and in those kaleidoscopic visions I walked on two paws and made love with Crash in a bright canopied room connected by mirrored corridors to the heaven that was Safety. I was wrapped in a heavenly prison of perfumed gauze, a prison from which I longed never to escape; and in the tiny, secret node that I'd created—my other mind, my doubled dog mind—I *knew* exactly what had happened: Crash had finally captured me so very securely in her anastamosing web...but the divine trap that had been created just for me (undoubtedly created by the kind, well-meaning, vivisectionist shadow-masters of Safety) had unintended consequences. What was meant to instill narcotic love had the opposite effect on the roving mutes.

They picked up her errant signals and were overcome with rage and hatred; and yes, even here, in the womb-stone damp depths of the cave, I could smell their lust-triggered hate and anger. Crash was now my telepathic conduit. What was hidden from her was now visible to me...or, rather, to the secret self I had created. Although the mutes felt only rage and hatred, they were drawn to Crash like iron particles to a lodestone. And if I was human, I would have smiled. Ah, the ironies of revelation: it turns out that *I* was the reason the rover gang had temporarily lost Crash's 'scent'. The spinal node of glia and neuroglia cells that I had created to shield my thoughts from Crash had also shielded her from the mutes. But now that Crash had ensnared, ensorcelled, and subjugated me; now that she had plundered my will (but for my aforementioned sequestered node, my doubled self), she was once again 'visible' to the mutes.

And like her, the mutes were telepathic.

They were more than a little like her, or so I had discovered by intercepting her neural action potentials: that treasure of information she didn't even know existed, that repository she wasn't supposed to be able to access. Just as I am an exemplar of canid augmentation, so was she the very picture of *homo augmentum*. And what about the poor dangle-armed, hump-backed, anthropophagous mutes that were tracking us?

Why they were the spawn of the unlucky ones that had been exiled from the subterranean halls of the City of Heaven.

Safety.

Seven:
Epiphanies of a Love Slave

OMNIA MAY VINCIT *amor* (you know, love conquers all), but as your Bard once wrote, "Unnatural deeds do breed unnatural troubles"; and so, bound by golden chains of love and adoration, we made our way south toward Safety. She knew the terrain far better than I did, and we skirted the coast. Our destination was 39°02'S 146°23'E, a peninsula that formed the southernmost part of the mainland, a coral-hued wilderness surrounded and protected by nano-wire and granite islands.

"*Once we reach that first tor, we will be safe.*"

She didn't have to point, for I was seeing through her eyes. I was but an appendage; and although she irradiated me with rosy love, she gave no more thought to me than she would the hair that tickled the back of her neck. I was enslaved, or so she thought…but she harbored neither guilt nor malice concerning my state. She loved me and had done what she had to do.

And now she was going to bring me to Safety.

I really did want to go wherever she might goest, for my brainwashed brain was brimming with love and devotion. Whatever eviscerations and vivisections might be in store for me was nothing compared to my new-found religion of love and servitude. I could easily recount ad infinitum the cliffs and valleys, the coves, beaches, dunes, inlets, swamps, and mudflats of my love; but I shall spare you…just as I will spare you an inventory of every footfall of our ill-fated attempt to reach Safety. Although every moment is burned into my mind and shall be forever, I will cut to the chase and tell you only what you need to know of love's labor lost.

Everything else is…mine alone.

So without the interference of grief or moral rationalization, herewith death without a number…

"**ONCE WE REACH** *that first tor, we will be safe.*"

Now if you follow Crash's imaginary gesture pointing out the best route to the tor, you'll see jade-rippled water washing over lichen-covered rock cascades. That was the nearest protection perimeter.

We moved quickly over dangerously exposed flat scrabble to the faux security of gum forest, which was cool, dark, and silent, but for the cracking and snapping of tiny, insectile fire-dragons. If we hadn't been ambushed, it would have taken us two days to reach safe ground.

But *I* knew we weren't going to reach safe ground…or rather my doubled self knew. Although I was deaf, dumb, and blind to what I was doing, my secret self was a planner; and it was not in the least constrained by any of those emotional ties that bind. I—or it (we'll call it 'it')— used Crash like a radio.

Here she is. Come and get her.

And, being a moderately fast learner, it learned how to manipulate Crash's sensorium—

I'm right here, darling, walking right beside you…

Good dog.

—and disengage me.

When the mutes closed in on her :: shot her :: broke her bones :: raped her :: ate her while she lived and breathed, I was running as fast as my heart could pump.

But fast as I might be, I couldn't escape her last thoughts, pain, and bewilderment.

WAITING FOR MEDUSA

AS I SAID before, every joyous, painful, life-changing moment of my time with Crash has been burned into my doubled mind. However, I'm considering letting go of that tiny node of grief and remembrance that is attached to my spinal cord.

After all, I can always grow another.

But…I'm of two minds about all that.

AFTERWORD TO "WAITING FOR MEDUSA"

RICHARD MCKENNA, AUTHOR of *The Sand Pebbles* and a handful of brilliant short stories such as "Casey Agonistes" and "The Secret Place", gave the unconscious part of the writing process form and personality. He called it the Little Man. "He it is who explores the caverns measureless to man and therein listens to ancestral voices. He is the sole author, the scenarist, and all of the actors in our private dreams."**

And he it is who insists that you buy a book you can't afford because it will be invaluable when you decide to write a novel you haven't even thought of yet. He it is who sends you to the keyboard at three o'clock in the morning to record that conversation you just had in a dream you can't remember. He it is who pushes those crazy ideas at you, those ideas that you really don't have time to write; but, dammit, you can't get anything *else* done until you...obey the little man.

When Kate Eltham, the director of the Brisbane Writers' Festival, asked me to write a story for a special issue of the *Australian Fiction Review*, I intended to write something out of genre, something personal, lyrical, and impressionistic, something that might reflect the light like some of Elizabeth Bowen's very short stories, something short and and literary and mainstream-ish. But the aforementioned little man, being of a perverse nature, had an entirely different idea: "*You've been invited to contribute to a literary journal. Why, Jack, that's just perfect! How about...a story about interspecies sex, mutants, cannibals, talking dogs, and the apocalypse*?"

---

* * Richard McKenna, "Journey With a Little Man," can be found in *Turning Points: Essays on the Art of Science Fiction*, ed. Damon Knight (New York: Harper & Row, 1977)

I said, "*No. Absolutely not!*"

I argued with him.

I mumbled something about being an *artiste*, but he ignored me as he always does. He sat down and began to write. In fact, he was having so much fun that I couldn't help myself: I just had to take a turn at the keyboard.

After all, it would be *my* name under the story title.

With all due respect, Kate and Elizabeth: the little man made me do it.

I might note that I was lucky with this story, for—after a bit of revision—I also sold it to Sheila Williams, the perspicacious editor of *Asimov's*.

JACK DANN has written or edited over eighty books, including the international bestseller *The Memory Cathedral: a Secret History of Leonardo da Vinci*, *The Rebel: an Imagined Life of James Dean*, *The Silent*, *Bad Medicine*, and *The Man Who Melted*. His work has been compared to Jorge Luis Borges, Roald Dahl, Lewis Carroll, Ray Bradbury, J. G. Ballard, Mark Twain, and Philip K. Dick. *Library Journal* called Dann "...a true poet who can create pictures with a few perfect words," and *Best Sellers* said that "Jack Dann is a mind-warlock whose magicks will confound, disorient, shock, and delight."

He is a recipient of the Nebula Award, the World Fantasy Award (twice), the Australian Aurealis Award (three times), the Chronos Award, the Darrell Award for Best Mid-South Novel, the Ditmar Award (five times), the Peter McNamara Achievement Award and the Peter McNamara Convenors' Award for Excellence, the Shirley Jackson Award, and the *Premios Gilgames de Narrativa Fantastica* award. He has also been honored by the Mark Twain Society (Esteemed Knight).

His latest novel is *Shadows in the Stone: a Book of Transformations*. *New York Times* bestselling author Kim Stanley Robinson called it "such a complete world that Italian history no longer seems comprehensible without his cosmic battle of spiritual entities behind and within every historical actor and event." His most recent collection is part of Centipede Press' *Masters of Science Fiction Series*. Forthcoming is *Islands of Time* (Cemetery Dance) and *The Writer's Guide to Alternate History* (Bloomsbury).

Dr. Dann is also an Adjunct Senior Research Fellow in the School of Communication and Arts at the University of Queensland. He lives in Australia on a farm overlooking the sea.

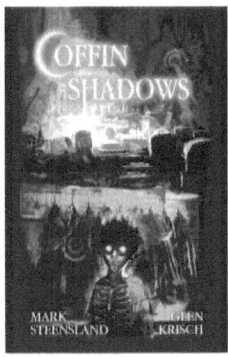

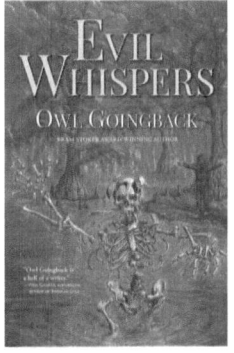

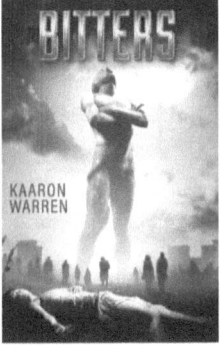

www.ingramcontent.com/pod-product-compliance
Lightning Source LLC
Chambersburg PA
CBHW031031030726
47497CB00004B/1098
9781587679230